PRAISE FOR BRIAN FREEMAN

"My discovery this year has been crime writer Brian Freeman...
Fleshed-out characters, high tension, and terrifying twists
put him up there with Harlan Coben in the psychological
crime stratosphere."

DAILY MAIL (LONDON)

"[Stride] is in the company of Bosch, Thorne, Tennison,
and Skinner, some of my other favorite detectives time
has not mellowed."

MINNEAPOLIS STAR TRIBUNE

praise for the series

"Excellent...A cleverly constructed, page-turning plot
and fleshed-out primary and secondary characters make
this a winner."

PUBLISHERS WEEKLY

(starred review) on *Alter Ego*

FUNERAL
FOR A
FRIEND

BRIAN FREEMAN

FUNERAL
FOR A
FRIEND

**BLACK
STONE**
PUBLISHING

Copyright © 2020 by Brian Freeman
Published in 2020 by Blackstone Publishing
Cover and book design by Kathryn Galloway English

Printed in the United States of America

First edition: 2020
ISBN 978-1-982663-72-8
Fiction / Mystery & Detective / Police Procedural

3 5 7 9 10 8 6 4 2

CIP data for this book is available
from the Library of Congress

Blackstone Publishing
31 Mistletoe Rd.
Ashland, OR 97520

www.BlackstonePublishing.com

For Marcia

"No one ever keeps a secret so well as a child."

—Victor Hugo, *Les Misérables*

Drip. Drip. Drip.

Water falling.

Jonathan Stride lay in bed, his dark eyes wide open, his body stretched atop the sheets. His bare leg brushed the bare leg of his wife, their skin damp with a sheen of sweat. Summer heat through the open window made the bedroom a sauna of wet, scorching air. He couldn't sleep.

Outside the old house, nothing moved on the lazy Duluth night. Nothing in the world made a sound. Not the pond frogs. Not the crickets. Not the spruces towering over the roof. Even Lake Superior, on the other side of the dunes, couldn't muster the energy to throw waves against the sand, and so the beach was silent.

When Stride listened, the only thing he heard was the slow drumbeat of water, driving him crazy.

He got out of bed and slipped a white T-shirt over his chest. In the moonlit glow of the bedroom, he watched his wife sleeping on her back in a pink nightgown, her breasts visible through the cups of lace. Her blond hair spilled in a tangle across her face. Her legs were slightly parted, one knee bent. She made an erotic sight that way, arousing him. He bent down and stroked his fingertips across her thigh.

"Andrea," he murmured.

His touch failed to stir her from sleep. She didn't move at all. She was like a wax figure, not even real.

And still the drip, drip, drip *of water filled his mind. He needed to make it stop.*

Stride went to the window and listened. There had been a torrent of rain for days, but it had stopped hours ago, and there was no longer a trickle from the gutters. He crossed to the bathroom and checked the faucet and shower, but both were dry. He returned to the bedroom, where he stood beside the closed door and held his breath.

The dripping of water came from the other side. A place where water shouldn't be. It was as if someone were standing there, soaking wet, each drop from their clothes making a splash on the wooden floor. He wasn't alone. He could feel the presence of an intruder in the house, and whoever it was must have heard Stride's footsteps walk right up to the bedroom door and stop.

The two of them faced each other from opposite sides of the door. Invisible antagonists.

His gaze shot to the chair in the corner of the bedroom, where he'd slung his holster and gun, as he always did. He was too far away to get to it. Instead, he reached slowly for the metal door knob and closed his fingers around it. In one smooth motion, he threw open the bedroom door. The knob rattled. The hinges squealed.

He was wrong.

No one was there. The drip, drip, drip *of water vanished, as if he had never heard it at all. His intruder was somehow a ghost.*

Stride didn't understand. He'd been so sure of his instincts, but the living room was hot, dark, and empty, and there had been no time for anyone to escape. At first, he assumed it was his imagination playing tricks on him. Then he knelt down and put his fingers on the floor, and they came away wet.

He glanced over his head. A leak from the unfinished attic?

No. The ceiling was dry.

He shut the bedroom door behind him as quietly as he could. When he turned on the living room lights, there they were. Footprints. Wet footprints, making a trail away from the bedroom door past the red leather furniture, beckoning him. He followed. The footprints led him to the dining room, glistening on the hardwood floor. Then to the kitchen. Then to the screened rear porch, where the air was damp and thick.

"This way."

Stride heard someone's voice, but it wasn't a voice he recognized. Or did he? There was something familiar about it.

A voice from a long time ago.

"This way," the man said again.

Stride went through the screen door and let it bang shut behind him. The door led into the small backyard that scraped along the slope of the sand dunes behind which, hidden from view like a vast beast, was Lake Superior. Nearly every day of his life, he went through that door, climbed the sandy trail, and hiked to the ribbon of beach where the waves lapped at his boots. He would stand there, soaking in the view of the huge blue lake, which constantly changed its moods like a beautiful woman. The skyline of Duluth clung to the steep hillside three miles away.

And yet that wasn't where he was now.

He went through the door and found himself in a completely different place. Looking back, he saw that his house was gone.

Instead, he now stood on a cliff of black granite, sixty feet over a raging river. The fullness of the summer forest surrounded him. He knew this place well; it was called the Deeps, where Amity Creek stampeded along Seven Bridges Road like a wild mustang, swirling in whirlpools and sucking tree limbs into its current before spitting them out in the cold water of Lake Superior. From this cliff, you could take a running leap into the water and swim in the black pool below. He'd done it himself dozens of times as a teenager. He and his best friend, Steve Garske, would shout, jump, fly through the air, crash into the water, and fight the undertow back to the surface. Over and over.

But sometimes, when the rains were heavy, the Deeps caught a body and didn't give it back.

Sometimes the flooded river held a body down and fed it to the lake.

Stride stared into the rapids, which boomed like deep rolls of thunder and erupted in silver waterfalls. He was right on the cliff's edge, where the spray made the stone slippery.

"Don't fall," a voice said.

Stride turned around.

"Don't fall. They'll never find you."

A man stood behind him. He was short, no more than five foot six, with a skinny build. He had thinning black hair and wide, staring eyes that looked like the mask of a raccoon. His skin was pale. His hair and clothes were soaking wet. He'd been diving into the swollen creek.

Drip. Drip. Drip.

Stride heard the noise in his head again, somehow louder than the violence of the river below him. But it wasn't water he heard. The man on the cliff had a bullet hole in the middle of his high forehead, a perfectly circular black-ringed wound that seeped a ribbon of blood down the man's nose, around his pale lips, and onto his chin, where it dripped onto the stone like chamber music.

Blood. That was what he'd heard all along. Blood.

Stride's right hand felt heavy. He lifted it and saw that a gun was in his hand, a wisp of smoke trailing from the barrel, a burnt smell in the air. He'd shot this man in the head. The wound was right there in his forehead, but the man still had his eyes open, still had a strange smile on his lips.

"You're dead," Stride told the man.

The smile on the man's face widened and turned into a mocking, cruel laugh that went on and on.

"You have to be dead," Stride insisted. "I shot you."

But the man raised his arm and extended a bony, brittle finger at Stride's chest.

Stride looked down.

His own shirt was soaked in blood. Fresh, cherry-red blood, growing and spreading into a misshapen stain. A mass of blood, the kind of loss no one should survive. And there was a bullet hole in his own chest, ripped through the fabric, right where his heart was.

"No," the man told him, still laughing. "You're the one who's dead."

1

"I had the dream again," Stride told his wife, Serena.

She sat in the passenger seat of his Ford Expedition and twisted a few strands of long black hair between her fingers. Her eyebrows arched in a teasing way above her green eyes, and her lips bent into a little smirk. "And were you still married to you-know-who?"

"Oh, yes."

"Should I be jealous?"

Stride chuckled quietly because Serena knew better than anyone that his second marriage, to a woman named Andrea Jantzik, had ended badly. Meeting and falling in love with Serena had been part of their breakup, but only part. Stride and Andrea had been mismatched lovers from the beginning, two wounded people looking for things the other couldn't give them. Their relationship hadn't even lasted four years.

"How many times is this?" Serena asked. "The dream, I mean."

"Every night for a week."

"Any idea why?"

Stride didn't answer at first. He stared through the truck window at the house across the street, where Steve Garske lived. They were parked a few blocks away from their own small cottage on the Point, which was the seven-mile narrow land barrier jutting out from downtown Duluth, creating a calm ship harbor protected from the assault of Lake Superior. Stride's house faced the lake, whereas Steve lived on the bay side. His friend's house was old, small, and needed work, as so many Point homes did, hammered throughout the year by floods and lake winds, frozen by bitter winter nights. A green picket fence and untrimmed hedges fronted the street. The house's wooden siding was painted to match the forest green of the fence, but the paint had weathered. A jumble of flagstones made a driveway that led to a single garage stall at the back of the house, steps from the bay.

"I met Steve at the Deeps when I was fifteen," Stride said finally. "In the dream, that's where I am. So I assume, in some way, it's about him. I haven't been thinking about much else this week."

"What about the gun? And the man you shot?"

Stride shook his head. "I don't know what that's about," he lied.

"And Andrea?"

"I don't know why she's there, either," he lied again.

There was something in the flicker of concern on Serena's face that said she knew he wasn't telling her everything. But for the moment, she didn't challenge him on it.

"I know how hard this is, Jonny," Serena said. "Do you want me to go with you?"

"No, I need to do this myself. You already said goodbye."

"Okay. I'll be here."

She slid across the seat, turned his face toward hers with both hands, and kissed him gently. Her lips were soft, as they always were. Her eyes were sad. She ran her fingers through his wavy black-and-gray hair, doing what she could to tame it, but it was a lost cause. He caught a glimpse of his face in the mirror. The weathered lines there were deeper and darker than usual.

"You look nice," she told him, being kind.

Stride wore his dress blues. He mostly did that for police ceremonies and funerals, but this day was a kind of funeral. It was the last time he would see his best friend. Steve was a doctor and a practical man about life and death, so he wanted no visitation, no church service, no wake, no gathering. When the time came, Stride would take his friend's ashes into the north woods to be scattered. And that night, at the coffeehouse in Canal Park called Amazing Grace, Steve's country band would play, with an empty chair on the stage.

He got out of the truck. The sun hid behind charcoal clouds, making the July afternoon unusually cool. The bay water behind Steve's house was motionless and slate gray. Standing on the street, he took a slow breath, trying to fight back tears. Then, drawing himself up straight to his full height, which was not quite six foot one, Stride crossed the street.

His number two on Duluth's detective force, Maggie Bei, was already inside. He passed her bright yellow Avalanche parked at the curb. The brand new truck replaced one that had been destroyed six months earlier, but in that short time, it was already missing its passenger-side mirror, had a crumpled rear fender, and bore the telltale dents and scrapes of Maggie's abysmal driving skills. Stride couldn't help but smile, even though it didn't last more than a moment.

Maggie met him at the door. She wore a little black dress, probably purchased in the teenage prom section at T. J. Maxx. She wasn't much bigger than a China doll, and had her dark hair pulled tightly back behind her head. Like him, she tried and failed to hide her tears.

"Hey, boss."

"Hey, Mags. How is he?"

"The nurse thinks it'll be tonight."

Stride bit down on his lip until it hurt. "Yeah."

"You want me to stick around?" she asked.

"No. That's okay. Thanks."

She caressed his arm briefly as she left the house. He could hear the sharp *crack* of her heels on the flagstones as she headed for the street. It was strange, the things that triggered memories. When his first wife, Cindy, had died, he spent the evening after the service here, in this house with Steve and Maggie, and he could remember the click of Maggie's heels then, too, when she'd left the two men alone on the back porch at midnight. Unfairly, he knew that the sound of Maggie's heels would always make him think of cancer.

Stride braced himself.

Thirty-six years. That was how long he'd known Steve Garske. They were as different as night and day: Stride, a closed-off cop who'd spent a lifetime building walls around himself, Steve, a guitar-playing family doctor who never left a room without making friends with everyone in it. At every crossroad with the important people in Stride's life, Steve had been there. Steve had been the one to see Cindy through the disease that took her away. He'd been the one to counsel Andrea on infertility at a time when they wanted kids. He'd been the one to see Cat Mateo, the teenage runaway who now lived with Stride and Serena, through the girl's pregnancy and delivery.

Steve had been best man at each of Stride's weddings. That said it all. And now he was dying.

He told Stride about it three months earlier, long after the initial diagnosis, when the outlook was terminal. He wanted no sympathy, no early grief, and so he'd kept it a secret from everyone. He'd spent the weeks since the announcement winding down his practice and finding new doctors for all of his patients. Stride and Steve had carved out one May weekend to take a last camping trip on the Gunflint Trail, and they spent three days fishing, swapping old stories, listening to Sara Evans songs, and completely ignoring the fact that they'd never do this again. When Stride dropped Steve back at his house, they exchanged a single look between them that said everything they failed to say in the woods. A look that said "thanks" and "I'm sorry" and "goodbye" and "I love you" all at the same time.

This house.

Stride inhaled the scent of it. Dust. Burnt coffee. Tuna fish on toast. That was Steve's life. It had smelled the same way for years.

Steve bought the ramshackle cottage on Park Point when he came back to Duluth after medical school and lived here ever since. It was a bachelor's house; Steve had never married, barely even dated. He'd never needed anything more than a small house on a small lot by the water. He wasn't addicted to material things, just medicine and music. The one change he'd made to the place over the years was to add a loft as a bedroom to give him a better view of the bay.

That was where he was now.

Stride climbed the stairs. As he went up, Steve's nurse passed him going down. She gave him a weak little smile and shook her head.

"It's good you're here," she said. "I don't think it will be long now."

He said nothing in reply. He paused on the stairs, letting a shudder of grief ripple through his body. Then he continued to the loft and hovered in the doorway, watching Steve in bed. The bed faced a picture window on the bay, and Stride could see one of the ore boats that had come off the lake through the city's lift bridge, heading for harbor on the Wisconsin side. To everyone else around Duluth, this was an ordinary day. Not the last day.

Steve didn't look like Steve. Not anymore. His wavy blond hair was gone. His tall frame had the bony look of a skeleton. His skin was pale and loose, like a suit that didn't fit anymore. Stride had been in too many rooms like this in his life. He didn't really mind death, but he hated the reality of dying.

He took a step closer, and the floor of the loft squealed under his feet. His friend's eyes fluttered open and took a moment to focus. The eyes, at least, were still Steve's eyes, smart and blue. Steve saw him and laughed out loud, which was an effort that ended in a cough. His voice had the rasp of an old wire brush.

"Holy shit. Dress blues. Is this heaven? Are you an angel?"

"Heaven can do better than me for angels," Stride said.

Steve had more to say, but it took him a long time to get out the words. "I'm picturing it like a Victoria's Secret commercial. Wings and all. Any chance Kathy Ireland is waiting for me up there?"

"Pretty sure she's still alive and kicking, Steve."

He laughed again. Coughed again. "Man, I cannot catch a break."

There was a wooden chair next to the bed, and Stride sat down. Wearing his uniform made him sit with perfect posture, which felt odd and uncomfortable. By instinct, he smoothed his sleeves and brushed away a loose thread. "So," Stride said.

"So. What's new?"

"Not much. You?"

"Busy. Lots of people."

"Yeah. Good."

"Maggie was here," Steve said.

"I know. I saw her."

"She brought a Big Mac. Ate it while we talked."

"She didn't," Stride said.

Another laugh. "No, but I could smell it on her."

"Yeah. Mags loves her Mickey D's." Stride shook his head and tried to think of something to say that wasn't banal. "Cat wanted to come, but … well, actually, I told her not to."

"Good. Keep her away. She doesn't need this. How is she?"

"She's pretending to be tough. She says she's over everything that happened to her in the winter, but she's not."

"She's a good kid."

"Yeah. She is."

Stride was angry with himself. This was the last time he was going to see his friend, and there was so much important ground to cover, so many memories to revisit, so many emotions to express. But all he could seem to do was make small talk, like they would do this again tomorrow, and the day after that, and the day after that. But they both knew they wouldn't.

They'd been friends for a long time, and Steve had a way of reading his mind. "It's okay, buddy."

Stride inhaled sharply. "No. It's not."

"Why don't you go home? You've done your duty."

"I can stay."

"No. Go. Really. I'm pretty tired."

"Are you sure?"

"I'm sure. Honestly, I think I'd rather be alone for the end."

"You don't have to be," Stride said. "I'll stay all night. Right here. You can sleep if you want, but I don't have to go anywhere."

"Yes, you do. Go home, Stride. Kiss Serena. Kiss Cat. Be happy, okay?"

"Son of a bitch, Steve."

"I know."

Stride got out of the chair. His friend's eyes blinked shut with exhaustion.

He leaned over and took hold of Steve's hand and clasped both of his hands around it. He held on, not wanting to let go, trying to cement the feel of his friend's skin, his grip, his warmth, in his memory forever.

"Tell Cindy I'm okay, will you?" Stride said.

"Count on it."

"Goodbye, buddy."

Stride choked out those words, but his friend didn't answer, as if he were already asleep. He put Steve's hand down on the bed and tucked the blanket around him, keeping him warm. He wanted to make it out of the room before he began to cry. He took one last look at Steve's face and headed for the door.

But Steve wasn't done.

He had more to say.

"Hey, Stride," Steve called after him in a voice that was barely there. "You're safe. You can let it go, okay?"

Stride stopped and turned around. Steve's eyes weren't open, but he was talking, murmuring, whispering so softly that Stride had to come back to the bed to hear him. "What did you say?"

"You're safe, buddy. I never told a soul."

"About what?"

"About the Deeps," Steve whispered.

Suddenly, Stride felt disoriented, as if he were back in his recurring dream. He looked down at his own chest, expecting to see blood on his uniform. A bullet hole. It was all so vivid. He could hear the surge of the river and feel the spray rising over him from the rapids like a cloud.

"What about the Deeps?" Stride asked.

Steve was quiet. His eyes were still closed. Stride knew he should let it go, but he couldn't. He had to know.

"Steve, what about the Deeps?" he repeated, more urgently.

His friend's lips moved. Steve spoke again, barely making a sound. "Nobody knows, buddy. Don't worry. I found the body after you left, and I took care of it. I buried him."

2

Darkness fell at the end of the long summer evening.

Stride stood on the narrow strip of beach that ran along the Point, the waves of Lake Superior crowding his feet. His face was damp from mist, which was the leading edge of a hard, steady rain approaching from the west. Grief and rain always seemed to go hand in hand. He hadn't eaten anything. All he'd done at home was hang up his dress uniform and change back into casual clothes, then head over the dunes to the lake. He'd been outside, alone, for more than an hour, watching the Duluth lights awaken on the hillside a few miles away. Serena knew to give him time and space.

He'd been visited by death many times before. Death always made him question his own life, but he never made any real changes when he lost someone. He'd considered moving away after Cindy died, but Duluth was home, no matter how many painful memories it carried. Going anywhere else would make him a foreigner, with no roots, and he couldn't handle that. A few years earlier, after falling in love with Serena, he tried moving to Las Vegas to be with her. But he was a fish out of water there. Not long after, rather than break up, the two of them had come back to the cold of northern Minnesota. Serena was better at being a stranger in a strange land than he was.

Now, as he was about to lose Steve, he found himself at a crossroads again. He wondered, not for the first time, about quitting his job. Changing careers. He'd put in his time; he could retire if he wanted. But no matter how restless he felt, he didn't know what he would do if he weren't a cop. He found it hard to imagine not getting up in the darkness every morning, not going to a job that took him all over the city. That had always been his life. He was addicted to what he did, and his colleagues were his family.

Regardless, every loss chipped away at his soul. The violence took its toll. He didn't know how long he could stay numb to it day after day.

"Stride?"

He turned around on the beach. Cat stood behind him. She held up a can of Bent Paddle. "I thought you could use a beer."

"You read my mind." He smiled as he took it from her. The can was open, and he weighed it in his hand, with a sharp eye at the eighteen-year-old. "Doesn't feel entirely full. I wonder why that would be."

"I may have tried a little. You know, to make sure it's fresh."

"Uh-huh."

"Just a little."

"Uh-huh."

Cat came up beside him, took hold of his arm, and leaned her head against his shoulder. Her long chestnut hair was loose. She wore shorts and a midriff-baring T-shirt, and her feet were bare, but the drizzle and the cold lake breeze didn't seem to bother her.

Catalina Mateo. The daughter of Michaela Mateo, a woman he had tried and failed to save from an abusive ex-husband. Michaela was another loss he carried with him that had begun to weigh him down. He looked at Cat and saw hints of her mother in her beautiful face.

"Are you okay?" Cat asked. "I mean, that's dumb. Of course, you're not okay."

"I've been better."

"I'm really sorry about Dr. Steve."

"Thanks."

They were quiet for a while. He drank his beer, while Cat stared at the water and held on to him. He thought it was sweet that she wanted to comfort him. Steve was right; she was a good kid. After more than two years with this girl in his life, it was hard for him to remember what it had been like before Cat. She'd hidden away in his house one night, terrified, homeless, pregnant, on the run from a killer. He and Serena had taken her in, and she'd lived with them ever since. Despite the ups and downs of that time, Stride saw something special in her, much more than she saw in herself. She was smart, beautiful, and brave, and at eighteen, she was quickly becoming more of a woman than a girl. But she'd grown up taking foolish risks, and that part of her personality still got her into trouble.

"Serena says you're still getting mail from strangers," he said.

"Some. Not a lot."

"Anything I should be worried about?"

"There are some weird ones, but it's no big deal."

"How about you show them to me, and let me decide about that?"

"Some guy in Estonia likes to send me dick pics. What are you going to do, Stride? Fly over there and kick the crap out of him?"

"I might," Stride said.

"He's like seventy years old."

"I still might."

"I'm fine. Really. Don't worry about me. You've got your own stuff."

Stride let it go. For now. Last year, he probably would have gone into her room and searched it to see what she was hiding from him. There had been issues all along with Cat keeping secrets. But she was eighteen now, and he and Serena were trying to give her more freedom.

It had been a difficult six months for Cat. In January, she'd been drugged and nearly raped by a Hollywood celebrity who was in town filming a movie. She exposed the actor's dark side to the world, and the resulting publicity made Cat a kind of celebrity herself. For a while, she'd thrived on the attention. She'd been on television. On magazine covers. But having people everywhere recognize her name and face carried its own dangers. She received thousands of messages, some from grateful #MeToo survivors, but many others from a parade of obsessive haters and stalkers.

"I can put the security back on for you, any time you want," Stride said, because he wasn't good at letting things go.

"And have some cop following me around all summer? No, thanks."

"Well, just be careful, okay?"

"I will."

"Thanks for the beer," Stride told her. "Why don't you go on back inside? It's cold out."

Cat didn't object. She gave him a hug before she left. He watched her silhouette as she hiked back through the sand and up the grassy slope toward their cottage. After she disappeared, he was alone again. The beach was empty. The lake waves kept rolling toward him. The lights of the city were a hazy blur through the mist. He thought about going back inside, but he felt as if he were waiting for something out here. Or someone. Really, he was waiting for Steve, to see if he would feel his friend's presence leave the world, to see if Steve would find a way to send him some kind of message.

But life didn't work like that.

Not long after, Stride felt the buzz of his phone and recognized the name on the caller ID. It was Steve's nurse. He allowed himself a moment to absorb the implications of her call. Then he answered the phone and got the news. Steve was gone. Peacefully. The nurse had checked on him minutes earlier and discovered that he passed away while she was out of the room. Alone, the way he'd wanted.

Stride thanked her for the call and hung up.

He scrolled to the pictures on his phone and found one of him and Steve together and thought about never hearing his jokes or seeing his smile again. In the time it took to blink, life came and went.

He texted Serena: *Can you come out here?*

She'd know why. She'd know what it meant.

As he waited for Serena, he called Maggie to give her the news. They exchanged awkward sympathies, because neither of them was good at it. After a long, long pause, he went on: "Listen, Mags, the timing is terrible, but this can't wait. We need to get a search warrant first thing in the morning. I can give you the details for everything you need, but the application should come from you, not me."

"A warrant?" Maggie asked in surprise. "To do what?"

"To dig up Steve's yard," Stride replied.

* * * * *

Cat still had trouble believing that she had appeared on the cover of *People* Magazine, but there she was. Her and that sleazebag actor, Dean Casperson. The man who slipped Rohypnol into her bottle of water, undressed her, and would have raped her if Stride hadn't arrived in time. Casperson was in jail now and would be staying there for a long time.

The headline on the magazine read: *The Teenager Who Exposed Hollywood's Dirtiest Secret.*

Serena had framed the cover for her, and it hung on her bedroom wall. The photo made her look a little unhinged, with a wild, angry look in her brown eyes. Some days Cat took it down, because she couldn't stare at it anymore. She really didn't want to remember that night, and she didn't want to be famous for it. Other days, she put it back up and thought about what Stride had told her. She'd done something completely stupid and unbelievably courageous, and he was proud of her. She didn't think anything else in her life had ever made her feel as good.

Serena was a like a mother to Cat, but Stride was—well, he was Stride. She was devoted to him, in love with him, in awe of him. He was her superhero, and she hated to see him in pain, the way he was now.

Cat lay in bed with the lights off. It was almost one in the morning, but she couldn't sleep. She was restless and bored, her knees twitching. Her corner bedroom faced the street, and the window was open. The drizzle outside had turned to rain. She saw the occasional gauzy flash of headlights from late-night cars passing on the street and heard the splash of their tires through puddles.

She thought about texting Curt Dickes to see if he wanted to get together. Curt was one of the only people from her bad days on the street who was still in her life. She'd always had a little bit of a crush on him, which irritated Serena, because Curt was nine years older and had been in and out of jail half a dozen times in his life. But Curt was also funny and cool and wild and a crazy dresser, and Cat liked him. She began tapping out a text, but then she stopped and deleted it. Curt was probably off with his girlfriend. They were probably having sex right now. The thought of it made Cat jealous. She'd hoped when she turned eighteen that Curt might see her as something more than a kid, but instead, he'd already hooked up with someone else.

It made for a lonely summer. She didn't have a lot of friends.

Cat turned on her nightstand lamp. She got out of bed and went to the window, where she stared at the rain. The air was sticky on her bare arms and legs. She tried to decide whether to sneak out to her car and head to a downtown club, but she didn't want to go out. Not tonight, not alone. But she was also wide awake.

She went back to her nightstand, opened the top drawer, and removed a stack of letters inside that were bound together with a rubber band. She'd told Stride that she wasn't receiving much fan mail anymore, but that wasn't true. Most days, she tried to get to the mailbox ahead of Stride or Serena, so they didn't see the dozens of letters addressed to her from people all over the world. Total strangers. They all treated her like a best friend. They all knew where she lived.

It was creepy.

Today's batch included almost twenty letters, plus a large manila envelope. She peeled off the rubber band and began opening the notes one by one. Most were harmless. People sent her the oddest things: photos of their pets, poems, cardinal feathers, loose change, pictures of Jesus. She put aside a few to send replies, because she felt bad for girls who wrote to her because they'd been raped, or abused, or assaulted. She'd been there herself, and she didn't want those girls to feel alone. Some of the notes she put directly in a shredder. Those were hate mail from Dean Casperson fans who accused her of trapping him and going after his money.

There were disgusting ones, too. It was unbelievable what people did. She'd told Stride about her Estonian pen pal who sent close-ups of his erections, complete with graying pubic hair, but she got others like that all the time. In today's stack, there was a soiled copy of her *People* magazine cover that a man in Kentucky had obviously used to masturbate. He sent her the results.

"Yuck yuck yuck yuck," Cat said aloud.

It wasn't the first time she'd gotten something like that. Holding it by the corner, she threw it away.

Then she got to the last item in the stack, which was the large manila envelope, hand-addressed to her in lime-green marker. She noted that the postmark was local. It had been sent to her by someone in Duluth.

When she opened the envelope, she immediately felt a shiver of alarm. Inside, she found an eight-by-ten photograph of *her*. It was a recent picture, taken at the house of Drew and Krista Olson, who'd adopted Cat's baby. The photo showed Cat in their backyard, her long hair flying, a big smile on her face as she played with her two-year-old son, Michael.

Whoever sent this had been watching her. Spying on her. But that wasn't even the worst part.

The photograph was covered in green marker, like the address on the outside of the envelope. One sentence was scribbled on the front and back of the picture over and over.

I love you I love you I love you I love you I love you I love you.

Cat had received personal messages before. Invitations to prom. Invitations to sex. Even marriage proposals and engagement rings. But this one was different. Something about it felt threatening, not just that the postmark was local, not just that it was a picture of her, not just that someone was watching her.

There was something else about it.

What?

And then her gaze drifted to the top of her dresser, and she knew. There it was, sitting upright next to her Bluetooth speakers, in plain sight. She hadn't noticed it before, but she knew she hadn't left it there herself.

A green marker.

He'd left behind the marker.

He'd written the message on the photograph right here in her bedroom.

3

Steve's yard was small and crowded with trees. There were only so many places to hide a body, and Stride knew where to tell the forensics team to dig.

He remembered the day seven years ago when Steve had added a picket fence and a small garden near the street. That was an unusual project for him, because Steve didn't exactly have a green thumb. He'd planted herbs like rosemary, parsley, and basil, because he said he was taking a cooking class and wanted to use fresh ingredients. The garden had lasted for all of one season, and since then, the rectangular plot had been nothing but a nest of weeds.

The ground in the yard was soft, thanks to the rain, and their officers had erected a tent over the garden. Under the tarp, men with shovels carefully scraped away the mud layer by layer. Stride sat with Maggie in her Avalanche as the team worked. He drank coffee; she ate McDonald's fries. Neither of them said a word, but he could feel her eyeing him across the truck. She was waiting for him to give her some kind of explanation for the search, but he couldn't do that.

Not yet.

Not until they found Ned Baer's body.

He'd recited Steve's dying words for Maggie exactly as he remembered them, leaving nothing out. He hadn't tried to protect himself. She'd taken his statement with an expressionless face and not asked any follow-up questions. Instead, she'd written up the warrant application based on Steve's confession and hand-delivered it to a friendly judge at the county courthouse. Now the search was underway. There was nothing to do but wait and see what the team found.

They weren't alone on the Point. Neighbors had already begun to gather near the house to observe the police activity. They all knew Steve and knew he had died the previous day. It hadn't taken long in the tight-knit Point community for word to spread that something unusual was happening. Sooner rather than later, the local media would also pick up the story and descend on the area.

The story of Ned Baer was going to be back in the news. This time, unlike seven years ago, Stride knew the truth was going to come out.

No more sins of omission. No more lies.

He needed to call Andrea and warn her.

Stride checked his watch. The forensics team had been digging for less than an hour, but if the body really was here, they'd get to it soon. He was impatient to know if he was right, so he got out of the Avalanche and stepped into the pouring rain. He wore a vinyl slicker and pulled up the hood. There was no wind, and the summer rain was warm, but he still shivered. This was one of those moments when he missed smoking. A cigarette in his hand would have gone a long way toward calming his nerves.

Maggie emptied the last few french fries into her mouth and joined him. She stood unprotected in the rain. He felt the weight of the silence between them, heavy and uncomfortable. He didn't like feeling that way with her. They'd been partners and friends for two decades; they'd even been lovers for a brief, uncomfortable stretch of months. He trusted Maggie more than anyone else in his life except Serena, but Maggie was also a cop, and Stride was acting like a witness with things to hide.

Under the tent on Steve's front lawn, Sergeant Max Guppo used two fingers to let out a loud whistle.

This was it. They'd found something.

Stride marched that way, head down, his hands in his pockets. He heard Maggie clear her throat behind him, and he knew she wanted him to stay back and let her talk to the forensics team alone. She was right. She was in charge here. He needed to keep this case at arm's length, but right now, he didn't care about protocol. He wanted to see what Steve had hidden in the ground.

His long legs carried him across the wet grass. Maggie hurried to catch up with him. The rain poured over the edges of the tent, and he crossed through a waterfall to the other side. Guppo was waiting beside a hole that went about two feet down into the wet soil. The other members of the team leaned on dirty shovels, and their faces were wet with sweat and rain.

Stride stared down into the hole, which was really a grave.

A skull stared back at him.

That was all that was visible right now, a white skull against the black dirt. In seven years, all the flesh had long since been eaten away. Its eye holes gaped. Where the nose had been was a dark, open triangle. The mouth of the skull was parted, its two rows of teeth separated as if in midscream. And in the middle of the forehead bone was a single, round hole.

A bullet hole.

The man in the ground had been shot in the head.

Maggie immediately grabbed Stride's arm and pulled him away. He resisted, unable to take his eyes off the skull, caught somewhere between his nightmares and his memories. Maggie pulled again, hard, but he remained rooted in place. Then she got on tiptoes and whispered in his ear.

"Stride, I'm not kidding around. You can't be here. You need to come with me *right now*."

This time, he let her drag him into the rain. His hood slipped from his head and the downpour drenched his face. The two of them hiked past Steve's old house, dodging the tall spruce trees until they got to the small backyard. They were steps from the bay. The water was dimpled, and fog and rain blocked the far Wisconsin shore from view. Maggie glanced over her shoulder, making sure that none of the other cops could see where they were.

"Okay, boss, what the hell?" she demanded in a loud voice. "What's going on?"

Stride understood Maggie's reaction. He would have been just as upset with her if the tables were turned. "You know as much as I do about this, Mags. The last thing Steve said to me was that he buried a body. I didn't know if it was real or not. For all I knew, he was delirious. Hallucinating. But it's not like I could ignore what he said. We had to check it out."

"Be straight with me, boss. Did you already know about this?"

"What do you mean?"

"Did you know about the body before yesterday?"

"No. Of course not."

Maggie shook her head. "Is that the truth? I can keep this off the record for now, but as soon as we go back out there, everything goes in the file. I have to know what happened."

"It's the truth, Mags. I didn't know about the body. Steve never said a word about it before now. This was a dying confession. I'm as shocked as you are."

Maggie swore. She bent down and picked up a thick branch that had blown off one of the trees and threw it into the water. "We're talking about a *murder* victim. Somebody shot this guy."

"I know that. Obviously."

She closed her eyes, wiping away the rain from her face with both hands. "It's Ned Baer, right?"

Stride shrugged. "I assume so. I don't see who else it could be."

"Did you know he was dead?"

"No, I didn't. I knew what you knew. What we all knew. Baer was missing. We assumed he'd drowned in the Deeps and the body was lost in the lake. I sure as hell didn't know he'd been shot."

"Do you think Steve killed him?" Maggie asked.

"Steve? No way."

"He buried the body. What the hell am I supposed to think?"

"Steve didn't even own a gun, Mags. As far as I know, he never fired a gun in his life."

"There's a first time for everything," Maggie replied.

"I'm telling you, Steve had no reason to kill Ned Baer. He didn't do it."

"So why hide the body? Why cover up a murder?"

"I don't know."

Maggie made sure they were still alone. They didn't have much time before the other cops got curious and came looking for them. Maggie leaned in close to Stride and jabbed a finger at his face. Her voice was an angry hiss.

"Like hell you don't know! You told me what Steve said. *You're safe, buddy*. If Steve didn't kill Ned Baer, then the only reason he hid the body was because he thought *you* did it. Now why the hell would he think that?"

"I'm telling you, Mags, *I don't know*. Steve and I never talked about Ned Baer. Not before he disappeared, not after. I had no idea that Steve even knew who the hell Ned was. There's no reason he would have thought that I killed him."

Maggie let a hostile silence draw out between them. "Did you?"

"Did I what?"

"Did you kill him?"

"Oh, come on. Are you serious, Mags? I can't believe you would ask me that."

"I'm totally serious."

"Well, what's next? Should I call a lawyer? I came to *you*. I told you what Steve said. If I killed Ned Baer, why wouldn't I just keep my mouth shut? No one would have known about the body if I hadn't told you to get the warrant."

"Yeah, until somebody bought the house and decided to plant a new garden, right? Come on, Stride. It's an official question, and I need an official answer. We're back on the record. This all goes in the file. I don't have any choice about this. Did you kill Ned Baer?"

"*No.* I did not."

"Do you know who did?"

"No, I don't. And obviously, Steve didn't know either, because if he thought it was me, he was *wrong*." Stride glanced over his shoulder and saw Max Guppo lumbering toward them. The sergeant's round face was furrowed with concern, watching the two of them argue. "But since we're back on the record, Mags, we might as well go to the station and make everything official. Interview me. Ask me whatever you want. I know you have more questions. Because even though I didn't kill him, we both know that I was the last person to see Ned Baer alive."

4

Stride had never spent any time on the opposite side of the witness table. He was typically the one conducting the interrogations, and he had a better sense now of what it was like to be on the receiving end of suspicion and mistrust from the police. Maggie sat across from him. Her face was a mask, the way it always was when she was in this room. No emotion, nothing personal between them. Except the two of them were close enough that they always knew what the other was thinking. She didn't believe for a moment that he'd murdered Ned Baer, but she also knew that he hadn't been honest with her when Ned disappeared.

Maggie had an overstuffed folder on the table. Two evidence boxes were stacked on the chairs on either side of her. He recognized all the materials they gathered seven years ago. This was the sum-total of what they learned while investigating the disappearance of Ned Baer.

An investigation he led.

An investigation that he'd deliberately obstructed.

He knew how this interview would go; he knew what he had to say. He was surprised to find himself oddly calm about admitting it after all this time.

Maggie opened the folder. On top was a photograph, which she removed and pinned to the bulletin board behind her. Stride recognized the picture. He'd long ago memorized the man's face.

Ned Baer had been a compact man, five foot six, with a scrawny, underfed frame. At the time he disappeared, he'd been thirty-nine years old. He had messy, receding black hair that left only a U-shaped tongue on his high forehead. His eyes were brown, with dark half-moons beneath them. He wore a wispy beard, and his lips were thin and unsmiling. In the picture, he wore hiker's clothes: boots, cargo pants, and a navy blue zipped REI jacket. The photo had been taken in the Colorado mountains, two hours from where Ned kept a Denver apartment.

"Are you ready?" Maggie asked.

"Sure. Let's go."

Maggie turned on a voice recorder in front of her and recited her name, Stride's name, and the date and time of the interview. She used her cop voice.

"Lieutenant Stride, can you confirm for me that you're conducting this interview willingly and under no duress?"

"I am." He added after a moment, "It was my idea."

"Do you want me to read you your rights?"

"No, that's not necessary. I'm pretty familiar with them."

Maggie hesitated, then turned off the recorder. When she spoke to him again, she was the snarky friend he'd known for two decades. "Just so we're clear, I know this is bullshit, boss."

"I know you do. Let's just get through it, Mags."

She switched the recorder back on, and her voice was professional again. "Lieutenant Stride, can you review the facts of Ned Baer's disappearance for me?"

He allowed himself a silent laugh. Maggie, who had a near-photographic memory, could have rattled off nearly every page of the investigative folder without so much as turning over a piece of paper. But this was official. This was about what *he* knew.

"Ned Baer was a writer for a journal called the Freedom Reporter Online," Stride replied. "FR Online is a conservative newspaper, and Ned was one of their investigative journalists. He lived in Colorado but traveled extensively on research projects around the country. His focus was primarily digging up dirt on left-leaning politicians. Seven years ago, in

July, Ned Baer came to Duluth and paid for an open-ended summer rental at a motel on the west end of Superior Street."

"Why was he in Duluth?"

Stride took a swallow from the can of Coke Maggie had given him before the interrogation. He eased back in the chair and rubbed his chin.

"Ned was investigating sexual assault allegations against a politician named Devin Card. The allegations had broken in the media the previous month. At the time, Card was the Minnesota Attorney General and was running for an open seat in the US House of Representatives. An anonymous woman alleged that Card had raped her more than twenty years earlier, while she was a high school student in Duluth. Ned was in town, along with half the political reporters in the country, to see if he could figure out who the woman was and whether there was any truth to the allegations."

"How long was Ned in Duluth?" Maggie asked.

"He disappeared the third week in August, so at that point, he'd been here for approximately one month."

"How did you become aware of his disappearance?"

"I received a call from Ned's editor, Debbi King. She told me that she hadn't had any communication with Ned in five days and that the voice mailbox on his cell phone was full. According to her, it was very unusual for Ned to be out of touch for so long, and she was concerned. At that point, I launched an investigation. Of course, you already know that, since we worked on it together."

Maggie ignored his comment. "Can you summarize how the investigation proceeded?"

"Yes. Our first step was to visit the motel where Ned was staying. You and I talked to the manager and the housekeeping staff, and we concluded that Ned hadn't been back to his room for several days. However, no one at the motel could tell us exactly when he'd last been there. We searched the room but found nothing to explain his whereabouts or what he'd been working on. There was no cell phone, no notes, no computer, no calendar, etc. At the same time, we ran a check on the credit card he'd used to pay for the room, and there had been no activity on the card in Duluth or anywhere else for nearly a week."

"And then what?" Maggie asked.

"We obtained records for Ned's cell phone, based on the number his editor gave us. The records indicated that Ned's phone had last been used for a call to his editor on the afternoon of Tuesday, August 24. That was also the last time he used his credit card; to purchase breakfast at the Duluth Grill. As a result, we began to focus on that time period as the likely point when Ned disappeared, although we didn't know what had happened to him. However, a series of incoming calls in his phone records gave us another clue."

"Where did those calls come from?"

"A rental car agency at the Minneapolis airport. Ned had a rental contract on a green Kia Rio, but as it turns out, we actually had the car in custody ourselves. That is, the police did. The car had been illegally parked, ticketed, and subsequently towed to an impound lot. When the officer who requested the tow ran the plates, he noted that it was a rental vehicle and contacted the agency. They started calling Ned to find out what was going on with their car."

"What information came out about the Kia?" Maggie asked.

"The parking ticket was written the morning of Wednesday, August 25. The car was towed the following day when it still hadn't been moved. This helped us confirm the timeframe when we believe Ned disappeared. It also told us what we believe was his last known location. The car had been parked off the shoulder on the south end of Seven Bridges Road, near a popular cliffside swimming area on Amity Creek, known as the Deeps."

"So the evidence suggested that Ned was at or near the Deeps shortly before he disappeared?"

"Yes. The location also suggested to me a possible explanation for Ned's disappearance. August 24 followed a period of heavy rain in the area. The currents were running high and fast, and the Deeps is extremely treacherous at times like that. We've lost swimmers there who didn't understand the power of the undertow and drowned after jumping from the cliff. Most of the victims eventually turn up at the mouth of the Lester River or in Lake Superior, but not all, especially if no one knows they're missing.

So the most likely explanation to me was that Ned—who was a stranger to Duluth and unfamiliar with the risks—may have drowned in the river and his body was subsequently lost in the lake."

"You believed that was what had happened to him?"

"Yes, I did."

"Was there any evidence of foul play?" Maggie asked.

"No. Well, sorry, that's not completely true. The passenger window on the Kia had been smashed, suggesting a break-in. However, we didn't find any evidence to suggest that the break-in and Ned's disappearance were connected. Vehicle smash-and-grabs aren't uncommon during the summer."

Maggie said nothing for a long, long time. She had a pen in her hand that she tapped slowly on the table.

"At that point in the investigation, did you share additional information with me about Ned Baer, based on your personal knowledge?"

Stride stared back at Maggie. She was a cool one. "Yes, I did."

"What was that information?"

"I told you that I had met with Ned Baer on the evening of Tuesday, August 24."

"In other words, on the night he disappeared," Maggie concluded.

"Apparently so."

"Where did this meeting take place?"

"At the Deeps," Stride said.

"So *you* met with him on the night he disappeared, in the place where he disappeared."

"That seems likely, yes."

"Did our investigation uncover anyone else who had met with Ned or saw him alive after the time you did?"

"No. We didn't locate anyone who reported seeing Ned after the evening of Tuesday, August 24. However, just to be absolutely clear about this, Ned was alive when I left him. Also, at the time of our investigation, I had no reason to suspect foul play. In fact, based on seeing him there, I was able to provide confirming evidence that Ned's disappearance was likely due to drowning."

"Namely?"

"He was soaking wet, presumably because he'd been diving in the Deeps. He was also drinking. He had a six-pack of beer with him. I warned him that it was a foolish thing to do. He didn't seem to take my warning seriously."

"And that's why you thought he drowned," Maggie said.

"Yes. Until yesterday, that was still what I thought."

"Were you acquainted with Ned prior to his disappearance? Did the two of you know each other or have any history together?"

"No, I met him that one time at the Deeps, and that was all. We had no other contact."

"You indicated to me at the time that you met with Ned to discuss his investigation into the allegations against Devin Card," Maggie said. "Were the police also investigating those allegations?"

"No. There was no basis to look into an anonymous claim of sexual assault from more than two decades earlier. Even if a victim had come forward, the accusation would have fallen outside the statute of limitations. Our hands were tied."

"So what did Ned want to know?" Maggie asked. "Why did he ask to meet with you?"

Stride felt as if he were a teenager atop the cliffs at the Deeps. Ready to jump. Unsure of what would happen when he hit the water. He'd avoided this moment for the last seven years.

"He didn't," Stride replied.

Maggie knitted her brow with confusion. "What?"

"Ned didn't contact me for a meeting. I was the one who sought him out."

His answer froze her into silence. She reached for the button on the voice recorder again, but Stride shook his head and wagged a finger at her, directing her to keep going. He watched emotions whipping in quick succession across her face. Uncertainty. Anxiety. Betrayal.

She reached into the folder in front of her and removed a single sheet of paper. She began talking faster and breathing hard.

"Lieutenant Stride, didn't you tell me seven years ago that Ned Baer contacted you about a meeting, because he wanted to discuss your personal memories of the time in which the alleged assault by Devin Card occurred? And didn't you tell me that the two of you had a brief conversation at the Deeps, lasting no more than five minutes, during which time you told him that you had no recollection of being at a party with Devin Card twenty-two years earlier and had no recollection of any rumors in Duluth that Attorney General Card had been involved in a sexual assault that summer?"

"Yes, I did tell you that."

"Are you saying that was not true?"

"It's true that I had no relationship with Devin Card and had no knowledge of any rumors about his behavior that summer. But that wasn't why I met with Ned Baer."

"You *lied* to me?"

"Yes, I did."

"Why did you meet with Ned Baer?" Maggie asked.

Stride shook his head and didn't answer.

"Stride?" Maggie demanded sharply, leaning across the table. "What was the meeting about?"

"I have nothing to say about that," he replied. "Ned and I had a conversation, and when it was over, I left. He was alive. As I've already told you several times, I didn't kill him. I also didn't see Steve Garske anywhere near the Deeps, and he and I never talked about Ned then or ever. I had no knowledge that Ned had been shot and no knowledge that Steve had found the body and buried it on his property. That's all I have to say."

"That's *all* …?" Maggie sprang to her feet and pounded her fist on the recorder to shut it off. "Boss, are you out of your damned mind?"

"Everything will be fine. It's okay, Mags."

"Okay? No. It is not okay. You do not sit here and tell me you lied to my face and then shut up when I ask you a question. That is not how you and I work. You do not hide shit from me. You tell me what's going on and then we figure out what to do about it. And if we need to smash this recorder into a million little pieces and start over, then that's what we do. Don't you get it? I'm trying to protect you."

He reached out and put a hand over hers. "I know you are. And you can't do that, Mags. I won't let you. This is my problem, not yours. Right now, your job is to figure out who murdered Ned Baer, and I can't help you with that. Now why don't you call the chief and get him down here? Because we both know that what happens next is me getting suspended from the department."

5

Peter Stanhope swirled Courvoisier in a bell-shaped glass and waited as the warmth of his hand raised the temperature of the brandy. Then he took a sip—the first sip was always the best—and tasted toffee on his lips and felt the glow spread throughout his chest. Afternoon brandy was one of the finest rituals of his day. He had another glass already poured and ready for Devin Card, but Card was usually late for their meetings. That was life in politics. Even the biggest donors had to wait.

Rain tapped against the glass of the top-floor windows in his downtown law office. Gray clouds stretched over Lake Superior like a circus big top, and he could see whitecaps dotting the vast expanse of water. The dark Duluth weather matched his mood. As a lawyer, he had a sixth sense for trouble, and trouble was definitely coming.

He tugged on the collar of his starched dress shirt. His office was warm. The air in the century-old stone building was always a little hot in the summer and a little cold in the winter. He could have moved to one of the modern bank buildings on Superior Street, but he liked sharing space with the ghosts of previous generations of his family. It kept him connected to his past.

The Stanhopes were Duluth royalty, alongside legendary names like Congdon, Merritt, and Cooke. Peter's great-grandfather had built

Stanhope Industries, one of the original companies on which Duluth's fortunes had been founded. That empire had made the family rich. But Peter had seen the writing on the wall when it came to the future of the steel business, and the writing was in Chinese. He sold off his interest in the family company when he was still in his twenties and opened a law firm instead, which would have horrified his father. Thirty years later, Peter had built an empire of his own. His litigation firm was one of the most successful and feared in Minnesota.

His money had also made him a kingmaker in the state's Democrat-Farmer-Labor party, and Peter had spent the last decade fitting a crown for his college roommate, Devin Card. The trouble with kings was that they had a nasty habit of getting their heads cut off. Peter had invested a lot of time and money getting Card into the US House of Representatives, and now his old friend was in the middle of a hotly contested campaign for the US Senate.

This was a bad time for old rumors to come back to life.

Peter had never craved the limelight of politics for himself. He liked power, not people, and he had no interest in worrying about how his personal life would look in the headlines. He bought what he wanted, traveled where he chose, and slept with women without caring who they would tell. He didn't apologize for his lifestyle or for being one of the richest men in the state. People called him cocky, which was true. He'd been comfortable with his privileges since he was a boy.

He wasn't tall, but he worked out daily and maintained a muscular physique, even at the age of fifty-one. He had Lasik surgery a few years back to correct his eyes, so he no longer wore glasses. His face was freckled, with a large nose and pronounced chin. His hair had gone prematurely silver at a young age, and he now kept it swept back so it wasn't readily apparent that he didn't have much of it left.

The intercom on Peter's desk buzzed. He heard the brittle voice of his assistant, Louise. "The Congressman is here for you, Mr. Stanhope."

Peter grabbed his suit coat off a hook and put it back on. He crossed the plush brown carpet and opened the office door. Devin Card leaned against Louise's desk as he flirted with the sixty-one-year-old assistant.

Two Congressional aides hovered nervously behind him. Card saw Peter, and his face lit up with a snow-white smile.

"There he is! Peter, how long has it been?"

"Almost a year, Congressman."

"Damn right. Way too long. I miss you! Phone calls aren't the same, you know. I'm in town all week. We need to squeeze in eighteen and have dinner at the Kitch."

"I'd like that. Louise will set it up."

"So what's the emergency?" Card asked. "What couldn't wait?"

Peter waved his old friend toward his office. "Let's talk in here. One-on-one today if you don't mind. No aides."

"Of course." Card added with a wink, "Mysterious."

The two of them went inside. Peter closed the door behind him, shooting a glance at Louise that meant there should be no interruptions. Card saw the brandy on the walnut conference table and didn't ask if it was for him; he picked it up and finished half with a single swallow. He went to the window and shook his head at the view over the lake and the lift bridge.

"Shit, Peter, you know how to live. Best view in the city up here. I'd never get anything done."

"It's not Capitol Hill," Peter replied diplomatically.

Card dismissed the comparison with a wave of his hand. "Ah, until you're in the White House, the view is the same. No, I'd rather be here than in Rayburn, I'll tell you that."

"Washington has other benefits. Another drink?"

"Definitely."

Peter retrieved the bottle of Courvoisier and topped off the Congressman's snifter. Card took another oversized swallow.

Devin Card was a big man in every way, tall and broad-shouldered, with a booming voice and a habit of gesticulating when he talked, as if every conversation were part of a campaign rally. He and Peter were the same age, but Card's hair was wavy and blond without a single gray strand anywhere. Peter was handsome in a refined, rich man's way, but Card was the college quarterback, chiseled and unforgettable, with a boyish smile and Paul Newman eyes. He had charisma. People were drawn to him as soon as he entered a room.

The two of them went back many years. They'd both grown up in Duluth, but in very different neighborhoods, Peter among the mansions along Congdon Parkway, Devin on the grittier streets of West Duluth. They hadn't met until they became freshman roommates at Minnesota's elite liberal arts school, Carleton College. The rich kid and the jock found that they clicked together. Card melded effortlessly into Peter's moneyed circle, and the two young men became a fixture at the trendiest parties in Minneapolis and Duluth. Throughout college and then law school at the University of Minnesota, they were inseparable.

Peter knew from his student days that he would open his own law firm. Card knew that he was destined for politics. It was the perfect strategic partnership, and Peter had been the silent navigator behind Card's steady rise for the past quarter-century, first as state auditor, then Attorney General, then US Representative.

In November, he'd add US Senator to his resume. And from there? There were no limits.

Unless it all came crashing down.

"Everything's set for the town hall at the DECC on Thursday," Card announced, wandering over to the large conference table and lowering his big frame into one of the leather chairs. "Polls are looking solid, too. We've been holding steady at four up for the past month."

Peter took a seat opposite Card. "I know. That's good news."

Card's bushy eyebrows did a little dance. "Maybe so, Peter, but you don't look like a man who's swayed by good news. Today you look like a lawyer. What's going on?"

"You're about to get hit," Peter replied.

"By what?"

"I have a police source who tells me that a dead body has been found. It hasn't broken in the media yet, but it will soon. And when it does, you'll be getting questions."

"A body?" Card asked, looking puzzled. "Who is it?"

"Positive identification will probably take a day or so, but the suspicion among the police is that it's Ned Baer."

Card tapped a finger against his lips as he processed the information. Then he said, "Drowned? Was he drowned? I remember everybody thought he went into the Deeps."

"No. If it really is Baer, he was murdered. Shot in the head."

Card closed his eyes. "*Shit.*"

"Needless to say, this is going to unleash a lot of crazy conspiracy theories. Everybody knows Baer was looking into the allegations against you when he disappeared. This is going to bring it all back."

Card finished his brandy and shoved his big body out of the chair again. He paced like a tiger. "No way the timing is coincidental. In the middle of the campaign? The GOP is orchestrating this."

"Normally I'd agree with you, but it sounds like the circumstances behind this coming to light are pretty random. Some doc on the Point confessed on his death bed to burying the body. Police dug it up earlier today."

"Why are they so sure it's Baer?"

"I gather this doctor said he found the body at the Deeps. That narrows it down, in terms of missing persons. There's more, but the cops are keeping the details close. Nobody's saying much."

"Did this doctor kill him?"

"No, it's not that neat and easy. Anyway, the timing of this discovery couldn't be worse."

"No shit. Who's investigating? Stride?"

"Actually, no. Word is, Stride has recused himself from the case, which I don't understand. His number two, Maggie Bei, is leading the investigation, but I hear the chief may bring in an outsider."

"Is there still bad blood between you and Stride?" Card asked.

"We're not exactly on good terms, but I'm hoping that time heals all wounds. His wife, Serena, did some work for me a few years ago. Stride was actually an ally for us on the Ned Baer case. When Baer disappeared, there was all sorts of online shit about you and me taking out a hit on him. Stride was the one who shut that down. He said the only evidence they had pointed to Baer taking a dive in the Deeps."

"Except now it looks like Baer really did get hit," Card said.

"Apparently."

"And Stride is off the case?"

"Officially, yes. I've got a call in to the chief to learn more."

Card shook his head. "I really thought we'd put all of this in the past."

"Nothing is ever past in politics," Peter replied.

The Congressman folded his arms over his chest. "Ned Baer murdered. I'd like to say I'm sorry, but the man was a prick. Whoever put a bullet in his head was doing a public service."

"I know."

Card stared down at Peter with his laser-like blue eyes. "Is there anything you and I need to talk about?"

"I think the less either of us says about this, the better."

"I agree," Card replied. He sat down again and picked up his empty glass. "Got any more of that brandy?"

"Of course."

"Think I should cancel the town hall?" Card asked.

Peter waited to answer while he went to his desk to get the bottle. He filled both of their glasses. "No. Doing that will make it look like you have something to hide. But you need to be prepared for uncomfortable questions."

"Yeah." Card stared into the amber liquid as if he were reading tea leaves. "It's not going to end with Baer, is it?"

"No."

"All of the other shit is coming back, too."

"Definitely."

Card exhaled in disgust. "An anonymous accusation. *Anonymous*. From almost thirty years ago. And that could be what costs me the election."

"It didn't cost you the House election seven years ago. If we handle it right, it won't now."

"Thirty years," Card murmured.

He eyed Peter across the table. A serious, regretful look came over his face, which was unusual. Peter had never known Devin Card to be troubled by self-reflection.

"I'm not saying we didn't do crazy things in college," Card said.

"There's a lot of stuff I would take back. It's the George Bush rule, you know? When we were young and stupid, we were young and stupid."

"You're right."

"I'd like to think we're better men now, Peter. Both of us."

"I'd like to think so, too."

Regret lingered on the Congressman's face. "Some of those parties, shit. I don't even remember them."

"Me neither. It was a long time ago."

"But I'd remember if I'd done *that*."

Peter realized that his friend was looking for reassurance. "Of course you would."

Card pounded back his brandy again. He wiped his mouth and got out of the chair. "I think we're done here. They've got me in back to back meetings until midnight."

"One more thing before you go, Devin," Peter said quietly. Using the Congressman's first name always got his attention. "This time around, the accusation may not stay anonymous. We have to be prepared that the press will find her. Or she may decide she's ready to come forward."

6

Serena revved her Mustang up the sharp incline of 1st Avenue, barely pausing at the stop signs. If you stopped on the slope, you could feel the car starting to roll back down the hill. The streets of downtown Duluth were like a Midwest version of San Francisco, but with snow and ice added into the mix for six months of the year. There was nothing but July rain for her to deal with today, but the pavement was still slick. Her sports car was notoriously impractical in this area, but the Mustang was one part of her Las Vegas past that she refused to give up.

Ahead of her, she saw Cascade Park, a steep patch of green land nestled under the high retaining wall of Mesaba Avenue. She spun the wheel and roared around the curves that wound to the top of the hill. When she got to the dead end, she saw Maggie's Avalanche parked at a careless angle, which was how Maggie always parked. Serena squeezed her Mustang next to the truck and got out. She untied her pony tail, stretched her long arms over her head, and loosened her hips. From up here, the Duluth skyline unfurled below her, and she could see the finger of the Point peninsula jutting into the lake.

Rain spat on her black hair. Her face was flushed. She'd been at a Michigan Street gym when Maggie called, and she still wore her workout outfit: cropped Lycra pants, a purple tank top, and neon pink sneakers.

Her damp clothes clung to her curves like a second skin. Summer was the time when she tried to sweat off the extra couple of pounds that always crept in during the winter months; rain didn't give her an excuse to skip a day.

Maggie waved from the stone gazebo that overlooked the city. The tiny cop sat on the wall with her back to the skyline, pedaling her legs and sipping a supersized McDonald's pop through a straw. The two of them had both passed the magic age of forty now, but somehow Maggie still consumed a daily menu of junk food without gaining weight. She didn't even drink diet pop, just full-octane, high-fructose corn syrup in all its glory. Serena found it annoying.

The two of them had had a complicated relationship from the beginning. For a while, they'd managed a wary friendship. Then, after Maggie slept with Stride, they'd become bitter enemies. Now, with the affair in the past and Stride and Serena married, they'd struck a kind of détente between them. They were both Duluth cops, and that meant they had to work together. They were both in Stride's life, too, and that wasn't going to change.

Serena, who was six inches taller than Maggie, took a seat next to her on the stone wall, her pink shoes flat on the ground. Maggie held out the pop to offer her a sip, and Serena shook her head.

"You want to tell me what's going on?" Serena said.

"That's what I was going to ask you."

Serena shook her head. "I don't know a thing. Jonny called, but he didn't give me any details. He said he had to meet someone and he'd fill me in tonight. He told me not to worry, but I'm worried."

"So am I. This whole thing is seriously messed up."

Serena shivered as the sweat made her cold. "So what the hell happened?"

"K-2 put him on paid leave. Suspended him. Stride *asked* him to do it. He said he can't be in the office while the Ned Baer case is under investigation, and he won't tell me why."

Kyle Kinnick, Duluth's deputy police chief, had gone by the nickname K-2 for most of his career. As long as Serena had known him, K-2 had run interference for Stride. They were a good team. K-2 loved the backslapping and backstabbing of city politics as much as Stride hated it. But the chief's ability to protect Stride only went so far.

"There's an explanation for all of this," Serena said. "There has to be."

"I agree, but I need to know what it is, if I'm going to help him. Did Stride ever talk to you about the Ned Baer case?"

Serena held up her left hand and wiggled her ring finger at Maggie. It was a cruel thing to do, given Maggie's own history with Stride, but she didn't care. "I'm his wife. Even if he told me anything about it, I couldn't say a word."

"This isn't a courtroom, Serena," Maggie replied coolly. "You don't have to pull spousal privilege on me. Come on, this is just you and me talking."

"That doesn't matter. Whatever's going on, there's a reason Jonny chose not to tell you about it, so I'm not going to say anything either. If he's on the outside in this case, so am I." Serena looked around the park and made sure they were alone. "Besides, the truth is, I'm in the dark, too. Jonny never mentioned Ned Baer to me."

"Don't you find that weird?"

"Not really. This all happened the year before I came to town. It's not like he rushes to tell me secrets from back then. You know him. I still have to drag things out of him, even after all this time. I'm sorry, but I don't know what was going on between him and Ned Baer. I don't know why he lied about it."

Maggie slurped her pop. "Seven years. Seven years, and all that time, Ned was buried in Steve's garden. It's crazy."

"If Jonny says he didn't know the body was there, then he didn't know."

"Maybe not, but he sure as hell knows something. I could really use your help. Nobody has to know that we're talking. Not even Stride."

"Jonny wouldn't like that. Neither do I."

"It's for his own good. Look, you and I both know he didn't kill anyone, but right now he's the prime suspect. He was the last one to see Ned alive. He lied about their meeting, and he won't tell me what it was about. And his best friend was so convinced that Stride killed the guy that he took away the body and buried it to keep him out of trouble."

"You tell me Jonny's a suspect, and you expect me to help you?" Serena asked. "Come on, Maggie."

"I'd never sandbag him. You know that. I'm just saying he needs an ally on the inside, but I can't be seen as helping him directly. That's why I need you to point me where I need to go. Anything you tell me stays between us."

Serena hesitated. "I'll think about it, but I can't make any promises."

"Well, think about this, too. K-2 is bringing in a special investigator to lead the case."

"It's not going to be you?" Serena asked.

"No. K-2 thinks I'm too close to Stride. The whole team is. He doesn't want any accusations that we're covering up for one of our own. So he's using an outsider to run the investigation, and I'll be reporting to him."

"Who?"

"You're not going to like it. It's Dan Erickson."

Serena slapped the stone wall with her hand. "Are you kidding me? *Dan Erickson?* Is K-2 out of his mind? No way he brings Dan back. I'm going to call him and get this stopped."

Maggie took hold of Serena's arm. "Wait. Don't do that. Interfering with K-2 will only make it worse. Look, Dan's the former county attorney. Regardless of what we both think of him, he's obviously qualified to do the job. Plus, everybody knows he hates Stride, so no one is going to think the chief is doing Stride any favors. That's why he wants him."

Serena shook her head in disgust. Dan Erickson.

Even hearing his name brought her back to the worst winter of her life. As county attorney, Dan had hired Serena to pay off a blackmailer who had unearthed the dirtiest secrets of Dan's personal life. But the blackmailer had come to town with motives of his own, and Serena had nearly died at his hands in a fish house out on a frozen lake. Her body still carried the memories of that torture.

She kicked up one of her bare calves that was mottled with discolored white streaks where she'd been burned by fire. "See those scars? I have those scars because of Dan Erickson."

"I know that, Serena. I know."

"*You* slept with him. Does K-2 know that?"

"No, and he's not going to, because if he finds out, he'll take me off the case, too. And we need me on the inside, where I can keep an eye on Dan. He's going to try to take down Stride if he can. I need to be able to stop him."

Serena stood up in frustration. "I can't be here anymore."

"Don't go yet. I get it, you have every reason to be upset about this. It pisses me off, too. But the only thing we can do now is find a way to have Stride's back during the investigation. That means I need to know what he's hiding. You can find out for me."

"I won't betray him."

"You're not betraying him. You're *helping* him. Stride didn't kill Ned Baer, Serena. Of course, he didn't. But you think that's going to matter to Dan if he sees a way to pin this on him? Look, Stride may not be the one who pulled the trigger, but he must have a pretty good idea who did. That's why he's not talking. He's also a pigheaded son of a bitch who wouldn't say a word, even if he ends up being the one to take the fall."

Serena stared at the ground. "I told you, no promises."

"I understand."

"I'll do what I can. *If* there's no other way to protect Jonny."

"Absolutely," Maggie told her.

"Keep Dan Erickson away from me. Otherwise, you may have another murder on your hands."

Maggie grinned. "Got it."

Serena marched toward her Mustang, ignoring the rain that washed over her. She tried to push aside her furious emotions and her bad memories and focus on the only thing that was important. Stride.

She knew that Maggie was right.

Jonny knew something about Ned Baer's murder. That was obvious. His subconscious had been taunting him with dreams about it, even before Ned's body was discovered. The only reason for Stride to lie was because he was covering for someone else, and Serena didn't need to talk to him to know who that was. There was only one person he'd still feel an obligation to protect after all this time.

His ex-wife.

She'd been in those dreams, too. Like unfinished business.

Serena had never met her. She'd avoided her for years, because she felt guilty about being the other woman in breaking up a marriage. Even a bad marriage. Serena had fallen in love with Stride, and Stride had fallen in love with Serena, but the reality for both of them was that he was still married when that happened.

She couldn't put it off any longer.

It was time for her to confront Andrea.

7

"I'm telling you, this is a million-dollar idea," Curt Dickes said to Cat. "It's big. The biggest thing I've ever come up with. Colleen thinks so, too."

Cat lay on a blanket stretched across the rocks at the Deeps. A few lingering raindrops broke through the tree branches and landed on her bare skin. She closed her eyes and said, "Uh-huh."

She didn't care what Curt's new girlfriend thought about anything, and she didn't want to hear him talking about her. She'd invited Curt to hang out specifically because he'd told her that Colleen had an art class on Monday evenings. So it was just the two of them near the river. She'd worn her sexiest bikini, the one Stride and Serena didn't know she had. The tiger print cups barely contained her breasts, and the cool air had worked its magic on them. The bottom was a black thong that flashed her cheeks to the world. She knew she looked hot, but Curt had barely given her the once-over before he started talking about his latest get rich quick scheme.

"Don't you want to hear about it?" he asked her impatiently.

"Uh-huh," she said again.

"Eyes … on … Duluth," Curt said, pausing dramatically between the words.

"What?"

"We build one of those big wheels. You know, like they have in London and Las Vegas. We put it over in Bayfront park. Can you imagine the tourists, Kitty Cat? Everybody will come to see it! This will be like the biggest thing in the whole Midwest! Suck it, Chicago!"

"Yeah, but doesn't Chicago already have one of those things?" Cat asked.

"I don't know. Whatever. Maybe they do. Anyway, it will definitely be the biggest thing in Minnesota."

"But those things cost like millions and millions of dollars to build," Cat pointed out. "Where are you going to get the money?"

"Oh, don't worry about that. I figure the business community will get on board, big time. The state, too. And the Indians, I mean, think of what it will do to the casino traffic. I just have to sell them on the idea and let them take over. They can do the rest. But I'll keep the rights to the name and sell all the merch. T-shirts, magnets, snow globes, you name it."

"Eyes on Duluth?" Cat asked.

"Exactly."

"Nice to know you've got your eyes on something," she murmured.

"What?"

"Nothing. Hey, if it's your project, why don't you name it after yourself?"

"After myself?" Curt said, looking puzzled. "Like what? What would you call it?"

"How about the Big Dickes?" Cat announced, giggling uncontrollably.

She expected Curt to laugh, too, but instead his face twisted into a sour expression. "I'm serious about this, Kitty Cat. This could be my big break, and all you can do is make fun of it?"

"I'm sorry," she said, although she was still laughing. "Really."

Curt lay back on the blanket with his arms behind his head and stared at the sky. He refused to look at her. When she propped herself on one elbow and reached for his hand, he pulled it away. For a scam artist who liked to think he was cool, Curt was actually pretty sensitive.

"Come on, Curt, I said I'm sorry," she repeated. "It sounds like a great idea."

His head turned. "You really think so?"

"I do."

"You're not just saying that?"

"I'm not. Eyes on Duluth. That's a moneymaker."

He scrambled to his feet on the rocks. "I know, right? It's huge!"

Curt wandered to the edge of the cliff and peered down at the rapids of Amity Creek, which roared through the narrows below them. He wore a black muscle shirt—although he didn't have much in the way of muscles—and a baggy yellow-striped swimsuit that hung to his knees. His feet were bare. He had tattoos over most of his body, and his straggly black hair fell below his shoulders.

Cat didn't know why she liked Curt so much. He was part of her past, and there wasn't much about her past that she wanted to remember. He helped her when she'd been on the streets, but the truth was, he hadn't always been nice to her. He made her laugh, mostly because each of his big ideas was sillier than the one before. Curt wasn't going anywhere in life, and she knew that, even if he didn't. But most days, she didn't think she deserved anyone better.

She got off the blanket and came up beside him on the rocks. Spray billowed up like a cloud from the river, high enough to dampen her face. They were alone out here, and though the sun hadn't set yet, it was shadowy and gray in the woods around them. The slight chill made her shiver. She thought about getting on tiptoes and kissing him and telling him that if he wanted to have sex with her, they could do it right now, right here on the wet grass. It didn't have to mean anything, and his girlfriend didn't need to find out. Cat was just lonely, and she wanted someone to make her feel good about herself.

But she didn't, because she didn't want him to reject her. She was a coward.

Instead, she said, "Got any weed?"

Curt eyed his backpack on the rocks. "Yeah."

"Want to?"

"I give you weed and Stride finds out, and I won't be able to call it the Big Dickes anymore," Curt said.

Cat giggled again. "He won't find out."

"Are you kidding? He probably knows already. He probably has that bikini of yours bugged, although I'm not sure where you could fit a bug on that thing."

"I didn't think you even noticed it," Cat said, putting her hands on her hips and arching her back.

"Oh, I noticed, Kitty Cat. Believe me, you're looking good. Too good. Thing is, I'm with Colleen now. She's really great. I don't want to screw it up."

"Right. Sure."

"Sorry," Curt said.

"No, that's okay. I get it. Does that mean we can't hang out anymore?"

"We're hanging out now."

"Yeah. I guess."

"Hey, come on, no Kitty Cat frowns," Curt said. "Actually, I want to hook you up with somebody. I've got a guy who wants to meet you. His name's Wyatt. He moved to town a month ago, and he's cool. He works at Hoops in Canal Park. I think you'll like him."

"I'm not looking to meet anybody," Cat said.

"No, really, you should. He's got dreads that are totally wild. Colleen and I are heading down there around ten for a drink. Wyatt'll be there. Come with us."

"Maybe."

"No maybes. You need to come. He said you were the prettiest chick in Duluth."

"He didn't," Cat said, with a little blush.

"He did, Kitty Cat, and he's right, because you are. I mean, don't tell Colleen I said that or anything."

Cat smiled. "Okay. Hoops it is."

"Good." Curt leaned over the cliff's edge again and whistled. "Holy moly, the river's really running."

"Yeah."

Curt gave her a wink. "What do you think? You want to make the jump?"

"Now? No way."

"I will if you will. Hell, I will even if you won't."

"It's not safe, Curt! You want to get killed?"

"Oh, come on! You only live once, Kitty Cat. I'm going to do it. The question is whether I'm doing it alone." Curt backed up from the edge so that he could take a running leap from the cliff. His mouth bent into a sly grin, and she didn't know if he was teasing her.

"Curt, don't you dare," Cat warned him.

"I'm gonna do it."

"No! Are you crazy? Don't!"

"Too late! Geronimo!"

Curt sprinted in his bare feet for the cliff's edge, and Cat was sure he was doing it just to scare her, that he would stop short before he jumped. But he didn't. Curt threw himself into the air with a loud *whoop*, his arms in the air, his toes pointed down. Cat screamed after him and watched helplessly as Curt plunged toward the river, hit with a splash, and disappeared below the frenzied surface. He didn't reappear right away. He was gone for way too long. She looked for him and waited, and waited, and waited, and her heart pounded before she finally saw Curt's head bob above the black-and-white water. He spit, coughed, and grinned up at her. The current carried him downstream, and he fought his way to the rocks on the shore and dragged himself out of the water. He waved at Cat on top of the cliff.

"Come on, do it! It's not so bad!"

"No!"

"Do, it, do, it, do, it!"

"No!"

Curt flapped his bent arms together and made chicken noises. Cat thought twice as she looked down, but then she backed up tentatively on the cliff. She chewed on a fingernail. Before she could stop herself, she ran straight for the edge and leaped high into the air as she flew. The air rushed past her. The thunder of the river boomed in her ears. She regretted the jump halfway down, but it was too late, and an instant later, her body slapped the cold water and shot downward. Her eyes were open, but she couldn't see. She kicked and kicked, but the river sucked on her body and didn't want to let go. Breath bubbled out of her lungs. She felt a shiver of panic creeping through her head, and she kicked again furiously and fought her way upward. Like a bathtub toy, Cat breached the surface. She gasped for air.

Curt applauded from the rocks. "Whoo-hoo! You did it, girl!"

Cat took a few seconds to get past her momentary terror, but when she did, she allowed the tiniest smile to break across her face. She'd braved the Deeps and won. She felt her body being carried along by the river, so she swam hard and made it to the bank a few yards downstream from Curt.

When she pulled herself out of the water, she heard him holler and let out a loud wolf whistle. She didn't understand, until she looked down at herself and realized that the jump from the cliff had torn off her bikini top, which was now somewhere in the river being carried toward Lake Superior. Her breasts were on full display, and she immediately wrapped her arms around her chest to cover herself.

"Don't look!" she screamed at Curt.

"Too late, Kitty Cat, and let me just say, meeee-owwww."

"Asshole!" she shouted, but part of her was secretly pleased. Once again, she couldn't quite keep the grin off her face. She trudged past him, blocking his view, and then climbed back up the rocks. At the top of the cliff, she dried herself with a towel and quickly got dressed again. By the time she was done, Curt had made it back to the top, too.

"You decent?" he called, with a hand over his eyes.

"Yeah."

"Damn!" he replied, and she swore at him again, but she didn't mean it.

They sat next to each other on the top of the cliff, not saying anything, still breathing hard from the climb. The river kept roaring below them. Cat could feel their hips brushing together. She felt a little embarrassed and a little proud of herself at the same time for having braved the Deeps. Once was enough, but she was happy that she'd done it. She felt another surge of desire for Curt, but before she could lean over and nibble his neck, he suddenly jumped to his feet.

"Oh, hell, I'm late!" he announced. "Sorry, Kitty Cat, I gotta run. If I'm not on time for Colleen, I'm in t-r-o-u-b-l-e."

"Sure. Okay. Go."

"You'll join us at Hoops later?"

"We'll see," Cat said.

Curt didn't take the time to convince her. He sprinted toward the footbridge over the river, waved at her one last time as he crossed the bridge, and disappeared toward his car, which was parked off the shoulder of Occidental Boulevard. A couple of minutes later, she heard the noisy growl of his Thunderbird as he peeled away.

Cat didn't leave immediately. The adrenaline of the jump had dissipated, and she felt a little sad and sorry for herself. As it got dark, she finally got to her feet and headed into the woods at a shuffling pace, kicking at the dirt and branches. Her own car was parked off Seven Bridges Road, so she didn't need to cross the river. Along the trail, birch trees and pines crowded her. The birds had gone quiet for the night, but the crickets had come alive.

Then, out of nowhere, she felt a strange uneasiness.

She stopped on the trail, listening. Her instincts from living on the street always kicked in and told her when something was wrong. It was a sixth sense that had kept her alive more than once. She walked faster, wanting to get in her car and go. She looked back as she hiked, peering into the trees and the overgrown brush, but no one was there. Even so, her anxiety grew. She was sure she wasn't alone.

Cat saw her car parked at the end of the trail. She began to breathe a little easier, and she broke into a run to reach it. Get in, lock the doors, drive away. But as she got close to the Civic in the semi-darkness, she stopped dead. Her mouth dropped open and she screamed.

Her car was covered in green paint. One message was written everywhere, all over the hood, the doors, the windshield, and the trunk. The same message over and over and over.

I love you I love you I love you I love you I love you.

As Cat stood on the trail, trembling and crying, her phone pinged. She had a new text. She opened it up and saw that someone had sent her a photograph from a number she didn't recognize. When she clicked on the picture, she saw herself standing on the riverbank near Curt, her almost nude body exposed.

Her stalker had been there, on top of the cliff, spying on her.

Below the photograph was a message.

You're so beautiful, Cat. Soon we'll be together forever.

8

The two-story house on 8th Street with the beige siding hadn't changed at all since Stride had last been here. Neither had the woman who owned it. When Andrea answered the door, he felt as if he'd gone back in time.

In that first moment seeing her again, he found himself reliving the ups and downs of their four years together. He remembered the first time they'd met, when he was up at Central High School investigating the disappearance of a teenage girl. Andrea was a chemistry teacher taking a break behind the school, with a cigarette in her hand and a cynical smile on her lips. The attraction between them had been immediate. She'd been pretty then and she still was, a pert, blue-eyed blond with a trim figure. He did a quick calculation in his head and realized that she must be forty-six years old now. She still looked young for her age and probably always would.

Young. Athletic. Unhappy.

In the early days of their marriage, he'd blamed Andrea's depression on being abandoned by her first husband. Then he'd blamed himself for not being able to give her what she needed. Finally, seven years ago, he learned the truth about her past, but the revelation had come too late to save their relationship.

"Hello, Andrea," Stride said.

She stared back at him and didn't say anything. Her face was distant. He'd wondered whether she would be angry at seeing her ex-husband again after so many years, but then he remembered: this was Andrea. She was the coldest woman he'd ever met. Cold in love. Cold in bed. She kept her emotions buried in a deep hole, like a prisoner she wouldn't set free.

"Hello, Jon," she said finally. "Long time."

"A very long time. How are you?"

"Same as ever. You?"

"I'm okay. I'm good."

"I heard you got married again," Andrea said.

"I did."

"The Vegas girl. Serena. The one you cheated on me with."

He frowned. "Yes."

"Well. Isn't that fucking terrific."

He didn't know what to say to that.

"Do you want to come in?" Andrea asked.

"I do."

She opened the door just far enough for him to squeeze past her, and he walked into the house where he'd lived while they were together. It was much bigger than his cottage on the Point, but being here again made him feel claustrophobic, stuck inside bad times. She'd changed almost nothing over the years. He recognized the same furniture and the same art on the walls. She'd recarpeted and repainted, but she hadn't even changed the colors. Andrea was like a cat, anxious and scared if anything disrupted her routines.

"Come back to the kitchen," she said.

He followed her. The kitchen was small, and there was an alcove where she had a dinette table near the windows. From there, he could barely see the lake like a gray smudge on the horizon. That was what he remembered about the house, how far away the lake seemed when he was in it. Stride could usually measure his own happiness by how close he was to Lake Superior.

"I made margaritas," Andrea said, pointing to a half-full pitcher on the table. "You want one?"

"No. Thanks."

"Too ironic?" she asked.

He let out a short, humorless laugh to tell her that he understood the joke. They'd gotten drunk on margaritas on their first date, and then they'd had sex on his back porch. That was how their relationship had started. For a long time, he'd regretted everything that followed that night—the marriage, the loneliness, the affair, the divorce—but there had come a point in his life when he had to make peace with his mistakes. It was obvious to him that Andrea had yet to do the same.

They both sat down at the table. She sipped her drink, licking salt off her lips each time. He noticed that the window behind her was decorated with suncatchers made of stained glass. They were all shaped in different designs, with a rainbow of colors. A hummingbird, a lighthouse, a rose, a frog, a mother and child, a sun, a heart, a butterfly, a dragonfly. As far as he could tell, they were the only decorations that had been added to the house since he left.

"Are you still teaching?" he asked.

"I switched to Denfeld when Central closed."

"Sure. Makes sense."

"I'm head of the department now."

"Good for you," he said.

"It's a little more money."

"That always helps."

"And a lot more school politics," she added.

"I'm sure. I try to steer clear of that."

"I remember."

"How's your sister?" Stride asked. "Is Denise okay?"

"She's fine. She moved back to Duluth this year."

"Really? Miami too hot for her?"

"Divorce," Andrea said.

"Sorry to hear it. Still, it must be nice having her closer."

Andrea shrugged. "It is. Except when it's not."

"Yeah. I get that. What about you? Are you seeing anyone?"

His ex-wife took another sip of her drink without answering, and he could see the manicured tips of her fingernails. Her blue eyes drifted away. He heard the thump of basketballs in the park next to the house. He remembered how the noise had driven him crazy when he lived here. And he remembered how he would find Andrea staring out the windows, watching the kids play.

"We really don't need to do the whole small-talk thing," Andrea said. "Just tell me what you want, Jon."

"Okay." Stride watched her face carefully. He was back to being a cop now, looking for the tiniest reactions. "I don't know if you heard, but Steve Garske died."

"Steve? Really? I'm sorry. I know you two were close. He was awfully young. What happened?"

"Cancer," Stride said.

"How sad."

"You used to go to him, didn't you?" he asked.

"Yes, but I switched doctors after you and I split. I figured staying with Steve would be uncomfortable for both of us."

"Sure."

"Is that what you came here to tell me? About Steve's death?"

"No. There's more."

Andrea tried out a false smile, but he could see the anxiety in her face as she wondered what he would say next. "Well, don't leave me in suspense, Jon."

"Steve did something bad a few years ago," Stride told her. "I only just found out about it."

"What did he do?"

"Actually, I thought you might already know," Stride said.

"Sorry, I don't."

"We found what we believe is the body of Ned Baer on his property," Stride went on. "Steve buried him there."

Andrea inhaled sharply. A little quiver rippled through her body. Her reaction definitely wasn't rehearsed. She took the pitcher of margaritas and refilled her glass to the top, and she shook the ice to chill the drink. "I see."

"He'd been shot in the head. Murdered."

Andrea put the glass down on the table. "Good."

"It's better if you don't say things like that."

"I don't care. I'm not going to pretend he wasn't a terrible human being. Ned Baer was trying to destroy my life. He was stalking me, following me wherever I went. He broke in here, do you remember that?"

"I remember that's what you told me."

"He was going to *expose* me, Jon. He was going to drag my name, my life, my past, through the dirt."

"I know."

Andrea stared at Stride. "Did you kill him?"

It was Stride's turn to be surprised. "Of course not."

She looked almost disappointed by his denial. "Really? I mean, to be totally honest, I always wondered if you did. We never talked about it after Ned disappeared. Although, I suppose we never talked about anything, did we? Ned just … went away. It always seemed way too convenient to me, the idea of him being lost in the Deeps. I thought that was just a story you made up to hide the truth. And you know, I never blamed you. That was probably the only time in our marriage when I began to think that you actually loved me. I mean, if you would do that … if you would go that far to save me …"

"I didn't kill him," Stride said again.

"No. I guess I was foolish to think that. You would never sacrifice yourself for me. For Cindy, definitely. For Serena, maybe. But not for me."

"We don't need to rehash the past, Andrea."

"No. We definitely do not. Well, if you didn't kill him, Jon, who did?"

Stride said nothing. He stared back at her and waited. She sipped her drink, as if she had no idea what he would say and why he was hesitating. Finally her eyes widened as she understood. Then she did something he didn't expect. She laughed.

"Oh, my God!" Andrea exclaimed. "Oh, my God, you think *I* did it! That is too funny."

"It's not funny at all, and it's *not* such an outrageous thought," Stride pointed out sharply. "Is it?"

Her laughter dissolved. She chewed on her lip in silence for a while.

"No. You're right. I'm only saying it's funny, because this is like a symbol of our whole marriage. I thought you killed him. You thought I killed him. And neither one of us said a word to the other."

"So you're saying you *didn't* kill him?" Stride asked.

"That's what I'm saying, Jon."

Stride saw no deception in her eyes. Even so, he wondered if she was lying. After all these years, he knew her well, or at least as well as any man could. And he knew from experience that if Andrea was pushed to a breaking point, she was capable of anything. She could be hysterical. She could be violent. That was how she'd been when she told him about Ned Baer. Desperate, out of control, willing to do anything to protect her secret.

"Do you have any idea who did kill him?" Stride asked.

"Maybe it was Steve," she suggested.

Stride shook his head. "No. He didn't do it."

"I don't think you can rule it out, Jon."

"Why? Steve had no motive."

Andrea leaned across the table. "I called him. That night, after you called me from Ned's motel, I called Steve."

"Why?"

"I was scared. You were *so* angry. I didn't know what you would do. I mean, I was frantic, and I told you to do whatever it would take to shut Ned up. But I didn't know how far you'd go, and I didn't want you to throw your whole life away. So I called Steve. I told him to go after you. I wanted him to cool you down and make sure you didn't do anything stupid."

"He knew about—?"

She nodded. "Of course, he did. He was my doctor. I told him every-thing. Later, after Ned disappeared, I asked if he knew what had happened. He said no. He said he never saw you at the Deeps. There was nobody there, not you, not Ned, not anybody. But I always wondered in the back of my head if he was protecting you."

Stride rubbed his fingers against his forehead, trying to push back a headache. "He *was* protecting me. Or that's what he thought."

"Maybe he protected both of us," Andrea said. "Maybe he killed Ned himself."

"Steve wasn't a murderer."

"Well, then I don't know what happened."

Stride nodded, because it made no sense to him either. He kept looking for an explanation and not finding one. Then he felt a buzzing on his phone and when he checked his messages, his face darkened with concern. He pushed back the chair and got to his feet. "Sorry, I have to go."

"Of course, you do. There's always something with you. Nothing changes."

"It's not me. There's a problem with Cat. She's a teenager who—"

"A teenager who lives with you," Andrea said. "Yes, I know about her. I read the story in the paper last winter. Talk about another irony, Jon. You never wanted to have kids, and now you and Serena have a teenager."

"That's not true about me not wanting kids."

"Oh, right. My mistake. You never wanted kids with *me*."

Stride's face clouded with anger, but he didn't have time for an old argument. "I have to go," he said again.

"So go."

He hesitated before he headed to the front door. "Listen, about this thing with Ned Baer. I'm not running the investigation. Maggie knows that I lied to her back then. I haven't told her what was really going on, but it won't be hard for her to figure it out. I won't be able to keep your name out of it this time."

"I understand, Jon," Andrea replied. "Believe me, I know what's coming. As soon as you said the name Ned Baer, I figured my life was over."

* * * * *

Serena waited in her Mustang, which was parked in the shadows two blocks away from Andrea's house. Dusk had fallen, but there were kids playing basketball in the waning light. She could see the front of the house from where she was, and she could see Stride's black Expedition parked outside, under the tall trees.

It confirmed to her that she was in the right place.

Whatever was going on, Andrea was in the middle of it.

Ten minutes after she arrived, she saw Jonny emerge from the house alone. He ran for his truck, fired the engine, and drove away at high speed. She thought about texting him to find out what was going on, but she didn't want him to know where she was. Not yet. She needed answers before they talked.

Serena steeled herself for what lay ahead. In no universe did she expect the next few minutes of her life to be pleasant.

She got out of the Mustang and headed for Andrea's front door.

9

Stride needed a flashlight to make his way to the Deeps. He swept the beam back and forth across the trail. Cat followed him, staying close enough that she could hang on to his belt. When they reached the cliff, wind howled through the gorge and the river rumbled with the low, angry growl of a tiger.

"You and Curt were up here?" Stride asked her.

Her voice was subdued. "Yes."

"Jumping?"

She didn't answer right away, and he waited without saying anything more.

"We jumped once," she admitted finally.

Stride pointed at the wild rapids. "Do you know how easy it would have been for one or both of you to have been swept away and drowned? Do you know how many times in my life I've had to pull bodies out of the lake because they went diving in this place?"

"I'm sorry." Then she zeroed in on his hypocrisy, the way she always did. "You used to jump here, didn't you? You and Steve?"

He sighed. "Yeah."

Cat didn't rub it in, but they both knew she'd chalked up a victory. Every generation had to make its own mistakes. His father had warned him about the Deeps when he was fifteen, and he hadn't listened either.

"Did you see anyone else while you were here?" Stride asked.

Cat shook her head. "No one."

"Nobody crossed the pedestrian bridge? You didn't see anyone in the woods on the other side of the river?"

"No, we were alone the whole time."

"What about when you were down by the water?"

"Well, somebody had to be up here," Cat said, "because that's where they took the picture. But I didn't see anyone."

Stride shined his flashlight around the rocks. He illuminated the crevices and checked the dirt for muddy footprints. When he found nothing, he hiked back to the pedestrian bridge over the river. The rough gravel showed no evidence of anyone coming or going.

"Let's go back to your car," Stride said.

They retraced their steps to where Cat's car was parked on the fringe of Seven Bridges Road. Max Guppo was there, along with a uniformed officer, examining the scene. Stride sent Cat across the street to wait in his Expedition, and then he gestured to Guppo. The oversized detective waddled up to him and offered a sympathetic smile. Guppo, who had five daughters, was familiar with the challenges of raising teenage girls.

"Find anything, Max?" Stride asked.

Guppo held up a plastic evidence bag that contained a can of green spray paint. "The guy left this behind. We can run it for prints and see if we get lucky, but I don't think he's going to make it easy for us."

"Oh?"

"Yeah, look at this." Guppo showed Stride another bag, which contained a crushed, muddy mass of blue plastic.

"What's that?"

"Shoe covers," Guppo told him. "That's why he didn't leave any footprints we can distinguish. Normally the mud would give us some clear tracks, but not this time. And the fact that he left them behind for us to find? I think it's kind of like sticking up a middle finger. He knew we'd be looking."

"This guy knows Cat lives with cops," Stride said.

"Could be."

"What about tire tracks?"

"Nothing so far. He probably parked on the road. We'll talk to the neighbors to see if they remember any cars, but kids park out here all the time."

"Thanks for jumping on this, Max. I know there's not a lot we can do, but this feels like more than just some creepy fan. I want to know who's doing this."

"We'll do everything we can, boss."

"I appreciate it." Stride put a hand on his friend's shoulder. He'd worked with Guppo since the day he joined the Duluth police thirty years earlier. "And you know that at this particular moment I'm not your boss, right? I'm just a concerned citizen."

"Whatever you say, boss."

Stride smiled at him. He shoved his hands in his jacket pockets and headed across the road to his truck. Cat sat inside in the passenger seat. She didn't look at him as he climbed behind the wheel. For an eighteen-year-old, she had the immature face of a little girl again, although Stride had learned through experience not to trust Cat's girlish looks. He reached out and gently tugged on her chin and turned her face toward him.

"Hey," he said. "How are you doing? Are you okay?"

"I guess."

"I know this is scary."

"Yeah, a little."

"Don't worry about your Civic. I've got a buddy at a garage who can take care of it. After Guppo is done with it, he'll get it towed and cleaned up. You should have it back by the end of the week."

"Thanks."

Stride gestured at the phone in Cat's hands. "I need to see the picture." She shook her head. "No."

"Cat, I don't care what it shows. The angle of the photo is important, and we may be able to get metadata off the image that will tell us who sent it."

"I don't want a bunch of cops staring at my tits."

"I'll make sure it's only women doing the analysis," Stride said.

"I don't want you seeing it either."

Stride took a deep breath. "Okay. You can hand your phone off to

Serena when you get home, and she can work with one of the women on the CSI team. No men involved at all. How about that?"

"I suppose."

"Let's talk about who could be doing this to you," Stride said.

"I have no idea."

"Do you still have the envelope and the photograph that was sent to you with the green marker on it?"

Cat nodded. "It's at home."

"You should have shown that to me *immediately*."

"Dr. Steve had just died. I didn't want to bother you. I told you, I get weird stuff sometimes. Most of it doesn't mean anything."

"Well, this one crosses the line way beyond weird stuff, Cat. Particularly if you think someone broke into our house and was in your room. That kind of obsession is dangerous. I'm not saying that to scare you. I just want you to appreciate the seriousness of it."

"I do now," she said.

"Okay, then let me ask you again. Do you have any idea who might be behind this?"

"I really don't, Stride."

"This photograph you got. The one with the local postmark and the green marker. Have you received anything similar to that before? It doesn't matter whether or not it was local. Have there been any letters, pictures, threats, anything that could have come from the same person?"

"I don't think so. This one was different. It felt different. It wasn't like the others."

"How so?"

"I'm not sure. It just felt more *real*."

"I want to go through all of the mail you've received," Stride said. "There could be something you missed."

"I toss most of the porn crap and the hate mail," Cat told him.

Stride frowned. "From now on, don't do that. When you get anything like that, show me. Or show Serena. And we'll still need to go through whatever you have, even the seemingly innocent letters. There could still be something in there."

"Yeah, all right."

"Whoever is doing this knows things about you, Cat. He showed up here tonight. Who knew you were getting together with Curt?"

"Nobody."

"Did you notice anyone following you?"

"No, but I don't think I would have."

"Have there been any strange cars parked near our house lately?"

"I don't know. I mean, a lot of tourists go up and down the Point. There are always different cars around."

"Have you met anyone lately who took an unusual interest in you?" Stride asked. "Even if it was a very brief encounter. It could have been entirely random for you, but not for them. Has anyone made you feel uncomfortable?"

Cat rolled her eyes. "Most men are like that with me. You don't know how many creeps are out there, Stride."

"I get it. But no one stands out? No one who was a little creepier than usual?"

She shook her head. "No."

"Okay, here's the thing, Cat," Stride went on, knowing he was about to endure a firestorm of protest. "Until we figure out who this person is and evaluate the nature of the threat, I don't want you leaving the house alone. When you're alone, you're at risk. What happened tonight proves that."

"Stride! No!"

"I'm sorry. I'm not taking any chances with your safety."

"It's summer!" Cat replied unhappily. "What do you want me to do, be a prisoner stuck inside all the time? That's not fair!"

"I'm not saying you have to stay inside, but I've arranged protection. If you want to go somewhere, he'll drive you. Wherever you go, he goes."

"Oh, great. Another cop babysitter. The last one was fatter than Guppo and ten years older. He wheezed trying to keep up with me. You think that's going to keep me safe? Can't I just agree not to go out alone? If I want to go somewhere, I'll meet friends."

"You mean friends like Curt? No. This isn't negotiable, Cat. It's a done deal. I already put out a call for volunteers in the department, and I found someone willing to help. His name's Brayden Pell. He's off-shift for the next few days, so he can be with you anytime. I'm sorry if it puts a crimp in your social life, but that's the way it is."

"I hate this," Cat said.

"I'm aware. Would you prefer it be *me* taking you everywhere? Would that be less intrusive?"

Cat frowned. "No."

"I didn't think so," Stride said with a smile. "Listen, give Brayden a chance. I've only met him once or twice, but I think you'll like him."

"Yeah, sure. When does Officer Nanny get here?"

Stride pointed to the other side of the road, near Cat's car, where a sunshine-orange Kia Soul, with a squat, boxy frame, pulled up behind Guppo's cruiser. "Brayden texted me he wasn't far away. I think that's him now."

"Are you kidding?" Cat asked. "A freaking orange Kia? I'm sorry, you want me driving around in a dork car like that? Come on Stride, if you just let me hang by myself, I promise that I'll—"

She stopped talking.

The door of the Kia opened, and a man in his late twenties got out, bathed in the glow of Stride's headlights. He had to unfold his legs to pry himself from the front seat, because when he stood up, it was clear that he was taller than six feet. He had blond hair shaved very short on both sides of his head but long and swept back on top. He had dark eyes, pale stubble on his beard line, and a sharp V-shaped chin. He wore an untucked dark blue jean shirt, sleeves rolled up, buttoned to the top, and tight fitting khakis. His build was lean but strong. He spotted Stride's truck and waved with a relaxed smile.

"Wow," Cat said under her breath, drawing out the word.

"That's Brayden Pell. Think you can manage to let him hang around with you for a few days?"

"Wow," Cat said again.

Stride chuckled. "I'll take that for a yes."

10

"Ms. Jantzik?" Serena said when Andrea opened the door. "My name is—"

"I know who you are," Andrea interrupted. Her blue eyes were hard, and her voice had all the ice of a Duluth January. "I'm not Ms. Jantzik anymore. I haven't been for years. Jantzik was my name when I was married to my first husband. I'm Andrea Forseth now."

"Of course."

"I was also Andrea *Stride* for a while, but you know that."

"Yes, I do."

"You've got a fucking lot of nerve coming here," she went on.

"I realize this is awkward—"

"Awkward? Is that what you call it? The bitch who stole my husband showing up at my door?"

"If I could just explain—"

"Does Jon know you're here?" Andrea interrupted again. "He just left. Is this supposed to be some sort of good cop–bad cop routine? First him and now you?"

"He doesn't know I'm here," Serena said.

Stride's ex-wife folded her arms across her chest. "Oh, so what, were you following him? Are you afraid he's cheating on *you*? Sleeping with *me*? That would be pretty ironic, wouldn't it?"

Serena felt slapped, but she hadn't expected anything less. "I'm really not here to talk about me and Stride, Ms. Forseth."

"Well, that's too bad, because I want to talk about it. I've wanted to talk about it for six years."

Serena nodded. "Okay. That's fair. Say whatever you want."

"I want to talk about you coming to Duluth and fucking my husband. Jon and I may not have had the best marriage, but that didn't give you the right to spread your legs for him."

"You're right," Serena admitted, doing her best to stay calm.

"You and your showgirl hair and big tits. Is that the way women get their men in Vegas? Because here in Minnesota, we call that being a whore and a slut."

"I understand that you may feel that way, and I don't blame you."

"I know what happened between Stride and Maggie, by the way. I saw that one coming a mile away. How did it feel, him cheating on you?"

"Awful. It felt awful."

"Good. Now you know how it was for me. Like I was dirt. Like I was worthless. And you married him anyway? Even after he slept with her? You're brave, thinking he won't do it again."

Serena waited for Andrea to run out of venom. This wasn't a time for explanations. She could have talked about the walls that she and Jonny had built for themselves, about the guilt and grief that had shadowed their attraction, about the many mistakes they'd both made on the way to realizing they were meant to be together. But none of that mattered. Not to this woman.

"I'm sorry," Serena said.

"Excuse me?"

"I'm sorry. That's all. I have no excuses. I'm six years late in apologizing. Jonny did that a long time ago, but I should have done it, too. In person. He and I made a terrible mistake back then. He felt that your marriage was over, and I think you felt the same way, but I was wrong to allow myself to get in the middle of it the way I did. I won't tell you that I feel bad or that I would take it back, because the fact is, I found the love of my life and I married him. But I'm still sorry."

"Do you think that changes anything?" Andrea asked.

"No. Not a thing."

Andrea breathed loudly through her nose. Her face twitched. She was still angry, but she'd already fired both barrels, and she looked too tired to reload.

"So what do you want?" Andrea asked. "Why are you here?"

"Do you mind if I come in? Just for a minute?"

Andrea made no move to open the door wider. "We can talk right here. What is this about?"

"I assume Stride told you about the discovery of Ned Baer's body."

The other woman shrugged without replying, but her body language said yes. Andrea knew.

"Did he tell you that he's been suspended from the department?" Serena asked. "He removed himself from the investigation, because he covered up facts seven years ago and lied about a meeting that he had with Baer shortly before he was killed."

"So what?" Andrea said.

"I think you know what that meeting was really about."

"Well, you'll have to ask him, not me."

Serena glanced at the quiet street behind her. She understood the dimensions of the challenge she faced. She needed Andrea to open up about the most wrenching personal experience of her life, and Serena was about the last person on earth this woman would ever choose to confide in.

"See, the thing is, Andrea," Serena went on, allowing herself to use her first name. "You and I both know Stride. No one knows him better than the two of us. No matter what mistakes he's made, he's an honorable man. If he lied in an investigation seven years ago, he had a reason for it. And the only reason I can imagine is to protect someone he loved. In other words, you."

Andrea shrugged. "I have nothing to say."

"Of course. I understand. I don't expect you to share your secrets with a stranger, particularly me. Except I did my research on Ned Baer. I know what he was doing in Duluth. I know he was here to identify the woman who made an anonymous allegation of rape against Devin Card. And I'm pretty sure that woman was you."

She could see the pieces of Andrea's composure breaking apart, and she didn't blame her for that.

"You need to leave," Andrea said.

"Please. Give me just another minute. I want to tell you a story."

"I'm not interested in your stories."

"Please," Serena said again. "After that, if you want me to go, I'll go."

Andrea held the front door tightly, as if her instinct was to slam it shut. "One minute."

"Thank you." Serena had to swallow hard and summon her own courage to get the words out. "I don't share this with many people, but I think you'll understand when I tell you. I grew up in Phoenix, not Las Vegas. Vegas was where I ran away to. You see, when I was fifteen years old, my mother became a drug addict. Addiction runs in our genes. I'm an alcoholic. My mother's drug problem destroyed our family. My father left. Ran away, left me alone with her. My mother blew through all the money, lost our house, lost her job, lost everything."

"I really don't see how—" Andrea began.

Serena held up a hand. "Wait. Please. Let me finish. After we were homeless, we moved in with her drug dealer. I was sixteen. My mother couldn't pay to feed her habit, so I became the payment. I became his property. I'm sure you can guess what that meant. For months, he raped me every day, and my mother did nothing. I had no way out. It wasn't until I got pregnant, and had an abortion, that I finally realized I had to run."

Andrea's face was pale and frozen. "Why are you telling *me* this?"

"Because there is not a day of my life, not one, that I don't carry the scars of what he did to me. For years, being raped as a teenager defined who I was. Even after I ran away to Vegas, I was always scared. I woke up angry every day. I still don't need to dig very far to find that anger. It destroyed how I thought about men for years. It ruined my sexuality for years. It almost killed me. I was suicidal. So when I meet another woman who has experienced that kind of horror, all I can say is, *I get it.*"

Andrea was silent, but a single teardrop slipped from her eye. She wiped it away and nervously smoothed her bobbed hair. She opened the door without a word and waved Serena into the living room that faced the street. Serena took a seat in a stiff backed, uncomfortable armchair near the window, and Andrea sat opposite her on a claw-foot beige sofa. The furniture didn't encourage guests to stay any longer than necessary.

"It *was* you, wasn't it?" Serena said softly. "You were the one who made the accusation. Devin Card raped you when you were a teenager."

Andrea didn't look at her, but her head nodded almost imperceptibly.

"I'm so sorry for what you went through," Serena said.

Andrea shook her head with a kind of wonder. "Jon said it was probably going to come out. Did he tell you? Is that how you knew?"

"No. He kept your secret. I just know Stride."

"I suppose you think I should have come forward years ago," Andrea said.

"I don't think that at all. I would never dream of judging a woman in your position."

Andrea peered back in time through a haze of memory. "I was seventeen when it happened. Jesus, I can't believe that was almost thirty years ago."

"The amount of time doesn't matter at all."

"No, it doesn't."

"I'm still that girl," Serena said.

Andrea nodded. "Me, too."

"I know it's hard, but can you tell me what happened?"

Andrea hesitated, but her demeanor had changed. Her anger had washed away for the moment. Then she started talking.

"I was shy. Into science, which made me a little weird for a girl back then. I tried fitting in—hell, I was even a cheerleader for a while—but I kept crawling back into my shell. I dated a few times, but never even felt comfortable kissing boys. My sister, Denise, was the party girl. She kept telling me I should let loose a little."

Serena waited. She watched Andrea gathering the emotional strength to go on.

"There was this party crawl one summer. It was sometime in August, I don't remember exactly when. I went with Denise and a bunch of her friends to a concert, and then we started going from house to house. There must have been a couple dozen of us. I'd never had alcohol before, but I drank a lot. You get that's why I didn't want to tell anybody, right? I knew they'd say it was my fault."

"I do," Serena said.

"It was after midnight. We were at somebody's house, but I really have no idea whose house it was. We'd been to so many. I was drunk. The lights were low. It was so crowded you could hardly move. The music was so loud you had to shout to the person next to you. And there were these two guys flirting with me. Older guys, college guys. One was Devin Card. The other was a friend of his, a rich kid, Peter Stanhope."

Serena closed her eyes. That was a name she didn't want to hear. "Peter Stanhope? Are you sure?"

"Yes, why?"

"Never mind. Go on, please."

Andrea shook her head bitterly. "See, I knew that's what everyone would ask me. Are you sure? Was it really them? Maybe you forgot. Maybe you made a mistake. How much did you have to drink? But I know it was those two. I knew Peter. Everybody did, because of his father. And I knew Devin, too."

"What happened?" Serena asked softly.

"Devin was handsome. The coolest kid at the party. He'd been drinking, I'd been drinking, and the next thing I knew, we were making out on the sofa. I'd never even had a boyfriend, and there I was, with this stud telling me how pretty I was, how soft my lips were, all that bullshit. He asked if I wanted to go upstairs with him, and I said sure. Yes. Absolutely. We went upstairs and found the master bedroom and started kissing on the bed. He began to take off my clothes. That's when I freaked. I was feeling sick from drinking, and suddenly I was lying on a bed with some guy I'd just met, and he was pulling off my shirt. So I told him no. I told him to stop. I said I didn't want to do this, that I was a virgin, that he needed to leave. I remember saying the magic word: *stop*. And then I don't remember exactly how it all happened after that. I think I passed out or something, but when I came to, I was naked, and he was on top of me. He was *inside* me. I was crying and saying no, no, no, but he kept going. And when he was finished, I just grabbed my clothes and ran out of there."

"Did anyone see you?" Serena asked.

"No. There was a balcony outside the bedroom right over the garage. I left that way. I had to jump down from the garage. I couldn't go back to the party. I didn't want anyone to see me."

Andrea got to her feet with a kind of proud stiffness. She went to the fireplace in the living room and rubbed a finger along the wooden mantel. There was no dust anywhere. Serena understood; everything had to be clean.

"Do you remember where the house was?" Serena asked.

"No."

"Do you remember anything about it?"

"No." Then Andrea blinked, as if a memory had come back like the flash of a camera. "There was a castle."

"A castle? Like a children's playhouse?"

She shrugged. "I guess. I don't know. I just remember running past a castle. It made me think of princesses locked away."

"Wasn't your sister worried when you disappeared from the party?" Serena asked.

"Denise? She probably didn't even notice I was gone."

"Where did you go?"

"I ran home. I just wanted to forget it. I wanted to pretend it had never happened. But you can't wish things like that away. I was like you. Every day, every single day, it was there with me. It was with me when I married Robin. It was with me when I married Jon. I didn't tell either of them. Nobody knew. It was my dirty little secret. As far as I was concerned, I was going to keep it forever. I probably would have, too, if Devin hadn't run for Congress. It was hard enough seeing him as the Attorney General. Really? Him? The state's top lawyer? But when he ran for Congress, I kept seeing his face on television, and I kept him hearing him pretend to be something he wasn't. A defender of women's rights. What a hypocrite. I had to do something. I couldn't stay quiet. I had an attorney draft a letter telling my story. I really just wanted to scare him. I thought if he knew I was out there, if he knew the truth might come out, he'd drop out of the race and save himself the scandal. Instead, someone leaked the letter to the press. All of a sudden, everyone was looking for me. The only story in the whole world seemed to be about the anonymous woman accusing Devin Card of rape. And if they found me—do you have any idea what that would have been like?"

"I think I do," Serena said.

"I was going to be crucified. They'd destroy me. If my name got out there, they'd tear open everything in my life. Believe me when I tell you I wasn't strong enough to handle it. I spent that whole summer living in terror that some reporter would figure out it was me."

Serena let the silence stretch out. "And Ned Baer did?"

Andrea nodded. "He came to see me. He had an old yearbook from my high school class. He said he was looking into a big party crawl that happened around the time of the allegations, and he had reason to think Peter Stanhope and Devin Card had been at some of the parties that night. He was interviewing girls from our high school yearbook to find out what they remembered. He had no idea *I* was the one, but I was panicked by his questions, and I think he could see that. I'm sure I gave it away. After that, he must have been looking for ways to confirm it was me. He began following me. I think he broke into my house, too. I kept waiting for him to come back, and a few weeks later, he did. That was late August. He said he knew it was me, that he wanted to interview me about the rape, but that he had enough evidence to print it one way or another. He was going to expose me. I was desperate, Serena."

Serena could see the fragility in this woman's face. Thirty years later, and she was still seventeen. She had never known this woman before; she'd only known the stories Stride had told, of her coldness, of her distance, of her obsession with her first husband. But suddenly Andrea Forseth was a real person. And they had something in common.

"What did you do?" Serena asked.

Andrea stared across the living room and said the last thing that Serena wanted to hear.

"I told Stride," she said. "I finally told him everything about my past, and I told him what Ned Baer was going to do to me. I begged him for help. I said if he loved me, he would find a way to make sure Ned Baer didn't print that story. I said he had to stop him."

11

Stride lay in bed with his hands laced behind his head. Cool air blew through the open windows in the small bedroom. He kept the lights off, with only a pale glow in the room from the streetlight outside the cottage. He stared at the rotating ceiling fan above him, not entirely sure if he was awake or asleep. He'd had the nightmare about Andrea and Ned so many times lately that he couldn't be certain what was real anymore. It made him reluctant to close his eyes.

The door opened with a ghostly *creak* of the hinges. Serena slipped into the bedroom, and he knew he was still awake. She was quiet as she undressed on the other side of the room. She peeled down her jeans, then pulled her T-shirt over her head, mussing her black hair. Her profile was a silhouette portrait. She grabbed one of his flannel shirts from the closet and slipped it over her shoulders, but she left the buttons undone.

"This thing with Cat scares me," she murmured, sitting next to him on the bed.

"It scares me, too, but we'll find whoever is doing this to her."

"My own experience with stalkers isn't good. I know how these things can end."

"I remember, believe me."

"Is Brayden reliable? Do you trust him?"

"All the reports on him are good. He's responsible. He promised me he wouldn't let Cat out of his sight."

"Okay." Serena was quiet for a while as she stroked his bare chest with her fingernails. "Confession time."

"You or me?"

"Me first," she said. "I know about Andrea and Devin Card and Ned Baer."

"Serves me right to marry a smart cop," Stride said. "I was going to tell you tonight. I wasn't going to keep it a secret."

"What about Maggie? Are you going to tell her the truth, too?"

"No. I'm sure the investigation will lead her to Andrea on her own. Until then, I don't want to be the one to expose her. In the end, it's still her secret, not mine."

Serena nodded. "Just so you know, Maggie asked me to be a spy. She wanted me to hand off information behind the scenes. To protect you."

"I'm not surprised."

"I won't tell her anything," Serena replied, "unless you end up at risk. Then all bets are off. I won't let you sacrifice yourself."

"I'm not at risk."

"I don't know, Jonny. Did you hear K-2 brought in Dan Erickson to lead the case?"

"I did. Dan still can't prove something that never happened."

"Maybe not, but the circumstantial evidence looks bad," Serena said. "Let's not kid ourselves. If the truth about Andrea comes out—and we both know it will—Dan will have a body, a motive, and a lie from the principal suspect, who also happens to be the last person to see the victim alive. Plus, you admitted to Maggie that Steve made a dying declaration that implicates you. Prosecutors have made cases with less. And even if Dan doesn't go after you with formal charges, the suspicion alone may make it impossible for K-2 to bring you back to the force."

"All true," Stride said.

"You don't even sound like you care."

"I don't know how I feel about it," he admitted.

"Well, I care. I care a lot."

"Then you and I better figure out what really happened," Stride said.

"Isn't that a little hard when we're both banned from the case?"

"Well, we can't investigate Ned's murder directly, but I'm pretty sure that the mystery didn't start seven years ago. It was *thirty* years ago. That's where we go."

"You mean Andrea's rape," Serena murmured.

"Yes."

"Then I have another confession," she went on. "I went to see her. Right after you did."

"She talked to you?"

"Not at first. At first, she just wanted to yell at me. But then she opened up. I think she began to realize that our backgrounds aren't totally dissimilar. We found some common ground."

"You and Andrea are *nothing* alike," Stride told her.

Serena leaned forward and kissed him, her dark hair falling across his face. "I know you'd like to think so, Jonny, but that's not entirely true. There's more of her in me than you might want to admit. We both come from the same place. We were both violated as teens. I didn't follow the road she did, but believe me, I know that road really well. I'm not going to blame her for how she turned out, because I could have gone there, too."

Stride knew that Serena was right. He'd seen Andrea's demons throughout their marriage, and he'd never been able to get around her walls. Eventually, he stopped trying. He'd failed her. It was something he still regretted.

"You also can't blame *yourself* for how she turned out," Serena went on, because she knew how to read the emotions on his face. "She was who she was long before you met her. Guess what, you can't fix everybody."

"Maybe not, but I did a lot of things wrong."

"We all do. Welcome to relationships."

His mind drifted to Cat and the way she'd brought him and Serena back together after his affair with Maggie. "Andrea talked about her and me not having kids. I wonder if that would have changed things."

"The trouble in your marriage wasn't about kids. She may have thought that was a magic bullet to make everything better, but you know that's not true. Her problems went deeper than that."

"So I take it you believe her about the rape."

"I believe something terrible happened to her. The details? I have no idea. She admits she was drunk. She admits she passed out. She doesn't remember where this happened or when it happened. On the other hand, she's certain it was Devin Card in that bedroom. That wouldn't be enough in a court of law, but it probably would have been enough to ruin Card politically if she came forward."

"Ned Baer certainly thought so," Stride said.

"And Ned found Andrea."

"Yes, he did, and he was planning to write the story."

"Do you think Ned told Devin Card that he'd located the woman behind the allegations?" Serena hesitated before saying the next name. "Or if not Card, did he tell Peter Stanhope?"

"I don't know. I couldn't ask either of them about it back then, because doing that would have risked exposing Andrea. And remember, I really thought Ned drowned at the Deeps. I had no reason to think he'd been murdered. It may have been in the back of my head, but I didn't want to believe it."

"Peter Stanhope texted me," Serena told him. "He wants to meet tomorrow. An off-the-record conversation."

"You said yes?"

"I want to hear what he has to say."

"He knows finding Ned's body will put a focus on Devin. And himself. They'll both be suspects. Of course, so am I."

"And Andrea, too."

"True."

"We both know she's capable of losing control," Serena murmured.

"I know that, but I don't think she did it."

Serena stretched out next to him in bed. She put a bare leg over his calf and molded her skin against his body. Her face was inches from his own. "Jonny, what really happened between you and Ned Baer?"

He closed his eyes and remembered that night. He could see it again, vividly, as if no time had passed. The Deeps. The boiling hot evening. Ned on the cliff, his clothes wet from diving.

Stride stared at his wife. "Honestly? I wanted to kill him."

* * * * *

As Stride crossed the footbridge over the Deeps, the river pounded through the narrows below him, erupting into foam. Its thunder was so loud that he couldn't hear anything else. The violence of the water fed the violence that pulsed in his chest, and the heat of the evening bathed his body in sweat. He made his way along the wet rocks on the cliff, and his hands clenched into fists as he saw Ned Baer. He'd never met this man, but he already hated him.

The water roared; his mind roared. He had to do something to protect Andrea. To save her. She'd disintegrated in front of him as she confessed the truth. She'd cried that she couldn't survive the humiliation, the lies, the attacks if her secret was exposed. Tears had poured down her face. She'd screamed and begged: stop him!

Do something. Anything. Whatever it takes.

You're my husband.

"Don't fall," *a voice said.*

Ned Baer grinned at him as he dried his thinning hair with a towel. His clothes were sopping wet, making him look even skinnier than he was.

"Don't fall," *Ned said again.* "I hear if you drown, they never find your body."

"You're right. You shouldn't be diving here. It's not safe."

"Gotta beat the heat somehow," *Ned replied, in a voice that whined like the chirp of a cricket.*

"I've pulled a lot of people out of the lake who thought that," *Stride replied.*

Ned focused on him with beady black eyes that looked too big for his face. "You sound like a cop."

"I am. You're Ned Baer, right?"

"Yeah. Who are you? What do you want?"

"My name's Jonathan Stride." *He paused and then told him,* "Andrea is my wife."

Ned slung the towel around his neck. He knelt down and grabbed a can of beer from a six-pack. One can was already empty and crumpled on the ground. "Really. No shit."

"I want to talk about the story you're writing."

"I don't think we have much to talk about. Your wife's the one who says Devin Card raped her when she was a teenager. You know it, I know it. I'm going to print it."

"You can't prove it was her," *Stride retorted.*

"Oh, I have enough to cover my ass. I can put Card and your wife in the same house at the same party."

"Along with how many others?"

"Doesn't matter. I have an anonymous source who saw them go upstairs together. Plus, your wife went to pieces when I confronted her. She said I'd ruin her life by printing her name. That sounds like an admission to me."

"And it doesn't matter to you if you ruin someone's life?"

"That's what shrinks are for. Look, once she sent the letter, she knew the risks. You go after a public figure, you better have a thick skin. Otherwise, keep your mouth shut."

Stride felt dizzy in the heat. "Andrea says you broke into our house. If that's true, I'll have you arrested."

Ned laughed. "That's weak, Stride. You try any bullshit like that and I'll have your badge."

"We could sue you."

"For printing the truth? Yeah, give that a try. That lasts all of five minutes until my lawyer asks your wife under oath if she sent the letter. The fact is, you're wasting my time here. Hollow threats aren't going to intimidate me."

Sweat burned in Stride's eyes, and he wiped it away. His voice was a low hiss. "If you print this, you're killing her."

Ned shrugged. "Fifty thousand."

"What?"

"Fifty thousand dollars, and I'll spike the story."

"You want a bribe? You're blackmailing me? Are you serious?"

"Hey, you want me to act dumb, that's not free. Talk it over with your wife. I'll hold the story for twenty-four hours if you want to think about it."

"Go to hell."

"Suit yourself. Then I run the piece." Ned squatted on the rocks and hunted inside a zippered hip pack. He took out a black digital watch, strapped it to his wrist, and checked the time. "I think we're done here, Stride. Why don't you go home and hold your wife's hand? Seems like she'll need it."

Stride felt another wave of violence wash over him like a flood. All of his muscles coiled into knots, ready to spring. It was easy to imagine his hands around this man's throat. It was easy to feel his slippery finger curling around the trigger of his gun and sending a bullet into this man's forehead.

No one would know. Ned Baer would simply disappear. The story would go away, and Andrea would keep her secret.

He heard his wife's voice again: "Save me!"

But he couldn't do that. There were lines he couldn't cross. What was going to happen was going to happen, and he had no way to stop it.

Stride didn't say anything more.

He turned around and left the Deeps, with Ned still on the cliff behind him.

* * * * *

"What did you do next?" Serena asked.

"I drove north. Alone. I'd never felt more powerless in my life. I drove up the lakeshore and sat by the water for hours. I didn't go back home until after midnight."

"Was Andrea there?"

"Yes. She was asleep. We didn't talk. The strange thing is, we never talked about it again. That was our style. By the next morning, it was like nothing had ever happened. Even when Ned disappeared, we pretended the whole thing didn't exist. She thought I'd killed him, but she never said a word to me about it."

"How did you find Ned at the Deeps?" Serena asked. "How did you know that's where he was?"

"I talked to the owner of the motel where he was staying. Ned asked him for directions."

"Did Andrea know that's where you were going?"

Stride nodded. "I called her. She was so out of control that night, I wanted to make sure she was still okay. That she hadn't done anything crazy. I told her that I was going to find Ned at the Deeps and do what I could to stop him from running the article. Except I think she already knew I wouldn't be able to do a thing."

"So she could have gone out there herself," Serena said.

"She could have, but I don't think she did. She said she called Steve and told him to follow me. That explains how Steve found the body."

Serena shook her head. She wasn't going to let Stride be noble, not when his whole future was at stake. "I'm sorry, Jonny, but you don't know that's how it happened. You don't know that at all. Andrea knew where Ned was. She was desperate to stop him. She could have followed you up there and confronted Ned herself after you left. With a gun. And when Ned was dead, *that's* when she called Steve to tell him she was afraid of what you were going to do. Because she knew when Steve found the body, he'd protect his best friend."

12

"Do you know who you remind me of?" Cat asked Brayden Pell a little breathlessly from across the long bench at Hoops brewery. "Ryan Tedder. You know, the singer from One Republic? I mean, I know he's a lot older, but you guys could be brothers."

"Actually, Ryan is my brother," Brayden replied.

Cat's eyes widened into saucers and she practically leaped across the table. "Oh, my God! Are you serious?"

Brayden winked. "No."

She sat back on the bench with a pout. "You're teasing me."

"A little."

His lips bent into a crooked smile, and his deep dark eyes twinkled at her. She had to look away in embarrassment, because she felt her face flushing deep red. Instead, she watched the crowd in the brewery. It was almost eleven o'clock, but the benches stretching across the beer hall were mostly full. Tourists stood two deep at the taps. The space was brightly lit with circular chandeliers and decorated in blond fir wood. Noise reverberated off the ceiling.

She fidgeted on the long bench and grabbed a square piece of Sammy's pizza they'd had delivered to the beer hall. She took a drink from a tall glass of pop and gestured at Brayden's mug of coffee. "You know, you can drink beer even if I can't. Stride said you're off-shift, right? I mean, babysitting me isn't really like being on duty."

"It is to me. And I'm not babysitting, Cat. You're under threat, and I'm here to make sure you're safe."

"So how does that work exactly?" she asked.

"I pick you up. I drive you where you want to go. I keep an eye on the surroundings wherever you are. Like here. I survey the people around us every few minutes, and I make sure no one's watching you. I note everyone who comes in and assess whether someone looks like a threat. But it's not like I have to be your shadow and constant companion, either. If you feel smothered, you're more likely to ditch me, and I don't want that. So if you want space around your friends, tell me, and I'll back off. Just be aware that I'll still be in the background."

"Okay. Thanks." She bit her lip and added, "You don't have to back off. I don't feel smothered."

"Good."

"Have you ever done this before? Protecting somebody?"

Brayden shook his head. "Not really. I'm a street cop. Mostly it's domestic disturbances and break-ins and drug busts."

"So why'd you volunteer to be with me on your days off?"

"Stride put out the word that he needed someone. I think you'll find that most of the cops on the force would do just about anything for him."

"I like that. I would, too."

She watched Brayden sip his coffee. As he did, his eyes checked out the beer hall again. He wasn't in uniform; no one would peg him as a cop. She knew she was staring at him, being way too obvious, but she couldn't help herself. He was *so* attractive. He was a decade older than she was, but she had never cared about age. There was something tough in his face when he looked at everyone else and something gentle when he looked at her.

"I guess you know the stories about me, huh?" Cat asked. "I mean, not just that actor and all the craziness last winter. I suppose Stride told you about my background before then."

"He did. A bit."

"I was basically a hooker when Stride and Serena took me in. I was on and off the streets. I just figured you should know who you're dealing with." She rolled her eyes and made an L on her forehead.

"Don't be so hard on yourself. Stride told me your mother was murdered when you were a kid, and you got shunted off to some awful foster parents. Now look at where you are. Sounds to me like you've come a long way."

She flushed again. "That's sweet. Thanks."

"I hear you have a kid," Brayden said.

"Yeah. Well, I let another family take him. They're great. I still see him all the time. But I know what you're thinking. A baby at seventeen, pretty stupid."

"I don't think that at all. You had a child and gave him a better future, but you're still involved in his life. He'll grow up knowing who you are and what you did for him. That takes a lot of guts."

"Stride gives me the same pep talk all the time."

"Well, he's right."

Cat offered up a half-smile and twisted a few strands of chestnut hair nervously between her fingers. She checked her phone. "I'm sorry we're just hanging out here. I don't know where Curt and Colleen are. They're late."

"That's okay. I'm enjoying getting to know you."

"Well, you know pretty much everything about me, but I don't know anything about you."

"What would you like to know?" Brayden asked. His dark eyes were so penetrating that she felt as if she had to look away again.

"Anything, I guess. Have you always lived in Duluth?"

"No. I grew up in Minneapolis. I moved up here when I was eighteen."

"Why Duluth?"

His mouth broke into a broader grin. He smoothed his blond hair back. "I wasn't exactly an angel back in high school. My father and I didn't see eye to eye on much of anything, and he didn't want me staying in the house after I graduated. I figured it was time for a do-over in my life. I love being around the lake, so I picked Duluth. I enrolled in police training classes, and I worked as a security guard for a few years in the interim. I've been on the force for five years."

"Do you like it?"

"I do."

Cat pushed the pizza box around with her fingers. "I don't see a ring." She tried to make it sound casual, and to her ears, she failed completely.

"No," he replied. "No ring."

"That's surprising. I mean, you must be—that is, you probably—oh, I don't know what I mean. I'm just surprised."

"I dated the same girl for several years after I came here," Brayden told her. "She's a nurse at Essentia. We lived together for a while. I figured we'd get married, but that's not how it went. She decided the life of a cop's wife wasn't for her. I respect that. It's definitely not for everyone."

Cat wanted him to keep talking to her. It didn't even matter what he said. His voice had a quiet music about it that made him sound like an artist or a teacher, not a tough cop. She liked it. She thought she could listen to him for hours. But before he could say anything more, a different voice cut through the beer hall like a shrill fire alarm.

"AHOY, HOOPS!"

It was Curt.

He stood in the doorway, arms over his head like an Olympic champion, the usual cocky grin on his face. He sidled through the brewery, slapping palms with his friends and with total strangers. Cat winced, and she wasn't even sure why. Her crush on Curt suddenly felt stupid and immature, as if Brayden would judge her for knowing him. All the cops in Duluth knew that Curt was a petty criminal.

"Kitty Cat!" Curt bellowed as he saw her.

He headed for the bench, dragging a short blond girl behind him. The two of them squeezed onto the wooden seat next to Cat. "Sorry we're late. Colleen was sketching down on the Point, and we got bridged. Two boats, took forever. Anyway, we're here! Colleen, Cat, Cat, Colleen."

Colleen reached across Curt to shake Cat's hand, and her grip was moist and limp. "The famous Cat," she said, in a girlish voice that was hard to hear. "I'm Colleen Hunt."

Curt's new girlfriend was not what Cat had expected. She couldn't be much older than Cat herself, definitely still in her teens. She was cute but not a beauty queen, and the intimidated look she shot Cat showed a combination of meekness and jealousy, which helped Cat's ego. Her blond hair was straight and parted in the middle, and she had pencil-thin dark eyebrows and chocolate brown eyes. Her skin was very pale. She wore a light blue summer dress that revealed matchstick arms and legs. She didn't look like Curt's type, and it occurred to Cat that if Curt was dating this girl, he must really feel something for her. A better question was what a white bread suburban flower like Colleen saw in a sleazy city boy like Curt. Then again, sweet girls liked to walk on the wild side sometimes.

"Who's the dude?" Curt asked, noticing Brayden for the first time and realizing that Cat and Brayden were together. She took a little pleasure in the fact that Curt didn't look entirely happy about it.

Brayden extended a hand. "Officer Brayden Pell."

Curt's eyes narrowed at the word *officer*. "Oh, yeah, yeah, I know you. One of Duluth's finest."

"Yes, I think we've met a couple of times, Curt," Brayden replied drily.

Curt didn't say anything, but he glanced at Cat, and his eyebrows asked the question: *What the hell is a cop doing here?* Cat explained, and to Curt's credit, he looked horrified to hear what had happened at the Deeps after he'd left.

"Holy hell! Are you okay, Kitty Cat?"

"I'm fine. But Stride wants Brayden to keep an eye on me for a few days."

"You never told me someone was stalking you," Curt complained.

"I didn't know myself. It's new."

Curt eyed the bar. "Well, yikes, I need a beer to handle this news. Colly, you want something?"

"Kombucha," Colleen replied.

"I don't even know what the hell that is, but I love saying it," Curt replied. He announced in a loud voice as he headed for the taps, "Kom-booooo-chaaaaahh!"

Now that Cat had Brayden with her, she felt a little more charitable about seeing Curt with his girlfriend. It wouldn't kill her to be friendly. She smiled at Colleen and patted the seat next to her, and Colleen slid nervously over on the bench to join her.

"You and Curt look good together," Cat said. "I'm glad to finally meet you."

"Oh, thanks. I'm glad to meet you, too. Curt talks about you all the time, you know."

"How'd you hook up with him?"

"I met him at the spaghetti dinner before the marathon."

"Oh, yeah, I was there, too. Did you run the marathon this year?"

Colleen laughed. "No way! I was just a volunteer."

"Serena runs it. She's my—well, she's not my mom, but she is. Anyway, she does the marathon every year now, but I think she's nuts."

"I'm with you on that," Colleen said.

"Do you still go to school? Are you off this summer?"

Colleen shook her head. "I work full-time. I graduated last year and didn't feel like college. I wanted to get my own apartment right away, so I found a cheap sublet in the Central Hillside, and I got a job at Miller Hill Mall. It's not much, just a kiosk thing, drawing caricatures. I've got a couple of other part-time gigs, too. I'd love to be an artist full-time, but that doesn't pay the bills."

"Wow, good for you." Cat was impressed on both counts. The Central Hillside was a rough area of downtown, and Colleen didn't look like Hillside material.

"Kitty Cat, over here!"

Cat glanced at the bar taps and saw Curt waving at her. He shouted across the beer hall, attracting attention.

"Over here!" he called again.

Colleen smirked. "Watch out. I think you're getting fixed up."

"What?"

"Curt has a friend working the taps. Wyatt. He's into you. Says he's seen you around."

"Oh, yeah. Curt mentioned him. Is he cute?"

"Well, he's a woodsy type."

"What does that mean?"

"Beard. Dreadlocks. Likes to hunt wabbits. I'm kidding about that. I mean, don't get me wrong, he's a nice guy, just quirky. Curt and I hang out with him at his place sometimes. He lives in my building, and he mostly listens to opera, plays with his cat, and smokes weed." She eyed Brayden across the table. "You didn't hear that."

The cop smiled. "Hear what?"

"Anyway, who knows?" Colleen went on. "Maybe you'll like him."

Cat sighed, because she didn't think that was likely, but she knew Curt wouldn't give up until she went over to the bar. She glanced at Brayden and said, "Do I need a permission slip to leave?"

The cop chuckled. "No, go have fun. I'll be here."

Cat got off the bench and pushed through the crowd. She drew stares from the men in the beer hall, as she always did. It didn't matter who they were, young, old, married, single. She was used to the looks. When she got to the taps, Curt took her by the shoulders and shoved her to the front. He waved at a skinny white boy in a tie-dye T-shirt and jeans, who was pouring a #21 ale. "Wyatt! She's here! Cat's here!"

Wyatt wandered her way with the bow-legged walk of a cowboy and handed the IPA across the bar to Curt. He wiped his hands on a towel and then extended one for Cat to shake. When he spoke, his boyish voice was more like a mumble. "Wyatt Miller. Really nice to meet you."

"Cat Mateo."

Curt picked up a glass of kombucha from the bar along with his beer and headed back to the bench. "You two talk! I have to get this to Colly."

Cat opened her mouth to protest being left alone, but Curt had already disappeared into the crowd. She forced a smile onto her face for Wyatt, and he smiled back at her. He wasn't bad-looking, but Colleen was right that he was woodsy. He wore an orange bandanna, and his reddish-blond dreadlocks dangled from his head and tumbled over his shoulders like a den of snakes. He had a gold, wispy beard. His nose was wide and flat, his cheeks sunburnt red, and he had very pale eyebrows over brown eyes. The smile he gave her was a little shy and reserved. He was probably in his early twenties.

"Can I get you something?" Wyatt asked. "I mean, not beer. I know you're only eighteen. But if you want pop or tea or coffee or whatever. On the house."

His nervousness made him ramble.

"I'm fine," Cat said. "Curt says you're new in town."

"Yeah, I got here a month ago. I used to live in Boulder, but I figured, water over mountains."

"Sure."

"What about you? You grow up here?"

"Yup, I'm a Duluth girl." She searched for something to say. "Colleen says you like opera."

"Love it. What about you?"

"Um, it's okay, I guess. I don't know much about it. I hear you have a cat."

"Me? No."

"Colleen said you liked to play with your cat."

"Well, my neighbors have a cat, and I let him into my apartment sometimes. He keeps me company."

"Uh-huh."

"What about you? Does Cat have a cat?"

"No. No cat."

A full minute of silence followed. This was unquestionably one of the least promising fix-ups of Cat's entire life.

"Well, I should get back to my friends," she said.

"Sure. Sure. I understand. Listen, do you mind if I call you sometime? The thing is, I've seen pictures and thought you were gorgeous, but meeting you in person, I was so wrong. You're like one of the most beautiful girls I've ever met."

Damn.

She couldn't simply dump him after he said that.

"Tell you what, give me your number, and I'll call you," Cat said.

"Cool."

Wyatt bent over and scribbled something on a small piece of paper. His dreadlocks dangled over his face as he wrote. He folded the note and pushed it across the bar. "It was great to meet you, Cat."

She fingered the paper in front of her. "Yeah. Same here."

"See ya," Wyatt said.

"See ya."

He headed down the row of taps to wait on another customer. Cat idly took the paper with his phone number in her hand. She didn't want to crumple it and throw it away in case Wyatt was still watching. Instead, she flipped it open.

When she did, her head shot up, looking to see if Wyatt was staring back at her. And he was. He poured beer at the other end of the bar, but he watched her with the same smile on his face he'd been wearing all along. Like he was waiting to see what she would do.

Like he was daring her to notice.

Cat tried to hide her reaction. She forced herself to smile back, and then she practically ran to get away from the bar.

She had the note in her hand with Wyatt's name and phone number.

It was written in lime-green marker.

13

Andrea awoke with a start in the middle of the night.

She always slept lightly, attuned to any unfamiliar sound. The bedroom was black except for the red glow of the clock on her nightstand, which told her it was nearly four in the morning. She stared at the ceiling, eyes wide open. Her ears pricked up, listening for whatever had awakened her. Her heart hammered in her chest. It didn't take much to bring the memories back.

A noise. A smell. A touch on the shoulder. And just like that, she'd be back in the darkness. Under him. Struggling.

It never went away.

You are not seventeen years old.

She climbed out of bed in her white silk pajamas. The master bedroom was at the back of the house, with windows on the rear wall facing the lake and windows on the adjacent corner looking down on the neighborhood basketball courts. Sometimes kids hung out there overnight. She swept aside the curtains but saw no teenagers in the park below her.

The bedroom felt colder than usual. She liked it warm, and she typically kept the heat on even during the summers, but she found herself shivering. When she went to the doorway, a draft sneaked up the stairs. Somewhere in the house, a window or door was open. That was never how she left it.

Then, below her, the downstairs floorboards shifted. Someone who was trying to be quiet gave themselves away. She wasn't alone.

He was back.

Andrea felt all of her emotions drain out of her. The panic left her entirely, and something robotic took over her mind like a strange, dead calm. She backed away from the bedroom door, conscious that she was making noise herself. She wanted him to know that she was awake. If he heard her, if he knew she was listening to him, then he would leave.

It always worked that way.

He never hurts you.

But Andrea took no chances. She opened the drawer of her nightstand and found her 9 mm pistol. She always kept it fully loaded, magazine in place. She pulled out the gun, which was heavy in her hand. The feel of it gave her strength. She had to use effort to drag back the slide and load a cartridge, but the click told her she was ready to shoot.

She carried the gun back to the doorway and stared into the gloom at the bottom of the stairs.

"I'm armed," she called. "I have a gun. You need to go."

If he was there, he held his breath, not making a sound. She flipped on the light switch, and bright light filled the foyer, making her squint. She anticipated a thunder of footfalls as he escaped, but the house was silent.

Andrea cradled the gun with both hands, her right index finger along the barrel. That was how Denise had taught her. She took the steps one at a time, stopping to listen. The air from outside got colder. Near the base of the stairs, she could see the front door, which was closed and locked. No one was waiting for her. The draft came from the other side, the back door in the kitchen. She got to the last step, swung left, and slipped her finger around the trigger.

She could see all the way to the rear of the house. It was empty. He'd stolen away while she was getting her gun. Still ready to fire, she continued to the end of the hallway and confirmed that no one was in the kitchen. The back door was ajar, letting in a whistle of wind.

He'd left a package for her on the kitchen table, the way he always did.

Andrea took the gun outside and descended the warped back steps in her bare feet and stood in the wet grass. The wind tore up the hillside and rattled the trees. She couldn't see much, but she knew he was still out here. Somewhere, he was watching her, because she could feel his eyes like fingertips on her neck.

"I know it's you," she called. "It's been a while. I didn't think you were coming back. Why now?"

She walked up to a rusted fence behind her property. Across a stretch of green grass was a cluster of trees. That was where he was, somewhere in those shadows.

"Who are you? Why do you do this?"

There was no answer. There never was. She turned away and walked back inside the house. She slammed the door behind her and locked it, although locks couldn't protect her. Somehow, he always knew how to get inside. She emptied the cartridge from the gun and laid it on the kitchen table, and at that point, she finally broke down. Her knees buckled, and she slid to the floor. Tears fell down her face. Her shoulders jerked as she sobbed, letting out all her fear.

When she was done, she wiped her face and got up again.

The foil box waited for her on the kitchen table. It was like all the others before, silver, with a yellow bow on top. Her fingers trembling, she took it and removed the lid. She knew what she would find inside. A suncatcher to add to the collection he'd created for her. This one was round, with a white dove in the center, its wings spread. The bird flew in front of a yellow sun, which gave out beams of light that broke into pieces of red, blue, green, orange, and purple glass.

The suncatchers had arrived many times in the past seven years. She'd never seen who it was; she'd never been able to catch him in the act. In the early days, he'd been discreet, leaving the boxes outside, on a doorstep, on the railing of her back porch. It had seemed like a game then, surprises from a secret admirer. Later, he'd grown bolder and darker, breaking inside her house to leave his tokens behind. That was when she was alone and divorced.

She had more than twenty of the suncatchers now. Instead of smashing them, instead of throwing them away, she kept them. At some point, she'd begun to hang them on her kitchen window. She couldn't even explain to herself why she did that. Maybe she wanted him to see them and realize she wasn't scared of his nighttime visits.

Or maybe it was something else.

It had been nearly a year since the last one arrived. That was the longest gap without receiving one, and she'd assumed he was done, or gone, or dead. Strangely, she'd almost missed him.

But now he was back.

The timing couldn't be a coincidence. He'd come back right after Ned Baer's body had been found, which had a strange symmetry. The very first of the suncatchers had shown up the summer that Ned Baer arrived on her doorstep. Someone had been sending her a message. He still was.

She took the suncatcher out of the box and held it in her hands, and then she looked for the note. There was always a note, written on a fold-over card in block handwriting.

It was the same message every time.

Forgive every sin.

14

Dan Erickson hadn't changed.

Maggie hadn't seen Dan in more than five years, but when he came into the conference room the next morning, it was as if no time had passed. His cologne always advertised his arrival. He wasn't tall, but if she measured by ego, he was a basketball player, and he walked into every room like he owned it. His skin had the artificial glow of hours spent in a tanning bed. His hair was blond, with a trimmed corporate cut. He wore a well-tailored dark suit with a loud red tie that made people notice him.

She couldn't deny to herself that he looked good. He always did. He still made her feel like a naïve kid, having sex with a married man, foolishly thinking he'd leave his wife to be with her. Dan slumped into a chair and leaned far back, putting his leather shoes on the table. His lips drew into a Tom Cruise grin.

"Maggie, Maggie, Maggie."

"Hello, Dan."

"I like the long hair. It looks good. I was never a fan of the bowl cut."

"I'm so relieved. If you didn't like it, I would have gone right out and cut it off."

He chuckled at her sarcasm. "Oh, Maggie, still the same. Still that sharp tongue of yours. Of course, I won't lie, your tongue was always one of your best features."

"Fuck you, Dan."

He didn't look offended. "And the nasty mouth, too! Dirty talk turns me on, but I'm sure you remember that. Come on, Maggie, lighten up. I was excited when K-2 said we'd be working together. You, me, just like the good old days."

"I don't remember the old days being very good," Maggie replied.

"Seriously? I'm disappointed. How many years has it been since we had our little fling? I assumed we were finally past the hard feelings. I mean, come on, it didn't last long."

"As I recall, nothing about you lasted very long."

"Ouch! Another poison arrow. Look, I know you and Stride were hoping you'd seen the last of me, but here I am. The bad penny back again."

He was right about that. Dan was a punching bag who kept bouncing back and never stayed down for too long. In his early years as the St. Louis County Attorney, he'd been buzzed about as a statewide political candidate. He had the right connections, the right look, the right wife, the right bank account. But when his appetites got the better of him, he'd lost it all, including his wife. Dan had resigned in disgrace, but he'd remade himself since then as a corporate lawyer. Judging by his appearance, he'd made back most of the money he lost.

Dan opened the thick police file in front of him. "Shall we get down to work? What do you think? Did Stride do it?"

Maggie gave him a frozen look. "Dan, if you can't be objective—"

"I'm being completely objective," he replied. "I read the file. I heard your interview. Stride's the obvious suspect."

"Well, he didn't do it. He told me flat out in my interview that he didn't do it."

"Oh, wow, a suspect denied committing murder during interrogation? Shut down the investigation and let's all go home. Is that the standard you'd apply in any other case, Maggie? Seems to me the only one not being objective here is you."

Maggie hated being outdueled, and she hated even more that Dan was right. "Okay. You're in charge, not me. How do you want to proceed?"

Dan's eyes glittered with satisfaction. "That's more like it. I like seeing the submissive side of you. Look, I know you and Stride go way back and you think he's innocent. I also won't deny that he and I have had our difficulties over the years. That doesn't mean I'm out to get him, but it also doesn't mean he gets a free pass. As far as I'm concerned, we treat him the way we would any other suspect. We go where the evidence takes us. Period. That work for you?"

"Fine."

"So what do we know? Not what do we think, not what do we assume, not what do we hope, not what anybody else tells us. What do we *know?*"

"Everything we know is thanks to Stride," Maggie replied. "He opened up the case himself, which he didn't need to do. He's the one who told us about Steve Garske's dying declaration. That's the only reason we found the body."

"Okay," Dan agreed. "Point goes to Stride. Have we heard anything from the medical examiner about the autopsy?"

"Yes, Violet just sent over her report. She confirmed the body is Ned Baer. We got records from Ned's dentist in Colorado, and the match is perfect. It's him. Cause of death was exactly what it looked like, 9 mm to the skull. Violet recovered the bullet, and we're sending it through the BCA to see if any matches show up in the system. That'll take a while."

"What else do we have?" Dan asked.

"Not much. Seven years ago, we were still trying to ascertain why Ned disappeared. We didn't uncover any evidence to suggest a crime had been committed, so we didn't investigate it as a murder. The circumstances suggested that it was probably an accidental death."

"Except Stride was the one who drew that conclusion, right?"

"So did I," Maggie said.

"But you based it on Stride's description of events," Dan said.

"Yes."

"A description we now know to be false."

Maggie frowned. "Yes."

"You still think he's not a suspect?"

Maggie said nothing.

Dan took his feet off the table and dropped them heavily on the floor. "Well, it's a homicide now, and we're starting from scratch. We need to build a picture of what this guy was doing before he got shot. We've already got his cell phone records in the file, so let's have Tubbo start following up on the calls Ned made to find out who he was talking to and what they were talking about."

"Guppo," Maggie snapped.

"Huh?"

"It's *Guppo*. Not Tubbo."

"Short guy? Mustache? Built like the Death Star?"

"Yes."

"Huh. I always thought it was Tubbo. Anyway, he can chase down the calls."

"What about me?" Maggie asked. "What do you want me to do?"

Dan gave her another wolfish grin. He opened up a laptop computer in front of him, and he patted the chair next to him. "I want you and me working together. Side by side. So close we can read each other's minds."

"Read my mind, Dan. What do you think it's saying?"

He patted the chair again. "Come on, sit over here. I set up a call with Debbi King. Ned's editor."

Unhappily, Maggie relocated to the chair next to Dan, where they were squeezed so closely at the end of the table that their legs were forced together. His thigh rubbed against hers. He booted up the MacBook and used FaceTime to dial a number. A few seconds later, they were connected with a woman in a Denver office. Through the window behind her, they had a blurry view of the foothills.

"Ms. King?" Dan said. "My name is Dan Erickson. I'm leading the investigation here in Duluth regarding Ned Baer. This is my partner on the case, Sergeant Maggie Bei. We appreciate your talking to us today."

"Your *investigation* is about seven years late, Mr. Erickson," King snapped.

"Yes, I understand that."

"Have you confirmed that the body you found is Ned?"

"We have. I'm very sorry."

King shook her head in dismay. She was quiet for a while, and then she looked out the window and wiped her face. Maggie guessed that the woman was around fifty years old, which was the same age Ned Baer would have been if he'd lived. She had a shock of curly gray hair, and her face looked weathered and lined from time in the Colorado sun. Her nose was short and hooked, and she had pale eyes.

"Is it true that Ned was murdered?" King went on.

"Yes, he was shot." When the editor didn't react, Dan went on. "You don't sound surprised to hear that."

"I'm not."

"Why is that?"

"Ned was an investigative reporter. It's a nasty business. We get threats all the time. They're usually just people trying to scare us off a story, but the risk is always there."

Maggie leaned forward. "Ms. King, can you give us some background on Ned Baer? Given that he wasn't from Duluth, we don't know very much about him. Had he worked for you for a long time?"

"Ned didn't work for me," King replied. "He was my business partner. He and I started FR Online together twelve years ago. Before that, we both worked at the *Post* for fifteen years until we were laid off."

"So you must have known him well," Maggie said.

"Of course. We were good friends. I met him while I was still in college in California. He was a roadie for ZZ Top one summer, and I met him backstage when the tour came through San Jose. We were both journalism majors and both archconservatives, which is a pretty rare combination. We hit it off. We spent the whole night talking about Reagan and Bush. We had a very similar philosophy. Even back then, we both believed the future of the media was in advocacy. Having a point of view. We were convinced that 'objectivity' was simply bullshit covering up a left wing bias. Seventeen years later, that's what led us to start FR Online."

"Did the two of you move to Colorado together after school?"

"That's right. The *Post* was hiring, and we both signed on. Like I said, we became close friends."

"Were you involved romantically?"

King chuckled. "Me and Ned? No, our friendship was purely platonic. Oh, he hit on me when we first met, but I shot him down. He wasn't the kind of man who gets my motor running. Honestly, Ned never dated much. He always had kind of an inferiority complex about his looks. Small guy, not much hair, beady eyes. So he never had much of a personal life. To be honest, he could be prickly, too. Angry, hard, always convinced the world was out to screw him. Not exactly the ideal e-Harmony profile. But that's also what made Ned a terrific reporter. He loved cutting powerful people down to size. I still miss him."

"Ms. King, can you tell us about that summer in Duluth?" Dan asked. "What exactly was Ned doing here?"

"Well, as you know, the Minnesota Attorney General, Devin Card, was running for the US House of Representatives. Card checked a lot of the Kennedy boxes. Liberal, good-looking, but also a reputation for bad behavior. When the anonymous rape accusation leaked to the press, there was a feeding frenzy to find out who was behind it and whether the allegation was true. Ned was convinced he could find the woman. He saw an opportunity to take down a rising Dem star."

"Did he?" Dan asked.

"Obviously not. Card won the election. Now he's running for the Senate."

"No, I meant, did Ned find the woman behind the accusation?"

King rocked back in her chair. "I don't know."

"You sound like you think it's possible?"

"Well, I told you, Ned was good at what he did. Unfortunately, he was also secretive. Reporters are competitive, and Ned usually didn't share stories with me until he was ready to go public. But he was dropping hints that he had something big."

Maggie's eyes narrowed. "What kind of hints?"

"Well, it was nothing he said. He never told me if he was close, or if he had the woman's name. That wasn't his style. But I'd worked with Ned for a long time. He had certain quirks. I knew his voice when he was onto something. He was like a puffer fish, and I could almost hear his ego inflating. That was how he was that August."

"How did Ned work when he was doing research?" Maggie asked.

"What do you mean?"

"Well, did he take paper notes? Use a laptop? Voice recordings?"

"Yes, all of those things, but Ned was old school. He still wrote things down. He'd fill dozens of yellow pads with ideas."

"We didn't find any notes in his motel room," Maggie told her. "No notebooks and nothing electronic either. His car was broken into, and we think his laptop could have been stolen. But there were no paper notes anywhere."

King didn't say anything immediately. She grabbed a pen from her desk and twisted it between her fingers. "So he had the story."

"What?"

"He had the story. That's what got him killed. Whoever did it took his notes. Did you talk to Devin Card? That son of a bitch had to be the one who killed Ned. If he thought his whole career was going down the crapper, he would have found a way to make Ned disappear."

"Do you have any proof of that?" Maggie asked. "Did Ned mention any conversations with Card?"

"No, but what else could it be? Damn it, I *knew* that was what happened. As soon as I heard he was missing, I figured it was because of the story. I've been waiting seven years to hear that Ned was murdered."

"I wish you'd shared your suspicions with us," Maggie said.

King's face screwed up with anger. "What are you talking about? I told the Duluth Police exactly what I'm telling you now. You were the ones insisting it was an accident, that Ned drowned in some river. I never believed that."

Dan shot a glance at Maggie. "Ms. King, do you remember who you talked to at the Duluth Police?"

"Sure I do," she replied. "I wrote it down. It was a police lieutenant named Jonathan Stride."

15

Stride found Andrea's sister, Denise, smoking outside the fence that bordered the runway at the Duluth airport. Crisp air blew across the hillside, making the long grass flutter. An F-16 from the National Guard unit was lined up for takeoff, and Stride waited to approach her until after the jet screamed into the air with a roar that he could feel under his feet like an earthquake. As the waves of noise faded, he crossed to the fence, and smoke from the woman's cigarette enveloped him.

He only met Denise a couple of times when he and Andrea were married, but he recognized her immediately, despite the years in between. Unlike Andrea, Denise had inherited the Forseth family height. She was several inches taller than Andrea and three years older, making her nearly fifty. Denise didn't color her hair; it was gray and short. Her physique was lean, with leathery skin heavily inked with tattoos. She wore a loose black T-shirt over camouflage cargo pants and work boots. Wire-rimmed sunglasses covered her eyes.

Two sisters who'd grown up in the same household couldn't be more dissimilar.

"Hello, Denise," he said.

She looked at him when she heard his voice. "Stride. What do *you* want?"

"Andrea told me you moved back to Duluth this year."

"So what are you, the rep for the welcome wagon?"

"I just wanted to talk," he said.

"Well, I'm not really interested in talking to you, Stride. You're not exactly one of my favorite people, given what you did to my sister."

"I understand that. I hurt Andrea, and I won't pretend otherwise."

"Do you expect to get points for honesty?"

"No."

She whipped off her sunglasses. Heavy bags sagged under her blue eyes. "Why'd you do it?"

"What?"

"Why'd you cheat on her?"

"I'm not sure how to answer that," he admitted. "I fell for someone else, and I made a mistake. Things between me and Andrea were bad, but that doesn't excuse it. I know that."

Denise put her sunglasses back on. She inhaled deeply on her cigarette, then coughed raggedly. "Well, if it makes you feel better, I'm a hypocrite to be blaming you."

"How so?"

"I cheated, too. A lot. Repeatedly, in fact. My husband finally got sick of it and threw me out."

"I'm sorry."

"Well, he was no prize, either. I wanted custody of our daughter, and he said, sure, fine, take her. Father of the year, that one. So Lexi and I moved back here. Thirty years away, but Duluth is still home."

"You left the Air Force?" Stride asked.

"Years ago. I put in my twenty." She gestured at the runway. "Sometimes I still miss it, though. I like to come up here and watch the jets."

"I went to your house. Your daughter told me you'd probably be here."

Denise turned around and leaned against the fence. She bent one leg and propped her boot against the mesh. "So why'd you want to talk to me?"

"Has Andrea told you what's going on?" Stride asked.

"About that body being found? Ned Baer? Yeah. She called me. Is she a suspect in the murder?"

"Actually, right now, the top suspect is probably me."

Her thin lips curled into a smile. "I heard that, too. Did you do it?"

"No."

"Too bad. Sounds like that asshole deserved what he got."

"I have to ask, do you know why Ned Baer was interested in Andrea?"

Denise tossed her cigarette butt to the ground and put her boot down and crushed it. "You mean, do I know about her and Devin Card? Yeah."

"Did she tell you about the assault when it happened?"

"Back then? No. She never said a word. I didn't have a clue."

"When did she tell you?"

Andrea's sister sighed and lit another cigarette. "Seven years ago, I got a strange call from her. She was asking me about the summer before I left for basic training. She made it sound casual, sort of nostalgic, but she was asking about parties we went to and where they were and who was there and what I remembered. I don't know, it sounded forced. I didn't think much about it, but then a few weeks later, I saw the news about Devin. Someone made an anonymous accusation that he raped a girl at a party that summer in Duluth. I put two and two together. I called Andrea and asked if she was the one behind the allegation, and she admitted it."

"Did you tell anyone else about it?" Stride asked.

"Not a soul."

"Do you know if Andrea told anyone else?"

"About being the one to make the accusation? I doubt it. She said our parents were the only ones who knew about the rape back then. She told them a few weeks after it happened, but my parents would have thought their daughter being raped was too shameful to admit to anyone. I'm sure they encouraged her not to talk to the police. Anyway, they're both dead, and I imagine they took it to their graves." Denise folded her arms across her chest. "Why are you asking me all this anyway?"

"I'm trying to figure out how Ned Baer found Andrea and who else knew the truth about her. That might give me a clue about who killed him."

"You think Andrea did it, don't you?"

"Actually, I don't," Stride replied. "On the other hand, I know it wasn't me, and Andrea was desperate to keep the secret concealed. But as far as I knew, she didn't have a gun. I don't think she even knew how to fire one."

Denise was quiet as he said this. He saw an uncomfortable expression on her face, and then she said, "Actually, that's not true."

"What?"

"Andrea knows how to shoot. Sometimes when I came home on leave, I'd take her to the range. I made her get a gun, too, for protection. That was long before the two of you met. She was single and living alone." Then Denise rushed on before Stride could say anything more. "But if you're asking if I think she killed him, the answer is no."

"Did she talk to you at all about Ned Baer?"

"Yeah. She called me in Miami, and she was pretty freaked out about him. She said this reporter knew it was her; she said he'd broken into her house and seen all of her private records. But she never said a word to me about killing him."

"Would she?"

Denise shrugged. "Probably not."

"What about the summer when she says she was assaulted? What do you remember from back then?"

"Come on, Stride. That was thirty years ago."

"I know, but whatever happened was important enough that it led to murder years later."

Denise waited through the roar of another plane taking off. Then she stared at the sky, as if she could clear her head and bring the memories back. "Andrea talked about a party crawl that summer. If that's when she was raped, I'm pretty sure I know when it was. I was heading out to basic in a few days, so that night was kind of a last hurrah with my friends. Go to a big concert, get drunk, stay out all night, whatever. I encouraged Andrea to come with us. She didn't go out very often, never did anything except run her science experiments. I pushed her to have some fun. If something bad happened to her that night, I feel responsible."

"If?" Stride asked. "Are you not sure she's telling the truth?"

"I don't know. I can't see her lying about it. Plus, it would explain a lot."

"What do you mean?"

"How she is. So closed off. After that summer, she barely talked to me for years. Her marriage to Robin failed. Her marriage to you failed. When she finally told me what she'd been through, her life began to make sense. And yet … I don't know."

"You still doubt her?" he asked.

Denise hesitated. "It's not that I doubt her. She's my sister. It's that I knew Devin. I can't picture him doing something like that."

"Take a college kid and add alcohol," Stride said.

"Oh, I get it. I'm not naïve. Believe me, I dealt with my share in the service. But Devin was a friend. I knew him pretty well throughout high school. He was a stud. No matter what party he was at, there were a dozen girls who would have spread their legs if he asked. He never had a reputation for pushing it too far, because he didn't need to."

"A kid who doesn't hear *no* very often might not think a girl is serious when she turns him down."

"Yeah. I get that."

"Do you remember who went with you on this party crawl? Or the houses you went to? I'd like to talk to some of your friends and see what they remember."

"Why?"

"To prove what really happened. And to figure out who murdered Ned Baer."

"In other words, you want to save your own neck," Denise said.

"I suppose that's part of it. But I also think Andrea deserves some closure."

Denise shrugged. "I can text you a few names. But honestly, the crowd got pretty big as the night went on. A lot of strangers joined us along the way. Plus, everybody drank *a lot*. Most of it's a blur. I wouldn't count on anyone being too clear about what happened."

"Are you sure Devin Card was there that night?" Stride asked.

"Oh yeah. Him and Peter both. They were there."

"You sound pretty certain for something that happened so long ago."

"I am."

"Why is that?"

Denise laughed bitterly to herself. "Like I said, we were all really drunk. Devin and Peter had a reputation for doing outrageous things at these parties.

They were always trying to top the other, coming up with wild new dares. And me, well, I had just broken up with my boyfriend, and I was heading into the military, so I didn't much care what I did or who I did it with."

"What did you do?" Stride asked.

"Peter said he'd give me two hundred bucks to have sex with him and let everybody watch. Let's just say we put on quite a show."

* * * * *

Peter Stanhope laughed. "Denise said that?"

"Yes, she did," Serena replied. "Stride talked to her, and that's what she told him. Are you saying it didn't happen?"

"Oh, no, no," Peter said, shaking his head. "If Denise said it happened, I believe her. It certainly sounds like a stunt I would have pulled. But honestly, I don't remember it. I've blacked out a lot of those days."

"If I were you, I wouldn't be laughing, Peter. According to Denise, Devin Card was with you at the same party. He was egging you on. Not many women voters are going to find stories like that amusing."

Her comment erased the smile from his face. Peter shoved his hands in his suit pockets as he stared at the lake. The bright sun glistened on his swept-back silver hair. The two of them stood in the Harbor Side Ballroom inside the DECC, Duluth's convention center, next to a wall of windows that overlooked the towering lift bridge that led to the Point. Boats dotted the expanse of blue water. The vast room was empty of furnishings, and no one else was inside. Their low voices echoed between the walls. In another two days, hundreds of people would be squeezed into the space for Devin Card's town hall meeting.

"You're right," Peter replied after a long stretch of silence. "I only laughed because that person is so far away from who I am now that I hardly even recognize him. I was twenty-one then. I'm over fifty now. Kids turn into adults, Serena. That's true of Devin, too."

"Maybe so, but it doesn't change what the two of you did back then."

"No, it doesn't. I'll be the first to admit it. Devin and I were both first-class pricks in college, and I'm sure he'd agree with that. Anyway, I appreciate your candor. I also appreciate your agreeing to an off-the-record meeting."

Serena shrugged. "If you hadn't called me, I was going to call you."

"I suppose that makes sense. I'm sure you weren't terribly surprised to hear *my* name in conjunction with this business. When you worked for me as a private investigator, I know you learned things about my past that didn't give you a very good impression of me. I don't suppose Stride is a fan, either."

"You're right, he's not," Serena replied. Then she added, "What did you want to see me about?"

"First of all, I wanted to tell you personally—and I hope you'll share this with Stride, too—that I find the whole idea of him killing Ned Baer to be completely ludicrous. I don't believe it for a moment. I know him, and he's not capable of anything like that."

"Thank you."

"I also wanted to pass along a very clear message that neither I nor Devin Card had anything to do with Baer's murder, either. That's equally ludicrous."

Serena's voice was cool. "Is it?"

"Yes. I know it's a stretch, but I'm asking you to trust me. You may not like me, Serena, but murder? I'd never do anything like that."

"Even if it meant saving Devin Card's career?"

"Yes, even then. Besides, it's a moot point. Neither Devin nor I ever met Ned Baer, so we had absolutely no reason to kill him."

"He never approached you?" Serena asked.

"No."

"He didn't tell you that he'd identified the woman behind the accusations?"

The smallest flinch crossed Peter's face. "He told us nothing, because we never met him. And if he'd actually found the woman, we would have been fine with him publishing the story. We *wanted* the name out there."

"Really," Serena said, not believing him.

"Really. It's easier to discredit a real person than an anonymous source."

"And by discredit you mean tear her life to shreds. Turn her into a whore. Make her wish she'd never been born."

Peter shrugged. "Basically."

"What if her story was convincing? What if Ned had proof?"

"He didn't, because the story wasn't true."

Serena shook her head. "I'm having a lot of trouble believing you about any of this, Peter. If you really had no connection at all with Ned Baer, then why are you so concerned with this investigation?"

"Because there were rumors and conspiracy theories floating around back then, and I know there will be again, now that we know Baer was murdered. People are going to call Devin a suspect. They'll say what you just did, that Devin must have been trying to keep the woman's name out of the papers. I want to get ahead of this story on his behalf and make it clear that the rumors are *false*. We had nothing to do with Ned Baer, and we had nothing to do with his death. Given the political sensitivities of the campaign, I'd like a little consideration."

Serena studied Peter's expression, but she knew from experience that his poker face told her nothing. The one thing she remembered from her work with him was that he was always too smooth. He could mix lies and truth so easily that it was impossible to tell one from the other.

Was he lying to her now? She didn't know.

"You realize that Stride and I aren't working on this case," Serena told him. "Officially, we're out of it."

"Yes, but I also know both of you well enough to assume that you'll find a way to stay in the middle of it anyway."

Serena nodded. "Okay. You've passed along your message. I'll make sure it gets to the police. Now I have a question for you."

"Go ahead."

"What about the rape?" Serena asked.

Peter stared back at her, and she thought again: *Too smooth.*

"I already told you, it never happened," he said flatly.

"The woman's lying?"

"I have no idea. Maybe the whole thing was a setup to take down Devin. Or maybe she's misremembering events from decades ago. Regardless, Devin is innocent. He didn't do it."

"You just told me about having blackouts, Peter. You didn't remember what went on between you and Denise. Isn't it possible that the same thing happened to Devin? He raped that girl while he was drunk and he doesn't even remember it?"

"No."

"That's not possible?"

"No. It's not."

Serena shook her head. "Maybe you don't want to believe that your best friend was capable of something evil."

Peter took a long time to reply. She tried to read his face for the truth, but if he had doubts, he would never admit them to her or say them out loud.

"You're right, Devin's my best friend," he told her. "That means I know him. Yes, we did some crazy things back then. Some highly offensive things, I'm sure. And you're right, I don't remember a lot of it. But rape? That's not who he is, and that's not who he was. I don't know why this woman thinks it was him, or what got twisted around in her mind, but she's wrong. If she was really assaulted, then someone else did it."

16

"It's *him*," Cat told Brayden. "I know it's him."

She picked at the cranberry wild rice French toast on her plate, but memories of the previous night distracted her, and all she could see was the face of Wyatt Miller behind the bar at Hoops. She sat with Brayden on an outdoor patio at a Duluth hot spot called At Sara's Table. It was almost noon, under a bright sun, and a green umbrella kept them in shade. She faced across the street toward a bus stop built at a corner lot that was overgrown and undeveloped.

This was a babysitting morning. Cat's two-year-old son, Michael, slept next to her in a stroller with the sun bonnet pulled down over his forehead. Michael's adoptive parents, Drew and Krista Olson, had a weekly staff meeting at their Canal Park camping store, and Cat took the boy whenever they needed help. She kept a protective eye on the sleeping child, and her face bloomed with love whenever she studied his face.

But even her son couldn't calm her today.

"He's taunting me," Cat went on softly, not wanting to wake up Michael. "He knows there's nothing we can do to him. This guy gets to stalk me, and I have to sit here and take it, because I can't prove it."

"I'm not saying you're wrong," Brayden replied. "Wyatt may be the guy."

"But a green marker isn't enough to search his place, right?"

"That's right. I'm sorry."

Cat shook her head. "You don't believe me, either, do you?"

Brayden reached across the table and put a hand over hers. She liked that his palm was warm, and she liked the calloused feel of his skin. "It's not that. If Wyatt is the one doing this to you, we'll find a way to prove it. But I won't pretend that it's going to be easy, unless he makes a mistake. I talked to him at Hoops last night. He said the green marker wasn't his. He said it was lying on the bar and could have come from anywhere."

"Sure, it's just a coincidence," Cat said sourly.

"Well, it could be. Or he could be the one. Or the real stalker could have planted it there. The thing is, if Wyatt *is* the one, now he knows you've got protection, and he knows I'm watching him. That may be enough to make him stop on his own. Most of these guys are cowards."

"It won't stop him," Cat said.

Brayden eased back in the patio chair. His eyes were always moving, watching their surroundings, which made her feel safe. "Look, after I dropped you at Stride's house last night, I went back to the department. I was there half the night, doing research on Wyatt Miller. There's nothing to find. He doesn't have a record here or in Boulder. No complaints, no assaults, no indications of any kind of violent behavior. Since he moved to Duluth, he's gotten an apartment, a job, and a driver's license. His background doesn't raise any red flags."

"I don't care about his background."

"Maybe not, but it limits what a judge will let us do."

Cat frowned in disgust. "Can I tell you something without offending you?"

"Go ahead."

"I hate men. I feel like men should come with warning labels, like they do with cigarettes. Slap a big label on their foreheads. 'Men Suck.' I mean, we'll date them anyway, but at least then we'd know the risks."

"You may be on to something."

"I'm pissed today, can you tell?"

"Yes, I can tell."

Michael fussed in the stroller and began to wake up. His eyes blinked, trying to find Cat among the strangers on the patio. Quickly, she reached under the boy's arms and pulled him into her lap. His face scrunched, threatening to cry, but she smoothly distracted him with Brayden's car keys and bounced the toddler on her knee. He settled calmly against her chest.

"You're good with him," Brayden said. "You're a natural mom."

She blushed. "Thanks."

"See, not all men suck. Michael doesn't suck."

"He's just a little boy."

"Well, men start out as boys. What happens after that is mostly because of their parents. So Michael is lucky to have a mom like you, along with his adoptive parents."

"You really are sweet."

"Was it hard?" Brayden asked with a quiet seriousness. "Did you struggle with letting the Olsons adopt your son?"

Cat's eyes never left the boy. "It was very hard. All along, when I was pregnant, I wanted to keep him. I thought if I let him go, that made me a failure. Eventually, Stride and Serena made me realize I had to think about what was best for him, not me. I met Drew and Krista, and I knew they'd be amazing parents, but it was still hard. I cried so much after they took him. But at least I still get to be a part of his life. That helps."

"It'll help him, too."

"I just hope he'll grow up okay. I told you, men suck." Cat inclined her head at the table next to them, where a woman was reading a copy of the *Duluth News-Tribune*. "Look at the headline. Everyone is talking about Devin Card. How he raped a high school girl while he was in college. I know so many pigs like that who think they can get away with anything. I don't want Michael to be one of them."

"He won't be."

Cat shrugged, because Brayden was just being kind. "I hope not, but he didn't exactly win the genetic lottery. His father paid to have sex with a teenager. And then there's me, the princess of poor choices."

"I couldn't disagree more," Brayden told her. "That actor who assaulted you? He was rich, entitled, and thought nobody could stop him. But *you* did. If Michael has half your courage, he'll make you proud."

Cat frowned at the compliment. "I wasn't brave or anything when I did that. I just jumped in, stupid and terrified. That's what I always do. I never learn."

"Being scared doesn't change what you did."

She looked at Brayden and then looked away. "I don't usually talk about this stuff with anyone. I've never told people how bad it really was. Not even Stride and Serena. But I like talking to you."

"What about going to a counselor?"

"I can't talk to shrinks. I had a shrink once. He abused me, too."

Brayden exhaled loudly. "Son of a bitch."

"Yeah. I've got the track record, huh? I just hope Michael grows up like Stride. Stride may be the only man I've ever met who isn't a complete and total jerk. And yeah, I know, not every guy is a Dean Casperson or a Devin Card. You're not."

"Devin Card was *accused* of rape. To be fair, that doesn't make him guilty."

"Don't tell me you think he's innocent."

"Well, I'm a cop. Everyone's innocent until proven guilty. I know false allegations happen, particularly in politics. And I know good people can make mistakes in identifying suspects."

"Rape victims don't make mistakes," Cat snapped.

Brayden hesitated, as if he were tiptoeing through a minefield. "Don't hate me for saying this, but yeah, sometimes they do. The wrong men have gone to jail."

"Now *you* sound like a jerk."

"Sorry."

Cat focused on Michael's face until she was calm again, then she looked up and stared across the table at Brayden and felt herself wrapped up in his eyes. Strands of his blond hair had fallen across his face, and she wanted to reach over and smooth them back. There was something so compassionate and strong about him. If anyone tried to harm her, he'd be all over them. He'd take them to the ground. And yet when he talked to her, he had this soft voice, never getting upset, never getting frustrated with her, always smiling at her jokes and rants. When he looked at her, he *saw* her. He didn't look through her as if she wasn't there.

The trouble was, she couldn't be with any man without seeing the other men she'd known in her life. They were all sitting behind Brayden in the cafe, hiding in his shadow. The ones who'd assaulted her, violated her, made her feel like nothing. They never left her. She didn't know how to send them away.

"No, I'm the one who's sorry," Cat said. "You've been nothing but great to me, and you're here giving up your free time to protect me, and what do I do? I call you a jerk."

"Don't worry about that. I've earned that label plenty of times. My father would be the first to tell you that, and he'd be right."

"What about your mom?" Cat asked.

Brayden shook his head, and Cat knew she'd touched a sore spot. "I was lucky like Michael was. The Pells were my adoptive parents. Grace Pell loved me just like Krista Olson loves this little guy. She was great. But she got ALS. Ugly, terrible, horrible disease. When she died, it was just me and Bob Pell. That wasn't a good fit. He was devastated after losing his wife, and I don't know, maybe looking at me always reminded him that she was gone. I loved him, he loved me, but we were like two dogs who growled at each other whenever we were in the same room. I had to get out of there."

Cat said nothing in reply. She sat there in silence.

"Cat?" Brayden said. "Are you okay?"

Still she didn't answer. She barely noticed Brayden opening up his heart to her. She was too focused on a bus coming and going at the stop on the other side of the intersection. As the bus pulled away from the curb, a man appeared like a ghost on the sidewalk, staring at the restaurant.

Staring at her.

"Oh, shit!" she murmured.

Brayden was instantly focused. "Cat, what is it?"

"It's him. Jesus, *it's him*."

Brayden swung around in his chair.

Wyatt Miller smiled at them, his red dreadlocks shining in the sunlight. His eyes were covered by sunglasses, and he had a backpack slung over one shoulder. As they watched, he began to cross the street diagonally toward them.

"I've got *Michael*," Cat said, her voice rising with fear. "He knows about my son! What if he comes after my son?"

"I'll deal with this."

"I can't look at him!"

"Take Michael, and go inside," Brayden told her. "He won't get anywhere near you."

Cat stumbled to her feet with her arms wrapped tightly around the boy. She hurried through the glass double doors, dragging the stroller behind her, but she found that she was too shaken to sit down. She went into a section of the restaurant lined with bookshelves, and she stood in the farthest corner, clinging to Michael and keeping her eyes tightly shut. She didn't know how much time passed. It felt like forever. She wanted to leave, to run, but she couldn't even open her eyes.

Then, finally, she heard a voice.

"Cat."

She shook her head, still staring at darkness.

"*Cat*," Brayden said again. He touched her face, and she finally opened her eyes.

"He's gone," Brayden told her. "I told him to leave. I said you didn't want to see him."

"What did he say?"

"He said *you* texted him and asked him to meet you here."

"What? That's a lie! I didn't!"

Michael picked up on her stress and began to cry, and she cooed in the boy's ear to soothe him. "I didn't," she said again, very quietly.

"He showed me his phone," Brayden said. "I took a picture of the message."

He enlarged the screen, and Cat read the text message from the photograph:

> Hey, Wyatt, it's Cat. Sorry about the mix-up at
> the bar last night. Some freaky stuff is going
> on with my life. Can I make it up to you with a
> late breakfast. At Sara's Table?

"I did *not* send that," Cat insisted. "It's a fake. That number's not even my phone."

"I know."

"The bastard must have sent it to himself," she went on.

"Maybe."

"But you can't prove it. You can't do anything."

"I'm sorry."

"Brayden, what does he want with me?" Cat asked, holding her son even tighter. "Why is he doing this?"

"I don't know, Cat. He swears he's not the one. He says meeting you last night was the first and only interaction he's had with you. And he promised me he'll stay away from you from now on. If he's lying, he's good at it. He seemed genuinely upset at the idea that someone was bothering you."

Cat realized that everyone in the restaurant was watching them.

"Can we go?" she asked. "I need to go. I need to get out of here."

"Of course."

She put Michael down in the stroller and followed Brayden toward the street.

Cat didn't know which was worse.

Either Wyatt Miller was an obsessive liar, and the police couldn't do a thing about it, or the person who was doing this to her was still out there.

And still unknown.

17

Maggie climbed out of her banged up yellow Avalanche in the parking lot of the Two Bridges Motel. The cheap truck stop was located in an industrial area south of the city, on the other side of a rusted fence from the speeding traffic on I-35. Warehouses and auto shops surrounded it, and a maze of power lines ran overhead. Rows of motel windows faced the freeway, with identical white curtains hung in each room. The baby-blue building needed new paint.

Dan Erickson got out, too, and put his hands on his hips. He chewed gum at a rapid clip. "This is where Ned Baer stayed that summer?"

"Yup."

"Man, the life of a reporter, huh?"

They headed for the motel office. It was mid-afternoon, and the parking lot was mostly empty, in the slump between checkouts and check-ins. The office was warm, and a fan with a noisy motor blew air around the snug space, but it couldn't get rid of the mildew smell. A faded print of Jesus in a cracked glass frame was hung on the wall above an array of tourist brochures. Maggie found herself thinking that Jesus had already suffered enough and didn't deserve to spend time here.

The motel owner sat behind the desk, his feet up, reading a library copy of a book called *Dead Man's Mistress*. He eyed Maggie and Dan from behind a pair of reading glasses.

"You guys want a room?" he asked in a rumbling voice.

Dan laughed cruelly. "Here? Yeah, no."

"So what do you want?"

"Dan Erickson. Maggie Bei. Duluth Police."

The owner got to his feet slowly, rubbing his back as he did. He checked out Dan's expensive suit. "Cops, huh?"

"We're here to talk about Ned Baer," Maggie told him. "You may not remember, but my partner Lieutenant Stride and I talked to you seven years ago when Mr. Baer first disappeared."

The man shrugged. "I saw on TV about his body being found. I figured you guys would be back here sooner or later, although I don't know what I can tell you that I didn't tell you then."

"It was a disappearance then," Dan said. "It's a murder case now."

"Well, I've owned this place for twenty-two years. This would be murder number four for people staying here. One more, and I think I get a ribbon or something from the motel association."

The man came out from behind the desk. He was tall and slightly bent over, and he wore a baggy Twins T-shirt and loose-fitting blue jeans. He couldn't have been more than fifty, but he had the weathered look of someone who'd led a hard life. He had milk chocolate brown hair that curled slightly where it fell below his ears. His eyes were dark and bloodshot, and his eyebrows were permanently arched into cynical question marks. He had a broad, prominent nose and jutting chin, with deep wrinkles on his face.

"What's your name?" Dan asked.

"Adam Halka," the man replied. "Look, not to be rude or anything, but how about you ask your questions and go? I've got a business to run."

"Ned Baer," Maggie said again. "Tell us what you remember."

Halka shrugged. "Baer showed up that summer, wanted an open-ended rental. I don't get too many of those. But his credit card was good. That's really all that matters to me."

"Anything unusual about his stay?" Maggie asked.

"Not really. He was a weird little guy, really paranoid. I remember he only wanted maid service once a week. The girls hated that. It takes twice as long to do a room when it hasn't been cleaned in a while."

"Is that all?"

Halka's eyes went back and forth from Maggie to Dan. "Well, one time he told me there was a break-in."

"Somebody broke into his room?"

"That's what he said."

"I don't recall you telling us this seven years ago," Maggie said.

"I guess it slipped my mind."

"What happened?"

"I have no idea," the motel owner replied. "I remember Baer stormed in here one night pretty late. My night guy was on, but Baer insisted on waking me up so he could talk to me. He was all on about someone being in his room, and was it me, or was it the maids, and did I have security cameras so he could figure out who was there. He was steamed."

"Do you have cameras?" Dan asked.

"No. If guests think I'm keeping too close an eye on them, that tends to hurt business."

"What did you do?"

"I went over with him and checked the door. It wasn't busted or anything. If someone got in, they picked the lock or had a key. Baer didn't invite me in or anything, but when he opened the door, I could see that nothing was torn apart."

"Did he say if anything was stolen?"

"No. It didn't sound like they took anything. He just said somebody was in there looking at his papers. I wasn't even sure how he knew, but he swore up and down it wasn't the way he'd left it. I told him if he felt that way, call the cops. But he didn't want to do that. Said there was nothing they could do. So I left. End of story."

"Did you know why Baer was in town?" Dan asked.

"Yeah, he told me. I made some comment one day about being a Duluth lifer, and he asked if I knew Devin Card. I said sure, I went to high school with him. He got real interested then. Started asking me a lot of questions about Card and some of the summer parties."

"What did you tell him?"

"Oh, hell, there wasn't much to tell. I was stoned and drunk most of the time. I don't remember those years too well."

"But you knew Devin Card?" Dan asked.

"It's not like we were buddies, but everybody knew Devin. Football quarterback. Girls hanging on him. I hoped he'd grow up fat and bald, but it didn't work out that way."

"What about the summer when the rape supposedly occurred?" Maggie asked. "That would have been a few years after you left high school, right?"

"I guess. That's what Baer said. I'd been out of school for three years by then, but you know, Duluth's a small town. Everybody still hung out together on the summer weekends. Concerts, parties, whatever. If there were girls anywhere, Devin was always around. Him and Peter Stanhope."

"Did Baer ask you about the rape?"

"Sure. I never heard about it. To me, that made the whole thing sound fishy. Devin Card raping a high school girl? Everyone would have heard about that."

"Did Baer ever tell you he found the woman who made the allegation?" Maggie asked.

"No. He didn't say anything like that."

"Do you remember him getting any visitors?"

Halka shoved his hands in his pockets. He took a little while to answer. "It was seven years ago. Are you kidding?"

"What happened after Baer disappeared?" Dan asked.

The man shrugged. "I didn't know anything about it until the cops showed up. I hadn't seen the guy coming or going for a few days, but I didn't give it any thought. Last time I saw him was when he was heading to the Deeps. Guess that's also when he kicked it, right? But I didn't know that."

"How did you know he was going to the Deeps?"

"He asked me how to find it."

"Why was he going there?"

"It was a hot day. I figured he wanted a swim. He didn't say anything else. Anyway, you guys already knew about that."

Maggie and Dan exchanged glances. "What do you mean?" Dan asked.

"A cop came by that night after Ned left. He wanted to know where Ned was, and I told him I thought he was heading to the Deeps."

"What did he look like?"

"The cop? I don't know. Plain clothes, like you. Seems to me he's the same guy who came here with you a few days later. He talked to me, and you went and talked to the housekeepers."

"Stride," Maggie said with a frown.

"If you say so."

"So you sent Lieutenant Stride to the Deeps to find Ned Baer," Dan concluded.

"He asked if I knew where Baer was. I told him."

"Did Stride tell you why he was looking for Ned Baer?"

"Not that I remember."

"What was his mood?" Dan asked. "Was he angry? Agitated?"

"I have no idea. He was a cop. Do cops have moods? He wasn't here more than a couple of minutes."

"And what happened after that?"

"Like I said, nothing. I had no idea Baer was gone until you showed up and said he was missing. I told you, the guy only wanted his room cleaned every week, so it's not like the maids would have noticed that he wasn't there. His bill was on the credit card, so I didn't care."

Maggie kept hearing Stride's voice in her head.

Ned didn't contact me for a meeting. I was the one who sought him out.

Stride had come to find Ned Baer at this motel, and the owner had steered him to the Deeps. And then what? All Maggie knew was that Ned Baer had never been seen again after that evening, until his body showed up in Steve Garske's yard with a bullet in his skull.

"When we visited you after Baer disappeared, his room was clean," Maggie said.

"Right. So? My girls went in and cleaned it."

"When I searched the room, I didn't find any papers, notebooks, computer equipment, anything like that," Maggie added. "There were just personal items. Clothes. Toiletries."

"Then that's all there was," Halka snapped. "My girls wouldn't have touched a thing, particularly because Baer was so paranoid. If the guy had papers, computers, whatever, they would have still been in the room."

"Could someone have broken in there without you knowing about it?" Dan asked.

"What, like after the guy disappeared?"

"Exactly."

Halka rubbed the back of his neck. "I guess. Hell, I don't know, if somebody killed him, maybe they grabbed his key. If they took any of Baer's stuff from his room, I wouldn't have known about it."

Maggie nodded. "But just to be clear, you and your staff never removed *anything* from Baer's room?"

"Not a thing." But the man suddenly looked uncomfortable, shifting back and forth on the balls of his feet. Maggie knew a lie when she saw it, and so did Dan.

"Mr. Halka?" he went on sharply. "Did you take something from Ned Baer's room?"

"What I took wasn't his," Halka said, with a pained expression on his face. "It was mine. I was entitled to take it."

"What was it?"

"My high school yearbook."

"Your yearbook? Why did he have that?"

"When Ned found out I went to the same school as Devin Card, he asked if I still had any of my yearbooks from back then. So I let him borrow the one from senior year. He had it for a couple of weeks, and I was getting worried about ever getting it back, you know? I didn't want him walking off with it. So one of the times that the maid went to do his room when he was gone, I went in and took it back. He never said anything about it. I figured either he didn't notice or he didn't care."

"Do you still have it?" Maggie asked.

"Yeah. Sure."

The motel owner disappeared into a back room. He was gone for a couple of minutes, and then he returned with an oversized book that had the team logo for Denfeld High School on the cover. Halka passed it to Dan, who began flipping through the pages.

"Can we take this with us?" Maggie asked.

"Yeah, but remember, I want it back."

Dan opened the book and laid it flat on the motel counter. "There are a bunch of girls from freshman and sophomore years with circles around their photographs. Some of them have X's through the pictures. Did you do that?"

Halka shook his head. "Nope. Pisses me off, too. Baer must have done that."

"All cute, all blond, all the right age," Dan said.

"He was looking for the girl," Maggie concluded. "He had a bunch of names, and he was crossing them off as he eliminated them. He was trying to find the one who made the allegation against Devin Card."

Dan kept flipping the pages. Then he whistled.

He picked up the yearbook from the counter so that only Maggie could see it, and he pointed at a photograph that had been circled several times, with an asterisk added to the book in a different color ink.

"Well, well, well," Dan said. "Look who we have here."

Maggie read the girl's name under the picture.

Andrea Forseth.

18

"We're looking for a needle in a haystack," Serena told Stride, as the two of them headed down the porch steps of an old bungalow high in the hills above Denfeld High School. They were deep in the trees, under a terraced section of the cliff where the railroad tracks ran above their heads. They'd just concluded an interview with a woman named Adella Oliver, who'd gone to high school with Denise. She was on the list of names that Denise had sent to Stride of the people she remembered being with her on the party crawl.

Her story was the same as everyone else they'd interviewed.

Yes, they'd gone to a lot of parties in those days.

No, she didn't remember any of the details.

"We're talking about one party thirty years ago where everybody was drunk," Serena went on. "We've talked to half a dozen people on Denise's list, and nobody remembers anything."

Stride nodded. "All we can do is cross them off one by one."

They reached Stride's Expedition, and Serena put a hand on his shoulder. He had the expression she recognized when he was deep inside himself, wrestling with the past. "Can I ask a question, Jonny?"

"Sure."

"What do you hope to prove by doing this? Confirming Andrea's story won't change anything about Ned Baer's murder. We already know she's the one who made the allegations against Card. Ned was threatening to expose her, and she was desperate to stop him. She was the only other person besides you who knew he was at the Deeps. And we both know *you* didn't kill him."

"You're right," Stride agreed.

"But you still don't think she did it."

"No."

Serena sighed. "I'm sorry, but why are you so sure? Are you just trying to convince yourself because she was your wife? The thing is, when I look at the evidence, *everything* points to her."

Stride didn't say anything right away. He went around to the driver's side of the truck, but he waited before opening the door. It was early evening, and the sun crept toward the peak of the hillside, throwing long shadows over their bodies.

"I know it does," he told her. "Look, you may be right. I'm thinking like an ex-husband, not a cop. But to me, it doesn't fit. It's too *calculated* for Andrea. She was running on emotion and adrenaline that day. I guess I can see her pulling the trigger, but if she killed Ned, she would have walked away and left the body where it was. On some level, I think she would have *wanted* me to know that she'd done it. I don't see her calling Steve and making him think I was the one who killed Ned. That's not her. No, she called Steve for the reason she said. She was afraid of what I'd do and she wanted Steve to stop me. And that tells me it wasn't her."

Serena climbed inside the truck, and so did Stride.

"Say you're right," she said. "Then who killed him?"

"I don't know. That's why I'm trying to figure out what really happened thirty years ago. And who knew the truth about it. Somebody had a secret they were willing to kill Baer to protect."

Serena squinted through the windshield at the hillside neighborhood. The streets were barely better than dirt roads, with chipped asphalt riddled by cracks. The houses were spread apart, hidden on wooded lots, with lawns that were a green-and-brown mixture of grass and weeds.

"All right," she said. "Who's next?"

Stride consulted the list that Denise had texted him, and then he steered the Expedition onto the bumpy street. The truck jolted as they headed down the hill. Before they'd even gone half a block, Serena grabbed his arm.

"Hang on, wait a second. Stop."

"What is it?"

"That house there. I'm curious. Is it on the list?"

She pointed at a large two-story set back from the street and almost invisible behind a row of large oak trees. The wood siding was painted an ugly shade of sea green, with windows trimmed in red and several gables on the second floor. The house was built with a sprawling front porch, and the yard backed up to the hillside below the train tracks. An old Chevy Impala sat in the driveway in front of a boxy two-car garage.

Stride checked Denise's list of names and locations. "No. It's not on the list."

"Can you find out who owns the place?"

He tapped a few keys on his dashboard computer. "Property records say the owner is a woman named Kathy Ford."

"Does that name ring a bell?"

He clicked for more information on the county records. "It looks like the place changed hands twelve years ago. The previous owners were Richard and Carol Godfrey. I remember a Kathy Godfrey from back in our school days. She didn't go to Central, but she and Cindy both waitressed at Grandma's on their summer breaks. But Kathy's not one of the names Denise gave me for the party crawl."

"Denise didn't say she remembered everyone, though, did she?"

"True. What are you thinking?"

Serena didn't answer right away. She got out of the Expedition and walked up the sloping driveway to where the Impala was parked. Stride followed. She studied a wide redwood balcony on the second story, which was built immediately above the roof of the garage.

"Andrea told me that after she was assaulted, she didn't go back to the party. She didn't want to face anybody. She left from the bedroom to an outside balcony, and from there, she jumped down from the garage. Seems like this house fits what she described."

"It fits a lot of houses," Stride said.

"Except she also mentioned a castle."

"What?"

"She had a memory of running past a castle." Serena pointed at the middle of the lawn. Among the towering oak trees was a varnished chainsaw sculpture that had been made out of the trunk of a fallen tree. The wood carving had been shaped like a fairy-tale castle, with high turrets, square grooves that resembled stone building blocks, and red conical roofs. Time had weathered it, wearing down the sharp edges and opening up cracks in the wood.

"I'll be damned," Stride said.

"Where did Andrea's parents live back then?" Serena asked.

"Near Cody and 59th."

"Well, she said she ran home afterward. That's not far."

Stride nodded. "You're right."

Serena stared at the bedroom windows on the second floor. She imagined a hot summer night decades ago and a hurt, crying teenage girl escaping onto that balcony. She could see the girl practically falling over the railing and dropping onto the dirty garage roof below her. And then, dangling from the roof's edge by her fingers, landing heavily on the wet grass. She could see the girl stumbling away, running through the dark streets down the hill, thinking of nothing except getting home, hiding in her bedroom, and sitting under the hot water of the shower until it washed her clean.

Which it never would.

Serena knew exactly how that girl felt.

"Can I help you?"

A voice called to them from the house's front door. Serena and Stride both looked in that direction and saw a middle-aged woman on the porch. She was tall but heavyset, with wavy brown hair. She wore an untucked button-down blue sweater over dark slacks.

"Ms. Ford?" Stride called.

"Yes."

"I'm Jonathan Stride. This is Serena Stride. We're with—"

"I know who you are, Jonathan," the woman interrupted, coming down the steps. "You were married to Cindy."

"That's right."

"I was at her funeral. I saw you then, but I'm sure you don't remember with all of the people there. That was so tragic to lose her so young. She was a lovely woman."

"Yes, she was. Actually, I'm married again. Serena is my wife. We're both with the police."

"I know that, too." The woman approached them in the driveway. Serena shook hands with her, and she gave Stride a brief hug. Behind her, in the house, a golden retriever pushed through the screen door and galloped across the yard to join them, its tail wagging wildly. Kathy Ford bent down next to her dog to pet him and then eyed Serena and Stride in turn.

"What's going on?" she asked. "Why are you here?"

"Ms. Ford, we'd like to ask you a few questions—" Serena began, but the woman stopped her with a smile.

"Oh, please. I'm not formal. Call me Kathy."

"Okay. Kathy. I know this was a long time ago, but we're looking into something that may have happened at a summer party almost thirty years ago. A sexual assault."

The woman frowned. "Is this about Devin? I know the allegations against him are back in the news."

"You're right. It is."

She hugged her dog and then pushed herself back to her feet with a little groan. "Well. I was wondering if someone would show up here eventually. When all those reporters were in town a few years ago, I assumed one of them would track me down, but nobody ever did. I guess I should have come forward myself, but I didn't want to get involved. That probably sounds selfish, but I really didn't want to see my life put through the ringer."

"You *know* what happened?" Stride asked.

"I have suspicions, but that's all."

"Please tell us whatever you can," Serena said.

Kathy Ford turned around and did what Serena had done. She stared at the upstairs bedroom window near the garage. "Did you talk to Adella Oliver?"

"Yes, we were just there," Stride replied. "She didn't remember anything."

"No, she never knew about this. Adella and I were best friends back in school. So funny, all these years later, we're still in the houses where we grew up. I guess that's Duluth. Parents die, and the kids move back in. Anyway, when the accusations first came out about Devin a few years ago, Adella asked me if I remembered anything. I lied and said I didn't."

Serena waited. She felt her own anxiety soaring, and then she realized. This was a story about assault. This was personal.

"It was August," Kathy went on. "I don't even remember the year. I'd been out of school for a while. A whole group of us decided to have a big blowout summer party crawl. Some big concert was in town at the DECC, and we all went there, and then afterward, we spent half the time going from house to house. Drinking. Doing crazy things. I was probably, what, twenty or twenty-one? But there were younger girls with us, too, some of them still in high school. It was a wild, wild night. I remember the party moved over to Adella's house, but then her parents came home and threw us all out, so we walked over here to my house. My folks were out of town. Not exactly my most mature decision, I'll say that."

"How many people were there?" Serena asked.

"Oh, I have no idea. Dozens."

"What about Devin Card?"

"Yes, Devin was there. Peter, too. Peter Stanhope."

"You're sure about that?" Stride asked her.

"Oh, yes. I remember the *incident*."

"What incident?"

"Peter was always throwing money around. I mean, you know his family, Jonathan. He had everything. He and Devin were both drunk. Well, we all were. Peter said he'd pay a girl to have sex with him and let the rest of us watch. And he did. It happened right inside on my parents' sofa. Believe me, I never forgot that."

"Do you remember who the girl was?" Stride asked quietly.

"I'm not sure I do. Oh, wait, no. Actually, I'm pretty sure it was Denise. Denise Forseth."

"Adella didn't mention anything about this," he said.

"No, like I said, she wasn't there. Her parents wouldn't let her go out after they came home and found the party at her place. So she didn't come with us."

"What about Devin Card?" Serena asked. "Was he with anyone?"

"Over the course of the night, I'm sure he was with lots of girls. That's the way Devin was. But I don't remember anyone specifically."

Serena hesitated. "I'm sorry, Kathy, but if you don't know anything about the alleged assault, why did you feel that you should come forward?"

The woman said nothing. She found a grimy chew toy in the grass, and she heaved it toward the back of the house and watched as her dog sprinted to retrieve it. Then she continued softly.

"When the allegations came out about Devin, I … I believed them. It's not like I could prove he did anything, but I'm pretty sure the woman is telling the truth. And I'm pretty sure the rape happened that night, here at my house."

"Why do you believe that?" Serena asked.

"I had to clean the house the next day," she replied. "It was a mess, as you'd expect. I didn't realize anyone from the party had gone upstairs, but then I went into my parents' bedroom. I found … I found the door to the balcony wide open. Someone had thrown up in the sink in the bathroom. And I had to wash the sheets from the bed. There was blood on them. And semen, too."

19

From behind his sunglasses, Brayden Pell surveyed the twilight swimmers at Brighton Beach. The evening temperatures were warm, but only a handful of people lingered on the rocky shore, and even fewer braved the cold lake water. A young couple lay on rainbow towels stretched across the granite slabs. Three children, none of them more than ten, hunted for pebbles along the beach below the tree line. An old man swam a slow breast stroke from south to north, unbothered by the chill.

Then there were the three people with Brayden.

He sat on the rocks next to Curt Dickes, who wore a swimsuit adorned with colorful pineapples that came down below his knees. He hadn't gone near the water; instead, he was glued to his phone. Curt kept the phone angled away so that Brayden couldn't see what he was typing, and Brayden assumed that Curt had probably committed half a dozen crimes just in the hour they'd been sitting there. It didn't really matter to him right now. Curt was a minor crook, mostly moving marijuana, fencing stolen merchandise, and running cons on tourists. Every now and then, he'd cross a line and spend a couple of months behind bars. But he wasn't violent. Brayden also had to admit that he found Curt's irrepressible self-confidence amusing to watch.

Curt's girlfriend, Colleen Hunt, waded in the lake with Cat, the two girls talking together as if they were old friends. The water came up to their thighs. Colleen wore a demure, one-piece polka dot swimsuit, and she held her skinny arms across her chest as if she were freezing. Her straight blond hair never got near the water. She looked as if she'd rather be on the beach, but Cat had dared her to swim, and Colleen seemed like a girl who went along with the crowd to be cool.

And then there was Cat.

Cat was dangerous.

Brayden knew that Cat had a crush on him. The girl couldn't be more obvious about it. He had no intention of doing anything to encourage her, both because of the age difference and because he wasn't about to incur Stride's wrath by getting involved with a girl who was the closest thing Stride had to a daughter. Brayden's only job was to keep the girl safe.

And yet he'd be lying to himself if he didn't admit that he was drawn to her. The attraction wasn't really sexual, although physically, she had a look that turned heads and stopped hearts, with her full, flowing chestnut hair, golden skin, and a body with every curve and swell in perfect proportion. She was showing it off now, in a bikini that barely covered anything. Any man who saw her would be hungry for her. As young as she was, Brayden knew that she'd been involved with men and sex in ways that would have shocked him, but it added to her appeal that she'd gone through all of that and could still seem innocent and sensitive.

He felt close to her; they had things in common. She'd gone through a troubled childhood, and so had he. They both had to rise above their pasts and become new people. Brayden knew that it would have been easy to get emotionally attached to this girl, but he couldn't afford to do that. She was a victim to protect, and that was all.

But even so, she was dangerous.

"She's something, huh?"

Brayden turned his head, and Curt grinned at him.

"I see you watching Kitty Cat," Curt went on. "Can't say I blame you. Girl's a stunner. Way out of my league."

"I'm just here to keep her safe," Brayden said, annoyed that he'd been caught out.

"Sure. Sweet gig. I mean, I love Colly, but Cat? Wow. Always felt good that she thought I was cool. Of course, Stride and Serena would slice me up like sushi if I laid a hand on her. So I don't go there, no way, no how."

"Smart choice," Brayden said.

"Yeah. By the way, I feel bad that Wyatt turned out to be a freak show. Colly and I never would have introduced him to Cat if we'd thought that."

"We still don't know if he's the one who's stalking her."

"Maybe so, but when it comes to Kitty Cat, I'd rather be safe than sorry. You keep him away from her, brother."

Brayden smiled. It was obvious that Curt had genuine affection for Cat. That was a point in the man's favor.

He glanced at the lake and saw Cat and Colleen emerging from the water, Colleen running for a towel on the rocks, Cat not hurrying at all as she squeezed her wet hair and adjusted both flimsy pieces of her bikini. Even if it was deliberate, she acted nonchalant about putting her body on display. Curt simply enjoyed the show, but Brayden made a point of looking away.

"Oh, man, that felt good!" Cat said as she headed up the rocks toward them. "I love summer."

"Looks to me like that water must have been pretty cold," Curt commented, drawing an evil glance from Colleen.

"You sure don't want to swim, Brayden?" Cat said. "I'd go back in with you."

"No. Thanks."

Cat gave a loud sigh, as if that was the answer she expected. "All right, Colly and I are going to get changed out of our suits. We'll be right back."

Brayden began to get to his feet to accompany them, but Cat giggled. "Really? You want to come with me for *that?*"

He felt a blush on his face, and he was sure Cat could see it, too. He looked over his shoulder at the parking lot beyond the trees, and he could see only a couple of cars in addition to his Kia and Colleen's old Rav4. He checked the tree line and the beach and felt secure.

"All right, go ahead. If you see anything strange up there, you shout, okay?"

"Yes, Stride," Cat said with a wink.

She grabbed Colleen's hand, and the two girls headed off together for the parking lot. Brayden followed them until they reached the path above the beach, and then he turned back to the water. He kept his eyes on the lake, because he didn't want Cat to think he was spying on her.

Curt, who'd been watching him the whole time, let out a long whistle. "Shit, you like her, too, don't you?"

"What?"

"You're into Kitty Cat."

"No, it's not that."

"Uh-huh, yeah, whatever you say. Word of warning, brother. Cat may not seem high maintenance, but trust me, she is. Be prepared. Skeletons rattle around in that pretty head of hers."

"I'm not into her," Brayden said, knowing he was protesting too much.

Curt grinned again and went back to his phone. Brayden hated telegraphing what he felt about anything, and if Curt could see it, then he was afraid that Cat could, too. And worse than that, so would Stride. He swore to himself to do better and shut it all down. To not let her tease him into conversation and then let out his secrets.

"By the way," Curt went on after a couple more minutes of silence between them, "you know she played you, right?"

"What?"

"Cat's gone."

"Excuse me?"

"I know the look. She's out of here. Colleen, too. I could see they were planning something. No boys allowed."

"Shit."

Brayden felt a wave of icy panic in his veins. He scrambled off the rocks and swore in frustration when he saw that Curt had pegged the girl perfectly. He'd been outsmarted, fooled, hung out to dry.

Colleen's Rav4 had disappeared from the parking lot. Neither girl was anywhere to be found.

* * * * *

"I know we talked about seeing a movie," Colleen said, as they drove out of the beachfront park in her SUV. "But actually, I was wondering if you were up for something a little more criminal."

"Criminal? What do you mean?"

A smirk crossed Colleen's face. "I have a key."

"A key to what?" Cat asked.

"Wyatt's place."

Cat froze, and her eyes widened. She stared across the front seat at Colleen. "Are you serious?"

"Yeah. He had a bunch of duplicates made when he moved in, and he gave me one so I could wait in his place while he was at work. He had a couple deliveries that needed a signature. He never asked for it back, and I forgot all about it. So I was thinking, if you want to search his place, well, the cops can't do it, but what's stopping us?"

Cat pursed her lips. "Well, holy shit. Now that's an idea."

"I know, right? What do you think? At least then you'd know if it was him."

"Is Wyatt home? What if he comes home?"

"No, I'm pretty sure he should be at work."

Cat reached across the car and shoved the other girl playfully. "You think like me. I like that."

"Ditto."

"Okay, I'm in," Cat said. "You be Thelma, I be Louise. Where do you live?"

"It's a four-story building on Third. Kinda sleazy, but I can't afford much. I'm on the ground floor. Wyatt's on the top floor."

Cat felt a flush of satisfaction, combined with a little wave of guilt at what she was doing. Guilt at the idea of running away from Brayden. Guilt at the idea of rushing into something that Stride would hate. But she was frustrated and had to know the truth. Wyatt could hide from the police, but not from her.

"By the way, I know what you're going through," Colleen commented, as she headed into the city. The lakeshore followed them on the left side of the street.

"What do you mean?"

"I was stalked in high school, too."

"It's horrible, isn't it? Did they get the guy?"

Colleen shook her head. "The cops couldn't do a thing."

"Yeah, they protect the creeps, not us."

"Are you done with school?" Colleen asked.

"No, I have one more year in the fall. I lost a lot of time because of my, well, my past. I'm still catching up."

"We were actually in one class together," Colleen said. "I was a junior then, and I think you were a sophomore. Math. Not that you'd remember, but I remember you. Man, you were smart."

Cat rolled her eyes. "That must been one of the few times I showed up. But yeah, math is my thing. My brain works that way."

"Art is my thing, math not so much," Colleen said. She eyed Cat across the seat. "So what's the deal with you and Brayden?"

"There's no deal." Cat grinned. "I mean, I'd like there to be. Wow, he's cute. But it probably won't happen."

"Don't be so sure. I see how he looks at you."

"You think?"

"Definitely."

"What about you and Curt?" Cat asked.

Colleen shrugged. "Oh, you know how Curt is. It's cool that he's a bad boy."

"He really likes you."

"Yeah, I know."

She said it in a way that made Cat think Colleen didn't feel the same way.

"I thought it was serious with you two," she said.

"No, not really. We have fun, but it's not serious."

Cat frowned, because she was pretty sure Curt would have given her a very different answer. "Well, if you dump him, let him down easy, okay? Curt acts tough, but he's pretty sensitive, actually."

"I hear you." Colleen swung the Rav to the curb. "Here we go. Home sweet home. You ready?"

Cat craned her neck to stare up at the austere, red brick building on the corner. Rows of individual windows faced the street, all the same, and she could see bent miniblinds and a few house plants on the ledges. It wasn't fully dark yet, but a few lights were on inside. The entrance had a faux glamour from the building's old days, decorated with stone columns and urns.

"Ready," Cat said.

The two of them got out of the Rav, and Colleen let them inside the building. The hallway carpet was worn. A wide set of wooden stairs, with carved bannisters in need of new varnish, led to the upper floors. Colleen led the way, and Cat followed, and when they got to the top floor, she stopped at the first door.

"This is Wyatt's place," she whispered.

"You have the key?"

Colleen dug in her pocket for her key ring, and she isolated a shiny silver key from the others. "Still got it. I'll knock. Stay on the other side in case he's home. I don't want him to see you."

Cat waited out of sight, and Colleen knocked sharply on the door. There was no answer, and she put her ear to the door and knocked again. Then, with a nervous grimace, she slid the key into the lock.

"Here we go," she said. "You sure about this?"

"I'm sure."

She opened the door to Wyatt's apartment, and they both crept inside. Colleen shut the door behind them.

Cat wasn't sure what she expected. Part of her thought that his obsession would be obvious as soon as she walked inside. That he would have pictures of her taped to all his walls. That half-written threats and green markers would be spread over his kitchen table. But there was nothing. It was an ordinary, uninteresting apartment, obviously belonging to a single man. Cookie-cutter laminate furniture and garage sale sofas and chairs. A flat screen television and a couple dozen warfare video games stacked next to it. Bose speakers. The floor was made up of checkerboard linoleum squares, and the kitchen cabinets and appliances were all white and dirty. The smell of old fast food and boy sweat made Cat wrinkle her nose.

"What do we look for?" Colleen asked.

"I don't know. Open some drawers. There has to be something."

They checked the kitchen and found nothing, and the living room had no places in which to hide anything. The two of them went into Wyatt's small bedroom, where a single window faced the street. He had a twin bed and a closet with bi-fold plywood doors. Cat opened every drawer in his oak dresser and found only clothes. She checked his nightstand and found a strip of condoms, a half empty bottle of hand lotion, pens, scissors, and some old electronics equipment. It was the usual junk.

"There's nothing in the bathroom," Colleen reported.

Cat opened the closet doors. Wyatt had a couple of dress shirts and a winter coat hung on hangers. Several pairs of hiking shoes sat on the shelf.

"I must be wrong," Cat murmured.

"Or he's careful."

"No, there would have to be something. Wouldn't there?"

She stood in the bedroom and bit her lip as she studied the room. There were simply no hiding places, and being here was beginning to make her nervous. "We better go," she added.

"Okay."

Then Cat thought of one more thing. She got down on her hands and knees and pushed up the blanket to look under Wyatt's twin bed. There, she saw an Amazon parcel box squeezed underneath, smiling at her. It was medium-size, about a foot high and a couple of feet long. She dragged it out and put it atop the bed. The box was light and taped shut, but the tape was loose, as if it had been done and undone many times.

Cat peeled away the tape and opened one flap of the box. "Oh, shit. Oh, Jesus."

The first thing she saw was the copy of *People* magazine with her on the cover. When she opened the box further, she saw an expensive Nikon camera with a zoom lens inside. The camera sat on top of a stack of photographs printed on computer paper. She slapped her hand over her mouth as she removed the pages one by one.

Next to her, Colleen stared at the photographs wide-eyed.

Every picture was of Cat. He'd followed her everywhere. To school. To the mall. To the movies. To restaurants. There were pictures of her on the beach behind Stride's cottage. At the Olson house, playing with her son. And more.

He'd been outside the house on the Point. Outside her window. He'd watched her dressing. Undressing. Dancing. Singing. Laughing.

He'd seen her in a towel, back from the shower. He'd seen her naked.

He'd been part of her entire life.

And when she got to the bottom, she found something else in the box. A gun.

"I'm going to be sick," Cat said.

But she had to hold back her nausea. As the two girls stood in the bedroom, they heard a noise from the other room. A muffled voice came through the apartment door in the hallway. She recognized it.

Wyatt.

"Shit, he's *back*," Cat said.

She shoved the photographs back in the box, carelessly retaped it, and shoved it under the bed. She looked around the bedroom for a way out, but they were trapped. The window offered no escape.

"The closet," Cat hissed.

The two of them ran for the small bedroom closet and squeezed inside. Cat nudged the bi-fold doors closed, but they were warped and didn't shut completely. A crack of light remained. Her back was against the wall, shoved in the middle of Wyatt's clothes, and she could smell him on the fabric. Colleen was right beside her, their bodies pushed together. The air was stifled and warm.

She held her breath.

It was hard to hear, but she could make out the rattle of the apartment door opening, and then she heard Wyatt's voice from the living room.

"You want to hang out with me tonight, buddy?"

There was no other voice to answer. Just Wyatt's.

The noise of footsteps got closer. He was in the bedroom now. She could hear the smallest gasp from Colleen, and she squeezed the girl's hand, not wanting her to make a sound. They could hear Wyatt moving around. Going into the bathroom. Going to the dresser. Cat tried to remember if she'd put everything back in the box and whether she'd shoved it completely out of sight beneath the bed.

Then they both jumped. Music filled the room. Loud, screeching music. Opera. The fat lady sang in some foreign language.

"You like it?" Wyatt asked. "I bet you could hit some of those high notes, huh?"

Who was he talking to? The only sounds in the apartment came from Wyatt. He was alone.

"I'm going to take a shower, and then we'll play some X-Box, okay?"

The loud music offered them cover, and Cat put her lips next to Colleen's ear. "When we hear the shower, we run."

In the darkness, Colleen nodded, her blond hair swishing against Cat's shoulder.

"Hey, what are you doing over there?" Wyatt asked.

Cat's mouth dropped open in horror as the closet doors began to rattle. When she looked at her feet, she saw something pushing through the crack where the doors didn't meet. Orange fur.

It was a cat's paw.

"Did you lose a toy in there?" Wyatt asked.

The cat kept pulling at the doors, which began to nudge apart, and Cat put out a hand to stop them from opening completely.

"You want me to see if it's in there, buddy?"

No!

Then, in the other room, a phone rang, rescuing them. Wyatt shut off the opera, restoring silence to the apartment. They heard his footsteps as he hurried to the other room to answer his cell phone. Wyatt began talking again.

"Hey, how are you, Sam? No, my shift got canceled tonight, so I went for a hike instead. I just got home. Yeah, sure, I can put in a couple of hours down there. I have to shower, but I'll be there in half an hour."

Wyatt hung up.

"Sorry, buddy, you're on your own tonight. Looks like I'll have to drop you back at your parents' place. I've got to go out."

They heard Wyatt return to the bedroom, and they heard the rustle of him taking off his clothes. His footsteps went into the bathroom, and the bang of water in the shower pipes followed. A minute later, they heard the shuffling of plastic shower curtain rings.

Cat silently pushed open the closet doors. An orange cat sat on Wyatt's bed, watching them curiously. She could see steam gathering on the mirror through the open bathroom door. In the shower, Wyatt began to sing opera himself, and his voice was surprisingly good.

"Come on."

She and Colleen tiptoed across the apartment and then silently let themselves out into the hallway. When they finally closed the door behind them, she began to breathe again.

"Holy shit, that was close."

Colleen looked pale, too. "But it's him?"

Cat felt sick again. "Yeah. It's him. And he's going to kill me."

20

The orange flames of a fire pit danced in the lake breeze behind the Canal Park Brewing Company. Maggie sat in an Adirondack chair as Serena arrived to join her, and the two of them had the outdoor patio to themselves in the darkness. Maggie had arrived early and was already on her second Stoned Surf IPA. Serena, who didn't drink, brought a raspberry lemonade from the bar. Behind them, Lake Superior threw waves against the rocks on the other side of the boardwalk. Sometimes the cascading spray made it all the way to where they sat.

Maggie kicked off her boots and propped her bare feet on the side of the fire pit, warming them. Both of them sat in silence for a while, entranced by the flames. Serena's eyes looked far away and a little cold.

It was awkward whenever they were together, and Maggie knew it. That was mostly her fault. They'd both been outsiders coming to Duluth, Maggie from China as a college student, Serena from Vegas as a cop. That shared bond could have brought them together, but instead, they'd ended up as rivals. Frenemies. Maybe it was inevitable because of the triangle they shared with Stride.

"How's he doing?" Maggie asked.

"He says he's calm. He acts calm."

"I don't know how he can be calm. I'm not."

"Me neither," Serena admitted.

"This thing isn't going away."

"He knows, but he doesn't seem to care."

Maggie hesitated, then said what was really on her mind. "I keep thinking, what if he never comes back? What if this is it? He's off the force. After all these years, he's gone."

"It's only been two days. It's way too early to worry about that."

"Yeah, but does he even *want* to come back?"

"Sure he does," Serena said. "That's crazy."

"Is it? Ever since the bombing at the marathon, he's been different. Burned out. I feel like the violence did something to him. You must have seen it, too."

Serena stared at her, and her green eyes had ice in them now. "Of course, I have. He's my *husband*. Look, the marathon bombing changed all of us. Jonny's different now. So am I. So are you. It doesn't mean he's going to walk away from his job. His job is who he is. I know that better than anyone."

Maggie bit her tongue. She wasn't about to tell Serena that she was wrong. That she didn't know her husband as well as she thought. But she *was* wrong. Maggie could see it in Stride's eyes. He was at a crossroads, thinking through choices he probably hadn't shared with anyone. Not even his wife.

"I almost walked away myself," Maggie said.

"What are you talking about?"

"You remember that Florida cop who was here this winter? Cab Bolton?"

"The one you slept with?" Serena asked.

"Yeah, but that doesn't narrow it down."

"True."

"He asked me to go to Florida with him. Leave Duluth. Be an investigator down there. I only thought about it for all of five seconds, but ever since, I've wondered if I should have done it. Made a change. Started over."

"You still could."

"I suppose you'd like that idea," Maggie said. "Me going away for good."

"Actually, no, I wouldn't."

She scoffed. "Yeah, right."

"It's true. Despite everything, I like having you around. Even when you annoy the hell out of me."

"Seriously?"

Serena reached out to tap Maggie's glass with her own. "Seriously."

"Well, it's a moot point. I'm not going anywhere. You're stuck with me."

"Good."

"We're perilously close to having a moment here," Maggie said.

"I guess so."

"Want to make out?" she joked.

"Pass," Serena replied.

Maggie chuckled. Then her face grew serious again. "Things are moving forward on the investigation. There's something you and Stride need to know. Dan and I found out about Andrea."

"We figured you would."

"She made the accusation against Devin Card, right? Stride was trying to keep her name out of the press when he talked to Ned Baer?"

"Yes."

"Damn, I should have seen that one coming. That should have been my first thought. You figured it out, didn't you? When we talked, you already knew she was involved."

"I guessed."

"Well, the trouble is, Dan now thinks Stride has a motive on top of everything else. That means we better start feeding him some other suspects fast."

"I think it's her," Serena said. "Andrea. She did it."

"She was a messed up bitch, that's for sure, but do you really think Mousy McBlonde would have the balls to shoot a guy?"

"Jonny and I know some things about her past that you don't. That's all I'll say."

Maggie arched an eyebrow but didn't pursue it. "Did Andrea know Ned was at the Deeps?" she asked.

"Yes. Stride told her."

"What about a gun?"

"Denise says she had one."

"Well, it makes her a suspect, but we have no proof that she went to the Deeps that night. Whereas Stride has already admitted it."

"I know. Plus, Jonny is convinced she didn't do it."

"Is that his famous gut talking?" Maggie asked.

"Pretty much."

"If not her, then who? Devin Card? Or Peter Stanhope? They had the most to lose if the story came out."

"Peter swears they weren't involved, for whatever that's worth," Serena replied. "He says they didn't know that Ned was getting ready to name the woman in his article."

"Do you believe him?"

"I'm not sure. Ned found Andrea, and I can't believe he wouldn't have gone to Devin for a comment, even if he didn't tell him who the woman was. But Peter must figure there's no way we can prove it one way or another. Maybe they scooped up all of Ned's notes after they had him killed."

Maggie shook her head. "Except there's zero evidence of that."

"I know. On the other hand, we do have evidence that Andrea was telling the truth about the rape. We found a witness who saw blood and semen in the sheets in an upstairs bedroom after one of the summer parties. It was in her parents' house in West Duluth."

"Did she see Devin and Andrea together?"

"No. So there's no proof that Devin was the one who did it. It's he said, she said. Then again, that probably would have been enough for the voters. If this woman had come forward seven years ago to verify the rape accusation, it would have been devastating for Devin's campaign. But Andrea says she never told anyone about it. Not Ned or anyone else."

Maggie frowned. "That means we're still left with Andrea, Devin, and Peter as the only people with motives to kill Ned. Other than Stride."

"So far."

"Having other credible suspects means reasonable doubt. That's a good thing."

"Yes, but unless we *clear* him, Jonny will always have a cloud over his head," Serena said. "He can't come back to the force while he's a suspect in a homicide."

"I know. That's what worries me. I don't see how we solve this."

"We have to be missing something," Serena went on, pursing her lips in frustration. "*How* did Ned find Andrea? How did he figure out it was her?"

"He's a reporter. That's what reporters do."

"Yes, but there were a lot of reporters in town trying to find the woman behind that letter. Ned's the only one who succeeded."

"Well, the motel owner where Ned was staying gave him a Denfeld yearbook," Maggie said. "Dan and I saw it. Ned put circles around the faces of dozens of girls. All the same general type. Blond, cute, the usual Scandinavian look. He researched each one name by name, crossing them out until he got to Andrea."

"And Andrea's reaction told him she was the one?" Serena said.

"Probably."

Serena shook her head. "Except how did he even know what she looked like? *Someone* must have seen Andrea with Devin at that party. Ned told Stride at the Deeps that he had a witness. Whoever it was must have given Ned a description, and that's why Ned started tracking down blond girls in the yearbook. That's what led him to Andrea."

"But he didn't tell Stride who the witness was?"

"No. He said he had an anonymous source. That's all."

Maggie pictured the circles and X's scribbled in Adam Halka's yearbook. She turned to face Serena in the firelight. "If you're a journalist following a tip from a witness, and you *think* you've found the right woman, what do you do next?"

Serena frowned as she put herself in Ned's shoes. "You go back to the witness and ask if this is the girl that he or she saw with Devin."

"Exactly."

"Somebody's hiding something, Maggie. Somebody talked to Ned Baer about that party, and they haven't come forward."

Maggie tapped her empty beer glass against her lips and thought about it. The lake breeze was cool on her neck. The fire jumped amid the red stones. "I'd really like to know who. And why they're so intent on staying anonymous."

* * * * *

Peter Stanhope made sure his Mercedes wasn't being followed as he left his Congdon Park mansion. These days, he never knew when he was safe from the prying eyes of the media. Online reporters and bloggers no longer played by the old rules. As he drove, he made a series of random turns, watching the headlights behind him. He didn't head out of the city until he was convinced he was alone.

He followed I-35 south to the Grand Avenue exit. Still eyeing his mirror, he drove another mile and then turned left across the railroad tracks into a quiet neighborhood near the water. Not far away, the road ended at the bay in the Indian Point campground. He took a dirt trail into the dense birch trees and parked where his car wouldn't be seen. From his glove compartment, he removed a compact Taurus pistol and secured it inside his jacket pocket.

This was a meeting where he took no chances.

Peter got out of the sedan and locked it. He made sure that no one else was nearby. The night was dark inside the trees, but pale moonlight shined on the water not even a hundred yards away. He could see silhouettes of campers dotting the woods, and he smelled the lingering smoke of fires. It was after midnight now, and he didn't think anyone would disturb them. He tramped across the soft ground, conscious that he was leaving footprints.

He found the RV where the man said it would be, in one of the campsites closest to the bay. A beige Buick was parked beside it. Peter climbed the steps of the RV and rapped his knuckles on the door.

Seconds later, the door opened. The smoke of a cigar drifted into a cloud outside.

"Pete," Adam Halka said. "Glad you could make it, man. Come on in."

The interior of the camper was humid and dank. None of the windows were open. Peter stood in the narrow corridor as Halka closed the door.

"Have a seat. You want a drink?"

"I won't be staying long," Peter replied.

The motel owner flopped down on a vinyl sofa and popped a can of Budweiser. He put his feet up. "Long time, huh, Pete?"

"What do you want, Adam? Why am I here?"

"I thought we should talk. It's been years since you and I talked."

"We never talked. We weren't friends. You said on the phone that this was important."

Halka shrugged. "Yeah, I get it, you don't like to slum it with the poor people. You're not part of the RV crowd. I usually stay at the motel, but during the summer, it's nice to get away and hang out by the water. Of course, your idea of a getaway is probably a private island somewhere, right? Must be nice."

Peter said nothing. He waited, because he knew Halka had to be leading up to something.

"Do you ever miss the old days?" the man asked. "High school? Summer parties? Those were wild times, huh? Lots of booze. Drugs. Sex."

"I don't recall partying with you, Adam. We played some baseball together in school. That's it."

"Oh, you may not have seen me at the parties, but I was there. I saw *you*. Devin, too."

"What's your point?" Peter asked.

Halka swigged his beer. "The point is, the police came to my motel today. They were asking about Ned Baer. You know, he stayed at my place that summer when he was in town."

"So what?"

"Ned heard I was part of the scene back then, so he asked me what I remembered from the party days. He wanted to know if I saw Devin with any girls. Whether I remembered any names."

"What did you tell him?"

"I told him no. Said that was way too long ago and my brain was fried. But the fact is, I saw Devin with *lots* of girls. I can't remember a party where he *wasn't* with a girl. More than one, usually. But that wasn't any of Neddy's business, was it? We hometown boys have to stick up for one another."

"Why are you telling me this?"

"I figured you should know that I'm able to keep my mouth shut. And also that I have a pretty good memory for details."

Peter's eyes narrowed with suspicion. "Meaning what?"

"Meaning the police are real interested in Ned Baer again, now that they know somebody killed him. They were asking me if Ned got any visitors while he was staying at my place. I said I didn't remember anybody. I didn't mention that I saw an old school buddy of mine hanging out near the motel right before Ned disappeared. I saw *you*, Pete. You were parked on the street in your Mercedes. Not exactly your neighborhood."

"Who's going to believe you, Adam?" Peter said after a pause. "You didn't tell anyone, and now you come up with this story? Without any proof?"

Halka laughed. "Who says I don't have proof?"

Peter froze where he was. "Excuse me?"

The motel owner dug a piece of paper out of his pocket and handed it to Peter. When he unfolded it, Peter saw a printout of a grainy nighttime photograph taken on a Duluth street near the motel.

It was himself. Sitting in his car.

"See, some things are weird enough that I like to document them," Halka went on, "just in case they ever come in handy someday. The Great Peter Stanhope hanging out near my fleabag motel? I definitely wanted a record of that. Good thing I had my phone with me. Of course, I never really thought it had anything to do with Ned back then. I didn't know anything had happened to him. But now?"

"What do you want, Adam?"

"You mean, to keep all of this to myself? To not talk to the police or the media about what I saw? Well, seems like we can come up with a fair price. I was thinking ten thousand dollars is a nice round number. Good for you and Devin. Good for me. Everybody wins."

Peter shook his head. "I have a counteroffer for you, Adam."

"Yeah? What do you have in mind?"

"Zero. That's what I have in mind. I pay you zero, and we forget this conversation ever happened, and I don't ask the police to charge you with extortion."

Halka slammed his beer can down on the table, and foam spurted from the top. He shouted loud enough to make the walls shake. "You think I won't send that photo to the cops? Just watch me. I'll do it! I'll take you down, Pete! I've waited a long time to get back at you, you arrogant prick!"

The motel owner sprang off the sofa, but just as quickly, Peter had his pistol in his hand. Halka stopped cold when he saw the gun. His upper lip snarled with hatred, but he backed away.

"That's right, sit yourself back down, Adam," Peter instructed him, keeping the gun aimed across the camper. "Here's what's going to happen. I'm going to walk out of here and forget I ever met you. You can do whatever you want with that photograph. Send it along to the police, I don't care. But if you think I won't put you in prison for blackmailing me, you're wrong. Don't play chicken with a lawyer, Adam. We don't blink."

Halka said nothing more. Peter waited to make sure the threat was gone, and then he turned around and left, slamming the door behind him as he did. He pocketed his gun as he descended the metal steps. He put on his best unconcerned smile as he marched across the wet ground back to his Mercedes, but he couldn't escape the reality of his situation.

Everything was unraveling, just as he'd predicted. The rats were coming out of the walls.

The police were going to find out the truth.

21

"We didn't break in to Wyatt's place," Cat told Stride. "Colleen had a key. He *gave* her a key. Doesn't that make it okay?"

Stride sighed in the doorway of her bedroom. "It wasn't her apartment. Colleen may have had a key, but she didn't have permission from Wyatt to go inside. So no. It's not okay."

He watched Cat twist her hair in exasperation. She got off her bed, went to the window and looked out at the street, and then came back. "But now we know it's him. I *saw* the pictures. He has a *gun*. You still can't do anything?"

"Like arrest him? I'm sorry. I wish I could, but no. As far as the police and the courts are concerned, nothing you saw in there actually exists."

"What if Colleen gives you a statement that Wyatt told her it was okay to go inside?"

"Is that true?" Stride asked.

"It could be true. I'm sure she'd say it was true."

"I don't play games like that, Cat. You know that."

"But what am I supposed to *do?*" she asked.

Stride sat down next to her on the bed. "The first thing you do is not ditch Brayden again. Got it? He's there to protect you. His job is to keep you safe. He can't do that if you disappear on him."

"I know. I'm sorry."

"Do the two of you not get along?" Stride asked. "I can find someone else to go with you if that's the problem."

"No, no, I like him a lot! I don't want him in trouble. This was my fault."

"Then let him do his job."

"And what about Wyatt?" Cat asked.

"I've asked Guppo to find out whatever he can about him, but like Brayden says, there doesn't seem to be much that's suspicious in his past. But we'll keep looking. If we find anything that would give us cause to get a search warrant, we'll go into his apartment. With the photos there, we'd be able to get a restraining order to keep him away from you. Maybe more. If there's evidence that he broke the law, we'll charge him."

"Like that'll stop him," Cat said, rolling her eyes.

"I know it doesn't seem like much. I wish the law worked better in these situations, but it doesn't. In the end, most of these people aren't actually dangerous, just confused, but we're not going to take any chances."

Cat shook her head. "Wyatt thinks he's in love with me, Stride. He's obsessed. You saw the note. You saw what he did to my car. Those pictures? He's been following me for weeks. He freaks me out."

"Believe me, I'm worried, too."

The girl got up again, and this time she pulled down the shades on all of the windows. "I hate living like this. He makes me feel like a prisoner in my own house."

"It won't be forever."

"Yeah. I know. But it never ends with me."

"Do you want me to stay with you for a while?"

She shook her head. "No. That's okay."

"Try to get some sleep."

Stride turned to leave, but Cat called after him. "Hey, Stride? Actually, can I ask you something before you go?"

"Sure. What is it?"

"Everything's been about me lately, but I know things are going on with you, too. I don't want you thinking I don't care. What's all this stuff about a body at Dr. Steve's place? And about you getting suspended from the police?"

"You don't need to worry about that," Stride assured her. "It's my problem, not yours."

He saw her face flush with anger. She crossed her arms tightly over her chest. "That's a terrible answer."

"What do you mean?"

"I mean, why do you shut me out like that? You do it to Serena, too."

Stride didn't know what to say. "Force of habit, I guess."

"I *hate* that you do that."

"I'm sorry, Cat."

"I know I'll always be a stupid little knocked up hooker to you. But give me some credit for growing up. I'm not the girl I used to be."

He was genuinely shocked to hear her say that. "I *never* thought that about you, Catalina. Not ever."

Cat got off the bed and marched up to him. "Then *talk to me!* Come on, Stride. Talk to me like I matter, not like I'm some charity case you dragged from the street. Talk to me like you really need me."

Stride put his arms around her. "Hey. You know how much I need you."

Cat held onto him, and they stayed that way a long time. A wave of regret washed over him, because she was right. He was doing to her what he'd done to people throughout his life. He shut them out from who he was. He built a wall to keep them safe. Except the wall wasn't there to protect anyone else; it was to protect himself.

He was always learning lessons from this girl.

Correction, he thought: *Woman.*

"Okay," he said. "You're right. Let's talk."

And he did. They sat down on her bed, and he told her everything, from start to finish. About his relationship with Andrea. About the Deeps. About Ned Baer. About lying to Maggie, about cheating on his wife, about things that had nothing to do with the investigation. He went back to his childhood and talked about people he hadn't thought about in years. He cried about Steve again. He cried about Cindy again. He opened up his heart and told her things he'd never told anyone else. And when he was done, Cat did what she always did. She cut like a surgeon through everything that didn't matter and went straight to what he was really hiding.

"You don't want to be a cop anymore, do you?" she asked, her eyes wide. "Is that what this is all about?"

He took a long, slow breath. The question was very simple and not simple at all. "Honestly? I don't know."

"You had to kill someone this year. Is it because of that?"

"Partly. It's about a lot of things. It's been gathering for a while, ever since the marathon bombing. And it's not like I have a plan to do anything, Cat. This is just something rolling around in my head. I guess being suspended didn't bother me like I assumed it would. The idea of being outside the police was always impossible for me to think about. Now here I am, and I realize it almost feels like a relief."

"Does Serena know?"

"Not yet."

"What would you do if you didn't go back?"

"I have no idea. I may feel differently about it tomorrow."

Cat leaned over and kissed his cheek. "Thank you for telling me."

"Thank *you*. I feel better talking about it."

"You make me feel special when you open up to me," she said.

"Well, you are special."

"I'm sorry for yelling," she added.

"Don't worry about it. Sometimes that's what it takes to get through to me."

"I meant what I said. I'm older now. I'm not a kid."

"I know that."

She looked down uncomfortably at her lap, and her voice took on a whole different cast. "I love you, you know. I always have."

Stride knew what she was saying. Her meaning was very clear.

He felt the delicacy of this moment, which as fragile as old china. He knew how easily he could hurt her, how profoundly he could damage their relationship if he patronized her or simply pretended that she meant something other than what she did. He had never been under any illusions about Cat and the sexuality hiding behind her feelings. That was part of who she was. When she'd first come into his house two years earlier, she'd made a clumsy attempt to seduce him, and after he shut her down, she'd never done anything like that again. But her feelings for him were still jumbled and confused by everything she'd been through in her life.

He took her chin and lifted it up so that she had to look into his eyes, which she didn't want to do. Her expression was full of shame. She was already regretting what she'd said, as if she wanted to squeeze the genie back in the bottle.

"Do you know who I love?" he asked her.

"Serena," she said.

"That's right. I love Serena. But that's not to say I don't love you, too. It's in a different way, but every bit as deep. You know that. You're like a daughter to me, and I never thought I'd be lucky enough to know what that felt like."

Cat nodded, biting her lip. She scooted away from him and wiped her face. "I shouldn't have said anything. I'm sorry."

"Don't be. You were being honest."

"I hope somebody loves me like you love her. Someday."

"Believe me," he told her. "Somebody will."

* * * * *

Stride very rarely got drunk, but that night, he decided that he wanted to get drunk. He took two six-packs of Bent Paddle onto the screened porch at the back of his cottage, and he sat on the old sofa and stared out at the darkness. The lake roared at him from behind the dunes, like an invitation to come to the beach, but he didn't even have the energy to walk outside and climb over the sand. He simply opened the first beer and drank half of it down.

Then, as if to remind him that drinking was a foolish plan, a tapping on the glass of the storm door interrupted his solitude. He looked over and saw Curt Dickes outside, shuffling back and forth on his feet as if dancing to music that only he could hear.

Stride groaned and got off the sofa and opened the door. "Curt. What the hell are you doing here?"

"Hey, Lieutenant. Can I come in?"

"Oh, sure," Stride replied acidly. "Why not?"

Curt wandered into the porch with his hands shoved in the pockets of his baggy shorts. He had his long, greasy black hair tied behind his head, and he wore a black T-shirt from Fitger's Inn. His eyes shot to the six-packs on the table next to the sofa. "Golden IPA," he said. "Cool. Can I have one?"

Stride rolled his eyes. "Knock yourself out."

Curt grabbed a can of beer and popped the top. He slouched on the sofa and stretched out his long legs. "How's Kitty Cat? I wanted to make sure she's okay."

Stride sat down on the sofa, too. "She'll be fine."

"Good. Good. That's great. I like her, you know. I like her a lot. Not that I'd ever touch her. No way. We're friends, and that's all."

Stride smiled. "You don't have to worry about me, Curt. Serena's the one to be concerned about."

"Oh, yeah. This I know."

"So what do you want?" Stride asked.

"Well, like I said, I wanted to check in about Cat. I figured you might be pissed about her running off with Colly. That's Colleen, my girlfriend. By the way, just so you know, your boy Brayden didn't do anything wrong. He was watching her like a hawk. I mean, really watching. But Cat never met a man she couldn't outsmart."

"I'm aware," Stride said.

Curt squirmed restlessly on the sofa. He drank his beer fast. When he was done, he eyed the six-pack again, and Stride shrugged. Curt belched and took another. "Word is, you can't really do anything about Wyatt stalking Cat. Not legally, I mean. No proof."

"For the moment."

"Uh-huh." Curt rolled the cold beer can around in his hands, and Stride could tell he was nervous. "You know, I like you, Lieutenant. Always have. Even when you're arresting me, you play fair. Maybe more than I deserve. Plus, you've got the hottest wife in town. Props for that."

"Thanks," Stride said warily.

"You're Duluth born and raised, like me. We lifers have to stick together, right? We help each other out. Somebody's in trouble, we do something about it."

"Meaning what?"

"Meaning if you can't touch Wyatt, maybe I can, know what I'm saying? I've got friends. No names or anything. But if you want the guy whacked, I can probably make that happen. Absolutely off the books. It would never come back on you."

Stride felt a headache coming on. He rubbed his fingers against his forehead. "Curt, did you really just go to a police officer's house and offer to have somebody *whacked?*"

"Hey, if you want, I could just have him roughed up. To send a message, you know?"

"I'm going to do both of us a favor and forget you ever said any of this, Curt. Okay? Just to be one hundred percent clear, you are *not* to touch Wyatt or solicit anyone else to harm him in any way. Got it?"

Curt shrugged. "Got it."

"Do you really? This is not a wink-wink kind of thing. Stay away from him."

"Yeah, okay. I was just thinking about Cat. I want to help her. Really."

"I get that, Curt."

Curt finished his next beer and belched again. He pushed himself off the sofa, but rather than leave, he stood on the porch looking uncomfortable.

"Is there something else?" Stride asked.

"Sort of. This isn't about Cat. I don't know if I should say anything."

"Well, it can't be worse than what you've said already."

Curt's lips pursed into a frown. "Except this involves kind of an on-going enterprise that could get me into trouble."

"Give me a clue. If it's not about Cat, what's it about?"

"That guy you found. Ned Baer."

Stride sat up straighter. "Talk to me."

"I would, except it might be bad for business."

Stride got off the sofa and put a firm hand on Curt's shoulder. "We'll call my porch the immunity zone. You get a free pass for anything you tell me here. What's going on?"

Curt's shoulders slumped in relief. "Okay, here's the thing. You know I have a lot of entrepreneurial ventures. Some a little more legal than others.

One of the things I do occasionally—and I'm talking *very* occasionally, hardly ever—is help people acquire handguns without a lot of red tape about permits and all. Especially out-of-towners who may be under time constraints about their purchases."

Stride's headache began to get worse. "I'm regretting my offer, Curt."

"Seriously, it's not often. Not anymore. In the old days, it was a bigger part of Curt, Inc., but not now. Anyway, the thing is, seven years ago, this guy Ned Baer bought a gun off me."

"Ned bought a *gun?*" Stride asked in surprise. "Are you sure it was him? That was a long time ago."

"I'm sure. His photo was in the paper, and I remember him clear as anything. When I met him, I was wearing a ZZ Top T-shirt, and he told me he was a roadie for the band back in college. So we spent a couple of hours comparing notes."

"Do you remember the gun you sold him?"

"H&K 9 mm. That's mostly what I sell."

"Did Ned say why he wanted a gun?"

Curt nodded. "Oh, yeah. He wanted protection. He said somebody was following him, and he thought they might try to kill him."

22

Maggie had never met Devin Card before, but when the Congressman walked into Peter Stanhope's office early in the morning, she could feel the electricity that he conveyed. You could hate politicians on television, but it was very hard to hate them face to face. His handshake was solid. His blue eyes were like lasers. His smile was focused on her and no one else, making her feel like the only person in the room. Plus, he was a big, handsome former quarterback, infectious in his self-confidence.

She had to remind herself: *Blood and semen on the sheets.*

"Sergeant, it's a pleasure to meet you," Card said. "I don't need to tell you how important the work you do is. It's an honor whenever I meet a police officer. And the team here in Duluth is truly the best."

"Thank you, Congressman."

Card's gaze shifted to Dan Erickson as if they were old friends, and he shouldered his way around the conference table with a big grin. "Dan, look at you, that suit, that tan. Making the most of the corporate deals, I see. You and Peter, I swear. If I'm reincarnated in my next life, I want to come back as a lawyer."

"Funny, I think I'd come back as a politician," Dan replied.

"Oh, no. You dodged a bullet, Dan. Trust me, it's like walking around with a permanent target on your chest. All you do is spend half your days and nights dialing for dollars."

Maggie heard the subtext in Card's comment. Once upon a time, Dan had been the golden boy with political ambitions and a shot at Congress, but then his career had imploded. She could see from the frozen expression on Dan's face that he hadn't missed Card's meaning.

"Why don't we sit down?" Peter Stanhope interrupted them. "We know the importance of your investigation, and we wanted to make sure you had a chance to ask your questions."

Dan took a seat on the opposite side of the conference table, and Maggie sat next to him. "You mean, so you can tell everyone how cooperative you're being?" he asked.

"We *are* being cooperative, Dan," Card replied with a smile. "We have nothing to hide."

Peter interjected again with his typical smoothness. "Look, the Congressman and I appreciate your willingness to have this conversation in my office and particularly for the two of you to come up here via the back elevator so that we don't have the media crawling all over us. In politics, how things look are often as important as how they really are."

"Understood," Dan said. "Well, here we are. Let's get started."

Maggie took out her phone. "Congressman, do you mind if we record this interview?"

Peter spoke again before Card could reply. "*I* mind, Sergeant. I'm sorry. Confidential recordings have a way of becoming not so confidential, even with the best of intentions. We have plenty of witnesses in this room to anything that's said, so let's stick with that."

She shrugged and took out a pen instead, and she opened a folder in front of her. "All right. Congressman, can you tell us where you were on the evening of Tuesday, August 24 seven years ago? We believe that's the night that Ned Baer was shot to death at the Deeps."

Card said nothing, but Peter pushed a piece of paper across the table at them.

"As you know, that time period was in the middle of a heated political campaign. Here's a copy of Devin's official schedule from that day.

You'll see that he had a fundraising dinner that evening at a private home in Cloquet at six-thirty."

"And after that?" Maggie asked.

"I have no idea," Card replied. "Typically, I'd be making phone calls to supporters until after midnight. On that specific evening? I couldn't possibly remember."

"So you have no actual alibi after, say, nine o'clock?"

"No, I'm sure I do have an alibi, because I was almost never alone that summer. I just don't know who was with me that night."

"What about you, Mr. Stanhope?" Maggie asked. "What were you doing that evening?"

"I checked my calendar for that night," Peter replied. "I figured you'd ask. I was here at the office preparing for a trial until very late."

"Would anyone be able to confirm that?"

"No. I was working alone."

"So no alibis for either of you," Dan concluded, with a glance at Maggie.

The Congressman rocked back in the chair, his arms behind his head. "I suppose I should say this at the outset, since this is why we're all here. I didn't kill Ned Baer. I didn't *arrange* for anyone else to kill Ned Baer. I have no idea who *did* kill Ned Baer. Is that clear enough for you?"

"Very," Dan replied. "Peter? What about you?"

"Same."

"See?" Card told them. "It's that simple. Are we done here?"

"I'm sorry, Congressman," Maggie told them, "but it's not quite that simple. We have more ground to cover."

Card shoved back the chair and got up from the table. He talked and moved quickly, as if he were always in a hurry, and his impatience made it impossible to sit still for any length of time. "I really don't see how we can help you, Sergeant. I just told you that neither Peter nor I know anything about this man's murder. It had nothing to do with me."

"Well, no offense, sir, but that's almost certainly not true."

Card froze. "Excuse me?"

"We all know why Ned Baer was in town," Maggie reminded him. "He was investigating rape allegations that had been made against you. He wasn't *from* Duluth; he was an outsider. So it's a good bet that whatever happened to him was somehow connected to the research he was doing on you. That's why we're here."

Card's warm blue eyes turned to stone. "False rape allegations."

"I'm sorry?"

"He was investigating *false* rape allegations. I never raped anyone."

Maggie stared back at him, and she felt herself stiffening with anger. "For now, the question of the rape is outside the scope of our investigation. All I'll tell you, Congressman, is that you should probably be grateful that's the case."

Card opened his mouth to object, but before he could say anything more, Peter interrupted sharply. "Hang on, hang on, what are you saying? Do you know who made the accusation? Have you identified the woman?"

"Yes," Dan replied.

"*Who?*" Card and Peter both shouted simultaneously.

"We're not releasing that information at this time," Dan told them.

But Maggie felt her rage bubbling over, and she couldn't keep her mouth closed. "We know who the woman is, Congressman. Not only that, we know where the rape occurred, and we have a witness who saw blood on the sheets in an upstairs bedroom, all of which supports the original allegation. We also believe that Ned Baer had a witness who saw you *with* the victim at the party where this all occurred. So forgive me if I tell you, as one of your constituents, that I think you're full of shit."

Card put his hands on his hips and didn't back down. "I don't know what information you think you have, but it's wrong, Sergeant. I am sick of these lies. I am sick of this dirt being spewed against me. I don't know who this woman is, or what happened to her, but she's either lying or she's mistaken. If Ned Baer told anyone about a witness who said otherwise, then that's a lie, too. This is all political filth, Ms. Bei. It's about destroying politicians for sport. Do you know what kind of man Ned Baer was? Did you investigate his history as a *journalist?* He wrote stories based on gossip and innuendo, and he didn't care whether it was true. His goal was to destroy candidates based on his political agenda. Period. He was a worthless, lying piece of shit, and I'm sorry somebody blew his brains out, but the world is a better place without people like him."

"*Devin,*" Peter snapped. "Dial it back. Calm down."

"No, I won't calm down, Peter. I'm sorry. These accusations have been chasing me for years, and they're bogus. They've been ruining my life. My family has had to put up with daily stories about what a monster I am. My *children* have had to read this! Hell, seven years ago, someone assaulted me on the street. And all over an anonymous allegation that has zero basis in fact."

Dan's brow furrowed. "Someone assaulted you?"

"That's right. We kept it out of the press, because we didn't think it would help my image, the former football star being sucker punched. We said I fell on the sidewalk. But the truth is, somebody jumped me outside the Sheraton and beat the shit out of me."

"Who?" Maggie asked.

"I don't know. He wore a mask. And do you know what he said to me? *Forgive every sin.* What the hell does that even mean?"

"*Devin,*" Peter said again. "Enough."

The Congressman finally realized he'd let his emotions carry him away. He unleashed a hiss of annoyance and then sat back down at the conference table without looking at Dan or Maggie.

Maggie let the silence stretch out for a while, and then she said, "So obviously you knew who Ned Baer was."

Card's eyes fired daggers at her. "Obviously."

"Did you know him before he came to Duluth that summer?"

Peter reached out and put a hand over Card's arm. "Actually, I think I'll advise Devin to let me answer the rest of your questions. I'm sure you can imagine how painful it is to deal with character assassination the way he has, and frankly, I want him to be in the right mental place for the town hall tonight. As for your question about Ned Baer, no, we didn't know about him prior to that summer. We did know FR Online, where he worked. Everyone in Democratic politics knows about that operation and their hatchet jobs. Shortly after Baer came to town, I got a call from a lawyer friend in Colorado who told me that Baer was coming after Devin and that we should be prepared. He told us about the man's unsavory reputation. So at that point, we did our homework on him."

"Did you talk to him?" Maggie asked.

Peter frowned and said nothing.

"Mr. Stanhope? Did you talk to Ned Baer?"

Peter was still silent, and she could see him working up answers in his head.

"Yesterday, you told Serena Stride that neither one of you had ever met him," Maggie went on. "Now you're talking about doing your homework on him, and you obviously were familiar enough with his work to consider him a liability. So I'll ask you again. Did you meet with him or talk with him that summer?"

"Yes," Peter replied in a crisp voice.

"*Peter?*" Card interrupted. "What the hell? You *met* with him?"

Peter shook his head and held up a hand, silencing the Congressman. "Yes, I did. Devin's surprise is genuine, by the way. I never told him about it. I wanted to protect him should it ever come out."

"Why did you lie to Serena?" Maggie asked.

"Since I wasn't involved in his murder, I didn't see any value in advertising the conversation I had with Mr. Baer. I didn't think anyone else knew about it. That was before someone tried to blackmail me."

"Blackmail you? About meeting Ned Baer? Who did that?"

"His name is Adam Halka. He owns the motel where Baer was staying that summer. He also knew me when we were teenagers in school. Halka saw me outside his motel, and he put two and two together about why I was there. He also had a picture of me in my car. Last night, he tried to extort me to keep the secret."

"When were you outside the motel?"

"August 23 seven years ago."

"The *day before* Ned Baer was murdered?" Dan asked.

"Apparently."

"Were you there to meet Baer?"

"Yes."

"How did that come about?"

"He dropped off a note at my office that day," Peter said. "He asked for a meeting. He told me that he'd identified the woman behind the anonymous allegation against Devin, and he wanted to talk about it."

"So you went?"

"Yes, I did."

"What happened?"

"Devin is right about Baer. He was a disgusting individual. Drunk. Almost violent. He was ranting about what shitholes Devin and I were and how he couldn't wait to see us twist when the news came out. He accused me of having him followed. Of breaking into his motel room to find out what he was working on."

"Did you do that?" Maggie asked.

"No."

"So what did he want?"

"He offered to spike the story if I gave him one hundred thousand dollars."

Dan made a silent whistle with his lips. "Baer wanted a bribe?"

"Yes."

"What did you say?" Maggie asked.

"I said no. I told him to publish whatever he wanted. Devin was innocent. I said we'd rather know who was behind the anonymous accusation, because then we could find a way to counter it. I told him he was doing us a favor. He didn't like that."

"Did he tell you who the woman was?"

"No."

"Did he tell you how he found her?"

"No."

"So what happened next?"

"I left."

"Did you talk to him again? Did you hear from him again after that night?"

"No. Never. The next time I heard his name was when I read a few days later that he'd disappeared. The police said he'd probably drowned."

"Did you believe that?" Maggie asked.

"I had no reason not to."

Maggie looked at Dan, whose eyebrows flicked a message at her: *We're done.*

"I think that's all of our questions for now," she told them. "Thank you both for your time."

"Actually, I have a question for you, Sergeant," the Congressman replied.

"What is it?"

"You said you know the identity of the woman who made the accusations. Have you talked to her?"

"Not personally, but one of my colleagues did, yes," Maggie said.

"Do you know if she plans to come forward?"

Maggie closed the folder in front of her and put the pen back in her pocket. She stood up, and so did Dan.

"I have no idea, Congressman," she told him. "I guess you'll find out soon enough."

23

High on the trail over Hawk Ridge, Cat felt as if she and Brayden were the only two people in the world. The dense brush made a little shelter where they sat on the rocks. Below them, the trees mostly blocked any views of the city, so all they could see were the green rolling hills of the northland heading to Canada and the great blue expanse of the lake. The morning air, only an hour after sunrise, was cool, with a breeze tumbling down the hillside and mussing her chestnut hair. The rush of the wind made the only sound, other than the occasional chatter of birds.

She plucked a stalk of white wildflowers that grew between the rocks and rubbed it along her cheek. She closed her eyes.

"You look relaxed," Brayden said.

Cat gave him a dreamy smile without opening her eyes. "Not really, but being here helps. I needed to get away from all of the craziness for a while. That's why I come here. To get away from everything. Hawk Ridge is my favorite place in the world."

"Do you hike up here with Stride?"

"Nope. Not Stride. Not Serena. Not Curt. I always come here alone. Just me. And now you."

"I'm honored."

"You should be," she replied, opening her eyes and giving him a smirk. "But you wouldn't have let me come by myself, would you?"

"No."

"There you go," Cat said.

She shrugged a small backpack off her shoulders and put it in her lap. She unzipped one of the pockets and dug out a granola bar from inside, and she held it out to Brayden. "You want one?"

"No, thanks."

"You don't eat. You don't drink. Are you always a good boy?"

Brayden laughed. "My father would roll his eyes at that idea, believe me. I was hell on wheels in school."

"How'd you get past it?"

"Who says I did? You're only seeing one side of me, Cat."

"I'd like to see the other side."

"No, you wouldn't. Trust me, tigers are best left in their cages."

"Oh, you're a tiger, huh? Now you really have me interested."

Brayden shook his head. "What is it with you? Do you flirt with every man you meet?"

Cat looked down at her lap, and her hair fell across her face.

"Sorry," Brayden said. "That was mean. I don't know why I said that."

"No. You're right. I'm screwed up when it comes to men. I probably always will be. Stride says I'll have a normal relationship someday, but I don't see it happening."

"Why not?"

"Because of my past."

"People change."

Cat pulled her legs up and hugged her knees. She stared at the sweeping view below them instead of at Brayden. "Do you have any idea how many men had fucked me by the time I was sixteen? I'm sorry, Stride hates it when I talk like that, but I don't know what else to call it. That's what it was. That's what they did. Guess how many."

"It's none of my business, and I don't need to know."

"Well, it was a lot. Most of them way older than you. That was my life, that was how I paid my way. The shrink I saw said I'd always be attracted to older men because of it. He said that while he was banging me in his office."

"Cat, I don't—"

"I had a boyfriend close to my age while I was pregnant," she went on. "Al. It didn't work out. I mean, he cheated on me, but even without that, I wasn't really into him. The shrink was right. I'm stuck on older guys, no matter how they treat me."

She could see that she was embarrassing him, but she charged ahead, the way she always did.

"Yesterday I told Stride I loved him. I mean, I do, and I always will, but he knew what I meant. He knew what I was offering if he wanted it. Can you believe I would say something so stupid? But that's me. I always do. If something's good in my life, I have to blow it up."

"I really doubt there's anything you could say that would blow up your relationship with Stride."

"Well, it's not like I don't try. Believe me, I try hard with everybody. Look at you and me. I like you, Brayden. I like you a lot. And here I go running off at the mouth and telling you all sorts of shit that pretty much guarantees you'll think I'm some kind of freak. Yeah, let's go out with the ex-hooker who has a crush on the fifty-year-old guy who's been like a father to her. I'm a prize. I really am. Did you know I'm a born-again virgin? It's true. I haven't had sex since I got off the street. I call it my second virginity. Which is a load of crap. I'm so horny I can't see straight. I really, really, really want to have sex. With somebody, with anybody. But you know what I think about when I think about sex? I wonder if the guy will give me money when we're done. I wonder if I'll blurt out, 'Hey that was fun, a hundred bucks please.' Nobody would want to have sex with me for free. Come on. Look at what I've—"

Cat stopped in mid-sentence. Her eyes grew wide as her brain caught up with everything she'd been saying, and then she buried her face in her hands.

"Oh, my God," she murmured, her voice muffled.

"It's okay."

She shook her head over and over. "Are you kidding? No, it's not okay.

I'm losing it. I'm sorry. I'm *so* sorry. It's the stalking, it's everything. This is more than I can take."

"Cat, I told you, it's *okay*."

She grabbed her backpack and scrambled to her feet. "Let's go. Can we go? I need to get out of here."

Brayden nodded. "Sure."

He got to his feet, too, and they stood in front of each other on the rocks, not even a foot apart. The wind whistled around them. Two hawks floated in the currents of air far above their heads, and insects whined in the brush. Somewhere nearby, something cracked, an animal tiptoeing through the fallen branches. She felt tears in her eyes, but she hadn't given in and cried yet. Brayden watched her, his blond hair swept back, a crooked smile on his face. He was tall, strong, beautiful.

"Kiss me," Cat said.

"I can't do that."

"You said you have another side. You said you're a tiger. Kiss me. No one will ever know. *Kiss me!*"

She didn't give him a choice.

She took a step and grabbed him roughly. One hand went around his neck, one went around his waist. She tilted her face to him and pulled his head down, and her mouth closed over his, pushing his lips apart, moving inside him with her tongue. Her arms wrapped him up in a fierce embrace, her breasts crushed against his chest. He reacted, he gave in, just as she knew he would. Men always did. His fingers spread her silky hair. They broke apart only long enough to catch their breath and gasp with passion and then kissed again, even harder and stronger than before, his grip so intense that she felt herself lifted off the ground. She could feel his arousal.

When they stopped, he took a step backward. Shock flooded his expression, and his eyes darkened. Cat put her hands over her mouth, astonished at what they'd done, in disbelief that it had really happened.

There was no time to say anything more to each other.

An instant later, blood sprayed over her face like a red cloud.

Brayden shuddered. He staggered, grabbing his arm. The crack of a gunshot rippled over the wind. Cat tried to scream and couldn't. She stood paralyzed, unable to move a muscle, until Brayden threw himself on top of her, pulling her to the rocks.

"Stay down, stay down!"

Another crack snapped through the air, and the ping of a bullet ricocheted off stone and sent up an explosion of dirt and dust. Then another. And another. Brayden slithered along the ground, taking Cat's arm and dragging her with him. He pulled her into a valley behind a moss-covered boulder jutting out of the hillside. Wildflowers grew around them.

Just as they took cover, another shot fired right over their heads.

Brayden had his gun out in his left hand now. His right arm was ribboned with blood. He stretched out his arm with the gun aimed forward and took a quick look over the rocks.

"I don't see anyone."

"Should we run?"

"Not yet. Keep your head down."

"But you've been shot!" she hissed. "Brayden, you've been shot! We need to get out of here!"

"I'm fine. Stay quiet, I need to listen."

Cat squeezed her eyes shut. She heard the breeze around them, but nothing else except the heavy noise of their breathing. Each second ticked by with excruciating slowness as she huddled in the brush. Whoever was hiding on the other side of the clearing was quiet, too.

"Is he still there?"

"I didn't hear anyone run away. I think he's between us and the trail. We need to go straight down the hill to the road. Can you do that?"

"Me, sure, but what about you?"

"I told you, I'm fine."

Brayden pointed across the flat ground. They were on a terraced, rocky section of the hillside, scattered with weeds and brush sprouting from the crevices. No more than twenty feet away, the land sloped downhill into a nest of tall bushes, spindly birches, and thick, conical evergreens. At the base of the hill was the narrow strip of road called Skyline Parkway.

"Once we reach the slope, we'll be fine," he told her. "But for a few seconds, we'll be in the open."

"What do we do?"

"When I say run, we run for the woods. Stay on my left side, and don't get ahead of me."

"But you'll be exposed!"

"Hitting a moving target with a handgun is a lot harder than you think. Are you ready?"

Cat bit her lip. "I'm ready."

"*Run!*"

With his left arm, Brayden yanked her to her feet, and the two of them took off across the rocks. Cat felt clumsy in her hiking boots, and when she stumbled, he had to keep her on her feet. His arm was around her waist. His body jigged, jumping and ducking across the uneven terrain as he guided her toward the trees. Gunfire erupted, little explosions that went wild. Cat's mouth opened into one loud, unending scream as they flew for the slope, and when they got there, she threw herself into the arms of the brush, not caring as sharp little branches scratched her skin. Brayden was right there with her. He got ahead of her and cleared the path, breaking through the woods as she clung to his belt and followed. Everything was a blur of leaves rushing past her face, of dirt under her feet.

Then, seconds later, they burst out of the foliage onto the gravel road. The panorama opened up ahead of them. The city. The lake. White clouds streaming with the wind toward the east. Brayden's Kia was parked on the shoulder twenty yards away. He kept his gun pointed into the trees as they hurried to the car.

"Get in the backseat," he told her. "Lie down and stay there."

She did as she was told, and she stretched out and covered her head. She heard Brayden's footsteps, heard him go around to the driver's side and fire the engine. The Kia accelerated with a *screech*. He sped around the curves, and the whole car shook, rolling her onto the floor.

It was only when they reached the city streets a mile later that he slowed down. Cat got up and tumbled awkwardly back into the front seat. She still had her backpack slung over her shoulders, and she grabbed it and found an extra T-shirt in one of the pockets. Brayden's right arm was caked in blood, and she wrapped the shirt tenderly around his skin. Even the gentle touch made him wince.

"Are you really okay?" she asked.

"The bullet gouged me. I think it's just a flesh wound."

"You're going to the hospital, right?"

"Yeah. Call Stride, tell him what happened. He should get a search party up on the ridge. The shooter won't stick around, but maybe he left some evidence behind."

Cat dug her phone out of her pocket, but before she could dial, she fell back against the seat and found herself struggling to breathe. She opened and closed her fists. The tears she'd been holding back ran like a river, and her whole body trembled.

Brayden saw her falling apart. "Cat, it's over. We're okay."

She knew he was right, but it didn't help.

"You're fine. I'm fine."

"He tried to kill me. He tried to kill both of us."

Brayden reached out gingerly with his hand and touched her cheek, leaving behind sticky blood. "I know."

"He saw us kiss," Cat said, wiping away the blood.

"What?"

"We kissed up there. That's what drove him crazy. He didn't like that. He wants me all to himself."

24

Andrea made pancakes on the griddle on her kitchen stove, mindlessly flipping them as they browned. The morning news droned in the background at a low volume. Her sister, Denise, stood near the rear window, drinking a mug of coffee and admiring the collection of suncatchers in the early light.

"These are pretty," she said. "I don't remember seeing these before."

"I'm not sure I had them up when you were last here."

"Well, I like them. They add color to the place. You need some color. Where do you get them?"

"A secret admirer," Andrea replied.

Denise turned around with the mug of coffee at her lips. "Sorry, what?"

"Someone sends them to me. I don't know who it is. It's been happening for years."

She didn't mention that her secret admirer also broke into her house to deliver his gifts and that they came with the same strange message each time.

Forgive every sin.

"That's sort of weird, isn't it?" Denise said.

"Well, it's probably a former student who's still bringing the teacher an apple. It doesn't really matter, does it?"

"I guess not."

Denise sat down at the table, and Andrea put a plate of pancakes in front of her, along with a glass of orange juice. She did the same for herself. For a few minutes, they ate without talking or looking at each other. Denise checked her phone; Andrea read the *News-Tribune*.

They had never been particularly close as sisters, and Denise moving back to Duluth hadn't changed that. Andrea wasn't looking for a confidant, and with their parents gone, it had been painfully obvious to both of them that they had little in common. Even so, they were taking baby steps toward a better relationship. The occasional breakfast together was part of that.

As she stabbed her pancakes with a fork, Andrea realized that Denise was staring at the television over her shoulder. She turned around and saw that the morning news program was broadcasting from inside Duluth's harborside convention center. The talk of the town was Devin Card's upcoming town hall meeting that night.

She turned up the volume and listened to what the news anchor was saying.

"Late last night, the Card campaign issued another press release emphatically denying the rape allegations that have dogged the Congressman for the past seven years. Regardless, the issue is sure to come up from constituents at tonight's town hall, along with questions about the unsolved murder of an online journalist named Ned Baer, who was attempting to identify the anonymous accuser. With the scandal back in the headlines, the question on many people's minds is this: Will the woman behind the allegations take this opportunity to finally come forward?"

Andrea picked up the remote control and muted the TV.

"So what are you going to do?" Denise asked.

"Nothing."

"Don't you want to tell your story?"

"I told my story. I talked to a lawyer. I wrote a letter. I never intended for any of it to become public."

"But it did. Without you to back up what you wrote, Devin can stand up there and call you a liar. Is that what you want?"

Andrea shot a look across the table. "Well, *you* think I'm a liar, don't you?"

Denise put down her fork and looked stricken. "Andrea, no. When have I ever said that?"

"I know your tone. You've never believed me."

"It isn't that—" Denise began, and then her words trailed off.

Andrea made a little snort of disgust, because she heard the same tone from Denise again. The tone that announced all of her doubts about Andrea's story. Her sister must have heard it in her own voice, because she stopped talking and took a minute to regroup. When she spoke again, she was firm. "I believe you."

"But?" Andrea said. "Because there's obviously a 'but.' Go on, fire away."

"It's not a 'but.' I'm not doubting you. I just want to know why didn't you tell me when it happened."

"You were gone, remember? You left for basic training two days later."

"We talked on the phone."

Andrea gave a sour laugh. "Yeah, how would that conversation have gone? 'Hey, Denise, how's Air Force life? By the way, Devin Card raped me at that party.' Don't you get it? You left, and by the time you came back, we were strangers. You have no idea what I went through. None."

"You're right. I'm sorry."

"It's not your fault, Denise. I don't blame you."

"But I pushed you to go to the concert and the party," her sister pointed out. "I didn't look after you while you were there."

"I went because I wanted to go. I wasn't looking for a chaperone."

Denise looked down at her plate and tilted it to make the syrup run. She didn't look up at Andrea. "Tell me what happened."

"You already know."

"Not the details. I don't."

Andrea shrugged. "It started after you had sex with Peter Stanhope. Remember that? You did it in front of everybody."

Denise closed her eyes. "I didn't realize you saw that."

"Of course, I did. Everybody did. You know what? I was jealous of you. My sister was cool and out there and willing to do all this shit that Mom and Dad didn't know about. And me, I was the good girl. The virgin. I was sick of it. So when Devin Card told me how pretty I was and started to make out with me, I thought it was the hottest thing ever. I'd never made out with anyone before, but *Devin Card?*"

"You're sure it was him?"

"One hundred percent."

"We were all drinking, Andrea. You'd hardly ever had a drink before, and you drank a lot."

"It was *him*. Do you think I wouldn't remember that? I was with the guy that all the girls wanted. You had sex with Peter Stanhope, but *I* was with Devin Card. Guys were watching us together and drooling over me. *Me*. So when he asked me to go upstairs, I said yes. I consented. But later, when it started to happen, I said *no*. I said *stop*."

"Maybe he didn't realize you were serious. I mean, sometimes guys—"

"Really, Denise? You're *defending* what he did to me?"

"No. I'm not."

"Yes, I was drunk. Yes, I agreed to go upstairs with him, and you know what? I probably thought I wanted sex. But when he started taking off my clothes, I *did not* consent. I told him to get out. He *raped* me! That's what happened!"

Her voice had gotten loud. Somewhere along the way, she'd stood up from the chair, and she was shouting and jabbing a finger at her sister. Tears came down her face. The memories roared back the way they always did. She stopped and shut her eyes tightly. Her body twitched, as if he were on top of her again in the dark bedroom. She could still feel him. She could still hear herself begging him to stop, to go away, to get off her. She could still smell the scent of him afterward as she lay there alone, with the awful ache between her legs and the stickiness of her own blood on her thighs.

Andrea opened her eyes.

Denise shook her head. "Jesus, sis. I'm so sorry."

"I know."

"I wish you'd told me. I would have tried to help."

"You couldn't have done anything. Nobody could. My life was already over."

Denise got up, too. She went over to Andrea and hugged her, and they stood there in that tight embrace for a long time. It felt good; it felt safe. Andrea couldn't remember the last time they'd done that.

Then, when they separated, Denise's face screwed up in disgust as she noticed the television. Andrea turned around, and there he was. Congressman Devin Card, perfectly dressed, serious and earnest, such a decent, moral man. She turned up the volume again.

"I'm not going to speculate on this person's motives. We're talking about an anonymous allegation. I don't even know how to respond to that, other than to say I've never done anything like what she says in my life. It did not happen. Is this whole thing political? Is this a smear? Who knows? Believe me, I would like nothing more than for this woman to come forward and tell all of us her name. To share her story in public. Because then maybe we can figure out the truth behind this mistake. And if she won't do that, then frankly, the voters can draw their own conclusions about her credibility. That's all I have to say."

This time Andrea switched off the set entirely.

She stood in the kitchen, breathing hard, still lost in the past.

"You can't let him say that about you," Denise told her. "You can't let him get away with it. Andrea, please. You can't stay quiet anymore."

Andrea inhaled, then exhaled.

It was like that moment right before you jumped out of the airplane. And once you did, there was no going back.

"You're right," she said to her sister. "I can't."

25

Cat huddled in a window seat in the far corner of the great room in Stride's cottage. She was invisible to everyone else. The police talked about her, but no one talked *to* her, and she hated that. She didn't like listening to other people making decisions about her future as if she was just a bystander.

Stride and Serena were both there. So were Guppo, Brayden, and four other uniformed officers. Brayden had a wrapped bandage extending below the cuff of his T-shirt. He was in pain where the bullet had grazed him, and she could see his mouth grimace when he moved. She kept trying to catch his eye. He knew she was there, but he refused to look her way. Now that it was over, he was pretending as if the kiss had never happened.

There was an urgency among the people in the room. She could feel it. Shots had been fired, a police officer had been wounded, and suddenly, this was about more than a stalker sending anonymous notes. She heard Serena talking about *attempted murder*. She heard her saying that if it was Wyatt Miller, he was not going to stop with one attempt. Cat believed her. She already had a sixth sense about the future that she wouldn't have admitted to anyone else.

People were going to get shot.

People were going to die.

Because of her.

"What did you find up on Hawk Ridge?" Stride asked.

Guppo shifted his girth in his chair. "We found where the shooter hid out on the hillside. There were lots of 9 mm shell casings. It looks like he unloaded the entire magazine at them. Brayden and Cat are lucky to be alive."

Lucky, Cat thought bitterly. Oh, yeah. She felt lucky.

"What else?" Stride asked.

"He tore his shirt on some sharp branches and left behind a patch of fabric. Tie-dye."

"Any DNA?"

"No, but I went over to Hoops, and two of the bartenders gave me affidavits that they remembered Wyatt Miller wearing tie-dye shirts. Brayden confirmed that Wyatt was wearing the same style the other night at the brewery. That was enough for Judge Edblad. He signed off on a warrant, and we went into Wyatt's apartment an hour ago."

Cat called from the corner. "Did you find the box under the bed? Did you find the photos he took?"

All the heads in the room snapped around to stare at her. It was as if they'd forgotten she was there.

"I'm sorry, Cat," Guppo replied. "No, the box wasn't there. Either he has it with him, or he moved it because he figured we might get in and do a search. But we did find something else. At the back of a kitchen drawer, we found an open package of green Sharpies that match what was used to write the notes to Cat. He was definitely lying when he told Brayden that he had no idea where the marker came from."

Stride shook his head. "Where the hell is this son of a bitch?"

"We don't know. We've got his photo out there and the license plate of his car. Everybody's looking for him, boss. I left a uniform to watch his apartment building, and we've got somebody down at Hoops. Apparently, Wyatt also does fill-in shifts at Va Bene, so we're watching there, too. As soon as we spot him, we'll bring him in. I got Judge Edblad to do a specific order for a GSR test. If we can establish that he fired a weapon, that should be enough to hold him over while we look for more evidence."

"That's good work, Max," Stride said. Then he called to Cat and jabbed a finger at her. "Until we find this guy, I don't want you leaving the house."

Cat shrugged. "Whatever."

He was treating her like a child again. For a few minutes the previous day, he'd talked to her like a real person. A woman, an adult, who was smart and sensitive and sexual. But not anymore.

"I bought a security system," Stride added. "We'll have motion-sensitive cameras on the front and back doors."

"Is that for him or for me?" Cat asked sullenly.

Her comment cast a pall of uncomfortable silence over the room. Stride didn't answer, and his face showed no apology. Cat shot a look at Serena, asking her to stand up for her, but Serena was in mother mode now.

"It's only until we have Wyatt in custody," she said to Cat. "We're trying to lock him up. Not you."

"Right."

Stride bulldozed over her unhappiness. "Is that everything, Max? Are we done?"

"Yes, sir. For now."

The meeting broke up, and everyone began to disperse. A few of them looked over at Cat and then looked quickly away. She expected something from Brayden, a smile, a glance, anything to acknowledge that things had changed between them, but he turned his back and headed for the front door without a word.

Cat refused to let him walk away from her. Not like that.

"*Brayden*."

The young cop stopped. He glanced at Stride, then headed across the room toward Cat. He made sure no one else was in earshot around them, but he also kept a safe distance, which matched the distance that she saw in his eyes.

"I can't talk, Cat," he said in a clipped voice. "I have to help Stride with the security cameras."

"That's it? That's all you have to say to me?"

"I'm sorry."

"Well, are you going to tell me if you're okay?"

"I'm fine," Brayden replied. "You don't need to be concerned. They patched me up and gave me an aspirin. That's all I needed."

Cat stood up from the window seat, and Brayden jumped backward as if she'd stepped out of the infectious disease ward. She kept her voice low. "I want to talk about what happened between us."

"Not now."

"Why, is this conversation going to take long, Brayden? I'm not an idiot. Obviously, you're going to tell me it was a mistake, a moment of weakness, you never should have let it happen. Right? How hard is that to say?"

"Cat, please."

"I *know* you liked it. I could feel it."

"Later. We'll talk about this later."

"Does Stride know?" she asked. "Did you tell him?"

"No."

"Well, I'm not going to tell him, either, if that's what you're worried about. I'm not going to get you fired."

"I'm not worried about that," he replied.

"Are you still my babysitter? Or did you make up an excuse to get out of it?"

Brayden took a step closer. His strength gave out a kind of aura that wrapped itself around her. "Stride gave me a chance to bail on this assignment. I said no, I wanted to keep going."

"Because you want to be with me?"

He ran his hands back through his hair and left it messy. He had the look of a man desperately searching for control. She'd seen that look on men's faces before, and they never found what they wanted. "Because I want to keep you safe. But there have to be ground rules, Cat. What happened between us can't happen again. If you can't accept that, then I'll ask someone else to take over. You're right, the kiss was a mistake. A huge mistake. That's just reality. My job is to protect you, and I can't do that if I lose my focus."

"Do I make you lose your focus, Brayden?"

He didn't answer, but she stared into his eyes and saw what she was looking for. He wanted her. Then he shook himself and broke the spell.

"I have to go," he said.

* * * * *

Colleen Hunt was so caught up in the sketch she was drawing that she didn't hear the knocking on her apartment door. When it stopped, and then started again, she finally looked up. The knock wasn't the big, confident pounding that Curt usually made when he came to pick her up. This was a nervous little scratching, like a stray dog begging to be let in out of the cold.

She put her sketch pad on the coffee table and went to the door, swaying a little as she did. Her feet were bare on the linoleum. She wore a knee length yellow wrap dress with a lily of the valley design. She was smoking her second joint, which gave her dreamy, staring eyes and a wicked little smile. Curt said she was at her prettiest when she had a post-weed glow. Colleen liked the confident feeling it gave her, as if she could get whatever she wanted. Her artwork was best when she was high, too.

"Who is it?" she asked.

A panicked, barely audible voice hissed back. "It's Wyatt."

Colleen hesitated, then opened the door a few inches. "What are *you* doing here?"

"Can I come in?"

"I don't think that's a good idea."

"*Please*, Colleen."

"I think you should go. I know you're a perv, Wyatt."

"Oh, man, not you, too. I'm not! I didn't do anything! The police searched my apartment, and they're trying to arrest me. A friend called from Va Bene. The cops are over there. Hoops, too. And there's a squad car across the street from the building. I had to sneak in through the back. I don't even want to go upstairs to my place, because someone might be inside. Just a few minutes? Please, Colleen, I need to think!"

She sighed and opened the door wider, and Wyatt came inside like a freight train careening off the tracks. He went to the blinds and peered outside, then backed away from the window. He sat down on the sofa but didn't stay there for more than a few seconds before he stood up again. He slipped his orange bandanna off his head and twisted it nervously between his hands.

"Jeez, Wyatt, chill," Colleen told him. She walked to the sofa and plucked her joint out of a heavy glass ashtray she'd sculpted in high school. "You want a puff? You need to relax."

He sat down again. "No. I can't do that now. I told you what's going on! It's nuts! I don't know what to do!"

"Talk to the police," Colleen replied.

"And tell them what? Do you know what they think I did? They think I shot a cop!"

"Did you?"

"No! I swear, no! I don't understand why any of this is happening to me!"

Colleen sat down next to him on the sofa. Wyatt was a wreck. She handed him a tissue to wipe his eyes and blow the snot from his nose. He hadn't showered, and he smelled. His sunburnt cheeks looked extra-pink, and she could see all of the tiny blood vessels. He tugged on his dreadlocks as if he were about to wrap the ropes around his throat. She smiled an airy, weedy smile at him, and her dark eyes sucked him in and calmed him down. She put a hand on his knee.

"Listen, Wyatt. There's no use pretending. I saw your pervy pics."

"What are you *talking* about?"

"The Amazon box you keep you under your bed. Cat and I went into your apartment. She found the box where you keep your stash, the one with all the pics. The evidence was all there. All the times you followed her. All the times you hung around outside her window. All those pictures you took of her naked. It was really creepy. And the gun, too. It was in the box. Is that the gun you shot the cop with?"

"I didn't do that! I don't even own a gun!"

"Well, what do you want me to say? We saw it, Wyatt."

"It's not mine!" he insisted. "There's no box! I don't have any box under my bed. There are no pics, no gun. This is a nightmare. Jesus!"

Colleen sucked in smoke from the joint between her fingers, and closed her eyes. "You're so tense. Come on, relax. Get high with me."

"Are you crazy? Not now!"

"Get high with me, and then we can fuck."

"What? What about Curt?"

"Oh, who cares about Curt? I broke it off with him."

"You did? When? Why?"

She shrugged. "I don't need him anymore. Come on, I'm horny, let's do it. I know that's what you want."

"You. Are. Nuts. I swear. You're out of your mind. I never should have listened to you. I wish you'd never told me about Cat."

"Me?" Colleen asked, as the corner of her lips bent curiously upward. "What on earth are you talking about?"

"What am I—" Wyatt began, his face a mask of incomprehension. "Come on, Colleen. This was all you. You told me about this incredible girl who was on the cover of *People* and how I should try to meet her. You said you and Curt could work it out for me."

Colleen blinked, and each blink felt slow in front of her eyes. "Wow, is that the story you're going to tell the police? Because they really aren't going to believe that."

"It's not a story. It's the truth!"

She shook her head carefully back and forth. "That's not how I remember it. I remember you had a copy of that magazine in your apartment, and you were going on and on to me about how amazing this girl was and how you absolutely had to meet her. Honestly, it was a little weird, Wyatt. It felt a little off."

"*What?*"

Colleen leaned forward and whispered. She licked his ear while she did. "But you're right, you know. You have good taste. Cat *is* the most beautiful girl ever."

Wyatt sprang off the sofa. He yanked at his beard with one hand as he paced. "What the hell is wrong with you today?"

"Nothing is wrong with me. I'm happy. I'm getting everything I want."

Colleen stared at Wyatt through a mellow haze. She got off the sofa and did a little pirouette on the floor, and then she picked up the heavy ashtray from the coffee table and held it up so that the colors shone. "I made this in high school. Isn't it pretty? It was supposed to be a gift. I made it for someone in my math class that I had this *huge* crush on. But I was too shy in those days to give it to them. I'm much better now."

"You're out of control. You need to come down." Then he stopped, as if a new thought had popped into his head. "Hey, wait a minute. How did you and Cat get into my apartment?"

"What do you mean?"

"You said you and Cat went into my apartment, and Cat found a box under my bed. How the heck did you get in?"

Colleen giggled. "I have a key, silly."

"What? No, you don't."

"Sure, I do. You gave me one."

"I gave you a key so you could wait for a delivery, but then you gave it back to me."

She laughed dismissively and waved her hand through the air. "Oh, that! I made a copy of the key before I gave it back to you. I figured it would come in handy someday. And I was right, it sure did."

She laughed again, watching Wyatt struggle to figure it all out. He was so stupid! So stupid and slow! But even dumb boys caught on eventually. Wyatt's face got this wonderful, horrified look as he put the pieces together of what she was saying. He glanced down at the coffee table and saw her sketch pad lying there, and Colleen just laughed and laughed as Wyatt picked it up and saw the sketch she'd drawn, the erotic, beautiful sketch of Cat in the nude. Just a few lines and shadows capturing the love of Colleen's life. The girl she'd been obsessed with for years.

Lines and shadows drawn with the fine tip of a lime-green marker.

Wyatt ran for the door, but she'd expected that. She was waiting for it. She swung the heavy ashtray right into the back of his head and dropped him where he stood. He crumpled face down on the linoleum and moaned. He was dazed but not unconscious. Blood oozed through his dreadlocks, as if all the snakes had just enjoyed a meal. Languidly, as if she were walking on a cloud, Colleen went into her bedroom and retrieved the Amazon box that she'd put back under her own bed. If she'd had time, she would have caressed the photos, the way she did every day. But that could wait. She got the gun. She'd reloaded it after the morning at Hawk Ridge. She took a pillow from her bed, too, white and soft, filled with goose feathers.

Wyatt had made it to his hands and knees and was trying to crawl away, but she put a foot on his ass and pushed, and he collapsed back to his stomach.

Colleen wandered to her apartment door, opened it, and looked outside. The hallway was empty and quiet. No one was around. She closed the door again and took her phone and cued a song to her speakers. "Stray Cat Strut." The name made her laugh. She turned up the volume as high as it could go and began singing along. Then she knelt beside Wyatt and put the pillow over the back of his head and shoved the barrel of the gun deep into the goose down.

"Meow," Colleen said.

She fired into Wyatt's head.

26

"Kathy Ford?" Maggie said, when the woman answered the door. "My name is Sergeant Maggie Bei with the Duluth Police. I believe you talked to Lieutenant Stride and Detective Serena Stride yesterday, and I was hoping you could answer a few more questions for me."

The woman smiled politely at her. "Well, look at me. I'm so popular with the police all of a sudden. My neighbors are going to start to wonder."

"This won't take long," Maggie told her.

"Is this still about what happened at the house? About the party?"

"In part."

Kathy frowned. "Well, I told Jonathan that I didn't want to get involved. I still don't. I'm afraid there's no gold star for trying to do the right thing anymore. If you get involved in a political controversy, it's like an invitation to have your life ruined. It's bad enough what they do to victims who come forward, but if you're a witness, you can expect the same treatment. I was sort of a wild child back then, Sergeant. There are plenty of things from those days that I wouldn't want to see out in public."

"I understand that," Maggie replied, "and if a thirty-year-old accusation were the only thing at stake here, I might not need to bother you. But there's more. I'm investigating a murder."

"I don't see how I can help you with that," Kathy said, but then she sighed and opened the door. "However, I'll tell you whatever I can. Come on in."

"Thank you."

"You're about to be assaulted, by the way."

"What?"

"My dog," the woman said with a smile.

Maggie followed Kathy Ford into the house's living room, which faced the street. The woman was right about the assault. A golden retriever galloped into the room and greeted Maggie with a wildly wagging tail, and she was forced to spend several minutes on the floor petting the dog. When she was finally able to take a seat on a sofa and wipe the slobber from her pants, she checked out the open floor plan of the Ford house. The living room and dining room led directly into the kitchen, and the kitchen gave way to a family room at the back. She tried to imagine the space filled with drunk young people and the walls shaking to the beat of Aerosmith.

From where she sat, she could also see stairs with worn carpeting leading to the second floor bedrooms. That was where Devin and Andrea would have slipped away.

And then what happened?

That was the question.

"The house hasn't changed," Kathy said, reading her mind. "Even the furniture was the same when I moved back in after my parents died. I'm trying to remodel, but my budget doesn't go very far."

"You grew up here?"

"Yes."

"Are you married, Ms. Ford? Do you have kids?"

"I was married for a long time, but not anymore. I have a son and a daughter. They're both in college now."

"I understand you knew Lieutenant Stride's first wife, Cindy."

"I did. Cindy and I were good friends a long, long time ago. It was shocking to lose her so young. I'm glad to see Jonathan has bounced back from the loss. Some people never get over those things."

"It took him a long time," Maggie said, without going into detail.

"His new wife is beautiful."

"Yes, she is."

"Well, how can I help you?" Kathy asked. "You said you're investigating a murder, and I assume you mean that reporter whose body was found recently. As I say, I really don't know what I can tell you. I told Jonathan that none of the reporters who were looking into the allegations about Devin ever came to my door. That includes the man who was killed. I never talked to anybody."

"I realize that, but I'm pretty sure that *someone* talked to Ned Baer—someone who had actual knowledge about the party that happened here. Whoever it is may know something that would be helpful in our investigation."

Kathy's dog curled up around her feet, and she reached down and scratched his head. "I'm afraid I have no idea who it could be."

"Well, the rumors about Devin Card were big news seven years ago," Maggie said. "I assume there must have been a fair amount of speculation among people who were kids in Duluth in those days. Do you remember talking to any old friends about what happened? Did anyone reach out to you—not reporters, but people who were in your circle from back then?"

Kathy pursed her lips as she thought about it. "A few, yes. Several of us reconnected. Everyone was trading guesses about the identity of the woman who'd made the accusation and debating whether she was telling the truth."

"Did anyone mention the party here at your house?"

"No. I was paying attention for that, believe me. It didn't come up."

"Did you tell anyone about your own suspicions? About what you— discovered—in the bedroom upstairs?"

She shook her head. "Not a soul."

"You kept the story to yourself?"

"Yes. As I told you, I didn't want to get involved. Nobody knew."

"Do you remember talking about it with anyone else over the years?"

"I'm sure I didn't. I had no reason to. I certainly wasn't going to tell my parents that I'd allowed a crazy party in the house while they were gone. And when I found blood on the sheets, I didn't think that anyone had been raped. I just assumed some high school virgin wasn't a virgin anymore. It was only when I heard the allegations about Devin that I began to think—well, that something else could have happened. It seemed like more than a coincidence."

Maggie glanced at the stairs. "Do you mind if I see the bedroom where it happened?"

Kathy shrugged. "If you'd like."

They got up from their seats in the living room, and when they reached the stairs, Maggie looked back to check the angles of sight. The stairs were visible to anyone sitting where she'd been on the sofa, but they would have been invisible to people who were deeper in the house. If Ned Baer had a witness who actually saw Devin and Andrea go upstairs together, that person would have been close by.

"Was it dark?" Maggie asked.

"What do you mean?"

"The party. Do you remember, were the lights on or off?"

"It was a party. People were making out. You know what all the songs say. Turn the lights down low."

Kathy led the way upstairs into a master bedroom that was small compared to what would be found in newer homes. Maggie eyed the queen-sized bed against the wall and the doorway to a small bathroom. On the left side wall, a doorway led outside to a small balcony, and she could see the roof of the garage below it.

"I suppose it would have been dark up here, too," Maggie said.

"I assume so. The party was late."

"Is the layout of the furniture basically the same as it was back then?"

"Basically. My parents had their bed on the same wall."

"You told Stride that you found the door to the balcony open? And someone had thrown up in the sink?"

"Yes. It was pretty disgusting. And like I said, there was blood and semen in the sheets. Not a lot, but enough to give me a clue of what happened."

"But you never told anyone what you found?"

"No. Literally the first people I told were Stride and his wife yesterday."

"Were there any rumors after the party? Was anyone talking about assault or rape?"

"No, I never heard anything like that," Kathy replied. "I'd remember, given what I saw. The word *rape* would have set off alarm bells with me. I'd like to think I would have talked to somebody."

Maggie shook her head and tried to figure it out. No one else that Stride and Serena had interviewed had talked about this particular party. Kathy Ford was the only one, and she'd kept quiet about it for three decades. And yet *somebody knew*. Somebody had talked to Ned Baer and told him what they'd seen. But who?

And why were they staying anonymous?

She realized that she had to say the name. There was no other way to learn more.

"Ms. Ford, do you remember a girl named Andrea Forseth back then? She would have been a few years younger than you. She was still in high school."

"I don't remember her, but the name Forseth? Are you talking about Denise's sister?"

"Yes."

"Well, I knew Denise had a sister, but I couldn't have told you her name, and I doubt I would have been able to pick her out in a crowd."

"Do you happen to remember whether Andrea was at that party?"

"I have no idea. You'd have to talk to her or Denise."

"Denise says that Andrea *was* there."

"Well, if she says so, I assume it's true. I told you, there were dozens of people in the house, and I was drunk, along with everyone else. I didn't recognize half the people who were there. When a big party crawl's going on, strangers show up out of nowhere. Word gets around."

"Sure."

"Why are you asking me about Denise's sister?" Then the woman stopped. Her mouth fell open, and she covered it with her hand. "Oh, no, was it *her*? Is she the one who was assaulted?"

Maggie said nothing, but her silence was as good as an admission.

Kathy wandered to the balcony door and opened it and stepped outside. She looked shaken by the news. Maggie joined her, and they stood in the warm air above the garage.

"I'm so sorry to hear that," Kathy went on. "I had no idea. I mean, it's not like I even knew the girl, but it's different when you can put a name to it, you know?"

"Yes, I understand."

"Denise never said anything to me."

"We don't think she knew, either," Maggie said.

"I feel so bad."

"Were you and Denise close friends?"

Kathy shrugged. "Oh, no, I wouldn't say close, but we were part of a group that hung out together. I mean, now that I think back, I'm sure I met her sister a few times. Shy, blond, that's all I remember."

"Do you think any of your other friends would have known Andrea better?"

"I doubt it. I'm sorry. A difference of three or four years in age doesn't sound like much now, but when you're young, it's practically another generation."

"Of course."

"I wish I could be more help, but if Denise doesn't remember, I can't think of anyone else who would."

Maggie nodded. "Well, I appreciate your time, Ms. Ford."

She turned for the door that led back to the bedroom, but as she did, Kathy put a hand on her shoulder. She still looked chastened by what had happened in her house. "I'm sorry, Sergeant, there's one other person you might want to talk to. He knew Denise well, so I suppose that means he'd know her sister, too. Probably better than any of our girlfriends, actually. He might remember something."

"Who's that?" Maggie asked.

"His name's Adam. Adam Halka. He owns a motel near the freeway."

Maggie froze where she was. "*Adam Halka* knew Denise? And you think he knew Andrea, too?"

"Well, I assume so. Adam would have been at Denise's house all the time, so he must have known her sister, too."

"Why was Adam at Denise's house?"

"He was her boyfriend," Kathy said. "They were hot and heavy for years, going back to high school. Most of us figured they'd get married after college, but Denise was the restless type. She dropped out of UMD after a couple of years and decided to join the Air Force instead."

"Do you remember if Adam was at the party that night?" Maggie asked.

"I have no idea. But let me put it this way, I hope not."

"Why do you say that?"

"Didn't Stride tell you about Denise and Peter Stanhope having sex? That would have driven Adam crazy if he saw it happen. Although who knows, maybe that's one of the reasons Denise did what she did. To shove it in Adam's face."

"Are you saying Denise cheated on Adam at the party?" Maggie asked.

Kathy shook her head. "Well, technically, no. Denise was a free bird at that point. You see, we were at a concert earlier in the evening, and Denise and Adam had a big fight. *Big* fight."

"What were they fighting about?"

"Denise was going into the service in a couple of days, so she told Adam they were over. She broke it off with him right there in front of everybody. He was mad about it. Seriously mad."

27

"You again," Denise said, seeing Stride on the doorstep at Andrea's house. "If you're looking for my sister, she's not here."

"Actually, I have a few more questions for you," Stride replied. "I stopped by your place and found out you were here. It's better if Andrea doesn't hear this conversation, so it's just as well that she's out."

"Interesting. Well, come on back. I imagine you know the way."

She led him through the house that he knew too well. The strange thing was that he could hardly remember himself *in* this place, other than a few isolated moments like photographs. He could remember Andrea. He could remember the house itself. He knew he'd lived here for three years, getting up every morning, eating, reading books, going to sleep in bed next to his wife, but he had no actual memories of doing any of those things. His time here had left no footprints.

Denise sat at the kitchen table with a beer in front of her. Before sitting down, he looked around the room, still trying to remember any moment or conversation with his ex-wife that had lingered in his head. Any image of himself with her that was meaningful enough to remember. But he had nothing. He went over to the suncatchers on the window and traced the outline of one with his fingers.

"They're lovely, aren't they?" Denise said.

"They are."

"Andrea tells me they come from a secret admirer. She doesn't know who."

He looked at her. "What?"

"She says they arrive anonymously. I told her it's a little strange."

"That is strange," Stride agreed.

"Well, she says it's probably a former student. I get the feeling she sort of likes the mystery of it."

Stride sat down at the table. "I want to talk about the night when Andrea was assaulted."

Denise swigged her bottle of beer. "I've told you everything I remember."

"Actually, you left something out," Stride said.

"Oh? What?"

"Adam Halka."

Denise stopped with the bottle at her lips. She put it back down on the table. "Ah. Adam."

"One of my police colleagues talked to a friend of yours from back then. She said you and Adam were an item."

"Oh, more than an item," Denise acknowledged. "Adam and I started dating when I was a sophomore in high school. He was my first … well, my first everything. First boyfriend, first lover. I assume I was his, too. You never know with guys, but I don't remember him being very experienced. When you're that age, you throw the word *love* around pretty easily, but Adam and I thought we were in love. We were joined at the hip throughout high school. After graduation, we got engaged. I went to college, and Adam didn't, but my plan was to marry him after I got my degree. Ah well, best-laid plans. Over the next couple of years, I came to the conclusion that I didn't like school, didn't like Duluth, didn't like my parents, and didn't like Adam."

"Any particular reason?"

Denise shrugged. "When you're twenty, do you need a reason?"

"I suppose not."

"Why do you care about Adam?" she asked.

"Because I hear you broke up with him on the night that Andrea was assaulted," Stride said.

Denise pushed the bottle around the table with her thumb. "Yeah, I think that's right. I guess it was the same night. So?"

"So that detail was worth mentioning," Stride replied. "He wasn't on your list of people we should talk to, but if anyone is likely to remember that particular night, it's Adam Halka. That was the night his fiancée dumped him. People don't forget things like that."

"We were kids. I doubt he's still pining for me."

"When did you last talk to him?"

"Adam? I don't know. It's been ages. I've been in the Air Force or in Miami for most of my life. Whenever I came back home for a visit, it's not like I made it a priority to look up my old boyfriend. I think I bumped into him when I came back for my twentieth reunion at Denfeld, but that was already more than a decade ago. I don't think we exchanged more than two words. Neither one of us was feeling nostalgic."

"Did you talk to him seven years ago when Andrea made the accusations against Devin Card?"

"No. Why would I? Andrea was keeping it a secret."

Stride nodded. "Tell me what happened with Adam that night."

"There's not much to tell. A whole bunch of us went to a concert. I broke up with Adam while we were there. I'm not proud of how I did it. I knew I was going to end it with him, because I was heading off to the service in a few days. But I figured I'd do it when we were alone. I didn't really plan to do it in front of all our friends. It just worked out that way. He started pressuring me about long-distance and saying why not get married before I left, and finally, I just dropped the bomb. I said it was over. I gave him the ring back. I think I may have said something about him putting it back in the Cracker Jack box where he found it. I was a real peach back then, I'll tell you."

"How did Adam react?" Stride asked.

"How do you think? Not well."

"What did he do?"

"He stormed off. I don't know where he went. He didn't come back to our seats."

"Did you see him again that night? Did he go on the party crawl?"

"I remember seeing him a couple of times, but we didn't talk. He was pissed."

"How pissed?"

"Furious. I can't blame him. I was a bitch."

Stride leaned across the table. "So the party where you 'put on a show' with Peter Stanhope. Was Adam there to see it?"

Her face darkened. "I don't remember."

"Denise," he murmured, because he could hear the lie in her voice.

She drank more beer, and then she got up from the table, obviously upset with herself. "Okay. Yeah. He was there. Why the hell do you think I was willing to do it, Stride? It wasn't just for the money. I wanted to shove it in Adam's face that I was done with him. I wanted to humiliate him. I told you, I was a bitch. I was also drunk and probably stoned."

"So the man you just dumped watched you have sex with another man in front of all your friends?"

"That's right," Denise snapped.

"Was Andrea there? Did she see it, too?"

Her chin sank into her neck. "Yeah, she did. I didn't know that. She just told me about it. Apparently, that's why she started hooking up with Devin, if you want the truth. She was jealous of me. She wanted to be just like her big sister. Like I'm such a great role model."

"What about Adam?" Stride asked.

"What about him?"

"Did he know Andrea?"

"Of course, he did."

"Did he see her at the party?"

Denise shrugged. "I have no idea. You'd have to ask him. Why, do you think Adam is the one who saw Devin assaulting her?"

"No, that's not what I'm thinking," Stride said.

"Then what—" Denise began, but she stopped in midsentence. Her lower lip quivered as she understood Stride's implication. Her eyes widened with a look of horror. "*Shit.* Oh, no, that can't be. Not Adam."

"Where's Andrea?" Stride asked. "I need to talk to her."

Denise sat down at the table again, as if it was too much effort to stand. Her whole body was trembling now. "She went to the DECC. She's going public. She's planning to confront Devin at the town hall."

* * * * *

Devin Card studied the camera feed from inside the convention center. Early attendees had begun to wander into the ballroom, and in two hours, when the town hall began, more than a thousand people would be squeezed inside, with hundreds more in the overflow space. There were a few chairs for disabled guests, but otherwise, the venue was standing room only. The people coming in now were the party faithful, invited to provide him with a cheering section. They'd be crowded near the front. But others would be there, too; the protesters always showed up, waving signs and jeering. The same posters drew his eyes at every event, paid for and distributed by his political opponents.

Rapist!

Resign!

A wide stage had been assembled at the front of the ballroom, adjacent to the arc of windows that overlooked the bay and the city's lift bridge. The microphone was there, where Card would face the crowd, with staff and security pushed out of sight to either side of the stage. It would be just him alone under the hot glow of the overhead lights. Cameras would be recording everything, taking note of every question and answer, every reaction, every word.

"This is going to be ugly," Peter Stanhope murmured as he stood next to him.

"Politics is always ugly."

"This is worse. It's politics and rape. That's a volatile combination. I was outside earlier, and it's getting pretty hot on the street. I'd feel better if we were screening people for weapons."

Card shrugged. "No. If I look scared, I lose."

"If someone shoots you, you lose, too."

"I'm not worried about that. Right now, I'm more worried about the woman. The media are all saying she's going to be there. Do you think it's true? Or is it a hoax?"

"I can't be sure. No one is releasing her name yet. This may just be a strategy to unnerve you before the event."

"Have your contacts inside the police told you anything?"

Peter shook his head. "They're playing it close to the vest."

"I know we said it would be better if she came forward, but not this way."

"Well, I'm sure she realizes that, too. If we know who she is in advance, we can dig up information and get it out to the press. If she stands up and starts accusing you here, she gets the first news cycle all to herself."

"Who the hell is she?" Card asked, shaking his head.

"She could be anyone. A girl with a grudge against you? We weren't exactly choir boys back then."

"No. We weren't." Card turned away from the cameras. "You know, you should have told me about Ned Baer seven years ago, Peter. About meeting him. About him looking for a bribe."

"You were better off not knowing," Peter replied. "If anything went wrong, I needed you to be able to say honestly that I hadn't told you a word about it."

Card put a strong hand on Peter's shoulder, which he did whenever he wanted to remind Peter who held the real power between the two of them. "We said we weren't going to talk about this, but I have to know. Were you involved in his death? Did you kill him? Or did you have him killed?"

"Is that really the kind of person you think I am, Devin?"

"I think you're loyal. I think you're the most loyal friend I've ever had."

"I am," Peter replied, "but I wouldn't take loyalty that far. Not even for you. I had nothing to do with his murder."

"I'm pleased to hear it."

Peter said nothing else, and the Congressman waited with curious anticipation on his face. "You're not going to ask me the same thing?" Card asked finally.

"No. I'm not."

"Because you're afraid of the answer?"

"Because I don't want to make you lie to me," Peter said.

"Well, I'm not lying. I didn't kill him, either. I had nothing to do with it."

"I never thought you did, but I've always been willing to let you have your secrets, Devin."

Card glanced at the video feed again. "Secrets like this woman?"

"You tell me. We've already admitted who we were back then. Sometimes things went too far at the parties."

"I have no recollection of doing anything like what she said," Card told him. "I truly don't believe I would have been capable of that."

Peter heard the subtle change in his story, the lack of an actual denial. "I wouldn't phrase it like that out there."

"I know."

"We can try to block her, you know. We can screen questions, try to figure out who she is."

Card shook his head. "You know that will never work."

"This is an ambush, Devin. You won't see it coming until it hits you. What are you going to do?"

"There's only one thing I can do," Card replied. "I have to let her talk."

28

Serena found Alice Frye where she always was, in the garden behind her house on Morgan Street in the flat lands above the city. Birches and maples made a ring around the yard, creating a private nook where Alice tended to her herbs and flowers. She had a small cottage behind her house, where Serena had seen her every other month for the last few years.

Alice was a therapist, well into her seventies. She was a pixie-sized widow with short dark hair and an endless supply of adrenaline. She had a deep reservoir of sexual anecdotes that always sounded shocking coming out of her sweet elderly mouth. Serena had heard more slang words for male genitalia in Alice's cottage than on the streets of Las Vegas. For all that, Alice was also smart, sensitive, and not shy about pointing out uncomfortable truths. Serena liked her.

She had tried therapy several times in her past, mostly with bad results. She didn't like to trust anyone with her secrets. However, after she and Jonny had broken up in the wake of his affair with Maggie, she'd tried again, at the suggestion of a woman she was living with in Grand Rapids at the time. The woman had recommended Alice, and Alice had kicked off their first session in the little cottage by asking flatly, "Okay, my dear, who put whose cock where?"

Right then, Serena knew the two of them were going to get along.

She'd told Jonny very little about her time in therapy. She'd never suggested that he join her. The sessions were for her and her alone. She'd talked a lot about him in the early days, but very quickly, she'd gone on to other parts of her life. Alice had taken her through her teenage years in Phoenix. They'd talked about Maggie. They'd talked about Cat and Serena's new role as a mother. With Alice, Serena had found a way to confront many of her demons. Even though she felt more in control of her problems, she still liked the validation of coming to Alice's place every other month, even if all they did was share stories about their sex lives.

Alice looked up with surprise as Serena came around the back of the house. She was on her knees in her flower garden, talking to the purple hydrangeas that had won ribbons at the state fair.

"Serena," Alice said, looking apologetic. "Did we have an appointment? I don't have anything on my calendar."

Serena smiled and shook her head. "No, I just stopped by."

"Is everything all right?"

"Yes, things are fine. I was hoping to get your opinion about something. It's related to a case I'm working on."

The therapist put down her gardening tools, stripped off her gloves, and rubbed her hands together. "Oh, I get to play Dr. Watson today. How exciting. Well, come on, come on, let's get to it."

Alice sprang to her feet with an agility that belied her age. She wiped the dirt from her knee pads and practically bounded in her muddy boots toward the little cottage near the trees. She unlocked the door and let the two of them inside, threw open all of the windows, and plopped into a wheely chair at her desk. By habit, Serena took her usual place on the sofa. The cottage was small, barely twelve square feet, decorated more like a children's playhouse than a therapist's office.

"Your husband has been in the news lately," Alice said, putting half-glasses on her face and fiddling with a shiny gray stone on her desk. She had a collection of polished rocks that she gave to patients to hold during their sessions, all inscribed with different words of encouragement. *Determination. Grace. Love. God. Memory.*

"Yes, he's in a difficult situation," Serena admitted.

"So I gather. Is he talking to you about it?"

"What do you think?"

"Stride? I imagine he's closed up like an oyster working on his pearl. Which means you're going to have to go in and pull him out."

"I know."

"When did the two of you last have sex?"

"A couple of weeks ago."

"Well, that's not acceptable," Alice snapped. "Who was on top?"

Serena chuckled. She was accustomed to Alice's explicit interrogations about the details of her lovemaking. "I think it was me."

"You need to be willing to use that lovely back of yours sometimes."

"I do, Alice. I promise."

"You don't always have to control everything, you know."

"I know. This isn't actually what I wanted to talk to you about. I'm not here about myself."

Alice delivered a pointed stare above the rims of her glasses. "You came to talk to *me*, Serena, not anybody else. So let's not pretend you have nothing to say about your own life. You're concerned about Stride, which means you're concerned about you *and* Stride."

Serena shrugged. "Okay, you're right. I'm worried about old habits. The easy thing for Jonny is not to talk, and I'm the same way. Sometimes I think he talks to Cat more readily than to me. Actually, it makes me a little jealous. I had a conversation with Maggie yesterday, too, and she told me Stride was burned out and not happy with himself. I told her she was wrong, but you know what? She's right. And it *really* pisses me off that she noticed it before I did."

Alice handed her the stone that she'd been rolling around between her thin fingers. The word inscribed on it was *Honesty*.

"Now we're getting somewhere," Alice said.

"I suppose I'll get a bill for this visit."

"No charge if you tell me more about the sex," she said with a wink.

"Send me a bill," Serena replied with a chuckle.

"All right, all right, I'll stop prying. So what's the issue today? What do you need my professional opinion on?"

"This is delicate," Serena replied.

"Ah, so we're back to sex."

"Sort of. There's a woman who has made an accusation of rape. It's an incident that occurred almost thirty years ago when she was a teenager."

"I assume we're talking about the Devin Card story," Alice replied.

"I can't say yes or no, but draw your own conclusions."

"Okay. As we talk about this hypothetical situation, would it be safe for me to rely on the details of that accusation as they've appeared in the media?"

"Yes."

"And you want to know whether this accusation can be considered credible despite how long ago this was," she said.

"You are too damn smart for your own good, Alice."

The therapist winked and picked up another rock from her desk, with the word *Intelligence* etched into the stone. "Tell me what you know. Have you talked to this woman?"

"Yes. She acknowledges that she was drunk the night of the assault. She says she threw up and may have passed out. We've been able to identify the likely time and place where it happened, but she can't verify those details herself. However, she is absolutely certain that she did *not* consent, that she *was* raped, and that she knows the identity of the man who did it."

"And you want to know whether this is a plausible set of circumstances?" Alice asked.

"Yes."

"Well, what do you think?"

"I think it's very plausible," Serena said.

"You would be correct. It's perfectly reasonable that a victim would have no clue about the time or place of an assault, or even that she would get many of the accompanying details wrong, particularly if alcohol or drugs are involved. But she could easily still remember being raped and who did it. In fact, I'd be surprised if she didn't."

Serena nodded. "Now comes the tough part."

"Namely?"

"Is it also plausible that she could have made a mistake?"

Alice drummed two of her fingers against her chin. "About which part?"

"Any of it."

"Well, about whether she was raped at all? That's extremely unlikely. Some women do *manufacture* stories of assault, but that's an entirely different set of circumstances and a very different pathology. If you believe she's sincere about her memories, then I would conclude that yes, she almost certainly was raped. As to whether she denied consent? That's much harder to know without context, and both the man and the woman might remember it very differently. On the other hand, if she specifically remembers using words like *No* and *Stop*, then I suspect it's likely that she did so, even if the man didn't hear it that way."

"And what about the identity of the man who did it?" Serena said.

Alice's face twisted into an expression of reluctant discomfort. "Oh, Serena. This is very difficult ground."

"I know."

"The overwhelming majority of victims don't make mistakes about who assaulted them. It's not a function of how much time has passed. The idea that a victim could be certain about the identity of her attacker decades later—while blocking out many of the other details—doesn't strike me as unusual in the least."

"But it does happen."

"Yes. It does happen. There have been instances where a victim was *absolutely certain* of her assailant's identity, and eventually, it turned out that she was mistaken. DNA proved it. In fact, certainty can be your worst enemy. It can feed on itself, making you squash out your doubts because you want to believe in the truth of your memories. On the other hand, that's far more likely to happen with a *stranger*, not someone the victim knows. In other words, if this woman actually knew Devin Card and specifically remembered going upstairs with him, I find it extremely unlikely that she made a mistake about that."

"Thank you, Alice," Serena said. "That's very helpful."

The therapist scooted her chair forward and leaned her elbows on her knees. "And yet you still think she made a mistake, don't you?"

"I really don't know. We've uncovered some evidence that someone else at the same party may have had a motive to assault her. It could have been an act of revenge against a girl who dumped him that night. And yet the victim knew this person, too, and his name never came up from her. She never mentioned him, never talked about seeing him there. If it was him, I can't believe she wouldn't have remembered. I don't see how she could have substituted someone else in her memory. It's hard for me to imagine a woman being wrong about that."

"Then what's your hesitation? I hope it's not that you think a man like Devin Card is incapable of behaving like that. Because we both know that isn't true. No man is truly the master of his dick, Serena. And it's not that I'm ganging up on Devin. In fairness, I believed the accusations against him seven years ago, but I voted for him anyway."

"Really?" Serena asked.

"Really. I had a client a few years ago who asked me if I thought it was possible to forgive every sin. I said not only was it possible, it was a human necessity. It doesn't mean we don't punish people for what they do, but we also have to accept that people grow and change. And that God's plan is infinitely more complex than we can understand."

"*Forgive every sin*," Serena said.

"Exactly."

"That's hard to do when it comes to rape."

Alice nodded. "Indeed. In fact, my client said the very same thing."

29

Curt sat next to Cat on Stride's sofa and sulked. His mouth was sunk into a permanent frown, and he'd barely said a word since he arrived. His legs were spread wide, showing off bony knees below his loose shorts. His long hair sat on his shoulders, limp and unwashed. With his body slumped, even his tattoos seemed to droop on his skin. He looked like a dog whose owner was away on a month-long vacation.

"Are you going to tell me what's wrong?" Cat asked.

"Nothing."

"It doesn't look like nothing."

"I'm fine."

"Do you want a drink? A beer or something?"

"No."

"Really? You don't want a drink, and you expect me to believe nothing's wrong?"

"Drop it, Kitty Cat."

Cat sighed loudly. When Curt got into one of his melancholy moods, he didn't do much more than grunt, and she'd learned over time to keep poking him until he opened up. Ironically, that always seemed to work with Stride, too, although he would have hated the comparison.

Outside, the early evening sky had turned dark, and none of the lights in the cottage were on, making it gloomy inside. Distant thunder rolled continuously, like a plane overhead making endless circles. The century-old walls rattled and shuddered. Cat could see a spatter of rain on the windows, and more was coming. A downpour.

"What's up with your Eyes on Duluth thing?" she asked. Then she giggled. "You know, the Big Dickes. Your Ferris wheel down in Canal Park."

"It's crap," Curt replied. "All my ideas are crap."

"Hey, don't say that. I like the idea. I think it's cool. You just need to get somebody with megabucks behind it."

Curt shrugged. "Don't lie to me. I'm not in the mood."

"I don't lie," Cat told him. "I mean, okay, I lie all the time. But not about this. I really think it's great."

"It's *stupid*."

Cat rolled her eyes. "Fine. Okay. Whatever. It's stupid. If that's what you want me to say, I'll say it. Is that the problem? You can't get anyone to buy your big Ferris wheel?"

Curt didn't say anything more, and Cat lost patience with his self-pity. She punched him in the shoulder, hard enough to make him flinch.

"Hey, you get that someone tried to kill me today, right?" she snapped, her voice rising. "Somebody unloaded a whole gun at me and Brayden, and he was *hit*. So how about you grow a pair and realize that I've got shit of my own to deal with. It's not all about you, Curt!"

That got through to him. His head turned slowly, and he focused his sad eyes on her. "Sorry, Kitty Cat. You're right. Are you okay?"

"No, I'm not okay. I'm seriously freaked."

"Yeah, I get that."

"Brayden was bleeding like crazy. I thought he was going to die."

"Shit. That's scary."

Cat glanced at the front door behind her to make sure Brayden was still outside. "We kissed."

"What?"

"Me and Brayden. We kissed."

Curt's eyes widened. "Well, that's not good."

"Why not?"

"He works for Stride. Plus, he's a lot older, right?"

"So what? He's the same age as you."

"Yeah, and if anything happened between us, Stride would kick the crap out of me. Assuming I was still alive after Serena got done with me."

She shrugged. "I don't care how old he is. I like Brayden. He makes me feel safe. And he's got this look in his eyes when he watches me, like he understands me. He gets why things are so hard for me. Not many people do."

"*I* understand you."

Cat thought about what to say, because she didn't want to hurt Curt's feelings. "No, you don't. You think you do, but you don't. I'm not trying to be a jerk, and you know I like you a lot, but you don't get who I am. You never did."

"Well, gee, thanks," he said bitterly.

"I'm sorry. It is what it is. You just can't relate. Look, it's not just you. Stride and Serena try, but they don't get me, either. I don't know how or why, but Brayden does. We've got a connection."

Curt picked up a paper clip from the coffee table and began playing with it between his fingers. His face still looked unhappy. "For what it's worth, I'm pretty sure he likes you, too."

"Really? He said that?"

"No, but he didn't need to say it out loud. Guys know the look. It's all over his face. Be careful, because if I can see it, Stride can, too, and he won't be happy."

"Thank you for telling me."

"You're right about me, you know. I don't get women at all. I never have. I suck at it."

"I wasn't trying to make you feel bad," Cat said.

"No, you nailed it. I'm a loser. Colly dumped me today."

Cat's mouth dropped open in surprise. Not hesitating, she reached out and pulled Curt into a tight hug. She knew this was the kind of blow that would shake him to his shoes. For all of his macho pretenses, Curt was a vulnerable little boy at heart.

"What happened?" Cat asked. "What did she say?"

"She called me this morning. Didn't even take five minutes. Said we were done."

"Did she say why?"

"She said it wasn't working out. She was bored."

"Bored? Really?" Cat frowned, because Curt was many things, but he was never boring. "Did you do something to upset her? Did you guys have a fight?"

"Nope. As far as I knew, everything was great."

She hesitated, biting her lip. "Do you think it could be somebody else?"

"I asked her that, and she ducked the question. That sure sounds like somebody else to me."

"Do you know who it could be?"

"No. It doesn't matter."

"Well, I'm really sorry, Curt. Honestly. You guys seemed good together."

"Yeah, I thought so, too. I mean, I know it hasn't been long, but I thought we had something. Hell, she really seemed like she was into me. Nine times out of ten, I have to make the first move, but she saw us talking at the spaghetti dinner and came over after. She said she went to school with you. Anyway, we started talking, and a couple of hours later, we were in bed at my place. It was amazing. I thought I'd hit the jackpot. And now we're over. One month together, and sayonara."

"Maybe she's just having a bad day," Cat said.

"It didn't sound like it."

"You should talk to her. Go over to her place."

"It won't make any difference."

"You want me to talk to her? Talk you up?"

Curt shook his head. "No, that's okay. I think I'm going to head out, actually. Not that I want to bail on you. I mean, I'll stay if you want me to."

"It's okay, Curt. Go."

"I just need to take a drive or something."

"I get it. If you need anything, call."

Cat leaned over and kissed his cheek, and he gave her a weak smile. She hated seeing Curt with his ego deflated, because he took it so hard. The two of them got up and hugged again, and then Cat walked him to the front door with her arm around his waist. They went outside, where Brayden leaned against the railing on the porch and studied his phone. The sky on the horizon was black, and Cat could see stabs of lightning over the bay water. The drizzle got harder.

"See ya, Kitty Cat," Curt mumbled, heading down the steps into the rain.

"Yeah, bye, Curt."

She watched him until he got into his car and headed down the Point toward the lift bridge. Even when he was gone, she didn't move from where she was. The storm rumbled closer, a shroud of dark, bubbled clouds. She was conscious of Brayden standing silently a few feet away. He'd put away his phone and was watching her, but she didn't look back at him. Without saying anything, she took a seat on one of the white Adirondack chairs, and Brayden sat down beside her. The wind was like a wave blowing up the street, tossing the trees.

"That was a quick visit," Brayden said eventually.

"Yeah."

"Everything okay?"

"Sure."

He squinted at the sky. "This is going to be a bad storm."

"Uh-huh."

"I like watching the storms."

"Me, too."

They were quiet for a while.

"Are you upset with me?" Brayden asked.

"No."

"Because you look upset."

"I'm not."

"Well, you're being so talkative, it's hard to tell."

Cat ignored his sarcasm. She pulled her knees up on the chair and wrapped her arms around them. Her voice was chilly. "I told Curt that you and I have a connection. I think you know that we do, but you're running away from it."

"I have a job to do."

"Does that mean you have to pretend not to feel anything for me?"

"It does sort of mean that, yes."

"What about when the job's done?" Cat asked.

"I'll cross that bridge later."

Cat shook her head. "Is it the age thing?"

"Partly. It's complicated."

"I don't know why age is a big deal. I'm young, but you know every-thing I've been through. That grew me up fast."

"I get that."

"Is it Stride? Does he scare you that much?"

"I'm not scared of Stride, Cat."

"Well, you can't be scared of me."

"Don't be so sure," Brayden told her with a smile. "I think you'd be surprised how many men find you absolutely terrifying."

"That's bullshit. Most men just want to have sex with me and then walk away. Is that what you want? Because I'm okay with that."

Brayden waited to reply until she turned and stared into his blue eyes. "You say things like that a lot, but I don't think you mean it. That's not the girl you are. Or who you want to be."

"You don't think so? Well, I'm telling you, I'm serious. I am. I'm going to go inside and take a shower now. You can join me if you want, and we can do whatever. It doesn't have to be anything more than that. It could be just like the kiss. We have sex, and then you pretend it didn't happen."

"That's not what I'm doing."

"Sure. Right."

"Look, I'm sorry, Cat. For a lot of things."

She pushed herself out of the chair and walked over to the railing. Rain dripped down from the roof, and she could feel the vibration of thunder under her feet. "I told Curt that you get me. You understand me. Was I wrong about that?"

Brayden exhaled slowly. He walked over to stand beside her. She could feel him trying to hold up the wall that kept them apart. "No, I don't think you're wrong about that. I do understand you. Your mother was killed when you were a little girl. You felt abandoned by her. You felt angry. And you blame yourself for feeling that way, because it's wrong, and it's not fair."

"That's exactly right."

"I'm the same way," Brayden told her. "I was abandoned twice. My birth mother gave me up, and then my adoptive mother died. So yes, I get you, because I've been where you are. And it's true, you and I have a connection, but two halves don't necessarily make a whole."

"What does that mean?"

"It means even if we understand each other, even if we share some bad things about our past, that doesn't mean we're good together."

"We might be."

"No. We're not. Right now, I have a job to do, and that's all."

Cat held back tears. "Fine. Whatever you want. I'm going to take that shower now."

"I'll be right here."

"My offer still stands. No strings."

"I'm sorry, Cat."

She left Brayden on the porch, and inside, she felt a rush of emptiness, like morphine numbing her pain. The cottage felt dark and deserted. She went to the bathroom and took off all her clothes, and she shivered as she waited for the trickle of water to heat up. When it finally did, she climbed into the tub and stood under the spray, eyes wide open, staring at the wall, wishing she were someone else. In her head were all of the people who meant something to her. Brayden, and Stride, and Serena, and Curt, and in back of all of them, Michaela.

Michaela. Her mother. Murdered by her father. Michaela existed now only in a couple of photographs from her childhood. Cat couldn't even call up a memory of her mother's face. She was gone for good.

Cat wasn't sure how long she stood under the shower, but eventually, the hot water ran out and turned cold. She shut it off and got out of the tub. She was shivering again, but she didn't even grab a towel to dry herself. She simply let the cold rattle her body, her knees knocking together. She dripped on the floor until the mat at her feet was soaking wet.

Fresh clothes were in her bedroom. She'd forgotten to bring them with her. Cat went and yanked open the bathroom door, which always stuck.

Then she screamed.

Colleen was standing in front of her.

30

Stride watched branches of lightning erupt over the lake like ribbons of fire, followed by a deafening boom of thunder. The clouds opened up; rain poured down, hammering the roof of his Expedition. The grayness of dusk in the sky had turned as black as night. His truck was parked on the sidewalk near the bay water. The immense Duluth convention center was on his left, and when he looked up at the tall windows of the ballroom, he could see the silhouettes of people staring out at the storm.

"Maggie's on her way to talk to Adam Halka," he told Serena. "Maybe we'll finally get some answers."

Serena didn't say anything for a long time. Her face was dark, like the evening sky, and she stared at the rain as if under a spell. "I don't know. It was thirty years ago, Jonny. Are there really any answers to get? Say we're right. Say Andrea was actually raped by Adam Halka, not Devin. We still can't touch him. The statute of limitations expired long ago."

"We can get him if he killed Ned Baer," Stride said. "Andrea and I weren't the only ones who knew that Ned was out at the Deeps that night. Adam knew it, too."

Serena nodded, but she looked distracted.

"What is it?" Stride asked.

"Even if we tell Andrea what we think, she won't believe it. She's certain it was Devin Card. Short of Adam admitting what happened—which he isn't likely to do—we're not going to change her mind."

"But Alice said it's possible that Andrea got it wrong."

"She did, but she also said it was very unlikely, particularly if we're not talking about a stranger rape. I mean, Andrea *knew* Adam. He'd been dating her sister for years. Adam and Devin look nothing alike. And Andrea specifically said she was making out with Devin, and *he* was the one who took her upstairs. It doesn't add up. I just don't see her blocking out one face and putting in another. If she was making out with her sister's ex-boyfriend, she'd sure as hell remember it."

"Well, let's wait and see what Adam says to Maggie."

"Yeah. Okay."

Stride hesitated before saying anything else. His instinct was to let it go, but he knew that his instincts sometimes led him down bad alleys when it came to emotion. "Do you still see Alice?" he asked. "I mean, do you still go to her for therapy?"

"Sometimes."

"Are you having problems?"

"I'll always have problems, Jonny. These things don't get cured."

"I mean problems with us."

Her fingers reached out and curled around his hand. She took a long time to reply. "I don't think so."

"That's not a rousing vote of confidence," Stride said.

"Well, I don't think I'm the one who's struggling," she replied, looking at him on the other side of the truck. "You tell me something, Jonny. Are you happy?"

"With you? Yes."

"I mean with everything. With life."

Stride had no idea how to answer that kind of question. He tried to find a way to put how he felt into words, but that had never been his strength. "I had to change my idea of what happiness was after Cindy died. You know that. No matter what I did, there would always be a dark cloud. I've had to make peace with that. But you make me happy. So does Cat."

"And the job?"

He shrugged. "I'm not sure anymore."

"What do you mean?"

"I mean, I've gotten up almost every day of my life and being a cop has been my whole identity. But lately, I stare in the mirror, and the person I think I am isn't the person who's staring back at me. It's someone different. Does that make any sense?"

"It does," Serena said.

"I'm sorry. I should have told you about this sooner."

"Yes, you should've." She added, "Have you talked to Cat about it?"

"She dragged it out of me."

"Of course, she did. Sometimes I envy how that girl can get you to open up."

"I wasn't trying to keep anything from you. I promise."

She nodded. "I know that."

"I think Cat has a crush on Brayden, by the way."

"Well, he's cute, I'll give her that. Do you think we need to be concerned?"

"Cat's going to make her own mistakes, regardless of what we say."

"What about Brayden?" Serena asked.

"I trust him."

"Are you sure? I admit, I wondered what they were doing up on Hawk Ridge together. It's kind of a romantic spot."

"I know. I wondered that, too. But Guppo says Brayden's not a player. Not like some of the young cowboys on the force. He's serious. Comes with some tough family issues, but worked hard to get past them. I think we have to respect that and hope he's mature enough to make the right choice."

"Okay."

Serena pulled down the visor in the Expedition and opened up the mirror, with barely enough light to cast a reflection. Her hair was damp and mussed, and she used a brush from the glove compartment to comb it out. She always frowned when she did that, and Stride wondered how she could see anything in her face that wasn't perfect. Because that was what he saw. But then he noticed Serena stop, put down the brush, and stare into the darkness of the mirror. He could see something working itself out behind her eyes.

"What's wrong?" he asked.

She flipped up the visor and twisted around in the seat. Something new was in her face. A quiet, intense revelation. "The person you're looking at isn't the person you think it is. It's someone different."

"What?"

"That's what you said about yourself, Jonny."

"Okay."

"Maybe *that's* what happened to Andrea," Serena said.

"I don't understand."

She hesitated, as if studying the pieces in a puzzle and trying to make them fit. "Andrea says she was making out with Devin Card at the party, and the two of them went upstairs to the bedroom together. There's no way she could be wrong about that. She wouldn't have mistaken Adam for Devin."

"That means Devin is the one who assaulted her," Stride concluded.

"Well, maybe not. What if it happened this way? Andrea's making out with Devin, and Adam is in the house, too. Watching them. He's pissed, upset, furious with Denise. He'd love to get back at her for dumping him. He sees Andrea and Devin go upstairs together, and a while later, Devin comes back down alone."

"Why?"

"Because Andrea told him to *stop*. Maybe that's what he did. He stopped. He left. Then Andrea went and threw up in the sink, and she came back and passed out on the bed. But if Adam *saw* Devin come back alone, he knew that meant Andrea was up there by herself. His ex-girlfriend's sister was all alone in the bedroom. So he goes upstairs and finds her passed out drunk. The room is dark. He rapes her. She wakes up in the middle, but she's still completely out of it, and she doesn't even realize that Devin is gone and someone else is in the room with her. Her brain never puts it together. Years later, all she knows is that she was raped, and Devin was the one who took her upstairs. She never knew that Adam took his place."

Stride frowned. "You could be right."

"Now flash forward to the accusation seven years ago. Ned told you he had a witness who saw Andrea and Devin together, right? Maybe the witness was *Adam*. He tells Ned that he saw Andrea go up to the bedroom with Devin Card. What better way to get a little payback against Peter and Devin than by ruining Devin's career? Except then Adam starts to get nervous. If it all comes out—if *he's* the witness—people may start asking questions. Maybe someone saw something or remembers something. Maybe Andrea's memory will start coming back when she sees his name. So Adam realizes he *can't* have Ned publish that story."

"He follows Ned to the Deeps. He kills him."

"Exactly."

Stride stared up at the bright windows in the convention center. He could see the people inside, but he couldn't see any faces. The rain sheeted down, harder than ever. "We need to talk to Andrea before she gets up on that stage," he said. "Once she tells her story, there's no going back."

* * * * *

Andrea could feel the pounding of her heart. She found it hard to breathe. She stood outside the Harbor Side ballroom, surrounded by hundreds of people pushing and shoving around her, and she couldn't move. Overlapping voices rang in her ears. Supporters carried signs. So did the protesters. They shouted and jeered at each other, and guards had to keep them apart.

"Ma'am?"

Andrea blinked in confusion when she heard a voice calling to her. Then she spotted a young woman at one of the check-in tables near the ballroom doors. She couldn't have been more than twenty years old. The woman wore a Devin Card button on her T-shirt, and the sight of Devin's smiling, arrogant face brought all of Andrea's anger back.

"Ma'am, are you planning to ask a question tonight?" the woman asked.

"I—I don't know. Maybe."

"Well, that's okay," she told her. "Just you know, it doesn't matter whether you plan to vote for Devin or not. The Congressman wants questions from all of his constituents, no matter what side they're on."

"All right."

"The town hall will start in about an hour. Find a place inside anywhere you can."

"Okay."

"Would you like a button, too?"

"*No!*" Andrea snapped, way too loudly. People around her stopped and looked. "No, I'm an independent."

"That's fine. Like I said, everybody's welcome."

"Thank you."

Andrea felt herself floating as she headed for the ballroom doors, practically carried along by the surge of the crowd. Inside, she wanted to cover her ears because of all the singing, shouting, and chanting. There was hardly a square inch free on the beige carpet, which was decorated with images of fall leaves. The curving windows showed the darkness outside, and rain pounded against the glass like machine gun fire. Lightning sparked almost continuously, causing a constant rumble of thunder that buzzed through her entire body.

She squeezed forward into the room, excusing herself as she went past dozens of people. She wanted to be right near the stage. She wanted to be close enough to see Devin's face. To stare into his eyes.

She wanted him to see *her*.

A microphone for the people who planned to ask questions had been mounted on a stand immediately in front of the stage. A velvet rope surrounded it, carving out a space for each person to come and introduce themselves. Not even ten feet away, up on the elevated platform, was another microphone, this one for Devin Card.

They would be face to face, but he would still be looking down at her. Still controlling her. Still on top of her.

She needed to purge that image from her mind once and for all.

Andrea staked out her place near the microphone and resisted every attempt by others to dislodge her. She wasn't going anywhere. She found herself watching every inch of the stage, wondering when it would all begin. When would she see him for the first time? When would he approach the microphone? There were steps on the far left that led off the stage and through the ballroom doors to the corridor. There were steps on the far right near the dark windows. Congressional staff walked back and forth, talking to each other and whispering into radios.

She imagined what they were saying.

Is she here?

Who is she?

What is she going to say?

"Ma'am?" another volunteer asked her as she held her ground near the velvet rope. He was a kid, too, hardly out of his teens. He wore a Devin Card T-shirt—again that awful, smiling face taunting her—and he held a clipboard and had a headset curled around his ear.

"Ma'am, are you planning to ask a question tonight?"

"Yes," Andrea replied. "Yes, I have a question for the Congressman."

31

"Wow, you surprised me," Cat told Colleen, covering her mouth after she screamed. "What are you doing here?"

Colleen gave her a little smirk. Her clothes and hair were wet from the rain, and she had a large satchel dangling from her shoulder. Cat was still naked in front of her, and Colleen reached out and playfully shoved Cat's wet arm. They were just a few inches apart in the bathroom doorway. "I thought we could hang out together, girlfriend. Just you and me."

"Does Brayden know you're here?"

"Tall, blond, and handsome? Your boy toy? Yeah, he's on the porch. I told him this was a girls' night. No dudes allowed. He said I could go in. Come on, you're up for that, aren't you? A little Cat and Colly time?"

"I guess. Sure."

"Look at you, you are so hot."

Cat had never felt uncomfortable being naked in front of another woman, but Colleen's eyes traveled up and down her body in a way that felt *off*. "Thanks. Listen, I forgot to get fresh clothes from my bedroom. Could you get some for me? I don't want to walk out there with Brayden outside."

"Yeah, of course. Whatever you want."

Colleen disappeared and returned a couple minutes later with a loose green tank top and frayed jean shorts, which Cat quickly put on. The two of them wandered into the cottage's living room, and Cat took one end of the red leather sofa while Colleen took the other. When Cat stretched out her legs, so did Colleen. The rain was loud on the roof above them, and wind shook the house.

"Any news on Wyatt?" Colleen asked her. "Have the police found him?"

Cat shook her head. "No."

"Well, I'm sure they'll get the son of a bitch soon."

"Yeah. I hope so."

"How about we sneak out again? Ditch boy toy and take my car?"

"I shouldn't," Cat said. "Stride wants me practically behind bars."

"You sure? I feel like doing something. We should go someplace."

"Where?"

"I don't know. Maybe find a club or something. We could dance."

"I'd love to, but Stride would kill me. He says I need to stick around here until they find Wyatt."

"Yeah, okay. I get it."

Cat noticed that Colleen's brown eyes never seemed to move or blink, and her smile was frozen on her face. The girl's chalky skin had a glistening fringe of sweat where her blond hair met her forehead.

"Curt came by," Cat told her. "He left right before you got here. He says you broke up with him."

"Yeah, I did. I was over him. Life moves on."

"He's pretty upset. I told you he wasn't as tough as he looks. I said you should let him down gently."

Colleen's smile twitched a bit, but that was her only reaction. "I know, but when you're getting rid of a guy, you need to do it quick like you're pulling off a bandage. Anything else just prolongs the pain."

"Are you really sure you're over him?"

"Very sure."

"Are you dating somebody else?" Cat asked. "Is there another guy?"

"Another guy?" Colleen giggled. "No, there's no other guy."

"Curt thought there was."

"Well, Curt's paranoid. Look, he's nice and all, but it was never going to be a long-term thing with him. If he didn't get that, that's on him."

"Okay. You know what you want, and it's none of my business. But listen, just so you know, Curt may try to get you back. I told him to talk to you. Go over to your place. I thought maybe there was still a chance for the two of you to make up."

"You told Curt to go to my place?" Colleen asked with an exaggerated pleasantness in her voice. Cat could tell she wasn't happy about it.

"Yeah. Sorry about that. I figured if you guys talked, you might change your mind. I shouldn't have gotten in the middle of it."

"It's okay. Don't worry about it." Colleen began to rub Cat's legs with her bare feet. "You want to put on some music?"

"Sure."

Colleen's eyes narrowed, and she cocked her head like a fortune teller trying to read her mind. "I'm betting you're a Chainsmokers fan."

"I am. I've got all their music."

"You like 'This Feeling'?"

Cat laughed. "Oh, yeah. I play it over and over. I drive Stride and Serena crazy with it sometimes. Do you like it, too?"

"*Love* it."

Cat didn't have to be asked twice. She retrieved her speakers from her bedroom, and she connected her phone and booted up the Chainsmokers song, letting Kelsea Ballerini belt out the opening lyrics. She saw Brayden glance inside through the rain-soaked front windows when he heard the music. When their eyes met, Cat deliberately swung her head away, ignoring him. She wanted him to know she was mad. She wanted to be a bitch.

Colleen got off the sofa and danced, singing the lyrics in an off-key voice. Cat danced, too, letting out some of her pent-up energy from being stuck inside the house. Colleen sidled up to dance behind her, and when Cat turned around, the other girl stayed right there, like they were squeezed together in a crowded club. Neither of them had much rhythm, but Cat didn't care. They swayed, they sang, they bumped together, and when the song was done, they played it again. And then again. Eventually, after the fourth time, Cat switched off the music and collapsed back on the sofa. She put her feet on the coffee table, and Colleen did the same, sitting right next to her. Both of them were sweaty and hot. Colleen put a warm hand on Cat's leg below her shorts.

"You got anything to drink around here?" Colleen asked.

"Sure, what do you want? We've got Coke, Mountain Dew, water."

"Got anything harder?"

Cat grinned. "I think that can be arranged. Like what?"

"Tequila."

"My kind of girl," Cat said.

She glanced over her shoulder to make sure Brayden wasn't watching, and then she went into the kitchen and retrieved a bottle of Jose Cuervo from Stride's stash in the cabinet. She grabbed two shot glasses and brought everything back to the other room. When she poured an inch for Colleen, the girl downed it in a single swallow, and Cat did the same for herself, enjoying the burn.

They did it again.

And again.

Cat began to feel happy. The alcohol went to her head. She relaxed, humming the way she always did when she was a little buzzed. She took the remote control for the television, turned it on, and muted the volume. Mindlessly, she flipped stations, not even spending a second or two at each one.

"Do you ever think about running away from here?" Colleen asked in a dreamy voice.

"What do you mean?"

"I don't know. Leave your life behind and go somewhere new. I've always thought it would be cool to vanish and leave a big mystery behind me. Magazines would write about it. Maybe they'd do those true crime TV shows, too. 'Whatever Became of Colleen Hunt?' That kind of thing."

"People talk about stuff like that, but they never do it," Cat said.

"Oh, yeah, that's because most people are cowards. Stuck in their *blah blah* lives. But I could. What about you? Do you think you could ever just pick up and go?"

"When I was on the streets, maybe I could. There were a lot of days back then when I wanted to take off."

"Well, see, we could do it together," Colleen said, and Cat couldn't tell if she was joking. "Run away, go off the grid. Cash only. Color our hair. We could be ghosts. No one would ever find us."

"You're crazy."

"Hey, when I make up my mind to do something, I do it. You want to go, we go. I've got my car on the street. I'm all packed."

Cat looked at her strangely. "I'm sorry, you're *packed?*"

"I just mean, I'm free to do whatever. No strings. So are you."

Cat shook her head and spoke softly, bringing reality into fantasy. "No, I'm not. I have a kid."

"So bring him with you."

"He doesn't belong to me. He's with the Olsons. Even so, I'd never go away and leave him behind."

"Well, like I said, bring him with you. He's still your kid, not anybody else's."

Cat frowned as she drank more tequila. "I don't like this conversation anymore."

"Sorry. I was just having fun."

Cat turned up the volume on the television, because she didn't want to talk for a while. The TV was tuned to a news channel broadcasting from inside the DECC. Hundreds of people filled the ballroom, and a countdown clock showed twenty minutes until the beginning of the event. A photograph of Devin Card filled a corner of the screen, and a message scrolled across the bottom: "Anonymous Accuser Promises Appearance at Town Hall."

"Wow, I'd love to see that," Cat murmured.

"What?"

"The woman Devin Card raped. Everybody says she's going to come forward tonight. She's going to confront him."

"No shit?"

"Yeah. That takes guts, huh? To stand up in front of all those people? I'd love to be there. I want to see him skewered. Men like that, they think they can get away with anything."

"So let's do it," Colleen said.

"What?"

"Let's go over there. I mean, it's five minutes away. Let's do it."

"Stride wants me to stay home. Wyatt's still out there."

"Oh come on, Cat. Look at all those people. Look at all the cops. It doesn't get much safer than that. Brayden can come along with us, so Stride can't complain. We can take my car."

Cat hesitated. "I don't know."

"We'll watch the fireworks as she comes forward. And then afterward, who knows? Maybe you'll change your mind about going someplace else."

Cat switched off the television. When the house was silent again, she could hear the thump of the driving rain not letting up. More lightning lit up the windows, and a drumbeat of thunder followed. Colleen was right. She felt trapped, and she wanted to be free.

"Sure, what the hell?" Cat said. "Let's go."

32

Maggie found Adam Halka throwing darts at a Superior Street bar a block from his motel. She shook the rain off her coat and waited while the man finished his game. He had a peculiar sidearm style, but he was good, landing all but one of the darts within an inch or so of the sweet spot in the center. A few of the drunk patrons gave a little cheer when he was done, and Halka took an exaggerated bow with his tall, stooped frame. Maggie got the feeling that Halka's proficiency at darts was one of the few highlights of his life.

The man sat down at a table behind a tall mug of beer and grabbed a handful of popcorn from a large basket. He ate it a kernel at a time. The gruff look on his wrinkled face didn't change. He wore what he had the first time she'd seen him, the same Twins shirt and jeans, both in need of a wash. A waitress came and planted a kiss on his cheek and put a burger in front of him. This was definitely his hangout place. In here, he was a star.

Maggie pushed a chair close enough to Halka that she didn't have to shout over the noise in the bar. Eighties rock music blared from the jukebox, but the television was on, too. On the screen, she saw the ballroom at the DECC and the impatient crowd waiting for Devin Card to approach the microphone and take questions. Halka showed no interest in the television.

"Seems like you've been busy, Mr. Halka," Maggie told him.

Halka adorned his burger with ketchup like a thick bloodstain. "Yeah? Busy doing what?"

"Trying to extort money out of Peter Stanhope."

The motel owner shrugged and didn't look concerned by the accusation. "Oh, that. He told you about that? Pete's exaggerating. I was blowing smoke up his ass, that's all. If you think you can make a thing out of it, arrest me, but I doubt 'ol Pete really wants this to go anywhere. It's not the kind of thing he wants to see in the papers."

"I'm not here to arrest you for extortion," Maggie said, putting a spin on the last word.

Halka's eyes narrowed as he took a big bite of his burger. He heard the hidden message in her voice. "Yeah?" he replied as he swallowed. "You got the idea I've done something else?"

"You tell me. Rape. Murder."

Halka put down the burger and wiped his mouth. "What the hell are you talking about? Do I need a lawyer or something?"

"That's up to you. You're not under arrest. You want to go? Go. You want me to go? Just say the word. I want to clear a few things up, but that's entirely up to you."

"I haven't done a damn thing," Halka insisted.

"Then answer some questions."

Halka rocked back in his chair and spread his arms. "Shoot."

"Ned Baer said he had a witness to back up his story," Maggie told him. "He had somebody who saw Devin Card going upstairs at a party with the woman who says she was raped. Were you the witness?"

"No. I didn't tell Baer a thing."

"*Did* you see Card going upstairs with a woman at one of the parties?"

"Who knows? It was thirty years ago. Card hung out with lots of girls."

"The night Ned Baer went to the Deeps, did you follow him?" Maggie asked.

"Follow him? Why the hell would I do that?"

"You tell me."

"No, I didn't. Ned drove off, and I never saw him again."

"Did you tell anyone else where he was going?"

"Other than your cop friend? No."

"Do you own a gun?"

Adam took another bite of his burger and chewed slowly as he considered his answer. "Several."

"Is one of them a 9 mm handgun?" Maggie asked.

"Yeah, I've got one of those. Me and a few million other people. Why?"

"Would you agree to let us run your pistol through ballistics? That way, we can rule it out as being the gun that killed Ned Baer."

"Well, I already know it's not, because the only place I fire that gun is at the range. As far as letting the police handle it, no, that wouldn't be tops on my list. I'm not really a trusting guy when it comes to the government. Tell you what, you come over to my place with a warrant, and you can test any of my guns that you like."

Maggie wasn't surprised that he didn't volunteer his guns. She gestured at the television screen over the bar. "The media are saying that the woman who made the accusation against Devin Card is coming forward tonight. She's going public."

"If you say so. I haven't paid any attention to that."

"Do you know who the woman is?"

"Don't know," Halka replied. "Don't care."

"Maybe I can refresh your memory," Maggie said.

"How do you plan on doing that?"

Maggie leaned closer. "Let's start with Denise Forseth. I'm sure you remember her."

Halka's mouth puckered like a dried grape. "Yeah. So?"

"Tell me about the two of you."

"There's not much to tell. Denise and I went together through most of high school. Kept going out while she was in college. We were going to get married, but Denise broke it off. End of story."

"Do you know she's back in Duluth?" Maggie asked.

Halka shrugged. "Yeah, I heard that."

"Have you seen her?"

"Nope. Why would I want to see her? Denise and me were ancient history."

"Tell me about the break-up," Maggie said.

Halka stared at her long and hard, as if he was trying to understand the rules of the game. "Why do you care about that?"

"Humor me. Do you remember when Denise ended your relationship?"

"Yeah, matter of fact, when your fiancée dumps you in front of all your friends, it kind of sticks in your head."

"So tell me about it."

Halka took a drink from his beer. "Denise was heading off to the Air Force. I didn't think that meant we had to break up. Looking back, I guess that was pretty stupid of me, but I was a kid. And I loved her. I thought we should do long-distance, or hell, I was ready to get married before she left. Instead, she said we were done. Gave me back the ring. Told me where to shove it."

"Where was this?"

"We were at a concert at the DECC. Big group of us."

"Was Devin Card there?"

"I don't remember."

"What happened next?" Maggie asked.

"What do you mean?"

"I mean, what did you do after Denise dumped you?"

"I have no idea," Halka replied. "I remember getting dumped, but that's all."

"I understand there was a party crawl after the concert. Did you go?"

Halka began to act squirrelly. "Who knows? Probably. I already told you, I spent a lot of time drunk or high in those days. I sure as hell wouldn't have stayed sober after what Denise did to me. But I don't remember any of it."

"None of it?"

He hesitated, and she knew he was about to lie. "Not a thing."

"Denise says there was an incident later that night at one of the parties. She says you saw the whole thing."

"What kind of incident?"

But Maggie could see it in his face. He knew.

"It involved Peter Stanhope," she said. "And Denise."

Halka froze. A kind of bloodlust filled his eyes. "Okay. She told you about that, huh? Yeah. I remember."

"Tell me what happened."

The man's voice came out in a strangled hiss. "I'm sure you already know what happened. Denise let Stanhope bang her in front of everyone."

"You saw it?"

"Oh, yeah. I saw it."

"This was the same night? The night she dumped you?"

"Same night."

"You must have been angry. Your fiancée dumps you and then has sex in front of you and your friends with another man? You must have wanted to get back at both of them."

"I wanted to rip their fucking heads off," Halka replied. "So what?"

"What did you do?"

"What the hell do you expect? I kept drinking."

"That's it?"

"Yeah, that's it. Did I think about going back home and getting a gun? You bet I did. But they weren't worth it."

Maggie let the silence stretch out between them. The only noise was the music of the bar and the mumble from the television. Then she said, "Did you know Denise's sister?"

Halka looked surprised by the change in direction. "Her sister? Andrea? Yeah, sure. I mean, she was around a lot when I was over at Denise's place. We talked every now and then, but not much. She was younger, brainy, kind of stuck up."

"Was Andrea at the party that night?" Maggie asked.

Halka shook his head. "Hell if I know."

"You don't remember seeing her?"

"No, I don't. Could she have been there? Sure, I guess. But I don't remember."

"Would you have recognized her if you saw her back then?"

"Denise's sister? Of course, I would've."

"Was Devin Card at the party?"

Halka nodded. "Oh, yeah. Devin was there. He was up in my face when Pete and Denise were doing it. Taunting me about it. That asshole."

"So you must have been pretty upset with him, too."

"Yeah. Him, too. All three of them."

"Did you see Devin become involved with anyone at the party? Did you see him go upstairs with anyone?"

"Jesus, how many times do I have to say it? *I don't remember.* For all I know, yeah, I saw Devin with his tongue in some girl's mouth, but I could have said that about fifty different parties."

"But this party was special," Maggie said. "This is the one where Denise humiliated you."

"Spell it out!" Halka growled. "Stop playing games. Exactly what the hell do you think I did?"

If he was going to crack, if he was going to admit anything, now was the time.

"Andrea *was* at that party, Mr. Halka," Maggie told him.

"Okay. If you tell me that, fine, maybe it's true, but I don't remember. So what?"

"Andrea says she was making out with Devin, and then she went upstairs to the bedroom with him."

Halka eyed the television over Maggie's shoulder. "*Her?* Shit, that was Denise's little sister? She's the one?"

"She's the one."

"Well, I'm sorry to hear that. Truly. I liked the kid. I still don't see what this has to do with me. She says Devin raped her, right? That's what this has been about for the past seven years. So why are you talking to me about it?"

"Andrea *thinks* it was Devin, but she'd been drinking a lot," Maggie told him. "She may have passed out. See, we're wondering if Devin Card came back downstairs and left her alone up in the bedroom. And there you were at the party, Adam. Drunk, pissed off, out of control. Suddenly, you realized that your ex-fiancée's sister was all by herself. Did you go upstairs, Adam? Did you figure if Denise was going to have sex with someone, you could do the same thing? Did you figure that's how you could get back at her for what she did to you? By *raping* her little sister?"

Halka's eyes widened in what could only be genuine shock. "You're out of your mind."

"You were there, and you had a hell of a motive."

"I didn't do it. You hear me? I *didn't* do it!"

"Maybe you were so drunk you blacked out and don't even remember."

"No fucking way."

"Can you be sure? Isn't that possible?"

"No. It wasn't me. Do you hear me? *No!*"

Halka lurched up from his chair, practically in a daze. He threw money on the table, left behind his beer and burger, and stumbled for the door of the bar. Several people shouted his name, but he ignored them. He punched through the door to the street and slammed it behind him.

Maggie rushed after him into the rain. Outside, she found Halka on the street corner, his back against the stone wall of the bar. He was bent over, his hands on his knees. The downpour flooded over him, soaking him to his skin. His face was red, and when he saw her, his features contorted. He straightened up and jabbed a finger at her, his voice like a primal scream. "Are you doing this because of Stanhope? Is this him getting back at me? He wants to get his buddy Devin off the hook, so he spoon-feeds this bullshit to you?"

"That's not what's going on here, Adam."

"He's rich, and I'm trash. He gets whatever he wants. He always has."

"Peter Stanhope doesn't know about any of this. Look, Adam, I just want the truth. After all this time, Andrea deserves the truth. And whatever you may think of Devin Card, he doesn't deserve to be destroyed over an accusation like this if he's innocent."

"It wasn't me!" Halka insisted again. "I don't know anything about a rape back then. I told you that. I told Ned that. If it happened at that party, okay, fine, whatever you say. But I didn't know, and I sure as hell had nothing to do with it."

Maggie blinked as rain ran down her face. She stared at Halka and realized that she believed him. He was innocent.

"Okay, Adam," she said. "Okay, you didn't do it."

"I loved Denise. Yeah, I was hurt by what she did to me, but I would never have taken it out on her sister. No way."

"So who assaulted her?"

Halka ran his hands through his wet hair. "If Andrea says it was Devin, it must been him."

"Can you think of *anyone* else who might have seen them together? Someone else who was at the party?"

"Nobody."

Maggie knew she was back at a dead end. "Thank you for talking to me, Adam."

Halka was still bent over, hyperventilating, trying to breathe.

"You okay?" she asked. "You need a doctor?"

He shook his head and waved her away. Maggie headed into the street, water pouring across her boots, the wind whipping around her hair. Her Avalanche was parked on the opposite curb. She hadn't even reached the middle of the street when Halka called after her in a raspy voice.

"Wait."

Maggie stopped. She marched back to the motel owner. "What is it?"

"There was another guy."

"Excuse me?"

"There was another guy at the party. A stranger."

"How do you know?"

"I brought him. He came with me. We left together, too. Actually, that's why I remember. I was too drunk to drive, so he drove instead. But he was jumpy and weird, and he crashed my dad's car. Drove it into a utility pole near the DECC. I knew I was going to catch hell. I wanted him to explain it to my dad, but the guy gave me two hundred bucks to say I did it. Then he ran. Just got out of the car and ran. I never saw him again."

"Who was he?"

"No idea. I don't think I ever knew his name. He was from out of town."

"Why was he with you?"

"I met him at the concert," Halka told her. "I wasn't going to sit with Denise after our fight, and I had a buddy who could always get me backstage. I hung out with the roadies. This guy and I hit it off, and when I mentioned the party crawl, he asked if he could come along. I said what the hell."

Maggie heard Halka's voice echoing in her head, and it triggered a memory.

I hung out with the roadies.

She felt a chill that had nothing to do with the cold rain.

"Adam, do you remember the concert that night? Do you remember the band you saw?"

Halka nodded. "Sure. It was ZZ Top."

33

A sea of people filled the DECC ballroom and squeezed into the overflow rooms and the corridors outside. Stride found it hard to make out
any faces. Serena stood next to him, and both of them got up on tiptoes
to survey the room, but if Andrea was here, she was lost among dozens of
blond-haired women. The deafening chatter in the room made it almost
impossible to hear. Most of the people inside were wet from the storm,
and the room had a pungent smell.

He dialed Andrea's number again, but the call went straight to
voice mail.

"We should split up," he told Serena, cupping his hands over her ear
so that she could hear him.

Serena nodded and leaned close to him. "If we find her, what do we
tell her? We have suspicions, but we can't prove what really happened."

"I guess we tell her that," Stride said. "This is the wrong time and place
for her to go public."

Serena headed toward the west end of the ballroom. Stride walked
the other way, toward the tall windows overlooking the rain-swept bay.
He checked his watch and knew he didn't have much time. The town hall
had been scheduled to start fifteen minutes earlier, and the crowd was
getting impatient. People had begun chanting Devin's name, and even

his supporters were wondering where he was. Stride didn't like the tone of the crowd around him. It was ugly, unsettled, with partisans on both sides veering close to physical confrontations. There were plenty of cops everywhere, but it still wouldn't take much for things to get out of control.

His phone rang in his pocket. When he answered it, he could make out Maggie's voice on the other end, but he could barely hear what she was saying. In a room with hundreds of phones, the choppy signal went in and out, and Maggie was obviously in her truck, with music blaring in the background. He kept asking her to repeat herself, but her voice was garbled, and then the call dropped.

All he was able to make out was "*Ned was there.*"

Stride didn't understand the message. He tried calling back, but the call failed to go through.

He reached the dark windows on the far side of the ballroom, but he still hadn't found Andrea. Staying next to the windows, he headed to the stage, which would give him a slightly elevated view. A gaggle of campaign workers clustered near the metal stairs, and a police officer noticed him and let him through. He climbed the steps and looked out over the seething crowd.

Finding one single person out there was impossible.

Stride felt a hand on his shoulder. When he turned around, he found Peter Stanhope, dressed as he always was: in a tailored suit. The room was warm, and the man's skin glowed under his swept-back mane of silver hair.

"Lieutenant."

"Hello, Peter," Stride said. They didn't smile at each other. They weren't enemies, but they definitely weren't friends. Stride had disliked Peter Stanhope going back to his teenage years, and little had happened in between to change his impression of the man.

"The crowd's getting restless," Stride went on. "You better get Devin out here."

"He's huddled with his campaign staff. They're still talking about the best strategy to deal with the woman if she shows up." Peter studied Stride's face. "Is she here?"

"I don't know. I haven't seen her yet."

"Can you tell me her name, Jonathan? It's not like we can do anything now, but Devin should know who he's dealing with."

"That's not up to me," Stride said. "It's up to her."

Peter shook his head. "Devin didn't do this, but he doesn't want to stand in front of a woman who claims she was victimized and call her a liar."

"Good call."

"Do you have any advice?" Peter asked. "You talk to witnesses with fragile memories all the time."

Stride stared across the hundreds of faces, barely visible in the low light of the ballroom. Thunder clapped like the thud of a bass drum outside. "My advice is, remember what the hell this is all about. Thirty years ago, someone did something terrible to her, Peter. I don't know whether it was Devin, but I know this woman's life was never the same. I want to protect her. I don't care about the politics."

"If you want to protect her, convince her to talk to us privately. No good will come of it in here. Not for any of us, including her."

Stride looked at Peter and knew he was a master of multiple agendas, and the man's loyalty was to whichever one served his interests at the moment. But he was also right. "That's exactly what I'm trying to do."

"Thank you, Jonathan."

Peter headed down the steps from the stage, back toward the private room where the candidate was waiting. Stride focused on the crowd again. Standing there alone, he had an odd sense of foreboding, like a shadow falling across him. Nothing felt right. Everything felt dangerous. The storm. The people.

No good will come of it.

He kept trying to find Andrea, but instead, he found someone else. Cat.

He saw her face and then lost her in the crowd, but it was definitely Cat. She was being pulled toward the far doors by another girl around the same age, with straight blond hair parted in the middle. At the same moment that Stride saw her, Cat looked up at the stage and saw him, and she couldn't get away fast enough.

Stride looked for Brayden. The young cop was close by, but he could tell from the look on Brayden's face that he'd lost Cat.

"*Brayden!*"

The cop twisted around and spotted Stride. His face fell. He pushed toward the stage, and Stride bent down to talk to him.

"What the hell is Cat doing here? She's supposed to be at home while we look for Wyatt."

"Yes, sir. I know. I told her not to leave, but the fact is, she was going to come here no matter what I said. At least here I knew there would be a lot of cops and security."

"They have their own jobs to do. They're not watching out for her. *You* are. Or at least, you're supposed to be."

"I realize that. I made a judgment call. By letting her go, I figured I could stay with her. Otherwise, I was afraid she'd slip out on her own, and I'd have no idea where she was."

"Meanwhile, you've *lost* her."

"Yes, sir."

"*Find* her, Brayden."

"Yes, sir."

"Once you do, keep her in sight. Keep her with you. I don't care if you have to cuff yourself to her. Got it?"

"Got it, sir."

Brayden began to turn back into the crowd, but Stride took hold of his shoulder.

"Who's the other girl?" he asked. "Who's Cat with? I've never seen her before."

"Her name's Colleen Hunt," Brayden told him. "She's Curt's girl-friend. Don't worry, she's harmless."

* * * * *

Curt sat in his old Thunderbird across from Colleen's building. He had the engine on, which coughed and rumbled. The driving rain pounded on the roof. He had the radio on loud, but he barely heard the songs. He'd been here for half an hour, trying to decide what to do, and every time he made up his mind to drive away and forget Colleen, he put the T-Bird back in park.

Light glowed in her apartment window, but no one moved behind the shade. He'd called her, and she didn't answer. He'd texted her, and he knew she'd read what he sent, but she didn't reply. She was ghosting him. The unspoken message couldn't be any clearer.

Go away, Curt.

He tried to figure out what had gone wrong between them. What he'd done this time. Sooner or later, he always screwed things up, but this time the break-up had come out of the blue. Just yesterday, they'd had loud, wild sex in the back seat of the T-bird, and now she was over him. No explanation.

He loved her. He really did, and that was a first. Colly was different from the girls he'd dated before. Sweeter. Classier. Smarter. They'd always had a good time together, but now he wondered if there had been something going on with her from the very beginning. She also had a cold side. There would be times when he'd look into her dark eyes and feel like she didn't even see him. Even when he was between her legs, he'd watch her face and get the feeling that she wasn't really there. Like she wanted someone else on top of her and he was just a stand-in.

Curt was no fool.

She'd been cheating on him all along. If that was the case, she could damn well tell him the truth.

He shut down the T-bird engine and got out of the car. Instantly, the rain drenched him. A car passed on Third Street, kicking up an ocean wave of spray. Curt jogged across the street and yanked on the building door, but it was locked. He buzzed Colleen's apartment but got no response.

"Come on, Colly!" he shouted into the intercom. "Come on, open up!"

He stormed down the steps onto the sidewalk. The third window past the door was her apartment, and he went and banged his fist on the glass. He called her name again. While he was doing that, he saw the building door open, and he shouted for the person to hold the door. He

ran back, made an excuse to the man at the door, and slipped inside. In
the hallway, he stood there, dripping on the floor. The apartment doors
were all closed. He heard the blare of televisions and someone practicing
an electric guitar.

Curt's feet squished on the carpet as he headed for Colleen's apartment. He thumped his knuckles on the door and listened, but he was
wasting his time. He realized he didn't have a key, which should have been
a red flag to him. He'd given her a key to his apartment, and she'd told
him how nice that was and how much she appreciated it. But she'd never
offered to give him her own key.

He was about to leave when he glanced down at his feet. The carpet
in the hallway was gray and worn, and the flimsy apartment door didn't
extend all the way to the floor. Where the crack was, he saw a wet, fresh
stain. Something dark. It had trickled along the linoleum inside. He squatted and rubbed the seam at the bottom of the door, and when he looked at
his hand, he found a red, sticky liquid streaking his fingertips.

Blood.

"*Colly?*" Curt called loudly. His heartbeat took off. "Colly? Are you in
there? Are you okay?"

Curt danced uncertainly in the hallway, trying to make up his mind,
and then he backed up and threw his shoulder against the door. He nearly
broke a bone, but the door held. The next time, he bent his leg and kicked,
and the lock shuddered. He kicked again, and the wood splintered away
from the lock and the door flew open.

He rushed inside the apartment and swore. "Holy shit!"

A body lay on the floor, a pillow covering its head. The pillow had a
burnt hole in it; feathers covered half the surfaces in the living room where
they'd been blown into the air, and a river of blood seeped from under the
pillow. He went over and used two fingers to peel the pillow back and saw
what was left of Wyatt Miller's face.

"What the fuck! Oh shit!"

Curt felt his stomach doing somersaults as he backed away from the
corpse. "Colly!" he screamed, trying not to throw up. "Colly! Jesus!"

He ran into her bedroom, expecting to find another body. Expecting to find his girlfriend murdered on the floor. Another gunshot. More blood. What he found was even worse.

Nearly every inch of Colleen's bedroom was covered with photographs thumb-tacked to the walls. The photographs were all of Cat. Cat inside, outside, Cat with her son, Cat in her bedroom. And across the pictures was the same message scrawled over and over in green marker, spilling from the pictures onto the walls.

I love you I love you I love you I love you I love you.

Curt covered his mouth with both hands and smelled his hot breath speeding in and out of his lungs.

"Oh, shit," he mumbled. "Oh, fuck. Colly, you crazy bitch."

34

ZZ Top.

Maggie didn't bother taking off her raincoat or turning on the light in her office at police headquarters. She crossed the room and dropped down in the chair, and then she dug through the file on her desk for the information on Ned Baer's Colorado editor. When she located Debbi King's phone number, she grabbed her cell phone and dialed.

"Ms. King?" she said, when the woman answered. "This is Sergeant Maggie Bei with the Duluth Police. We talked about Ned Baer a couple of days ago."

"Yes, of course, Sergeant. Do you have news for me?"

"About his death? Not yet. But I do have a few more questions."

"Of course. Anything."

"This will sound like a strange question, but I remember you telling us that you met Ned backstage at a ZZ Top concert in San Jose one summer when you were in college. He was a roadie for the band that year. Is that correct?"

"Yes, that's right."

Maggie could hear puzzlement in her voice. "Do you remember what year that was?"

King hesitated. "Well, hang on, let me think. That was the summer after my junior year at San Jose State."

She rattled off the year, and Maggie wrote down the numbers on the notepad in front of her. It was the year she'd expected the woman to say. That was the same year Denise Forseth had left home to join the Air Force. The same year that the party crawl happened. The same year Andrea Forseth had been raped on the second floor of a house in West Duluth. There were no coincidences.

"Tell me what you remember about Ned back then."

"What do you mean?"

"Well, you said he didn't date much, had an inferiority complex, no personal life. Was that true when you first met him?"

"I guess so, yes."

"Was he a jealous type? Did he resent men who had better luck with women?"

"I don't understand what this has to do with anything, Sergeant."

"I know, Ms. King, but please just answer my question."

"Okay. Yes, Ned could be very bitter about things like that. That was one of the less attractive sides of his personality."

"One more question. Before Ned came out to do the investigation into Devin Card, did he mention whether he'd ever been to Duluth?"

"In fact, he told me a couple of times that he'd never visited Duluth before. Now what is this about, Sergeant?"

"When I can tell you more, I'll be in touch," Maggie replied.

She hung up the phone.

The next thing she did was run a Google search to track down a Wikipedia listing of concert dates for the ZZ Top tour thirty years earlier. Everything in the world was online. She ran through the tour dates for that summer, and there it was.

August 21.

Duluth, Minnesota. The DECC Arena.

Ned Baer had lied to his editor. He'd been in Duluth when he was a roadie for the band. He'd been in Duluth the exact same night that Andrea had been raped.

No coincidences.

"Hello, Maggie. Working late?"

She looked up and saw the trim figure of Dan Erickson in her doorway, with the lights of police headquarters glowing behind him. He came
into her dark office, sat down across from her, and put his glistening
leather shoes on her desk. She was soaking wet from being outside in the
storm, but Dan was dry and perfect. He gave her his usual cocky grin.

"Was that Debbi King you were talking to? What's going on? Did you
learn something new?"

"There was no witness," Maggie told him.

"What?"

Maggie got up from her chair and leaned on the corner of her desk
next to Dan, not caring that her wet hair dripped on his shoes. "Ned told
Stride that he had an anonymous witness who saw Devin and Andrea go
upstairs together. He didn't. *He* was the witness."

"What the hell are you saying?"

She explained everything she'd discovered. Her conversation with Adam
Halka. The stranger from the ZZ Top concert tour tagging along on the party
crawl. That same stranger—jumpy and weird—hauling Adam out of the
party and crashing his father's car on his way home because he was so upset.

"It was Ned Baer," Maggie insisted. "He was there. He was at that
same party. Think about it. Here's this guy who's a stranger in town, drunk,
sexually frustrated, bitter, angry. He sees Devin and Andrea making out,
and he's wild with jealousy. They go upstairs, but then Devin comes back
alone. So he figures he has a golden opportunity. He goes upstairs and
finds the girl passed out on the bed. The room is dark. He assaults her. *Ned
Baer* is the one who raped Andrea."

"You'll never prove that."

"Maybe not, but it makes sense. It fits. Years later, Ned reads the story
about the rape accusation against Devin Card, and he realizes that he
knows all about it. All the details match with what happened that night.
He knows that *he* was the one up in that bedroom, not Devin. For years,
he's been worried about the rape being exposed, but instead, he finds out
that Andrea thought it was someone else the whole time! She was so drunk
that she never realized that Devin left and a stranger came up to the room
and took his place."

Dan frowned, but Maggie knew that frown. He knew she was right.

"As a journalist, Ned figures this is a gift wrapped story," she went on. "He knows details about the assault that nobody else does. He knows when the party happened. He knows what the girl looked like. He's got a head start in trying to find her. That's why he was able to locate Andrea when none of the other reporters could."

Dan pursed his lips. "You really think you're right about this?"

"Yes, I do."

"Devin's innocent? Ned's the one who actually raped her?"

"Right. Ned was all set to destroy Devin's career for a crime he committed himself."

"Twisted son of a bitch." Dan stood up and grabbed a tissue from her desk and wiped off each of his shoes individually. Then he stood uncomfortably close to her, the way he always did.

"We still have a problem," he said.

Maggie nodded. "I know. We still have no idea who killed him."

* * * * *

Colleen held Cat's hand as she dragged her through the crowd. Cat looked back over her shoulder, knowing that Stride had spotted her. Over the heads of the people around them, she saw Stride talking to Brayden from the stage, and she could read his face. He was furious. She tried to slow Colleen down, but the other girl had surprising strength.

"Where are we going?" Cat asked impatiently.

"Bathroom. Come on. If we lose each other in here, we'll never find each other again."

Colleen yanked Cat through the open doors on the west side of the ballroom. In the corridor, there was a little bit more breathing space among the people and more fresh air. Behind them, Cat could hear an eruption of cheers and jeers and the boom of a microphone over the speakers. The town hall was finally getting underway. Devin Card was being introduced.

"It's starting," Cat said. "We should go back in."

"Two minutes."

Colleen aimed for the door to the women's restroom, and she and Cat went inside. Two other women left as they entered, and they had the bathroom to themselves, just a line-up of sinks and two rows of empty stalls. In here, the voices from the convention center were a muffled, indistinct chatter. Colleen put a finger over her lips to keep Cat quiet, then went into one of the middle stalls. Instead of letting go, she hauled Cat inside with her and locked the door behind them.

"You can't do this yourself?" Cat asked, with a crinkle of annoyance on her forehead. Her back was to the door.

Colleen whispered, and her voice had a hollow echo. "No, silly. I need to tell you something. It's important."

"What is it?"

"It's a *secret*."

"Are you drunk, Colly? Because you're acting weird."

"No, no, no, no, oh Cat, this is so important. I know you don't remember me, but I remember the very first time I saw you in math class. I couldn't take my eyes off you! You looked so amazing, you were so smart. But I couldn't even talk to you. I was too tongue-tied. I get that way sometimes, or at least, I used to. It was that way with Karen, too."

"Who's Karen?"

"Karen! I told you about Karen! Before I came to Duluth, I lived in Madison. That was during my first two years in high school. There was this girl, Karen, and same thing like you, she was so pretty, so smart. My sophomore year, we took all the same classes, went out for the same teams, hung out in the same coffee shops. I told you, she was stalking me!"

"*She?* Your stalker was a girl?"

"Yeah, but Karen told the police it was *me*. She told them I kept sending her notes, kept following her. But she had it all wrong. That was my way of letting her know how cool she was. How much I loved her. She didn't want to admit that she loved me, too. That she was obsessed with me. But I knew."

A tremble wracked Cat's body down to her toes. The truth washed over her like cold rain. "I need to go. Let me out of here."

But Colleen was in front of her, backing Cat up to the door of the stall, her hands pinning Cat's arms against her body. "No, no, no, I haven't told you the *secret* yet! You can't leave! Oh, I was such a mess back then, so shy. I've grown up since then. I'm different now, but you can see that, can't you? Karen didn't understand. She didn't appreciate what was going on between us. But that was my fault, because I couldn't tell her face to face. That would have made all the difference. If you love someone, you have to *tell* them. That was why it didn't work out with Karen."

"What happened to her?" Cat asked in a stricken voice.

"Karen? She disappeared. She was one of those people in the magazines. You know, like I told you about. 'Whatever Happened to Karen Lopez?' Of course, the police thought *I* had something to do with it. Everybody in school did. But that was silly, they could never prove anything. Even so, I decided it was better for me to leave. I was done with Madison, so that's when I came to Duluth. I just packed up everything and went away."

"You left? What about your parents?"

"Oh, my dad died when I was twelve. Somebody shot him. The stupid police never figured out who. And then the same thing happened to my mom right when I was moving to Duluth. Weird, huh? But I didn't need her anymore. I just buried her in a field and left town."

"Holy shit," Cat murmured. She tried to push Colleen away, but the girl grabbed Cat's wrists and held on tight.

"Where are you going, sweetheart? We're finally together! I've waited so long! Seeing you at the cottage today? I could barely stop myself from making love to you right then and there. But I knew we needed to get away first. Soon, darling. Soon we'll be together forever. I told you, I'm packed, just like I was in Madison. We can go tonight."

Colleen kissed Cat roughly and molded her body against her. She let go of one of Cat's wrists and stroked her body everywhere. Under her shirt. Down the back of her shorts. And then in the front, invading between her legs. Cat squirmed to get away, but Colleen had her imprisoned.

"See? I can tell you the secret now. I can finally *show* you. I love you, Cat. I love you, I love you, I love you, I love you, I love you. And you don't have to pretend anymore. You love me, too. I know you do. That first night at Hoops, I could see how you looked at me. Wow, what a relief that was! To see how much you wanted me, just like I wanted you!"

"You're nuts," Cat said. "You're out of your mind. Let me go!"

Colleen's face twisted in unhappy confusion. "What's the matter, my love? What's wrong? Are you still scared of Wyatt? Do you think he's going to come between us? You don't have to worry about him. I took care of him for you."

"You took care of him? Oh, my God, what did you do?"

Colleen squeezed Cat into the corner of the stall. The girl dug into her purse and came out with a black semi-automatic pistol in her hand. She placed the side of the barrel gently against Cat's temple. The burnt smell of the gun was in Cat's nose, and she knew it had been fired recently.

"Wyatt won't bother you anymore, my love."

"Oh, shit, you killed him!"

"I had to! I didn't have a choice! He'll never stalk you again."

"But that was *you!*"

"Me? No, no, what I sent you were *love* letters. I could see how Wyatt looked at you. He was obviously infatuated with you, that little pervert. I had to do something about that. The same with that cop, Brayden. The two of you kissing on the hillside? That was very naughty, Cat. I was pretty upset with you for cheating on me like that. I confess I lost my temper. But then I realized it was his fault, not yours. You're too pure. You're too beautiful. He's the one who tempted you. I was shooting at him, not you."

Cat felt tears running down her face. "Colleen, put down the gun. Please. Put it away."

"I need the gun to protect us, Cat! This way, no one will stop us or get in our way. I told you, we can go right now. My car's outside. It will be hours before anyone realizes we're missing. By that time, we can be anywhere. It's going to be amazing, Cat. You and me on the road. Like ghosts. You'll be on the cover of *People* again, and this time, *I'll* be with you. Everyone will be looking for us, but no one will ever find us. We'll be legends. Come away with me, Cat!"

Cat breathed hard. She needed an escape. Just one moment to buy her freedom. "Okay."

"Really?"

"Yes. You're right. Let's go quickly. Before anyone sees us."

"Oh, Cat, *yes!* I knew you'd understand. But first, tell me you love me. Please, sweetheart. I need to hear you say it. I need to see those perfect lips of yours form the words."

"With a gun to my head, Colly? Really?"

Colleen giggled. "Oh, sorry! I forgot!"

She pointed the barrel of the gun at the bathroom floor. She took a step back, and Cat came forward, her fingers around the girl's neck, caressing her skin. She leaned in, her lips breathing warmly on Colleen's mouth.

"I love you," Cat said.

"I knew you did. I knew it. Say my name."

"I love you, Colly."

"Yes, oh yes, kiss me. Kiss me."

Colleen closed her eyes, waiting breathlessly, hungrily. Cat brushed her lips against the other girl's mouth, and Colleen sank backward on weak knees. This was the moment.

With a hand on the girl's cheek, Cat slammed Colleen's head into the metal wall of the stall as hard as she could.

Blood flew. Bone cracked. Colleen unleashed a guttural scream of pain and rage.

Cat spun around, unlocked the door of the stall, and ran.

35

Devin Card stared at the unruly crowd, the way he had hundreds of times in his career. The supporters tried to drown out the protesters, and the protesters raised their voices in response. Card tightened the knot in his tie, smiled, waved, and walked from one end of the stage to the other, bending down to shake hands. Town halls fed his ego, regardless of whether people were cheering him or screaming at him, but tonight he was nervous. He wondered if it showed on his face as he sweated under the bright lights.

For the first time in his career, he didn't know what to say. His entire future hung in the balance in the next few minutes, and the pressure weighed on him. Every word, every expression, every twitch of his mouth or blink of his eyes, would be analyzed and reanalyzed by the press in the months ahead.

Come November, he would either be Senator Devin Card, or Devin Card, private citizen.

Devin Card, rapist.

He stepped up to the microphone in the very center of the stage and held up both hands for quiet, but that didn't work. The roar became rhythmic chanting. Loyalists shouted his name: "*De-vin, De-vin, De-vin, De-vin.*" He grinned, soaking it all in. When he glanced to his right, he saw Peter Stanhope and several of his senior aides waiting on the far side of the stage. They smiled back at him and gave him the thumbs up. But they were nervous, too.

"Hello, Duluth!" Card bellowed into the microphone, his voice booming through the convention center.

The crowd wouldn't let him talk. The noise got louder.

"It's great to be back home in the Zenith City!" he said, trying again, smiling as the shouts drowned him out. He raised his hands to settle them down, and he repeated his greeting multiple times. It took several minutes before the deafening tumult in the ballroom began to fade, like the keynote at a political convention.

Finally, he had the floor.

"Hello, Duluth!" Card said again, trying to sound casual and relaxed. "And thank you to everyone for showing up here tonight, with your questions, with your encouragement, with your support. And yes, with your opposition, too."

A small spat broke out in the crowd but was silenced. Card used the pause to focus on the faces nearest to the front of the stage. In his mind, he isolated the women who were the right age and tried to read their eyes. He tried to see what they were thinking as they looked at him. Was she there? Was the woman looking back at him right now? He needed to decide how to react when she stood up and announced herself, and he still didn't know.

What to do. What to say.

His staff had told him: *Wait.*

Don't bring it up. Wait until the woman comes forward. Maybe she won't show. Maybe this was all a ruse, another chance to change the subject from politics to his past. Until there was a real human being to put a face to the accusation, he should pretend it didn't exist.

He took a deep breath. He launched into his remarks, using the script his staff had worked up for him. The teleprompter scrolled the words, and he followed the plan.

"An election isn't about me," Card told the crowd. "It may be my name on the ballot, but elections are about all of you. They're about making choices. Making sacrifices. Deciding the kind of life we want for ourselves, for our families, for our friends and neighbors, and figuring out how to lay the groundwork for the next generation. We don't always agree about the best ways to do that, but that's okay. As long as we listen to each other, disagreement makes us stronger. Addressing the concerns of our opponents makes our plans better. That's why I'm here. To talk about those things. To listen to you. To hear what you think, what you have to say, what you like and don't like, what you're afraid of, and what you're excited about."

Card stopped.

He had a lot more to say, but he let the silence draw out. The teleprompter froze where it was, waiting for him to continue. His staff exchanged uncomfortable glances. So did the people in the crowd. The longer he stood there without speaking, the more people began to shuffle on their feet and wonder what was going.

"Okay, look," Card told them, going off the prepared script. He took the microphone off its stand and walked to the front of the stage. "Here's the thing. I really believe elections are about you, but this town hall, right now, right here ... well, let's face it. We all know it's about me. It's about an anonymous accusation from back when I was in college. An accusation that I have said over and over is *not* true. But you've seen what they're saying in the media. So have I. Supposedly, the person who made that accusation is here tonight. Some people have suggested that I should pretend like this situation doesn't exist, but I'm not going to do that. I want to talk to this woman directly. If you're here, I invite you to come up here on stage and say what you want to say. Let's not wait. Let's deal with this right now."

People began to look around, and an expectant hush fell across the crowd.

"I get it, you may be reluctant to do that," Card continued. "I've said harsh things about this accusation in the past, and that's not because I don't believe women. It's because politics can be an ugly business. When you're accused of something but you can't put a name to the person behind it, well, you start to wonder if it was all made up just to tear you down. Believe me, there are radicals on both sides of the political aisle who will do those things. It happens. Still, I understand. If you're sincere, if this was a genuine accusation, then you're probably thinking to yourself: He knows who I am. He knows what he did. All I can tell you is, I really don't. I'm not diminishing whatever happened to you or saying I don't believe you, but I think there has been some kind of terrible misunderstanding here, and I'd like to clear it up. This may not be the best forum to do that, but here we are. So if you're in this room, please, come up and talk to me. You talk, I'll listen. The stage is yours."

Devin put the microphone down and looked out across the crowd. He waited.

Everyone waited.

It was now or never.

* * * * *

Stride felt his phone vibrating. He stood on a corner of the stage and backed up into the shadows as he pulled it out. Outside, the storm raged on, lightning flashing on the tall windows, thunder making the building shake. The entire room seemed to be holding its breath.

He checked the caller ID.

"Mags," he whispered into the phone.

"I've been calling you for half an hour and couldn't get through," she told him.

"Signal's terrible. What's going on?"

"Have you found her? Have you found Andrea at the DECC?"

Stride shook his head. "No, Serena and I have both been looking, but we haven't located her yet. It's a madhouse in here."

"You have to stop her. Don't let her go public."

"We're trying, but why? What have you found? Did you talk to Halka?"

Maggie's words tumbled out. "It wasn't him, boss. Halka didn't do it. It was Ned Baer. Ned was a roadie at the big ZZ Top concert in Duluth that night. He was *there*. He went to the party with Halka, the one where Andrea was assaulted. You know what that means. It was him. It had to be him."

Stride closed his eyes and silently swore.

"How sure are you about this, Mags?"

"As sure as I can be after thirty years. Do you believe in coincidences?

Because I don't. Baer kept it a secret. He didn't want anyone to know he was in Duluth that night, because *he did it*."

Stride could see Ned Baer's face in his head again. He could see him at the Deeps, that nasty smile on his face, proud of what he'd done. That man had violated Andrea as a girl and then violated her all over again years later by coming to town to expose her secret.

It made Stride wish he'd been the one to pull the trigger.

"Andrea won't believe it," he went on.

"Maybe not, but if she goes up there and confronts Devin, and then this all comes out, it will destroy her," Maggie went on. "You can't let her do it."

Stride stared across the stage, and his heart fell.

"Too late," he said. "She's here."

* * * * *

Andrea held her breath at the top of the steps on the west side of the ballroom stage. It took a while for anyone to realize she was there. For that fleeting moment, she was still anonymous. She froze where she was, gathering her strength, debating whether to turn and walk away while she still had time to stay out of the spotlight.

She could go back home if she changed her mind right now. She could live her life. It was sad, it was shadowed, but it was still a life. She could make peace with who she was and what she'd done. *Forgive every sin*. She almost turned around and preserved all of that, but she waited too long, and circumstances made the decision for her. One second of hesitation passed, and there was no going back.

Peter Stanhope noticed her first. His gaze passed across her without really seeing her, but then, as if by instinct, it went back and stopped. He stared at her with a kind of curious horror. She could tell. He knew, watching her face. She could see him whisper to the person next to him, could see his lips form the words.

It's her.

Someone with a camera noticed her next. A journalist. He took a picture. The pop of the flash, as bright as the lightning storm, made her squint and cover her eyes, and suddenly, others began to look her way. Murmurings began, a growing undercurrent, a rumor that became a living thing in the ballroom. People pointed at her. Every gaze shot toward her. More cameras flashed, and video cameras swung toward the end of the stage. The staff saw her, the crowd saw her, the seas began to part to let her through. A long stretch of empty stage opened up in front of her, a clear path for her to walk toward Devin Card.

He was the last one to realize she was there.

For a long moment, he was oblivious, trying to understand the changed dynamic in the ballroom. Everything was different, and he obviously didn't know why. Then, finally, Devin saw her, too. They stared at each other. He studied her like a scientist discovering an unusual new species. It was all too obvious that he knew she was *the one*, and it was equally obvious that he had no idea who she was. No idea at all. She was a total stranger to him. That, more than anything else, made her furious. This man had been the central figure in her entire life, had dominated her thoughts every day, and he didn't even recognize her. He had used her and thrown her away and forgotten her. His life had gone on, a life in which she didn't matter at all. Meanwhile, she hadn't been able to get his face out of her mind. He'd always been there, tormenting her, reminding her of what she'd lost, of what she'd given up.

Andrea started across the stage. She didn't hurry. Someone, from somewhere, came up and handed her a microphone. She held it in her hand and thought: *I have a voice now.* It made her feel strong, made her walk with a confident step. All the years had led her to this moment. Devin watched her come, and she could see uncertainty cross his face, confusion fill his eyes. He was racking his brain, hunting to find her there, trying to pull her out of some dusty drawer in the back of his head.

Do you know me?

There were thousands of people in the room, but now it was just the two of them.

She stopped when she was six feet away. Devin didn't say a word. He was waiting for her to begin. The whole ballroom waited for her, wanting to see what would happen next.

"My name is Andrea Forseth," she said into the microphone.

Just like that, a thousand journalists keyed her name into search engines. She would never be anonymous again. The first line in her obituary had just been written.

"Hello, Ms. Forseth," Devin Card replied. "Thank you for coming forward. I know this must be hard for you."

Her mouth was dry. She had trouble forming words.

"I know you won't admit what you did to me," Andrea said, hearing her voice in the room like the voice of a stranger. "I know you can't. But that's not even why I'm here. That's not what I want. After all this time, it doesn't even matter to me to hear you say it. I know what happened to me. I know how my life changed that night. You can deny it, or say I made a mistake, or say I never told you to stop even though I did, but I don't care. Like I said, that's not what I want from you."

Devin waited a long time before he said anything. He wasn't going to interrupt her.

"What *do* you want from me, Ms. Forseth?" he asked.

She stared into the face that had haunted her dreams for decades. It was an older face now, but still with the same wavy blond hair, still with the same movie star blue eyes, the same masculine confidence that life would give him whatever he wanted. He was the football quarterback and always would be.

Andrea inhaled and put down the microphone, so that he was the only one who could hear her. "I want you to say that you remember me."

36

Brayden stared, transfixed, at the blond woman on the stage in front of Devin Card. In the midst of looking for Cat, he simply stopped what he was doing and couldn't take his eyes off her. She came out of nowhere, emerging from the crowd of people crushed around the west-side steps. She had a kind of simple grace, not like a victim and not like a hero. And yet her presence electrified the room, as if royalty had joined them. She was right there above Brayden, barely twenty feet away from him, staring straight ahead at the man she'd accused. He felt others pushing to get closer to the stage, wanting to see her face.

The whispers began.

That's her. She's the one. Who is she?

Then she answered the question for them.

"My name is Andrea Forseth."

Brayden heard her speak, and she had a surprisingly powerful voice. He thought about the courage it took for her to be here. To stand up for herself in this place. All day long, he'd heard reports in the media that the anonymous victim would finally come forward, and he hadn't believed it would really happen. There was no way she would put herself through this circus. But here she was. Looking at her now and seeing the wolves gather, he could only wish she'd stayed away. She would never have peace again. They would rip apart her life, pry open every secret.

There was no reward for trying to do the right thing. Only regret.

When she put down the microphone, he was near enough to her to read her lips. *I want you to tell me that you remember me.*

But she already knew the truth. Devin Card didn't remember her at all. The look on her face was eloquent, the look that said she'd made a mistake by opening Pandora's box. Better to keep the demons locked inside.

The emotional drama up on the stage made Brayden want to close his eyes. This was too painful to see.

Then his phone interrupted him, the ring tone muffled in his pocket. He wanted to ignore it, wanted to stay focused on the woman just above him, but he knew he couldn't. He covered one ear with his hand and looked away as he answered the phone. It was a 911 dispatcher, transferring an emergency call to him.

As the transfer came through, he began to say his name, but he didn't even get it out before a voice erupted over the line.

"Shit, man, it's her! You've got stop her! It's Colleen! It's Colly!"

Brayden winced at the shouting. "Who is this? Curt? Is that you?"

"Yeah, it's me, man. She killed him. She fucking killed Wyatt, man! Blew his head off! I found his body in her apartment!"

"Curt, what the hell are you talking about?"

"*Colleen!*" Curt bellowed into the phone. "Damn it, aren't you listening to me? It was her, man, it was never Wyatt. *She's* the one stalking Cat. Colly's the one obsessed with her. You've got to get Cat away from that girl, man! That bitch is going to kill her!"

"*Shit!*"

Brayden shoved the phone back in his pocket.

He pushed through the crowd in a panic, shoving people aside, shouting for everyone to get out of his way, but he had no idea where to go. He'd lost her. He'd failed.

Cat needed him, and he'd failed.

Where was she?

* * * * *

Devin didn't remember her. She was a fool to think he would.

All these years, Andrea had harbored the notion that when Devin finally came face to face with her, he would recognize the girl he'd assaulted. She would see an awakening in his eyes as he studied her features. You couldn't rape someone and forget who she was. You couldn't erase that person completely from your memory.

But he had. His face was completely blank as he shook his head. She was a nobody to him. As far as Devin Card was concerned, he'd never seen her before.

Andrea lifted the microphone again.

"You were the first boy I ever kissed," she said. "Did you know that? I don't remember whether I told you that at the time. You said I reminded you of Nicole Kidman. You said I was even prettier than she was, and you asked if I wanted to make out, and I said yes. You asked me if I wanted to go upstairs, and I said yes. I thought that's what I wanted. I mean, I was with *Devin Card*. That was every girl's fantasy back then. But later, I said *no*. I told you that I wanted you to *stop*. And you didn't listen to me."

Card said nothing. She could see him clenching his jaw shut as his face turned to stone. He knew she wasn't lying. He might not recognize her, but he recognized *himself* in her description. He knew she was talking about him, not anybody else. *That line about Nicole Kidman. How many times did you use that one, Devin? It wasn't just with me. You said that to all the girls, didn't you?*

"I'm sure there were so many of us back then. That's the problem, isn't it? So many parties. So many conquests." She put down the microphone and stepped closer and spoke under her breath. "Do you need a clue about when it was? Peter Stanhope fucked my sister in front of everybody that night. Don't tell me you forgot that, Devin. That's when it happened."

She watched his mind working furiously.

Oh yes, he remembered that. She could see a new awakening in his eyes. He felt doubt. She was pushing buttons, reminding him of things he'd done, things he'd seen. Maybe it had really happened just the way she said.

Nicole Kidman. Peter and Denise.

Is any of it coming back now, Devin?

Card took a step away from her. She could see him breathing slowly in and out. She waited. Everyone waited. What would he say? He put the microphone to his mouth, then put it down. Impatience spread through the ballroom like a virus. He had to say something. Here she was, in front of him. She'd done what he asked her to do; she'd come forward, identified herself, and told her story. Not one word of it had changed.

You know I'm telling the truth, Devin.

But as Andrea waited in the silence, she saw someone out of the corner of her eye. Stride. Her ex-husband. The man she'd tried to love, the man she'd kept all of her secrets from, the man who'd cheated on her, the man she'd lost. He was on stage, walking toward her, beckoning her. The cameras hadn't noticed him yet. Only she had. His presence distracted her, tore her away from her focus on Devin. She wanted Stride gone, wanted no one else to be part of this moment. She needed to hear what Devin would say. This was the moment she'd wanted for years.

Go away!

But he kept coming closer. Andrea's gaze bounced away from Devin, over to Stride, and then back. Stride wanted to talk to her, but she couldn't imagine *why*. Not now. Not in the middle of this. His expression was inscrutable, the way it always was, sharing nothing.

"Andrea," he murmured.

Her whole body tensed. She needed him to *leave*. He was ruining everything. Devin was about to talk, but then he saw Stride, too, and he knew that something was wrong; something strange was happening. He put down the microphone, and Andrea wilted with dismay. She'd missed her chance. The moment was gone, and moments like that never came back.

She found herself unable to move. She stood where she was, waiting, feeling the tears come. Stride came closer and closer, until he was right next to her. His body close to her, still familiar after all this time. Everyone saw him; everyone had the same question about why he was there. She tried to summon her voice to tell him to go, to shout at him, but she knew, she knew, he had something to tell her.

Something that she didn't want to hear.

He leaned in so close that no one else could hear him speak.

"Andrea, I'm sorry. You need to know this. We think *Ned Baer* was in Duluth that night thirty years ago. We think he was *at* the party where you were assaulted. I just wanted you to be aware of that. Because maybe … maybe somewhere in your mind, it means something to you."

She heard the words he said, but she hardly heard them at all.

She blinked over and over.

"Ned Baer," she murmured. And then again. "Ned Baer."

That man. That man had come into her house seven years ago, with his questions, with his prying and prodding about her past. With things he *knew*, things no one else knew. She'd tried to stay calm, to deflect and deny, but the more she told him that she didn't know what he was talking about, the more she fell to pieces and gave away the truth. He was going to expose her secret. Everything was going to come out.

And yet there was something more.

There had always been something more about him.

There was this smell about him that instinctively made her sick. The touch when he shook her hand made her skin crawl. Seeing him, hearing the raspy noise of his breath, made her want to run and hide. And as she fell apart, as she admitted to him without saying a word that this had all happened to *her*, there was the strangest vibe about him, something twitchy and aroused and afraid.

She knew what it was now.

It was the look she'd wanted to see from Devin Card. The look of truth. The admission of guilt.

Ned Baer *remembered her.*

"Oh, my God," she said aloud, her hand flying to cover her mouth.

She didn't have time to say anything more.

Behind her, the screaming began.

37

Cat pushed through the people that filled the corridor. She made it into the chaos of the ballroom, but when she looked over her shoulder, she saw Colleen not far behind. The girl emerged from the bathroom with a ribbon of blood dripping through her hair and down her pale cheek. Her gaze traveled with the coldness of a robot from person to person until it landed on Cat, and their eyes met across the crowd. The tiny smile on Colleen's face lusted after her, but her stare had the sharpness of a hawk's talons, ready to cut into prey.

The densely packed men and women formed a wall in front of Cat. She shoved against it, trying to get through, but she felt mired in quicksand as she fought her way deeper into the ballroom. She looked for Brayden, she looked for a police officer, a security guard—someone, anyone—but all the people blurred into a single mass in front of her eyes, and she could barely see who was around her.

"*Cat.*"

The other girl's voice trailed her like the sultry whisper of a lover. Cat looked back again, and Colleen was barely even six feet behind her now, calmly threading the maze and catching up with her.

"Cat, don't run from this," Colleen told her. "Don't run from me. I don't want to hurt you."

Other voices bubbled up around them. They saw the blood on Colleen's face, and fear spread from body to body. *That girl. Look at her. What's going on? Find the police!* In their confusion, they squeezed together, tightening the web around Cat and giving her nowhere to go. She beat her fists to get them to separate, but the crowd drew in like a claustrophobic mass of strange faces and eyes that made her dizzy.

"Cat."

She tried to scream and couldn't even muster the sound. The bodies around her held her in place. Colleen floated toward her; one moment, she was a few steps away, and the next, she was in front of her, pulling Cat to her with a hand around her neck. Colleen's blood smeared on Cat's cheek as their faces came together. The girl's other hand came up, and Cat felt the gun press into her chest below the swell of her breasts, hidden from view. The barrel pointed upward, where the bullet would sever bones and arteries on its way through her. Colleen spoke into her ear.

"Cat, why are you running from me?"

"Let me go. You're crazy!"

"Cat, I don't blame you. You've been poisoned against me. Curt, Brayden, Wyatt, Stride, everyone, they all want to keep us apart. They don't realize that we're meant to be together. I wanted us to run away. You and me. I wanted us to be ghosts. Mysteries. Legends, remembered forever. It would have been amazing. But I guess we'll have to jump to the very end. We'll die in each other's arms. Your blood and my blood, mingled together."

"Colleen, don't do this. Please, stop, don't do this."

Cat tried to wriggle away, but the girl held her tightly and pressed against her. The gun pushed harder into her chest. Cat stared into Colleen's eyes and saw there was no hope. No escape and no way out. Those frozen, dark brown eyes came from another world.

"This will be quick. No pain. Then I'll join you. Don't worry, you won't be alone, my love."

This was the last moment. Colleen's eyes drifted shut. Cat knew the next thing that happened would be Colleen squeezing the trigger and the bullet ripping through her body.

Then, out of nowhere, a man in the crowd stumbled heavily into Colleen. Like a miracle, the gun swung away from Cat's chest. Cat grabbed Colleen's wrist and hung on, and a woman near them looked over and saw the two girls struggling over the pistol.

"*Gun!*" she screamed.

Someone else shouted it, too. "*Gun!*"

"*Police!*"

With Colleen's arm swinging back and forth and Cat desperately trying to hang on, the girl squeezed the trigger. A man in the crowd lurched back, a bullet searing through his shoulder. The explosion echoed against the ceiling, and screams and wails rose out of a thousand throats. Panic seized the ballroom, and a stampede began. Running bodies spilled against them, driving the two of them apart. Cat had an instant of freedom where she could see the steps to the stage right in front of her, and she ran. She bolted up the stairs, knowing Colleen was behind her, knowing she had only seconds to save herself. She didn't look back.

Cat burst onto the stage, where she saw a long stretch of empty space ahead of her and three people standing apart from all the others, bathed under the hot glow of lights.

One of them was the man who had saved her life over and over and over. Stride.

Cat sprinted for him.

* * * * *

Stride looked up as the gun went off, as pandemonium set in, and had the strangest experience of his life. He didn't know whether it was a vision, or a hallucination, or a waking dream. He looked across the empty stage, and there was Ned Baer, soaking wet the way he'd been at the Deeps, with a bullet wound oozing blood from the center of his forehead.

Ned's lips pulled back into a skeletal grin. The smile on the man's face widened and turned into a mocking, cruel laugh. Ned raised his arm and extended a bony, brittle finger at Stride's chest, and he shouted across the stage.

"*You're the one who's dead!*"

Then the hallucination vanished.

Ned disappeared from Stride's sight, and where he'd been, Stride saw Cat running across the stage, her hair flying, her face twisted with terror. Stride ran, too, meeting the girl halfway and gathering her up in his arms. Her heart beat wildly against his chest as he held her, and she clung to him as if he could save her from everything.

"Cat, what's going on?" he heard himself say. The words seemed to come from someone else, sounds that were disconnected from his body.

Stride looked around the stage. The world slowed down, and every tick of the clock took forever. He heard a roaring in his ears, as if his body had crashed underwater. Everything seemed so crisp, so clear, a film moving a single frame at a time. He saw it all in slow motion, saw everything happening around him in the span of a few heartbeats.

There was Andrea, paralyzed in the middle of the stage with a look of confusion and fear. He could hear himself shouting at her to duck, to get down, but she stayed where she was, as if rooted to the ground.

There was Devin Card bolting to the front of the stage with the microphone in his hand, his voice booming through the ballroom, telling everyone to stay calm, not to panic.

There was Serena leaping up the steps on the east end of the stage, her arms and legs pumping as she ran. And yet every step she made happened at a glacial pace in Stride's mind. She hardly moved at all; she was still so far away. She had a gun in her hand, and as he watched, she sank to one knee and aimed.

She screamed.

"*Stop! Drop it! Drop it!*"

There was Brayden, the young cop, on the ballroom floor below the stage. Sweat poured down the man's face. He had his gun in hand, too, pointed where Serena was pointing, and he screamed just as she did.

"*Colleen, put the gun down! Put it down!*"

Slow, slow, slow.

The world hardly moved at all.

Stride felt his head rotating ever so slowly like the wheel of an overturned car. He followed Serena's eyes, followed Brayden's eyes, followed the direction of their guns, and they all led him to a girl walking calmly across the stage. No one else was around her. Everyone else had jumped from the stage or dived to the floor. She was a pretty blond girl, not even twenty years old, with brown eyes and a cryptic smile and blood on her face.

She had a pistol at the end of her outstretched arms.

Pointed at Cat. Pointed at Stride.

Stride heard the muffled noise of his own voice from deep in that ocean inside his mind. "*No!*"

Slow oh so slow, the world hardly moved at all.

His body had the thickness of honey as he tried to react. He felt himself pushing Cat down, throwing her to the ground, felt himself stepping over her, kneeling, and blocking her with his body.

Then it was just the two of them, the girl with the gun and Stride acting as a shield between her and Cat.

The world sped up again.

Everyone began to fire.

38

Brayden steadied his gun arm and fired once, twice, three times, four times, five times. So did Serena, from her higher angle on the stage. It happened so fast that his head spun; it happened as everyone else ran, ducked down, fell, and jumped to get free. Brayden tried to quash his adrenaline and aim, to focus every shot on the girl and not the people that interrupted his line of sight. Bodies came and went like flashes of light; people screamed. He couldn't tell whose bullets hit home, but he saw gunfire riddle Colleen, striking her in the chest, stomach, and legs, drawing blood and making her limbs jump like a marionette.

But Colleen fired, too.

She squeezed off multiple shots as her arm went wild, as bullets flew up, down, and sideways. A deadly crossfire laced the stage. Then one shot in the middle of her forehead ended the battle in an instant. Brayden didn't know whose gun caused her death. Their fire overlapped, as if timed with the thunder of the storm. Colleen's gun dropped from her hand to the floor. Her body pitched straight forward, like a pencil falling.

Even with the gunfire over, panic gripped the ballroom. The crowd flooded for the doors, trampling over abandoned political signs. Police and security fought past them in the opposite direction, heading for the stage. Screams lingered, and peopled huddled near the walls, crying.

Brayden holstered his gun and boosted himself onto the stage platform. He walked toward Colleen's prone body, first securing the gun that lay near her hand, and then squatting next to the body to confirm that the girl was dead. Her face was sideways on the floor, her frozen eyes still wide open, the same tiny smile lingering on her lips. Blood made a widening pool beneath her and red stripes down her forehead.

He got to his feet and studied the rest of the stage. Not far away, he saw Serena Stride kneeling over a body, touching her fingers to someone's neck, trying to get a pulse.

Who was it?

It was a woman's body, and he thought: *Cat*.

Brayden ran over there, his breath leaving his chest. He stared down, shaking his head, not believing what he saw. The woman at his feet wasn't Cat. It was Andrea Forseth. She lay on her back, eyes closed, her face at peace. A bullet had penetrated the side of her skull, and her blond hair was crimson with blood.

He opened his mouth to ask if she was dead, but he didn't need to ask. She was gone.

Serena looked up. "You're Brayden, aren't you?"

"Yes."

He watched her mouth tighten as she held back the things she wanted to say. To throw blame at him for not protecting Cat, for letting everything spin out of control. He wanted her to scream at him, but she looked away and focused on the body.

"The girl didn't shoot her," Serena said.

"What?"

"The angle's wrong. I'm pretty sure it was one of us."

"*What?*"

"I'm afraid we killed her, Brayden. Either you or me."

"No. No, that can't be true."

Her voice had the dead dullness of someone forcing down her emotions. "That's what it looks like. When we run ballistics, we'll know for sure."

Brayden blinked over and over. "I killed her?"

"She strayed into the line of fire. It was an accident. We had an active shooter, Brayden. People panic. They lurch one way or another. Sometimes terrible things happen."

Tears leached down his face. "*I killed her.*"

"We don't know that yet. It might have been me. No matter who it was, it wasn't your fault."

Brayden looked down at Andrea, and then he looked at the position of Colleen's body. He stared down at the ballroom floor, where he'd aimed his gun across the stage. Those seconds of gunfire had felt like hours. People had run, blocked him, forced him to stutter his shots. Even so, he knew. In the whirl of adrenaline, he knew. He could see it happen.

He'd been pulling the trigger as Andrea awakened from her trance and tried to flee the stage.

"I did it," he said. "I tried to hold back the shot, but I was too late."

Serena stood up and squeezed his shoulder. "Find a place to sit down for a while. It's going to be a long night."

Brayden felt dazed. His brain began to spin, and acid bubbled into his mouth, making him want to vomit. He tried to walk, but he nearly lost his footing, and Serena had to hold him up.

"What about Cat?" he asked, trying to make sense of what was happening to him. "Is she okay? Where's Cat?"

* * * * *

Cat lay on her stomach, her hands over her head, not daring to move. She waited for the gunfire to stop, but then she realized it already had, and she wasn't hearing bullets anymore. The crack she heard was thunder, rattling the building like ice calving from a glacier. A downpour of rain tapped on the windows. The smell of smoke tainted the air, bitter and sharp. She heard voices talking; she heard the thump of footsteps on the stage. The screams of the crowd had quieted.

It was over.

She opened her eyes. Stride was next to her, but the first thing she saw was Colleen's face. The girl lay on the stage twenty feet away, eyes fixed, staring back at her even though she was dead. That image, that look, was going to linger in her dreams. She could still taste Colleen on her lips and smell her on her clothes. She still expected the girl's mouth to open and for her to start talking from the grave.

I love you, Cat.

We'll be ghosts together.

Cat stood up slowly, her legs wobbling. She tried to take a step and had to steady herself. She saw Brayden, his face stricken, his eyes full of tears, but he didn't see her. When she tried to call his name, she found that her voice was missing, unable to form words. She saw Serena kneeling by a body, and she realized that people had been shot. People had died.

Then someone pointed at her. Some stranger. Shouts and screams traveled across the room at her, and people began to run her way. She didn't know why until she looked down at her clothes and saw that she was covered in blood. When she glanced at her feet, there was more blood there. Blood was on the stage; she was standing in it. She patted herself all over, certain she'd been shot, but she felt no pain, no injury; she saw no wounds or bullet holes, and when she peeled up her shirt, her skin was unharmed.

And yet she was covered in blood.

"Am I hit, Stride?" Cat murmured. "Did Colleen shoot me?"

Stride didn't answer.

She noticed him, as if for the first time. He still lay on the stage, where he'd been when she opened her eyes. He wasn't moving.

"Stride?"

Cat's whole body began to shake uncontrollably, like a young tree bending in a wind storm. She saw blood on the stage, saw blood where she was standing, and she realized it was coming from beneath Stride. From his body. Her hands tore at her hair, and she sank down to the ground in disbelief. She knelt in the blood and grabbed Stride's shoulder, and with a fierce energy, she pushed him over, so that he lay on his back. His eyes were closed, his face pale.

His chest was covered in blood. Fresh, cherry-red blood, growing and spreading into a misshapen stain. A mass of blood, the kind of loss no one should survive. And amid all the blood, there was a scorched bullet hole in his chest, ripped through the fabric, right where his heart was.

"Stride? *Stride?* Oh, my God, no! No, no, no!"

Tears spilled from her eyes like a flood. Her fists squeezed open and closed. She cupped her hands under his head, shook him, and tried to wake him up, but he wouldn't move. Her body twisted around, and her voice filled the room with her scream.

"*Serena!*"

39

"He's in emergency surgery," Serena told Maggie, her voice drained of all inflexion. "They said even if it goes well, it's likely to be a while until we know anything. If it doesn't go well, I guess we'll know quickly."

She stood by the hospital windows and stared with dead eyes at the blackness of the night, which was interrupted by lightning over the lake. The storm refused to move off, and heavy rain beat against the glass. The waiting room was warm and hushed.

Maggie slung an arm around Serena's waist and held on tight. Serena hardly even felt it. She didn't feel anything.

"Where was he hit?" Maggie asked softly.

"The heart."

She heard Maggie suck in a long, ragged breath.

"They say it's a single chamber injury, which apparently is a good thing," Serena went on, mouthing the words and barely hearing them. "If multiple chambers were affected, he'd have almost no chance. They also said he wasn't in cardiac arrest when they took him into surgery, and that's a good thing, too."

"Okay."

Serena's lower lip trembled. "I asked the surgeon to give me odds. She didn't want to, but I pushed her."

"What did she say?"

"One in four."

"That he dies?"

"That he lives."

Beside her, Maggie began to cry, and tears crept down Serena's face, too, as if all the emotion she was keeping inside had to find a way to get out. The two of them stood like that for a long time, in silence, in tears. Serena had always heard about people in near-death experiences seeing their lives pass before their eyes, but she found that her own life passed in front of her now.

Instead of the Duluth night, she saw her past with Jonny go through her mind, one memory after another.

Getting off the plane at the Duluth airport, seeing Stride and Maggie for the first time, not realizing that her life had just changed permanently.

Making love with him on the cold beach of the Point in the darkness.

Jonny rescuing her from a burning shanty in the middle of a frozen lake, where she'd been held captive and tortured. The sight of his face, the love in his eyes, as he took her in his arms.

The awfulness of him confessing that he'd slept with Maggie, the bitter separation that followed, the reunion that finally came when Cat entered their lives.

And that moment at the green bench at the end of the Point—the sacred place where Stride confronted everything that was good and bad in his life—when he'd finally said goodbye to Cindy's ghost and gone down on one knee to ask Serena to marry him.

All those memories came and went in an instant, and she was right back where she was, in the hospital, waiting to see whether her husband lived or died.

"Half the police force is in the lobby downstairs," Maggie told her. In her own Maggie way, she added a joke. "Honestly, if you want to commit a crime in Duluth, this is a pretty good time."

Serena tried to find a smile, but it wasn't there.

"Everyone is praying for him," Maggie went on. "He's the toughest man I know, Serena. Not just physically tough, but soul tough. He's determined. He never gives up. I don't care what anyone says the odds are. He won't leave you."

"Except we both know that's not how life works," Serena murmured.

Maggie shook her head fiercely. "I don't know that at all. Not tonight. I may be a cynical bitch most days of my life, and I may think the universe is mostly playing a big joke on us, but not tonight. I prayed, too. For both of you. I had to introduce myself to God, because it's not like we're best friends or anything, but I prayed."

"Thank you, Maggie."

Serena wanted to find comfort in the idea that the city was praying for Stride, but she didn't know how to take any comfort in anything now. Her own soul was as alone and black as the night. The only glimmers she saw were the flashes of lightning on the other side of the rain-swept glass, and those bursts made her think of shocks of electricity trying and failing to start a heart.

"I told Guppo I'd give him an update," Maggie said. "I should probably find him."

Serena nodded. "Sure. Go."

Maggie turned to leave, but then she stopped. "You know, Serena, for what it's worth, I remember when *you* were shot in the graffiti graveyard and almost died. I don't know if Stride ever told you, but he and Cat prayed for you. They held hands and prayed. He swears that's what brought you back."

"He told me," Serena murmured, but she didn't say anything more than that.

Maggie squeezed her shoulder and left the small waiting room. Serena stayed by the window. She wasn't even sure how much time passed, standing there in a kind of suspended animation. The room was silent, and silence was good, because the only thing that could interrupt the silence now was a door opening, and a surgeon coming in to deliver bad news.

Right now, silence was keeping her alive. Silence meant Jonny hadn't left her.

Except it was too quiet. She cast her gaze around the waiting room and realized that she was alone. Cat had disappeared. The girl had been sitting on the sofa, and now she was gone. Serena spotted the door to the bathroom and saw that it was closed but unlocked. She went over, knocked gently on the door, and called Cat's name. When she got no answer, she slowly pushed open the door. The overhead lights of the bathroom were harsh and bright.

Cat sat on the tiled floor in the corner, her knees pulled up. Her cheeks were flushed beet red from crying, and strands of her chestnut hair fell across her face. She stared straight ahead with vacant, empty, horrified eyes. Serena went over and sat down next to her. She put an arm around the girl's shoulder and stroked her fingers through Cat's hair.

"This is my fault," Cat murmured.

"It's not. Not in any way."

"If he dies, I'm going to kill myself," the girl said.

Serena realized how selfish she'd been, thinking she was alone. Instead, she dug down into herself and summoned words. "No, you're not going to do that. Neither am I. That's not how this goes."

"How can you be calm about this?"

"I'm not calm, Catalina. I'm terrified. But I'm not going to sit here and let you blame yourself. Whatever happens, we need to stay strong. I'm going to be there for you, and you need to be there for me, too. Got it?"

Cat didn't answer, but she felt the girl's shoulders quivering as she cried.

Serena waited a long time to say anything more. "It's okay if you want to pray. You should."

"It won't do any good. It's a waste of time."

"Since when?"

"Since always. Nobody's out there. Nobody cares. You know what I told Stride when I first met him? I said death was just a cold nowhere. No heaven, no hell, no God. Nothing. I was a fool to start believing anything else. I mean, that's what you think, isn't it? You don't believe in any of that."

"It doesn't matter what I believe."

"When's the last time you prayed? I mean, really prayed. God, please help me. Like that."

Serena hesitated. "In Phoenix. When I was being abused."

"Did it work? Did it save you?"

"No."

"Well, see? It's a waste of time."

Serena could almost see the girl's faith taking flight, like a departing angel into the sky. The strange thing was, as Cat's soul grew emptier, Serena felt something taking hold inside herself that she hadn't felt since she was a small child. A belief in something other than what she could touch, hear, and see. It spread throughout her body, and she wanted to wrap Cat up in its warmth.

"I have no idea what's true or what isn't," Serena told her. "But one thing I do know is that if those terrible things hadn't happened to me as a child, I wouldn't be where I am today. I wouldn't know Jonny. I wouldn't know you. That's the reality of my life. Does that make any of it better? Or less painful? No. Of course not. But I guess I've learned something in all my years of being hurt and angry. You have to be a little humble about knowing what it means to have your prayers answered. It may look very different from what you expect."

Cat shook her head. "There's nothing good in this. There's no plan."

"All we can do is wait and see. And hope."

She heard the girl's voice grow shrill with despair. "There's no hope. He's going away."

"Don't say that."

Cat twisted around in her lap and stared up at her. "He's not here anymore! He's somewhere else. I can feel it, and I know you can, too. Don't lie to me. I can feel him going away from us."

"Shh. Don't talk anymore."

Cat buried her face again, and Serena kept stroking the girl's hair as Cat sobbed. The light in the bathroom felt way too bright, and Serena closed her eyes so that she didn't have to see it. With her eyes closed, words simply sprang into her head, and she moved her lips to murmur them aloud.

"God, please help me."

* * * * *

Stride stood in the middle of Minnesota Avenue on the Point.

He was alone. The world had turned black and white, all of the color sucked away. The trees and lawns had no green; the flowers and the sky were white; the houses were all painted in shades of gray. Not a single car drove up and down the street. He listened for the roar of the lake behind the dunes, but the water seemed frozen into silence. He felt no wind, no warmth, no cold, as if this were nothing but a photograph of Duluth, not the place where he'd lived. He felt out of place here, a stranger. But along with it, he also felt no hunger and no pain. Every weight and care had been lifted from his shoulders.

He walked down the street, passing houses he'd known for years, but they looked abandoned. All the doors and windows stood open, inviting visitors, but with no one coming or going. No one worked in the gardens or sat by the bay shore. When he walked up to one of the doors, he looked inside and saw no furniture, just empty rooms perfectly free of dust. The people had gone away and left only skeletons of their lives behind them.

But not entirely.

As he walked, he heard something human. *Music. He heard the* plink-plink *of someone picking out a country tune on a guitar. He walked faster, because he knew who it was. He'd heard that melody hundreds of times before. When he got to the next block, he recognized Steve Garske's house, and there was his old friend on a three-legged stool in the middle of his yard, strumming chords. Unlike everything else around him, Steve was in color, his flannel shirt patterned in green and red, his torn jeans a stone-washed blue. He wore leather cowboy boots, and his foot tapped along with the music he made.*

"Steve," Stride said.

His friend looked up. "Well, hey, buddy. Welcome."

"What is this place?"

"Don't you recognize it?"

"I don't. It's not the Point. Not really. I don't know what it is."

"Well, you brought us here. You chose the place."

"For what?" Stride asked.

"For your funeral," Steve told him. "We all got our invitations, so we're here to welcome you. The living say goodbye, but the dead say welcome. We'd never miss a funeral for a friend, Stride."

"I don't understand."

"Don't worry. She'll explain it to you. She's here along with the rest of us."

"Who?"

"The one you love. The one you miss."

"Where do I go?"

Steve gestured down the Point. "Green bench, buddy. The usual place. She's waiting."

Stride stared down the colorless road that led to the bench by the water. He felt an urge to keep going, to find her, to see her. He knew the face that would be there. And yet he didn't want to leave.

"I miss you, Steve."

His friend chuckled and kept playing the guitar. "Back at ya, buddy. Right back at ya."

Stride kept walking. Now he saw that he wasn't alone. The farther he went, the more others appeared to welcome him. People from his past. The ones who were gone. The victims. He saw a teenage girl jogging the opposite way on the street, wearing a sports bra and shorts, her hair tied in a pony tail. She was soaking wet, even though it wasn't raining. He'd never met her, but he knew who she was. He'd been trying to solve her murder when Cindy died. And he'd only done so years later, after he met Serena.

"Kerry?" he called. "Kerry McGrath?"

The teenage girl smiled with a sweet face he knew from photographs, but she didn't break pace. She kept running, as if she had somewhere to go and would never get there. She pointed the other way, toward the end of the Point, because that was where he needed to be, and he was only halfway there.

She ran past him, and when he looked back again, she was gone.

Still he walked farther into the black-and-white world. More people came from the shadows. More of the dead. They emerged one by one, the people he'd left behind. The innocent ones, taken too soon. The deaths he'd investigated.

Michaela Mateo stood by the side of the street. All of the bruises and wounds had healed where her ex-husband had beaten and stabbed her. Her chestnut hair blew into swirls, but he still felt not even a breath of wind around him. She was beautiful again, perfect, the spitting image of her daughter, Cat.

"Oh, Jonathan, welcome!" she told him. "It's so lovely to see your face again. Thank you for rescuing Catalina! Thank you for saving my girl! I wish you could stay here with me, but she waits for you. The green bench. She is there for you! Hurry!"

Stride walked faster, as if he could lift off the ground and fly.

He saw others returning to him, ghosts reminding him of their stories. Ahdia Rashid and her child, Pak, who had died in a gallery fire after the marathon bombing. Clark Biggs, whose heart had stopped in a lightning strike.

So many others.

Helen Danning.

Tanjy Powell.

Peach Piper.

And Andrea.

Andrea came out to see him, too. He didn't understand why she was here. She had something in her hands, and he realized it was a suncatcher, looking vibrant in many colors against the whites, blacks, and grays of this world. She held it up to the light, and he could see images in the stained glass with a strange clarity. On her face was something he hadn't seen in a long time. A smile. She was happy, as if somehow she'd been given a do-over for all of the things she'd missed in life.

"I should have told you," Andrea said to him.

"Told me what?"

"What I did."

"What did you do?"

She shook her head. "Forgive every sin."

"I don't understand."

Andrea kept smiling as she waved him down the Point. "You need to keep going, Jon. There isn't much time now. She's on the green bench. She's waiting for you."

And she was.

The next moment, Stride reached the park where the road ended, frozen in black and white. The only splash of color he saw was the green bench by the bay. This was the bench that marked every crossroad in his life. The place of death, the place of new beginnings. Time had destroyed it in real life, but here, the bench looked as if it could withstand generations of winter and storms.

Cindy sat on the bench.

She looked as young and healthy as the day he'd married her, with her long, long black hair, parted in the middle and utterly straight. A sprite, hardly more than a hundred pounds. Her little nose, sharply angled like the blade of a knife. Her big brown eyes, always teasing him.

"Jonny," she said, in a voice he'd never thought he would hear again.

He sat down next to her, drinking her in with his eyes, glorying that she was so vivid and alive. Over the years, his memories had grown blurry, and he'd had to take out pictures to remind himself of the details of her face. But here she was, back with him again. He never wanted to leave. He never wanted to see that picture fade from his mind.

"Why are you here?" Stride asked. "Why am I here?"

"Don't you know by now?"

"Steve said this was my funeral."

"Well, it is if you want it to be. Or maybe it's your wake. Or maybe it's your waking up."

"I don't understand."

She made fun of him with a musical laugh. "Really, pirate eyes? You can't figure it out? You take one bullet in the heart, and all your detective skills disappear. I'm disappointed in you, Jonny."

Stride looked at the black-and-white world around him. "I'm dead."

"Dead? Yes and no. I'm dead. Steve's dead. Everyone around here is dead. You, you're only halfway there. It's up to you whether to stay or go."

"Is this real?"

"What do you think, Jonny?"

He searched his broken, wounded heart for the truth. "I think I'm dreaming."

"*Maybe. Or maybe not. Who's to say?*"

"*I think I was shot. I'm on an operating table with my chest cracked open. I think my heart stopped, and the doctors are trying to get it started again.*"

"*So what are you going to do about that? You have to make a choice.*"

He looked around at the gray world of the Point, a place that he loved but that now existed only like a painting in a frame. This wasn't his home. But then he saw his late wife in full color, exactly as she'd always been, and his heart ached. It literally ached.

His heart felt shot through with pain, over and over and over.

No heartbeat. We're losing him.

"*I don't want to leave you behind again,*" Stride said.

"*I left you behind, my love. The question is whether you're ready to do to Serena what I did to you.*"

"*What will happen to her?*"

"*What happens to anyone who suffers a terrible loss? If you give in, if you die, Serena and Cat will be left alone. Hurt, angry, devastated, the way you were after I died. But they'll go on. You went on eventually, too.*"

"*It took me a long time,*" Stride said.

"*I know. I'm sorry about that. But you didn't help matters, did you? I sent you Serena, and you nearly screwed it up with her. I wasn't sure the two of you would ever get there. I can't believe you slept with Maggie, by the way. How many times did I warn you about that?*"

"*Oh, hell, not you, too.*"

Cindy laughed again. He'd missed that laugh so much. He wanted this moment with her to go on forever, but then she said, "It's time to decide, Jonny."

"*I can't.*"

"*Stay or go, my love. Those are the only two choices.*"

"*I want to stay with you,*" he said.

"*Then stay. Here I am. But Serena's back there. She's waiting for you, too.*"

"*I can't leave her behind.*"

"*Then go.*"

"*How do I decide?*"

Cindy leaned over and kissed him, and he could feel the touch of her lips like a jolt of electricity in his heart.

"That's up to you," she said. "I can't tell you what to do."

Another smile. Another kiss.

Another jolt that made his whole body shiver.

"Every story ends, Jonny," Cindy said. "It's all a question of when. So here we are. Is this the end of your story?"

40

Stride opened his eyes.

The first thing he felt was pain. A deep ache radiated through his entire chest. When he took a breath, a stab like the sharp prick of a knife made him wince. He blinked, trying to focus, trying to understand where he was. Lights were low, and he lay on his back, staring at the ceiling. He tried to get up, but his body immediately protested with an even worse shiver of agony.

"Hey, take it easy," a voice said.

He looked up and saw Serena standing next to him. She sat down in a chair and took his hand. He noticed that her face was a study in contradictions. She wore a smile of pure happiness, but her eyes were glassy with tears.

"Look at you," she went on. "All alive and everything."

Stride croaked out a word. The breath that went with it was painful, and he felt a lingering soreness in his throat. "Hey."

"Easy on the talking," Serena told him. "Your chest is going to hurt for a while. If your throat hurts, too, that's from the breathing tube. Other than that, the doctors say you're on the road to recovery. They call it a miracle, and I don't think they throw that word around here lightly."

He tried to cut through the fog in his brain. "How long?"

"Almost three days."

His head turned slowly. He could see a sofa near the window and the brightness of sunshine outside. Pillows and blankets were strewn across the sofa, along with a cafeteria tray and a half-eaten meal.

"Yeah, I've been here the whole time," Serena said. "I haven't left. You woke up a few times, but you were pretty out of it. Do you remember anything? Do you remember what happened?"

Stride shook his head. "Tell me."

"We don't have to do this right now. Let's wait until you're stronger."

"No. I need to know. Tell me."

She smiled at his stubbornness. "Okay. The person stalking Cat was a girl named Colleen Hunt. Actually, that's not her real name. She took that name when she came here from Madison, where she was a suspect in at least three murders. Cat tried to get away from her at the town hall, and Colleen chased her on stage and opened fire. I fired back, and so did Brayden. Colleen was killed. It was Brayden who got her. You protected Cat—she's fine—but you were shot in the heart, Jonny." Her voice choked up as she tried to go on. "They had to perform an emergency thoracotomy. Basically, they cut open your whole chest cavity in order to stitch up your heart."

Stride closed his eyes. Then he struggled to speak again. "I died."

Serena struggled to speak, too. "Yeah. You did. Your heart stopped during the operation, and they had to revive you. You didn't come back right away. Any longer, and they were going to call it. I almost lost you, Jonny."

"Sorry."

She laughed through her tears. "Don't scare me like that again."

He managed a smile.

"Cat?" he said.

"I sent her home. She couldn't handle seeing you like this. She was falling to pieces. I just texted her that you're awake. She'll be here soon."

Stride let his mind drift backward, but there was nothing to find in the moments before he was shot. That night inside the convention center, the town hall, everything was gone. The last thing he remembered was sitting outside the DECC with Serena in the pouring rain and listening to the thunder. And then, just a blink later, he was here.

"Others hurt?" he said.

Her face bent into a frown. "Well, the good news is, it could have been much worse than it was. One of the men in the crowd took a round in the shoulder, but he's already out of the hospital and doing well. Colleen's shots on stage were basically aimed at you and Cat, and other than the shot that hit you in the chest, all of her other rounds missed. She didn't hit anyone else."

Somehow, Stride knew there was more. He could read the look on Serena's face.

"But," she said.

He already knew what was coming next. The memory of her face was in his head. "Andrea."

"How did you know?"

Stride didn't answer. He simply waited.

"Yes, I'm sorry, Jonny. Andrea froze when the shooting began, and then she tried to run. She ended up in the crossfire, and she was hit. She was killed instantly. We got the ballistics report back. The bullet came from Brayden's gun, but it wasn't his fault. Andrea was in the wrong place at the wrong time."

Stride nodded.

He thought about Andrea, gone. They'd shared years together, most of them unhappy, but he felt sad that she'd lost any last chance to make peace with her past. And yet, somehow, he also believed that death had brought her that peace. He'd seen it in her face.

He'd seen it in the suncatcher she held.

"How did you know Andrea was dead?" Serena asked again. "You'd already been hit. You were unconscious."

"I saw her."

"Where?"

"A dream."

"While you were …?"

Stride nodded, feeling the exhaustion of trying to speak and the weight of sleep closing in on him again. Even so, he forced himself to say what he wanted to say. "I saw the dead with me. Steve. Michaela. And Andrea. So I knew."

"Wow." She reached out and stroked his face with the back of her hand. "Tell me something. Was ... she ... there with you, too?"

He knew who she meant, and he nodded.

"You saw Cindy, and you still came back to me," Serena murmured. There was a little bit of wonder in her voice, and he watched tears silently move down her cheeks again.

He squeezed her hand, because he couldn't do much more.

"I'll let you sleep," she went on, seeing his eyes blink closed. "Cat will be here soon."

Stride shook his head firmly, despite the pain it caused. He moved one finger to beckon her closer, and he managed another word. "Autopsy?"

"What? Who?"

"Andrea."

Serena nodded with a little confusion. "Sure, we did an autopsy. Maggie called with the ballistics report, but I haven't seen the autopsy report itself. Why? There's no mystery about how she died."

He wasn't sure if he was already asleep, but in his head, he heard himself telling Serena, "Check it."

* * * * *

Maggie emptied the dregs from the bottle of champagne into the last of the plastic glasses and made an announcement to the police officers gathered in the conference room. "Ladies and gentlemen, a toast. To the Unsinkable, Indestructible, Very Much Alive Jonathan Stride."

A cheer arose from the cops. They downed their champagne and launched into a round of applause. Maggie grinned as she studied their faces. She wasn't surprised to see a lot of big, tough cops working hard to hold back tears. She'd known every one of them for years, and she knew they would all risk their lives for Stride. They knew how close they'd come to losing him.

Guppo didn't even try to hide his emotions. He simply blubbered. Maggie wandered over and gave him a hug, and she found herself brushing tears of relief from her own cheeks, too.

It was a happy moment, but then the devil walked in to spoil it.

"Maggie."

She glanced at the doorway of the conference room and saw Dan Erickson signaling to her. He wore a phony smile of sympathy. Maggie rolled her eyes, then grabbed the remnants of another glass of champagne from the table and swallowed it down to give herself strength. She joined Dan in the hallway outside the room.

"You want some bubbly?" she asked. "If you do, too bad, because we're all out."

"I'm fine, thanks."

"We're celebrating, you know."

"Yes, I know."

"What do you want, Dan? Because right now, all I want to do is go to Sammy's and get a pizza and drink a lot of beer."

He shrugged. "Can we talk?"

"Now? Really?"

"Really."

Maggie sighed. "Yeah, sure, whatever you want."

She led him to her office, and she noticed that he closed the door when they went inside. She didn't particularly enjoy being in a closed room with Dan, but she consoled herself with the idea that if he tried anything, she had no qualms at all about kneeing him in the groin.

"What's up?" she asked, sitting behind her desk.

"It's good news about Stride, obviously. What a relief."

"I'm sure he'll be touched by your concern, Dan."

"You may find it hard to believe, but I've always respected Stride, and I'd never want to see something bad happen to him. I couldn't be happier that he survived. However, good news or not, I wanted to check in with you about the future. Are you ready?"

"Ready for what?"

"Come on, Maggie. Stride's alive, but this was an extremely serious injury. He'll need months to recover. He's not coming back to the force anytime soon. I assume K-2 will be making you the new lieutenant."

"I've given that exactly zero thought," she snapped.

"Well, you should. It's reality."

Maggie scoffed, but without saying so out loud, she knew that Dan was right. K-2 had already told her the same thing. She'd assumed that the chief would eventually relent and bring Stride back with a reprimand, regardless of whether the Baer case was resolved. But the shooting had changed everything. Stride wouldn't be in any shape to return to the job for the foreseeable future.

Assuming he wanted to come back at all.

She was going to be in charge of the detective division. She was taking over. It scared the hell out of her.

"Let's focus on Ned Baer, okay?" she said. "We still have a murder to solve. That's my priority right now."

"Have you learned anything more?" Dan asked.

"Well, gee, the last couple of days have been a little busy, but actually, yes, I have. Debbi King tracked down a photo of Ned Baer from his college days, and Guppo showed it to Adam Halka. Halka identified him. Ned was definitely the roadie he brought to the party that summer. It doesn't give us any conclusive evidence that Ned assaulted Andrea, but as far as the murder investigation goes, I think it's reasonable to suspect he did. The question is whether that changes anything or gives us any new suspects. Unfortunately, I'm not sure it does."

"It gives Andrea an even more powerful motive to kill him," Dan pointed out. "Stride, too. What would he have done if he found out that he was confronting the man who'd raped his wife as a teenager?"

"Stride didn't know."

"So he says."

"No one knew, Dan. Ned had every reason to keep it a secret."

"Maybe so, but we can't be one hundred percent certain that no one remembered him. Particularly Andrea. If she was face-to-face with her rapist, even after all those years, maybe it triggered a memory."

Maggie shook her head. "Then why would she go to the town hall to confront Devin? That makes no sense. She obviously still thought Devin assaulted her. No, Andrea didn't know about Ned, and I honestly don't see how anyone else could have known, either. It was a fluke that we even discovered it."

"And yet of all the motives we've talked about, I like that one the best," Dan said. "It's the only one worth killing over. If Devin or Peter wanted to quash Ned's story, I think they would have paid him the blackmail to spike it, not killed him. And as much as Andrea wanted to protect her privacy, I can't really see her or Stride going as far as murder to keep her name out of the papers. But rape? That changes everything."

Maggie frowned. Once again, Dan was right. "I agree, but it's too late to ask Andrea about it."

"So where does that leave us?"

Maggie rocked back in her chair. She knew where that left them. Nowhere. With an unsolved cold case that would be put back in the files. She chewed her lip and tried to think of something she'd missed, and as she did, her gaze drifted to a folder on her desk. She pulled it toward her and flipped open the cover. The printed contents stared back at her.

"What's that?" Dan asked.

"Andrea's autopsy summary. Serena said that Stride thought we should check it. She didn't know why or what he thought we would find. He was still pretty groggy from the surgery."

"Did you look it over?"

"Sure, but there was nothing unusual about the external examination. It shows what you'd expect. Single GSW to the head."

"What about the internals?"

Maggie shrugged. She flipped open the report and turned to the page that summarized the internal findings. "Nothing strange there, and I don't know why there would be. She was a healthy forty-six-year-old female. Lungs normal, gastro normal, endocrine normal, genitourinary shows—"

She stopped in mid-sentence.

"Hang on. Wait a minute."

"What is it?" Dan asked.

Maggie picked up the report and reread the postmortem examination of the genital organs and reproductive system. After she did, she put the report down and scoured her memory for what she knew about Andrea Forseth. She went over everything that Stride had told her years earlier. About himself and Andrea and their marriage. About her earlier marriage and divorce to Robin Jantzik.

She knew she was remembering the facts correctly. It had come up too many times for her to be mistaken about it. Stride had always told her that the problem in both of Andrea's marriages had stemmed from her not being able to get pregnant. She was desperate to have a child, and she never did.

And yet there it was in black and white.

"Something's wrong," Maggie said. "This doesn't make any sense. According to the autopsy, at some point in her life, Andrea delivered a baby."

41

"A *baby?*" Denise said. "No, that's not right. That's impossible. My sister never had a baby."

Serena and Maggie exchanged a glance with each other, because that was the reaction they'd expected. Denise didn't know. No one knew. It had been the secret of Andrea's life.

"I'm sorry, but the evidence is conclusive," Maggie told her. "I checked with the medical examiner again to make absolutely certain there was no mistake. She told me that her analysis of the pelvic area during the autopsy left no room for doubt. Andrea had gone through childbirth. If it wasn't with Stride or Robin, then when did it happen?"

Denise got up from the kitchen chair in Andrea's house with a start. Her fingers twitched. She went to the back door, opened it, and lit a cigarette from the pack in her pocket. After she inhaled, she tilted her head and blew smoke into the air. Her chest rattled with a cough. "I can't believe this."

Maggie joined her in the doorway and waited as Denise tried to process the shock. "She never said a word about it? She never gave you any hint?"

"None."

"What about your parents?"

"They didn't say a thing to me. But I don't suppose they would."

Serena got up, too, and looked around the kitchen. She saw it in a new light, now that Andrea was gone. She always felt a keen sense of loss when she entered the house of someone who had recently died. Everything still spoke of their presence. The food in the refrigerator. The mail on the counter. The coffee cup in the sink. The house still acted as if someone would be coming back soon and picking up where they left off. Knowing the truth about Andrea's life made it even worse.

She wandered to the window, where Andrea had kept her array of suncatchers. She spotted the one that Stride had remembered, the one he'd seen Andrea holding in his dream while under surgery. The sun catcher had been sending him a message.

The stained glass, molded in chips of blue and red, showed a mother holding a baby.

"You said Andrea didn't know where these sun catchers came from?" she said to Denise.

"No. She said a secret admirer sent them to her. Apparently, it had been happening for years."

"We're going to have to take them with us," Serena said.

"Why?"

"To look for prints. To see if we can figure out who sent them."

"Why does that even matter?" Denise asked.

"Because there was someone in Andrea's life that no one knew anything about. It's important that we find out who it was. Particularly if it's possible that it was her child."

A flood of emotions crossed Denise's face. Confusion. Anger. Regret. And ultimately grief. "My whole life, Andrea and I only saw each other every couple of years. When we did, we had practically nothing in common. I thought when I came back to Duluth, we'd find a way to be sisters again. These last few months, I was hoping we were finally getting closer. Now I realize I didn't know a thing about her."

"When did that start?" Serena asked. "When did the two of you begin to grow apart?"

Denise threw down her cigarette and began to cry. "After that fucking party."

They waited for Denise to get control of herself. She stood outside for a while, staring at the lake on the horizon, her lips pushed together in a hard line. Then she came back inside and slammed the door, and she sat down at the kitchen table again.

"We need to know what really happened, Denise," Serena said. "Is it possible that Andrea ended up pregnant after the rape?"

Denise gave a long sigh. "Possible? I suppose so. I left town a couple of days later. It was probably two years before I came back for a visit. I'm not the nostalgic type, and I was looking to get out of Duluth. I called home every few weeks, but nobody said a thing. That doesn't surprise me. This would have been horrifying for my parents. Their little angel getting pregnant? They would have kept it a secret any way they could. But I do remember one thing—"

She stopped.

"What is it?" Serena asked.

"I remember they pulled Andrea out of school in the second semester that year. After Christmas. They told me it was mono. She finished the year at home."

Serena did the math in her head. "She would have been starting to show."

"We know she carried the baby to term," Maggie said. "Assuming the child survived, it seems likely that the baby was adopted. Do you remember any relatives, cousins, neighbors, who had a baby around that time? Someone who might have taken custody of Andrea's child?"

Denise shook her head. "No. You have to understand what my parents were like. They wouldn't have wanted that baby anywhere close to the family. They would have acted as if it had never existed. Hell, to me, the baby never did. They never even told me that I had a niece or nephew. So whoever took it, I doubt they were in Duluth, and I doubt they let Andrea knew who it was."

"We'd like to search the house," Maggie said. "She must have kept something from back then. Something that would give us a clue what really happened. And maybe where the baby went."

"Go ahead, search all you want," Denise replied. She gestured toward the stairs. "Andrea has a spare bedroom that she used as an office. If she kept anything, it's probably in there."

Serena and Maggie made their way to the stairs together. They found Andrea's office in a small bedroom that faced the basketball courts beside the house. She had a wall of built-in bookshelves, mostly filled with science textbooks, three steel file cabinets on the adjacent wall, and a weathered oak desk in front of the bedroom's small window. When Andrea sat at the desk, she could turn around and stare outside at the park next door.

"She used to watch the kids playing," Serena murmured. "Stride said she did that all the time. Imagine spending every day of your life thinking about the child you gave up."

"Do you think Steve Garske knew?" Maggie asked.

"He was her doctor. I'm sure he did. He would have been talking to her about secondary infertility when she couldn't get pregnant again. So he knew why the threat of exposure was so traumatic to her. He wasn't just protecting Stride by hiding Ned Baer's body. He was protecting Andrea, too."

Maggie began opening drawers in the desk. "I confess I never liked her. I said some pretty mean things about her to Stride. Now I feel a little bad about that."

"Take a number," Serena replied. "I'm the one who broke up their marriage."

Maggie stopped and looked up. "Don't put that on yourself. Their relationship was broken long before you came to town. She and Stride were wrong from the beginning."

"I know, but still, it's a little weird being here," Serena admitted, opening a drawer in the first filing cabinet and pawing through the contents, which were mostly biology quizzes and tests that Andrea had prepared for her classes over the years. "I feel strange trying to find secrets about my husband's ex-wife."

"I'm sure."

She noticed that Maggie had stopped searching and was staring out the window instead. "You okay? Is something wrong?"

Maggie didn't look at her. She had her badge in her hands and began turning it over in her fingers. "Do you think Stride will ever come back?"

"I have no idea. I hope so."

"K-2 wants me to take over while he's gone."

"Of course, he does. You're the natural choice."

"He already made the promotion official. I'm Lieutenant Bei now."

"Congratulations."

Maggie kept rubbing her badge in her hands. "I know we've had our problems. Me being a cheating whore. You being an ice-cold bitch. That sort of thing. How is it going to work with you reporting to me?"

Serena chuckled softly. "We'll be fine, Maggie."

"I need a partner, and I know who I want," she said.

"I'll think about it."

"You know, as soon as Stride wants the job back, it's his," Maggie went on. "I'd never stand in the way."

"I guess we'll all cross that bridge when we come to it."

Maggie chewed on her lip. Serena knew that, in her heart, Maggie was a more vulnerable person than she let anyone else see. Her prickly sarcasm was a shield. "If Stride had died, I'm not sure what I would have done."

"Me neither," Serena replied. "I'm glad we didn't have to find out."

They kept searching in silence. Maggie went through all of the desk drawers, finding nothing. Serena did the same with the filing cabinets. They had no luck. Everything that Andrea kept in the office was related to her work at the high school, or to her financial records, but there was nothing personal about any of it. It was as if her distant past had been completely erased and she didn't want to remember anything from her earlier life.

"If Andrea didn't keep records from back then, it's going to be difficult to find what we need," Maggie said. "We have no idea what hospital she would have used, if they used a hospital at all. Or when the actual birth was. Or what adoption agency they used. We're looking for a needle in a haystack after thirty years."

Serena shook her head. "Something's here."

"You sound pretty sure. This was a child of rape. Maybe she wanted to forget what happened."

"No way."

"Okay. Where do we look? A safe deposit box?"

Serena stood in the middle of the office and thought about it. "No, let's check her bedroom. She would have kept the memories of her child there. Not in the office. She would have kept it close to her."

"You think so?"

Serena didn't answer. Instead, she continued down the hallway to the master bedroom that overlooked the lake, and she went directly to the nightstand next to Andrea's bed. When she opened the top drawer, the first thing she found was a stack of folded white cards made of heavy stock. She pulled them out and opened the first card. Inside was a hand-written message in block letters.

Forgive every sin.

She opened the other cards one by one and found the same message inside each of them.

"'Forgive every sin,'" Serena murmured.

"Devin Card used the same phrase a couple of days ago," Maggie said. "He was assaulted seven years ago when the accusations came out. Somebody jumped him on the street one night and beat the hell out of him. He said that's what the man told him as he did it. 'Forgive every sin.'"

"I think these notes came with the suncatchers," Serena said. "There's a box in here from one of the suncatchers and another of the cards inside."

"So what sin?" Maggie asked. "The sin of rape?"

"Or the sin of giving away your baby."

"You think these came from Andrea's child?"

Serena stared at the neat stack of notes that had kept in the night-stand. "I think Andrea thought so. She kept every one."

"Is there anything else in there?"

Serena dug into the nightstand again and found a handgun in the top drawer, but nothing else of interest. As soon she opened the second drawer, she discovered a metal lock box, which she removed and placed on the bed. The box was secured with a combination lock, but when she pushed the latch aside, she found that the numbers on the lock had been left at the correct combination.

She opened the lid.

"Oh, hell," Maggie said. "Look at that."

Inside, they found dozens of photographs, the brightness of their color fading after decades had passed. All of the pictures showed the same thing: Andrea as a teenager, holding a newborn baby in her arms. A boy. The photos showed her feeding her child. Changing him. Grinning as she held her son in the air. The two of them asleep on a blanket in the grass. Serena didn't think she'd ever seen such happiness and love on a face as she saw in Andrea in those pictures. And it occurred to her that Andrea probably hadn't had that look of happiness on her face again in the decades since then.

"She didn't want to give him up," Maggie said.

"No. That's obvious."

"I wonder how long she kept him before her parents made her let him go."

Serena turned over the pictures and saw dates written in ink on the back. "The photo of her with the newborn is in May. May 14. This one here in the grass is late July."

"Two months with a child, and then you have to give him up?" Maggie said.

Serena shook her head. "I can't imagine it."

"Is there anything about the adoption? The name of the agency? Anything about where the boy went?"

"No. I wonder if her parents even told her. I wonder if they just took him away."

"Oh my God."

Serena dug down to the bottom of the lock box. Amid the memorabilia of the few weeks that a young mother had shared with her son, she found a birth certificate. She pulled it out and examined the text. She didn't notice the hospital, or the doctor, or the time of birth.

Instead, she focused on the one detail that told her everything she needed to know.

"Andrea gave him a name," Serena said.

Maggie looked at the faded print on the birth certificate where Serena was pointing. "Son of a bitch," she gasped. "*Brayden.*"

42

Cat sat with Brayden on the clifftop overlooking the Deeps.

The recent storms had swelled the current, making it a maelstrom of whitewater and whirlpools surging toward the lake. Late afternoon shadows draped the rocks. The river looked angry, and Cat could see a reflection of the water in Brayden's turbulent mood. His dark eyes had a sunken quality, like twin caves. Greasy cowlicks hung from his hair, and he hadn't shaved in days. When she put an arm around his shoulder, she could feel his whole body tensed into knots.

"Stride had to kill someone this year," Cat told him softly. "I saw what it did to him. I saw how it haunted him."

Brayden shook his head, not wanting comfort. "That was a good shoot. This isn't the same thing at all. I made a mistake. I killed my—I killed an innocent person. She should be alive right now."

"You also saved *me*."

"Stride did that, not me. And he nearly died in the process."

"Colly would have kept shooting. Who knows how many others she might have killed? You stopped her."

"I screwed up," Brayden insisted.

"I understand that you're upset. It's natural."

He shook his head. "I don't think I can live with this."

"Don't talk like that."

"I'm sorry, but you have no idea what I'm feeling. You don't under-stand. You don't know what I *did*."

"Try me."

But Brayden said nothing. He looked lost in a maze, with no way forward. As they sat there, he got a text on his phone, which he read with an expression that somehow deepened the darkness he felt. He shoved his phone back in his pocket without telling Cat who it was, or what it was.

Only seconds later, her own phone rang. It was Serena.

"Is Stride okay?" Cat asked, without even saying hello.

"He's fine, Cat. This isn't about him. Where are you?"

"At the Deeps."

"Is Brayden Pell with you?"

"Yeah."

"Cat, I want you to leave right now," Serena told her. "Don't ask any questions, and don't say anything. Just come back home."

"Why?"

"I'll explain when you get here. Don't tell Brayden about this call, please. Just leave the Deeps by yourself."

"Sure. Okay."

Cat hung up the phone, but she made no effort to get up or leave. Instead, she twisted her body around on the rocks and sat cross-legged next to Brayden. Calmly, she brushed back her chestnut hair. She knew he could feel her looking at him, but he stared at the waterfall without acknowledging her.

"So do you want to tell me what's going on?" Cat asked. "That was Serena. She wants me to leave right away. It's about you."

He shrugged. "They know. That was the text I got. They know."

"Know what?"

"Who I am. I figured they'd find out eventually. Honestly, I've thought about coming forward for years, but if I did that, I knew she'd be exposed, too. It wasn't my secret to share. I knew she didn't want anyone to know about me. I didn't care about myself or what would happen to me. I was trying to protect *her*."

"Protect who?" Cat asked.

"Andrea."

"I don't understand."

"Andrea Forseth was my birth mother," Brayden told her. "She had a baby, and no one knew about it. She had me."

Cat's eyes widened with shock. Her lips parted, and she covered her mouth with her hand. Then, as the dimensions of the tragedy settled over her, she reached out and put her arms around Brayden's neck. "*No.*"

He nodded, his face like granite. "Now she's dead because of me."

"Brayden, that was a terrible accident."

"Really? Because it doesn't feel like an accident. It feels like fate. Like I'm being punished for what I did seven years ago."

"What did you do?"

Brayden looked around at the Deeps, as if he could see things here that she couldn't. "I guess it doesn't matter who I tell anymore. Now that they know, they won't have any trouble proving it. I kept everything. It's all in a box in my attic. Ned's laptop. His papers. His gun. I guess I thought one day I'd tell Andrea what I did, how I'd saved her. Avenged her. But I can't tell her about it now, can I? It's too late."

"Tell *me*," Cat said.

Brayden lay back, stretching out on the rocks. He put his hands behind his head and stared at the trees and sky. He spoke quietly, his voice barely louder than the thunder of the river.

"I didn't know I was adopted until I was in high school," he said. "Grace and Bob Pell kept it a secret. It only slipped out when I was a senior, and Bob and I were having one of our usual arguments. He made some comment about someone like me never coming from his blood, and then he told me the truth. That was the first time I knew that I had another mother somewhere else. A mother who'd given me up."

Cat stayed silent and let him speak.

"Bob Pell didn't know who she was, how old she was, why she gave me up, anything like that. It was a closed adoption. The only thing he knew was that my birth mother was from Duluth. The weird thing is, knowing all of this finally gave me a purpose in life that I'd never had before.

After high school, I moved to Duluth. I loved the lake, and God knows I wanted to get away from my father, but somewhere in my head, I also thought I could track down my birth mother. I wanted answers about where I came from. About why she abandoned me."

"And you found her?" Cat murmured.

"It took me a while, because I had so little to go on. I started dating a nurse, and she helped me get access to hospital records. The thing is, the Pells had always told me that my birthday was in the summer. That was when they adopted me. Later, I discovered that Andrea had kept me for more than two months before giving me up. I guess when she had to go back to school, her parents told her she couldn't keep me. I was looking in the wrong time frame and didn't even know it, so for a long time I was at a dead end. Anyway, it took me three years, but eventually, the search led me to Andrea. A thirty-nine-year-old woman, married to a cop. She would have been seventeen when she had me."

"Like me," Cat said, with a new sense of wonder. "She was just like me."

"That's right."

Suddenly, Cat pulled away from him and sprang to her feet. "That's why you felt a connection with me, isn't it? That's why there was never anything between us. I reminded you of *her*. A teenager who gave away her baby. Just like your mother."

"I told you it was complicated."

"I can't believe I acted like such a fool," Cat said.

"You didn't. Believe me. This was my problem."

Cat sat down next to him again. "What did you do when you found out who she was?"

"I watched her. That's all. I got to know her from a distance. I'd sit outside her house on the weekends when I had time. Or I'd follow her to the high school where she worked. I just wanted to get a sense of who she was. I thought about introducing myself, but I wasn't ready to do that. And I was pretty sure that she wasn't ready, either. A part of me was angry, too. How could she have given me up?"

"Because she loved you," Cat said. "Because she wanted a better life for you. That's why I did it."

"I know. But understanding it isn't the same thing as forgiving it. I spent some time with a therapist, trying to figure out how to forgive my mother. She told me the same thing. That sometimes letting a child go is an act of love."

"Don't think the guilt ever goes away," Cat told him. "It doesn't."

He said nothing. His face was dark with his memories.

"One day that summer, early in August, I saw a man show up at her door. After he left, Andrea went outside and sat on the front steps, and I could tell she was very upset. Crying. I didn't like seeing her that way. I wanted to know this man and what he'd said to her. So I tracked him down by the car he was driving, and I located the motel where he was staying. He was a journalist. His name was Ned Baer."

Brayden's fists clenched, and then he released them. He sat in silence for a little while.

"I found out what Baer was doing in town—that he was researching the rape accusation against Devin Card. You can't imagine what a thunderbolt that was for me. Suddenly, everything made sense. I realized that Andrea was the one behind the accusation. That she'd been *raped*. That was how she got pregnant. That was how I came into the world. I was born of violence. And Devin Card was my father. I didn't know what to do. I was so furious. I needed to know more. I broke into Andrea's house when she and Stride were away, so I could find out what happened. I found a box she'd hid, with pictures of her and me, and I realized she loved me. Despite what had been done to her, she *loved* me. I was going to pieces, Cat. My whole identity had been stripped away from me. And I felt so bad for my mother, for what she'd been through. I bought her something—a suncatcher—and left it for her anonymously with a note. *Forgive every sin.* I knew, somehow I just knew, that she blamed herself for letting me go. I didn't want her to do that. But I also couldn't come forward. Not when I knew she was so desperate to keep what had happened a secret."

"What happened next?" Cat asked.

"I took out all my rage on Devin Card. I was obsessed with what he'd done to her. It killed me to see him stand up there and *deny* the accusation, when I knew it was true. When I could prove it! That drove me crazy. One night, I followed him, and when he was alone, I jumped him and beat the hell out of him. I almost told him who I was, too. But I already had what I really wanted. His *blood*. To confirm everything. I had this idea that I could force Card to drop out of the race, just like Andrea wanted, if he knew there was a way to prove what he'd done. But instead, I got the paternity test back, and it was negative. Devin wasn't my father. I didn't understand. It made no sense. Andrea *was* my mother, but if Devin didn't assault her, who was my father? How could she have been wrong about that?"

"What did you do?"

"I broke into Ned Baer's hotel room," Devin said. "All I really wanted was to see what information he'd discovered about the party and the rape, because somehow he'd been able to find Andrea when no one else had. I thought I could find a clue to figure out what had really happened. So I began going through his papers, everything he'd collected. That's when I realized he knew things he shouldn't have known. Before he came to Duluth, on his very first page of notes, he'd written down the *date* when Andrea was raped. How could he possibly know that? No one did—not even Andrea. He had a yearbook, and he'd only circled girls who looked like her. How did he know what she looked like? But what really sealed it was a picture I found of him. I could see myself in his face. There was just enough resemblance that I *knew*. So I took a tissue from the motel wastebasket, and I ran another test. This time, it came back positive. Ned Baer was my father. He's the one who raped my mother."

"Oh, Brayden. I'm so sorry."

"I needed to confront him. I couldn't think about anything else. Imagine him doing what he did years ago—and then coming back to torment my mother all over again. I wasn't going to let him get away with it. So I called him. I lied and said I had information about the party for his article. We arranged to meet that night."

"Here at the Deeps," Cat said.

Brayden nodded. "Yes. I got here first and waited for him in the woods. It was such a hot, hot night, absolutely broiling. I watched as he got here and drank beer and went diving in the creek. He kept checking his watch, wondering where I was, but somehow, I couldn't bring myself to go out and talk to him. And then just when I finally decided I was ready, someone else showed up."

"Stride."

"Yes. I watched Stride confront him. Ned was such a son of a bitch. Arrogant. A vicious liar, a rapist, and he thought no one knew. Stride was trying to talk him out of exposing Andrea, but Ned didn't care about that at all. It didn't matter whose lives he destroyed. After Stride left, I came out of the woods. Ned was pretty drunk at that point. But when I told him who I was, when I told him what I *knew*, he sobered up fast. At first, he didn't believe it, but I told him about the paternity test. It was a shock. He didn't care that I was his son. That wasn't important to him at all. He cared that I could *prove* what he'd done. I could ruin his whole life. And I was going to. I told him that. I was going to make sure everyone knew what kind of a man he was."

"What did he do?" Cat asked.

"He pulled out a gun. Pointed it in my face. He was going to shoot me and dump my body somewhere. That was how much he cared about me."

"What happened?"

"We struggled." Brayden took a deep breath before going on. "We wrestled over the gun. In the fight, he got shot in the head."

"So it was self-defense," Cat said. "He was trying to kill you, and you killed him. Nobody can blame you for that."

Brayden stood up on the rocks. He stared over the cliff's edge at the roiling waters below them. "I don't know, Cat. Was it really self-defense? I was bigger than he was. Stronger than he was. He was drunk. I should have been able to take the gun away from him without a fight. But I wanted him dead. I wanted revenge for my mother. I don't remember exactly how it happened, but when it was over, I stared at the body at my feet, and I didn't feel a thing. Actually, no, that's not true. I was *glad*. I felt like I'd finally done something to help

Andrea. I'd kept her secret, and I'd made sure the man who raped her was gone."

Cat got up from the rocks, too. "Then what?"

"I was going to take the body away, but I saw headlights. Someone else was coming. So I grabbed the gun and hid in the woods again. This man came over to the rocks—I had no idea who he was—and he found Ned's body. I figured he'd call the police. But he didn't. He took away the body. He dragged it back to his car and drove away. I didn't understand why, but I didn't care. All I knew was that he'd solved a problem for me. I found Ned's car parked off Seven Bridges Road and broke inside; I took his laptop, his notes. Then I went over to his motel room that night and cleared it out. I didn't want anyone to know what he'd discovered. I didn't want anything that would point the police to Andrea. I figured they'd find the body soon enough, but they never did. Ned vanished. He was gone. The story went out a few days later that the police believed he'd drowned in the Deeps and his body was lost in the lake. Until a few days ago, that was what everyone thought. We were safe. Both of us, me and Andrea. But then it came back to life again."

Cat touched his shoulder. "When Stride put out a call for someone to help me with my stalker, you volunteered. Why?"

"I wanted to keep tabs on the case. I thought you could help me find out what Stride knew and how close they were to the truth. But that was just the beginning, Cat. Believe me. Very quickly, I felt close to you."

"You need to tell them what happened, Brayden. It *was* self-defense."

"No, it's too late for that. I killed Andrea. I killed my mother. There's no going back."

"That's not your fault."

"What difference does that make? Instead of protecting her, I *killed* her. How do you expect me to live with that?"

"With help," Cat said.

Brayden shook his head firmly. He backed away from her and inched closer to the cliff, where the pound of the spray was so strong it rose up high enough to dampen their faces. "No, it's better like this. Better for everyone."

"What the hell are you saying?"

Then Cat understood.

"*No!*" she screamed. She ran up to him and grabbed both of his arms. "No, don't you do it, don't you jump. I won't let you go. Do you hear me? If you jump, I'll go over the edge, too. I swear it. Are you ready for that? Are you ready for both of us to die?"

"Cat, let go of me. *Please.*"

But she held on even tighter. She felt her feet slipping on the wet edge of the rocks, and she looked down into the beast of the rapids, which growled up at them so loudly she wanted to cover her ears. "I'm not going anywhere, Brayden. You fall, so do I. We leave here together, or we drown together. It's your choice."

"You have a *son.*"

"Yes, I do. Just like your mother had a son. Are you going to take me away from him? Is killing yourself worth that much to you?"

"Cat, *stop.*"

He tried to separate himself from her, but she squirmed and held on. Their bodies swayed on the cliff. A hurricane of water cascaded through the canyon, a vortex ready to suck them in.

"No, I won't let you go," Cat insisted. "I am not going to let you do this. Don't you understand? I'm eighteen years old, and I'm sick of people dying around me. I'm sick of losing everyone. *I* lost *my* mother, too, do you remember that? I bring death with me everywhere I go, and it ends right now. No more. I'm done with it. You don't get to die on me. You don't get to leave me with that."

She laced her damp fingers tightly with his. She pulled his hand and began to walk away toward the trail.

"Are you coming?" she asked him.

Cat didn't allow any doubt in her voice, but she was filled with doubts about what would happen next. She knew, if he wanted, that he could break away from her and jump into the canyon. There was nothing she could do to stop him. She knew, too, that her threats were hollow. She wouldn't follow him over the edge. Not now or ever. She wouldn't leave Serena and Stride. She wouldn't give up her life and leave her son behind.

"Are you coming?" she asked again. "Because I'm ready to go home."

Brayden took her hand and brought it to his lips and kissed her fingers one at a time. She held her breath, waiting to see if he chose life or death. Her eyes pleaded with him. He cast a last look over his shoulder at the torrents of the river below them and hovered on the brink, a heartbeat from falling to the rocks.

Then he gave Cat a broken smile.

"Okay," he said. "I can't say no to you."

He came away from the edge and let her lead him from the Deeps.

43

"You're officially cleared in Ned's murder," Maggie told Stride. "Brayden gave us a full statement. He supplied all of the evidence he took from Ned's car and motel room—including the gun. So even Dan was forced to grudgingly admit that you had nothing to do with Ned's death."

"Poor Dan," Stride said. "What a disappointment for him."

"Yeah. I'd like to say we'll never see him again, but every time I think I'm finally done with him, he comes back. He's like the road company for *Les*-frickin'-*Mis*. As he was leaving, he actually had the balls to ask me out again. Can you believe that?"

"Coming from Dan? Yes, I can."

"Well, I'm just glad this case is over," she said. "For a lot of reasons."

"Me too." He was quiet for a while, and then he said, "It doesn't change the fact that I lied to you back then, Mags. I kept you in the dark, and I'm sorry about that."

"Apology accepted, boss."

Stride shook his head and gave her a wicked laugh. "Oh, no, no, you're the boss now. I suppose I need to get used to calling you Lieutenant Mags."

"Ha. Like I wanted any of this."

The two of them sat in chairs pushed into the sand on the beach behind Stride's cottage. A warm August sun beat down on the Point, and sailboats dotted the lake. Not far away, he saw Serena and Cat walking through the wet surf, as the waves licked at their ankles. Two beautiful women, side by side, hand in hand. He was lucky to have them in his life. He was lucky to be alive at all.

"I'm going to need help with the job," Maggie added.

"You? I doubt that."

"I'm not crazy about doing it alone."

"Then maybe you should let some other people in," Stride told her. "You don't have to be an island."

"Yeah. Maybe."

"The fact is, I'm not going anywhere, Mags. I'm here if you need me."

"Thanks. Boss."

Stride smiled, but he didn't tell her that he felt a wave of relief that the job was hers now, not his. He didn't know what that meant for the future. He shifted in the chair, and a stabbing pain in his chest reminded him of what he'd been through. He'd been home for several days now, but his surgeon had warned him that recovery was going to be slow. It would be months before he felt like the man he'd been. If he ever felt that way again.

And then? He didn't know.

"What's going to happen to Brayden?" Stride asked.

"It doesn't look like the county attorney is going to file murder or manslaughter charges against him. She thinks a jury's more likely to conclude that Brayden acted in self-defense. There's no forensic evidence to suggest otherwise, and Curt told you that he sold Ned the gun. That reinforces Brayden's story that Ned was the one who pulled the weapon. And Ned isn't exactly a sympathetic victim, what with him being a rapist and blackmailer. We'll work out a plea on lesser charges related to the obstruction, but I don't think it will mean jail time. He'll be forced to resign from the force, though."

"What about Devin Card?"

"We got test results back to confirm that Andrea was Brayden's mother and Devin was *not* his father. He's holding a press conference about it tonight. I suppose this will give him a bump in the polls."

"Don't be so sure," Stride said. "Assault or not, Devin and Peter were sleazy, awful boys in their youth. Voters don't like that."

Maggie checked her watch and got out of the chair. She stared at the water, which she'd done a million times, but to Stride, she looked older now, more weighed down by the world. Whereas he felt free enough to float away.

"Anyway, I better go. Meeting with K-2."

"Welcome to my world, Lieutenant," Stride said.

"Yeah. Thanks for that. You need anything?"

"Not a thing," he told her.

She waved at Serena and Cat on the beach. She put on her sunglasses, but before she headed back across the dunes, she squatted in front of his chair. If this hadn't been the cool, cynical Maggie Bei, he would have sworn there were tears choking her voice.

"Take all the time you need, Stride. Get stronger. Then you come back to me, okay? I like having you on my island."

He leaned forward with a wince and kissed her cheek. "Keep your feet off my desk."

She gave him a grin and trudged up the grassy hill with her hands in her pockets.

Stride waited for Serena and Cat, enjoying their smiles from a distance. The days since he returned home had made both of them look free, too, as if they'd all been given a second chance. They wandered away from the water and joined him, sitting down in chairs on either side of him. Sand clung to their wet bare feet. Cat leaned over and put her head on his shoulder, and Serena took his hand. The three of them sat there in silence, with the waves rolling in and out, leaving sparks of sunlight in the surf. To their left, the city skyline sprawled across the hillside. On the horizon, he could see an ore boat muscling through the water toward the lift bridge.

It was a perfect Duluth day.

"I'm going over to Drew and Krista's," Cat said, when half an hour had passed. "I told them I'd watch Michael for the evening."

"Have fun," he told her.

"Do you need anything?" she asked, which was the question he now heard fifty times a day.

"Not a thing," he said again.

"Did you hear about Brayden? Looks like he's going to be okay."

"He is. Thanks to you."

"I didn't do anything."

"One of these days, Cat, you're going to realize how much you do."

The girl shrugged as she got out of the chair, as if she didn't believe what he said, but he knew she was secretly pleased. She tilted her chin and closed her eyes against the sun, and the breeze rustled her chestnut hair. Looking like that, she was an adult, ready to take on the entire world. Then, with a smile that was girlish again, she bent down and put one hand lightly against Stride's chest with her fingers spread wide, and she cupped her hand behind her ear, as if listening to something.

"What are you doing?" he asked.

"Heart's still beating," she said. "Just checking."

"Oh, go away."

Cat giggled and ran away like a teenager, her hair flying. His eyes followed her until she disappeared over the dunes back to the cottage.

Then he was alone with Serena.

He was alone with his wife.

She took out something from her pocket, and he realized it was a suncatcher, shaped like a dragonfly, its wings spread, its tail like tiny jewels.

"Keepsake?" he asked.

"It belonged to Andrea," she said. "I asked Denise if I could have it."

"Why?"

"I don't know, I felt like I wanted something to remember her by. We were more alike than I ever would have thought."

Serena held it up to the sunlight, where he saw the glass glinting in purple, orange, pink, and blue.

Stride smiled. "Forgive every sin."

The perfect day went on. They needn't say anything more to each other. The sun cast shadows over the beach as it waned, and the people began to turn into silhouettes. He felt Serena's hand around his in a light, loving touch. Soon enough, they'd have to get on with life. Soon enough, he'd need to think about what came next. But not now. Not yet. He'd never really understood the idea of living for every moment as it happened. He'd always been too busy thinking about the next one to stop the carousel. Until he was shot. Until he died. Then, when he opened his eyes in the recovery room and saw Serena standing over him, he'd finally understood what an incredible gift a single moment could be.

Stride savored the colors he saw, the liquid blue of the lake, the chocolate brown of wet sand, the gold of the dunes. Color was so much better than the deadness of black and white in his dream. Even so, he found that he kept going back to that experience. When he closed his eyes, he could picture the faces he'd seen, each in their own private world. The dream was always with him. If it really was a dream. If it wasn't something else altogether. A part of him couldn't be sure.

What had happened to his soul at that moment when his heart stopped?

That moment when he was dead, not living?

All he knew was that he could still hear Cindy's voice in his head, as she sat next to him on the green bench. So familiar. So real. It didn't feel like a vision, it felt like *her*. As if they'd been given one more moment. He kept going back to what she told him, because what she said had made all of the years since she left him take on a whole new meaning.

It was such a simple thing. Why hadn't he realized it before?

I sent you Serena.

A gift.

A gift from death to life.

"Do you want to go inside, Jonny?" Serena asked him, turning her head and staring at him with her emerald eyes.

Oh, the color of those eyes.

Stride shook his head and didn't let go of her hand. "Not yet. One more moment."

ACKNOWLEDGMENTS

Jonathan Stride is having an anniversary—and so am I! It's now been fifteen years since the release of my debut novel, *Immoral*, which was also the first book in the Jonathan Stride series. Some great people have been with me all along the way.

Blackstone published the audio edition of *Immoral* in 2005 and has produced the audio books for every Stride novel since then. Now, with *Funeral for a Friend*, they are also publishing my print and e-book editions. I have had such a rewarding partnership with them since the very beginning of my career—and I'm honored to have worked with so many talented people there. A big thanks to Haila Williams at Blackstone, who has long been an amazing supporter, friend, and fan. And a special nod to the Blackstone head of library sales, Stephanie Hall, who has not only been a huge advocate for my books, but has become a wonderful friend to me and Marcia (and our cats).

I'm grateful to have tremendous people working on my behalf. Deborah Schneider and her colleagues at Gelfman Schneider, ICM, and Curtis Brown have been my agents, allies, advocates, and friends for more than fifteen years. Special thanks to Cathy Gleason, Alice Lutyens, Josie Freedman, Penelope Burns, Claire Nozieres, and Lucy Morris.

My wife, Marcia, is my partner in everything I do, and she's been at my side through more than thirty-five years of marriage. She's not only the first and best advance reader of every new manuscript, she's also my creative sounding board, my events manager, and my social media guru. I couldn't do anything without her love and support.

Marcia and I are fortunate to have some amazing friends who provide support for us, including Ann Sullivan (not only a friend but a great advance reader!), Barb and Jerry, Kathy, Sandee, Chuck, Rebecca, Sally, Matt and Paula, and many others. Thanks to them and my whole family for being such a wonderful part of our lives.

And a big, big thanks to the many readers, librarians, book reviewers, booksellers, and bloggers who have joined us on this journey during the last fifteen years. From the people of Duluth to readers across the country and around the world, Marcia and I are so grateful for your enthusiasm and excitement about my books, your help in spreading the word, and your friendship on social media and at events. We look forward to sharing books with you for a long time to come!

FROM THE AUTHOR

Thanks for reading the latest Jonathan Stride novel.

If you like this novel, be sure to check out all of my other books, too. Visit my website at BFreemanBooks.com to join my mailing list, get book club discussion questions, and find out more about me and my books.

Also, if you enjoy my books, please post your reviews online at Amazon, Goodreads, Audible, and other sites for book lovers—and spread the word to your reader friends. Thanks!

You can write to me with your feedback at Brian@BFreemanBooks. com. I love to get e-mails from listeners and readers around the world, and yes, I reply personally. You can also "like" my official fan page on Facebook at facebook.com/BFreemanFans or follow me on Twitter or Instagram using the handle BFreemanBooks. For a look at the fun side of the author's life, you can also "like" my wife Marcia's Facebook page at facebook.com/TheAuthorsWife.

ALSO BY BRIAN FREEMAN